24-4.

INQUISITION

By David Gibbins

The *Jack Howard* Series
Atlantis
Crusader Gold
The Last Gospel
The Tiger Warrior
The Mask of Troy
The Gods of Atlantis
Pharaoh
Pyramid
Testament
Inquisition

The *Total War* Series
Destroy Carthage
The Sword of Attila

DAVID GIBBINS
INQUISITION

HEADLINE

First published in Great Britain in 2017 by
HEADLINE PUBLISHING GROUP

1

Cataloguing in Publication Data is available from the British Library

ISBN 978 1 4722 3023 2 (Hardback)
ISBN 978 1 4722 3022 5 (Trade paperback)

Typeset in Aldine 401BT by Avon DataSet Ltd, Bidford-on-Avon, Warwickshire

Printed and bound in Great Britain by Clays Ltd, St Ives plc

HEADLINE PUBLISHING GROUP
An Hachette UK Company
Carmelite House
50 Victoria Embankment
London EC4Y 0DZ

www.headline.co.uk
www.hachette.co.uk

Acknowledgements

I'm very grateful to my agent, Luigi Bonomi of Luigi Bonomi Associates (LBA); to my editors, Sherise Hobbs at Headline in London and Peter Wolverton at Thomas Dunne Books in New York; to my former editor Martin Fletcher, and to Ann Verrinder Gibbins; to Jane Selley for her copyediting; to the rest of the teams at Headline and at Thomas Dunne Books, including Emily Gowers, Patrick Insole and Jennifer Donovan; to Lee Gibbons for his excellent cover art for my books; to Alison Bonomi, Ajda Vucicevic and Danielle Zigner at LBA; to Nicki Kennedy, Sam Edenborough, Katherine West, Simone Smith and Alice Natali at the Intercontinental Literary Agency; and to my many foreign publishers and their translators.

In my previous novel, *Testament*, Jack Howard and his team discover an amazing shipwreck of Phoenician date off the west coast of Cornwall in England. That wreck was fictional, but their exploration was closely based on my own diving over the past few years on shipwrecks off Gunwalloe Church Cove on the west side of the Lizard peninsula. In *Inquisition*, Jack moves even closer to real life, as the wreck that he finds in the first chapters of the novel, the *Schiedam*, is one that I myself rediscovered with Mark Milburn in 2016 – a Dutch merchant-man captured by Barbary pirates and then by the Royal Navy that was used in the evacuation of the English colony at Tangier in 1684. I'm very grateful to Mark and all the divers with Cornwall Maritime Archaeology, the organisation Mark and I set up that parallels Jack's International Maritime University. The *Schiedam* is a protected wreck under UK law, and I'm indebted to Historic England for authorising us to carry out archaeological work on the site and to the National Trust for their support, as well as to the British Library, the National Archives and Cornwall County Archives in Truro for facilitating documentary research on the wreck.

Just as Jack's discoveries always excite press interest, so did ours in late 2016, when the BBC and many other news media featured our discovery of the *Schiedam* as a top story. You can read all about that on my website, www.davidgibbins.com. Thanks go to Mark Milburn and Jeff Goodman for their excellent video and still photography on the site. I'm very grateful to my brother Alan for taking the photo of me under-water that appears on the cover of this novel, and to our mother Ann – indispensable proofreader of all of my novels – and my daughter Molly for joining me on a diving expedition to the wrecks of Tobermory in Canada to mark the completion of this novel, and the beginning of exciting new adventures ahead.

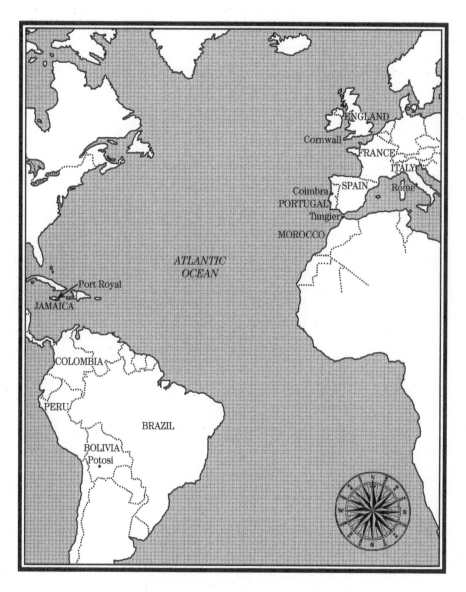

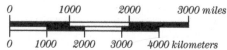

Map showing the main places mentioned in the novel, including the site of
the persecution of Christians in 4th century Rome, the 17th century shipwreck
off Cornwall in England, the Court of the Inquisition at Coimbra in Portugal,
the English colony at Tangier in North Africa, the pirate city of Port Royal in
Jamaica and the Spanish silver mines at Potosi in South America.

And he took a cup, and gave thanks, and gave it to them, saying, Drink ye all of it; for this is my blood of the covenant, which is shed for many unto remission of sins. But I say unto you, I will not drink henceforth of this fruit of the vine, until that day when I drink of it new with you in my Father's kingdom.

Matthew 26: 27–29 (King James Version)

The table was not of silver, the chalice was not of gold in which Christ gave His blood to His disciples to drink, and yet everything there was precious and truly fit to inspire awe . . .

St John Chrysostom (late fourth century AD), on the Gospel of Matthew

By the King's Direction there were buried among the Ruins a considerable Number of mill'd Crown Pieces of his Majestie's Coin, which haply, many Centuries hence when other Memory of it shall be lost, may declare to succeeding Ages that that place was once a Member of the British Empire . . .

Josiah Burchett, *A Complete History of the Most Remarkable Transactions at Sea* (1720), on Tangier

Prologue

The man with the sword stumbled along the rock-cut tunnel as fast as he could, the dull echo of his footsteps resounding down the passageways filled with burial niches that extended off on either side. He had entered the catacombs by a secret portal, pausing only to glance one last time at the shooting stars that filled the sky to the north-west before plunging into the sepulchral gloom of the tunnel. The skylights that had lit his way by moonlight since the entrance had ended some way back, and the only light now was the smudge from a distant oil lamp in the darkness ahead. A few minutes later he reached it, and stood panting, hunched over with his hands on his knees. He had only been this deep into the catacombs once before, when he had been shown the secret place. Beyond the lamp the tunnel split, one passage veering off to the left, the other to the right. His mind had gone blank, paralysed by the horrors he had witnessed on the execution ground only hours before, and he had forgotten the way. He knew that his choice would make little difference to his chance of escape from those who were following him. They would come like a rushing torrent through the catacombs, filling every passage, every space. But it made all the difference to the task that he, Proselius, legionary of Rome and soldier of Christ, had sworn to undertake that day, that the others had entrusted to him as they were led off to martyrdom. The very future of the Church was at stake. *He had to remember*.

He tried to control his breathing, and closed his eyes. Despite all that he had seen as a soldier, all the horrors of war, he had not been able to watch what they were doing to Laurentius, his friend and teacher; he had turned from it and gone to prayer, but another of the brethren had sought him out and brought the message: *passus est* – he is martyred. Proselius had rushed to the catacombs as soon as it was dark, through the city walls and down the Appian Way, trusting his memory of the time he had been brought to the secret place by Laurentius and Sixtus all those years before, when he had sworn to undertake this task should the worst happen to them. And now, his mind devoid of direction, he felt that he had betrayed them, had betrayed Christ himself.

He forced himself to recall what Laurentius had taught him: in times of duress he needed to remember what had led him to Christ, what had given him the strength to reject the old gods and accept the new. *He needed to remember his moment of revelation*. He clutched at the crude metal cross that hung from his neck, forged from two Roman spear points he had picked up from the battlefield at Abritus. He, Proselius, standard-bearer of the Second Legion, had been the last of his cohort left alive, the sole survivor of the Scythian onslaught that had killed the emperor, Trajan Decius. As he had stood over his emperor's body, sword dripping with Scythian blood, ready for a renewed assault and certain death, the clouds had parted in the shape of a cross and a sudden deluge had cast the enemy into disarray, a miracle from heaven.

As he remembered that moment, he raised the cross and kissed it, pressing the cold metal against his lips, then thought again of the shooting stars. Laurentius had said they were the tears of Christ himself, shed for those who would suffer during the persecution. And two days ago they had seen another omen, in the place where Christians were executed as common criminals: the Colosseum of the gladiators was struck by a bolt of lightning that had left the wooden upper tiers of seating a smouldering ruin, as if God himself had smitten the place from heaven and lit the fires of martyrdom.

But they had not needed omens to know what was coming: that the new emperor, Valerian, would wish to stamp his mark on the Christians of Rome. From his beleaguered outpost with the Army of the East, hemmed in on all sides by the Persians, Valerian had issued his edicts, the words of an emperor terrified that in his absence the people of Rome would rise up against him, would cast away the last vestiges of the old religion and declare Christ supreme. At first, all who refused to sacrifice to the Roman gods would face banishment; senators and knights who professed Christianity would be dispossessed of their property and rank, servants of the

3

imperial household would be reduced to slavery, and the treasures of the Church would be confiscated and locked in the imperial coffers. But everyone knew that these words were a smokescreen for what was to come, that banishment and slavery meant execution and slaughter. And everyone feared Valerian's enforcers, the Altamanus, the Black Hand, so named for the image that was burned into the flesh of their palms. They were former Christians among the Praetorian Guard, men who had faced banishment for their beliefs but had been offered an alternative, for whom the dishonour of discharge from the Guard had proved greater than the draw of Christ; they combined the unswerving loyalty of the Praetorians with the special edge of men who had deviated from a military code but then recovered their way, who would drive themselves relentlessly to seek vengeance on those who had led them astray. Valerian had known how to shape them, and Proselius had seen the fear among his fellow legionaries, many of them secret Christians but without the urge to martyrdom. They knew it was better for their own survival to join the persecution rather than risk revealing their true allegiance and suffering hideous retribution themselves.

Pope Sixtus had gone readily to his death, beheaded two days ago outside the entrance to these very catacombs, as had Laurentius, roasted alive on a metal grille in the arena of the gladiators. Proselius recalled what the presiding tribune had told Sixtus as they had held him over the scaffold: 'You have drawn together men bound by unlawful association, and professed yourself an enemy to the gods and religion of Rome; the most pious, most sacred and most august Emperor has endeavoured in vain to bring you back to conformity with the rites of Rome, but you have persisted as chief in these crimes. You shall be made an example to those who have associated with you, and the authority of the law shall be ratified in your blood.' Sixtus had looked up towards those gathered around, then smiled, raised his arms to the sky and declared: 'Thanks be to God.'

Earlier, as his followers had tried to stop him from giving himself up, as Proselius himself had begged and implored him to go into hiding, Sixtus had reassured them that in recompense for being the first to offer his neck to the sword, Christ would reward his merit as a martyr, and would preserve the rest of his flock. Proselius had known that this would not be so; that with the first sight of blood the crowd would be baying for more. It was the Roman way, and would be so until Christ was ascendant in Rome. He had watched as the executioner hacked at Sixtus's neck with a blunt blade, and then butchered his servants and family, unleashing an orgy of blood-letting that he had only ever seen before at the end of a triumphant battle.

And now the men of the Altamanus were back at the gates of the catacombs, having purged the streets of Rome and returned to the last refuge of the faithful, to the place where two centuries earlier the followers of Peter and Paul had gathered in secret for the first time to worship under the noses of the emperors, in the burial grounds of their ancestors. Both Sixtus and Laurentius had been willing martyrs, knowing that Proselius would carry the torch forward, that the light that shone through the tears of Christ would not be diminished, that their greatest treasure, their covenant with the Lord, would be spirited away to keep the forces of darkness at bay until Christ should come amongst them again. Proselius felt as if the weight of the world rested on him now, and yet he felt immobilised, unable to remember which passageway to choose.

A violent tremor shook the ground. He opened his eyes and thrust the cross back under his tunic. He heard distant echoes, an unearthly, terrifying sound, and then a high-pitched shriek. He had known that they would not be far behind him, that the death of Laurentius would lead to a murderous rampage, to the wholesale slaughter of anyone found in the catacombs. He suddenly had a vision of Laurentius before him, peering ahead as he had done when he and Sixtus had first brought him here, and all at once he remembered: *it was the right-hand passage*. He whispered a quick prayer of thanks, sheathed his sword and took the lamp from its holder, shielding the flame with his hand and making his way forward.

The reek of recent death was overpowering, a sickly-sweet stench that had filled the catacombs over the past few days. Here in the deepest recesses they had brought the executed and the slaughtered: Sixtus's decapitated body, Laurentius's roasted corpse, innumerable others, mangled and mutilated, retrieved from where they had been dumped outside the city walls, brought here under the cover of darkness by grieving relatives. This was the true smell of martyrdom; not the smell of blood and burning flesh, the reek of the spectacle, but the stench of decay, of people whose sacrifice would be forgotten as quickly as they had been condemned if he did not fulfil his mission, if he did not carry it forward.

He passed musty piles of bones and rags on the floor, pulled from the niches and dumped unceremoniously to make way for the hastily laid-out corpses of the last few days, their bloody shrouds still visible where there had been no time to seal them in with fresh plaster. Rats scurried by, feasting on flesh, and then a bat brushed his face, swooping low from its perch on the ceiling above. Another tremor shook the ground, this time closer, followed by a distant roaring sound, and he sensed the air draw back down the tunnel. *Now he knew what they were doing.* They were using Greek fire, pumping jets of burning naphtha through the catacombs to clear out anyone who had come from the city to take refuge in this place of the dead. He had seen Greek fire used in battle by the Persians, had watched his comrades burn like human torches, had felt the air sucked from his lungs. He knew that the flames would lick down every tunnel, seeking air, drawn further by the piles of rags and bones that would ignite like kindling, suffocating anyone who had not already burned to death. He could hear other, more distinct sounds, eerie drawn-out cries, the noise of clashing. They were coming down the main passageway, clearing out the tunnels on either side. It could only be a matter of minutes before they reached the place where he had paused, where the tunnel split. He had no time to lose.

He stumbled on, ever deeper into the catacombs, and then rounded a bend and saw it, just visible in the smudge of moonlight from the end of the tunnel ahead that marked his escape route. In an alcove to the right was a larger niche, the plaster still mercifully intact. Those who had come here in the last few days seeking resting places for their loved ones had known to leave this one alone, to venerate the image painted on the plaster above it even though none of them could have known what lay sealed within. He reached the niche and raised the lamp for a better view. In the centre, high above, was a crudely painted image of Christ, facing out, the reflection from the lamp seeming to radiate from his head over the others in the scene. It showed the Last Supper, the apostles ranged on either side beneath the semicircular curve of the niche, a table in front of them. The figure of Christ held a loaf of bread in one hand, and in the other a cup. Laurentius had told him that the image had been daubed into the wet plaster by the apostle Peter, when he had fled to Rome from Judaea bearing the relics of the Messiah. For a split second Proselius felt as if Peter were there still, standing beside him, united in the task of preserving what lay inside from those who would attempt to submerge the light of the Lord in a new darkness.

The whooshing sound of fire was closer, and the acrid smell of burning naphtha filled his nostrils. He dropped to his knees and placed the lamp on the ground. He could not risk using his sword to cut through into the niche in case he damaged what lay within, so he scraped at the plaster beneath the painting with his bare hands, grimacing as he broke his nails on it. Small pieces came off, and then larger chunks, stained by the blood that was dripping from his fingers. Beneath the outer crust the plaster was damp, permeated by the pigments from the painting, and he was able to drive his fingers in deeper. He broke through into the cavity beyond, reaching as far as he could and pulling out a swaddled package, bound in old leather. He saw the marks on the leather that Laurentius had told him to look for: the fish symbol of the Christians, with the Greek letter alpha on one side and omega on the other. He knew that he had found it.

He struggled upright with the package in his hands. As he opened the satchel on his belt, a figure came stumbling down the tunnel from the direction of the noise, a woman, her gown and hair smouldering and one leg dragging behind her, welted and blackened. She collapsed in front of him, retching and coughing up blood, and looked up imploringly, her gaze shifting from him to the image of Christ that was still intact above the hole he had dug in the plaster. For a moment he stood transfixed. His mind flashed back to that afternoon, when Laurentius had been brought before the tribunal and the prefect had demanded that he hand over the treasures of the Church. Laurentius had opened his empty hands and gestured to the crowd that thronged around them, kept at bay by the line of soldiers, and then proclaimed: 'These are the treasures of the Church. The Church is truly rich, far richer than your emperor.'

The words had enraged the prefect and sealed Laurentius's fate, but they had empowered all those who heard them, both the faithful and those still wavering in their beliefs. The woman in front of him now was one of those treasures; she *was* the richness of the Church, and yet she was also one of the multitude who knew, like Laurentius, that they might have to sacrifice their lives for the greater good of the Church. Proselius knew that he could not save her; she could barely walk, and the flames would be on them before they reached the end of the tunnel. He put the swaddled package in his satchel, then pulled the cross on its leather thong over his head and passed it to her, placing it in her palm and clasping his own hand around it for a moment. The cross was forged of the strongest steel, the steel of a legionary's spear, and would survive the flames and the destruction, a small symbol of hope in this place just as the treasure he was carrying would be an inspiration for all who followed the sign of the cross in the future, those still alive and those not yet born.

He remembered what Laurentius had prophesied. Valerian would never return to Rome; he and his legions would be destroyed in Persia. His son Gallienus would rescind the persecution, and within a generation the cross would be raised over all the pagan places, over the Temple of Jupiter and even the Colosseum itself. By then Proselius would have taken the treasure across the sea to Spain, to the town in the foothills of the mountains where he and Laurentius had grown up together. He would entrust it to the community of Jews sympathetic to Christianity who had been there since the Emperor Titus had brought down the Temple in Jerusalem almost two hundred years before, who had fled west and sought refuge in the borderlands of the Empire. They would keep it concealed from the forces of darkness, the men with the black mark upon their souls, who would never relent in their quest to find and obliterate the symbols of belief that gave such power to those they were seeking to destroy.

He remembered the Gospel of Matthew, first read to him by Laurentius when Proselius had sought him out in Rome after his revelation on the battlefield. Matthew told how Christ had raised the cup that Laurentius, using the Greek words of the Gospels, had called it *poterion*, and said: 'I will not drink henceforth of this fruit of the vine, until that day when I drink of it new with you in my Father's kingdom.' That promise had been their clarion call, their covenant with the Lord, the reason why Proselius was here now. It was essential that they preserve the cup for the Second Coming, as a beacon of hope during the trials they all knew lay ahead, when the power of the cross and of true belief would be put to the test over and over again as the tides of history swept against them.

Proselius looked one last time at the image of Christ on the painting above the tomb, and then at the woman. She had drawn the hood of her cape over her head, and was kneeling in front of the image, clutching the cross. Behind her a flame licked down the tunnel, wreathed in black smoke, vivid red like the tongue of a serpent. He turned towards the light, drew his sword and began to run.

Part 1

1

Off Cornwall, south-west England, present day

'Jack, I can see silver. It's fantastic. It looks like a piece of eight.'

Jack Howard stared at the diver wedged into the cleft in the rock in front of him. More accurately, he stared at the backside of the diver, coming ever closer with each surge of the sea behind them. Another wave hit him, forcing him further up Costas's legs, and he braced himself against the rock as the water boiled around them and then subsided, draining off with a giant sucking sound. 'Are you sure?' he shouted, his voice sounding hollow in the cleft. 'You sure it's not just another shiny pebble stuck in the rock?'

'I'm no archaeologist, Jack, but I know treasure when I see it.' Jack braced himself, knowing to trust his friend's judgement. Costas might be a submersibles engineer by profession, but after twenty years of diving together, a little bit of Jack's passion for archaeology had rubbed off.

Another surge hit them, and Jack struggled to keep his mouth above water. 'Can you get it out?'

'I've got the tool, but my arms aren't long enough.'

'You're saying you're stuck.'

'I didn't say that.'

'I knew I shouldn't have let you go in first.'

'If you'd gone first, the surge would have pushed you beyond the pool in front of me now, and you'd never have seen it. With my more muscular physique, I was able to stop in time.'

'You mean you got stuck.'

A large wave broke over the rocks in front of the cliff behind them, rolled down the gully that led to the cleft and smacked into the entrance, spraying Jack with flecks of foam before the water hit him. The big waves came with every ten or twelve oscillations of the swell, the residue from some distant mid-Atlantic storm. Jack dipped his face into the water to clear the foam from his mask and turned to look back at the sea, his wetsuit scraping against the rock as he did so. He could see line-of-sight down the cleft to the entrance in the cliff some ten metres back, and then down the gully beyond the cliff base for another twenty metres or so to the open sea, the grey clouds visible above the distant lines of whitecaps. From where they were on the coast of Cornwall, the next stop down that line-of-sight was the northern coast of South America, some five thousand nautical miles distant. It was an astonishing thought, one that excited the explorer in Jack, as if he were looking through a porthole into the unknown, into the vast expanse of ocean that had drawn his ancestors and generations of other mariners to set off from these shores on voyages of discovery and revelation.

That line-of-sight was why he and Costas were wedged into one of the most unlikely dive locations in their twenty-five-year career together, not in the sea itself, but inside a crack in a cliff that was actually several metres above sea level when the tide was out. Jack had first discovered it years before, as a boy, when he had explored these cliffs searching for smugglers' caves and collecting points for wreckage, but it had always seemed too perilous to venture inside alone. The Cornish name for the headland in the old maps even referred to it: *Carrack y pilau*, meaning 'the undermined rocks'. At some point millions of years ago, titanic forces had split the cliff between the headland and the adjacent cove, leaving a fracture line in the serpentine that ran from the seaward gully some fifty metres through the cliff to an opening beside the cove. He had remembered it two weeks ago, when a storm had shifted the sand on the seabed and exposed a solitary cannon on a shallow reef beyond the gully, a discovery made by his daughter Rebecca and her friend Jeremy when they had been snorkelling around the headland. It had been a hugely exciting find, bolstering Jack's theory that the seventeenth-century wreck they had been excavating for several months around the other side of the headland had been of a ship that had broken in two, and that the lost part was at their current location.

Something had been missing from that wreck, a mother lode of silver bullion that Jack knew must have been on board, and there was every chance that this new location would provide the key. But with the cannon being too eroded to date closely, the reef being surrounded by deep sand and late autumn storms being forecast for the weeks ahead, there was little sense in shifting the excavation team to a new site, where they might be digging blindly for nothing and be blown off by adverse winds at any time. Jack's idea would have to remain a hunch, one that would be impossible to test until they were able to get back to the site for more sustained excavation after the winter months.

But then the previous evening, he had stood on the cliff above the cannon and remembered the cleft. Ships wrecked against this coast were almost invariably caught in a south-westerly gale, blowing in from mid-Atlantic. Looking down at the rocks below him, he had realised that the cannon and the gully were on the same alignment as the cleft. He had been here before during storms and had seen the violence of the sea, with the swell piling into the cliffs and the spray hitting him thirty metres above. If the ship had wrecked in those conditions, then the part of the hull that might have impacted here would have smashed against the rocks and been driven up the gully, with smaller items such as coins being thrown down that cleft. A single datable coin could give all the proof that was needed to bolster Jack's theory and justify a return in better conditions to search for the rest of the treasure in the sand outside. If Costas was right, if Jack's hunch had been correct, they might just have hit pay dirt.

Another wave smashed against the cliff, and he turned back towards Costas just in time to brace himself for impact. Despite its height above low tide, the cleft contained a permanent sump of water, a result of the surge that ran constantly through it when the tide was high. Where Jack was now, the water was only about half a metre deep, allowing him to crawl and scrape his way to his present position with his head above water, but beyond Costas he had spotted a larger pool that might be considerably deeper, a likely location for heavy objects such as coins to have sunk into fissures. The problem now was that the tide was coming in and the swell was growing stronger. It had been a squeeze getting into the cleft, and rather than returning the same way, they had planned to carry on and exit from the cave on the other side, a protected location in the cove. But with Costas stuck and no way of backtracking, they had a situation on their hands, one that was becoming more serious as the surges became stronger.

He watched Costas pull down the zipper on the off-white boiler suit he was wearing over his wetsuit. 'I'm going to have to shed my skin,' he said, wriggling around as he pushed the suit down. 'That should give me the leeway I need.'

'I did warn you that wearing that suit might be a bit much in this space,' Jack said. 'Bearing in mind your muscular girth.'

'I never dive without it. You should know that by now. Even if this isn't really a dive. And anyway, if you can reach that coin, you'll be thankful for the tool belt. It'll have to be you that digs it out, by the way. My arms aren't long enough.'

Jack helped by hauling on the suit as another surge enveloped them, pulling it down over Costas's feet and then pushing it forward into the gap so that Costas could take it out with him. They waited for the next surge and then let the water move them forward together, Costas into a recess just ahead of the constriction and Jack alongside him, his head poking out above the pool where Costas had left his torch shining into the fissure at the bottom. Another more violent surge brought them face to face, Jack's cheek scraping against Costas's chin as they wedged together again on the far side of the pool. The water burst over them once more, submerging Jack completely, and then drained off down the cleft, leaving them high and dripping in an awkward embrace. Jack stared at his friend's stubbled face, only inches away and looking at him deadpan, and tried to suppress a laugh. 'We must stop meeting like this.'

'This was your idea, not mine. I was quite happy tinkering with the remote-operated vehicle in the equipment tent.'

'You need a shave.'

'I'm a Greek sponge-diver, remember? Got to keep up appearances.'

'Maybe your grandfather was, but you're a PhD from MiT in submersibles technology and you were brought up in the Bronx.'

'What are you, then?'

'Just a diver. Nothing fancy.'

'With a PhD in archaeology from Cambridge University. And a commission in the Royal Naval Reserve.'

Jack pushed hard to try to disengage, wincing as a barnacled outcrop dug into his hip. 'When have we ever been in a jam like this before?'

'Huh? Like this? Well, let's see. Last year, defusing a torpedo inside a sunken Second World War freighter.'

'That was your idea. Defusing the torpedo, I mean. Completely unnecessary.'

'I'd never done a Mark VII before. Anyway, you have to allow me some fun.'

'And?'

'Other jams? Inside a sacred Mayan well in Mexico. Nearly drowning in the ancient sewer under Rome. That was a good one. Oh, and diving into a live underwater volcano. The list goes on. I'm writing it all up, you know.'

'Come again?'

'I'm writing it up. My take on our adventures. A kind of alternative view of Dr Jack Howard and the International Maritime University, not focusing so much on the archaeology.'

'That should be interesting,' Jack said, grimacing as he strained to move forward.

'Don't sound so excited.'

'I'm serious. I mean, from a technological point of view. Looking at the equipment, the logistics. Your kind of thing.'

'Exactly. Lanowski's going to help me. He's doing the chapters on computer simulation and robotic nanotechnology.'

'Should be a humdinger,' Jack said, remembering the first time he had met Jacob Lanowski, at an archaeological science conference. It had quickly become clear that they would need him at IMU, but it had taken most of one afternoon for Jack to extricate himself from Lanowski's passionate attempt to explain the mathematics of 3-D modelling using a portable blackboard that seemed to go everywhere with him.

'And Rebecca's going to contribute a chapter on your relationships,' Costas added. 'I mean, with Katya and then Maria. Always good to have a daughter's perspective. She really has a pretty good take on you by now. I mean, the first

21

half of her life spent in Naples with her mother, and then in New York with her guardians, followed by the tragedy of her mother's murder by the Mafia, and then you find out that you have a daughter and she moves in here. It's been pretty intensive for her, but it's left her with a keen eye for people. And Jeremy's going to add his angle too. You know, from his work with Maria at the Institute of Palaeography in Oxford. Jeremy may be Rebecca's boyfriend, but actually I think he knows Maria just as well. After all, she supervised him when he first came over from the States as a graduate student. He must really have the lowdown on what she thinks.'

Before Jack could reply, another surge swept violently over them, and he felt Costas moving. He pushed himself hard against the rock behind him, and as the surge dissipated he saw that Costas was ahead of him, the daylight from the cove at the end of the tunnel clearly visible ahead. Costas swept up his boiler suit in front of him, fumbled in the belt and reached back, thrusting a tool into Jack's hand. 'This should help to get it out. Remember to bring my torch. Brace yourself against the next surge, otherwise you'll be coming with me. Okay, I'm out of here.'

A wall of water boiled and hissed along the cleft towards them, and Jack wedged himself into the recess that Costas had just vacated. With the plug removed, the danger now was not so much getting stuck again as being thrown uncontrollably against bone-shattering rock, and Jack knew that he could not afford to linger longer than was absolutely necessary. The water hit him with the force of a body blow, and he saw Costas being swept on down the cleft. In the lull that followed, he dropped into the pool, floating for a moment on the turbulent surface. It was little more than a widening in the cleft, just long enough for him to stretch out, but it was easily two metres deep, the rock walls smoothed and sculpted by millennia of storms and tides. Costas had perched his torch in a crack, illuminating most of the pool, and Jack could see the problem he would have had in reaching into the fissure at the bottom; his own longer arms meant that he might just be able to do it.

He waited for the next surge to wash over him and then put on his snorkel, staring along the length of the pool. After only a few seconds he saw it, a distinct metallic reflection in the torchlight, wedged among worn pebbles in the bottom of the fissure. He weighed up the tool, a metal crowbar with a rubber-padded clamp at the other end, something that Costas had knocked up in the engineering lab specifically to loosen wedged coins and then extract them with minimal damage. He tried to relax, taking deep breaths, and then held his breath and plunged down, just avoiding being pummelled again. He kicked hard against the buoyancy of his wetsuit and held on to an outcrop of rock at the bottom, drawing himself down and poking the bar as far as he could into the cleft, pushing the sharp end into the accreted pebbles on either side of the shiny object. When he could see that it had loosened, he pulled the bar out, spun it round and dropped the clamp around it, closing the simple lever handle and pulling until it gave way. He raised it, opened the clamp, dropped the object into his hand and grabbed the torch, rising to the surface as he did so and clearing his snorkel. Then he braced himself against the sides of the cleft with his legs, opened his hand and shone the torch on his palm.

He let out a whoop of excitement through his snorkel. There was no doubt about it. They had found a Spanish silver coin at least three hundred years old, a crudely struck cob typical of the millions minted from New World silver at the time of the Spanish Main, the period of the Spanish Empire during the sixteenth and seventeenth centuries when the vast wealth of the Americas fuelled the economic and political upheavals not only of Spain but of the entire Old World.

He took the coin carefully between his fingers and inspected it. He could clearly see the snip marks where the planchet, the coin flan, had been cut from a rolled bar of silver, and then further small snips where it had been trimmed to the correct weight. He knew from its size that it was a four-real coin; not a piece of eight as Costas had supposed, but identical to the larger coin in all its main features. Most silver coins that Jack had found on wrecks were encased in corrosion or worn so thin by centuries in shifting sand that they were little more than thin discs of metal. This one, though, was in good condition, having become embedded in the fissure before it could be tumbled around too much; the constant water movement in the cleft since then had kept its metallic surface clear and shiny, with a dark patina only in the impressed parts of the design.

He could see immediately that it was a 'shield' coin of the design specified under Philip II of Spain in 1570, giving a clear *terminus post quem* for the coin. The exergue, the lettering around the edges naming the king and his empire, HISPANIARUM ET INDIARUM – of Spain and the Indies – was mostly lost, as was typical of these coins; getting the planchet exactly positioned between the dies during the strike would always have been a hit-and-miss affair. What mattered most was the design in the middle, a quartered shield showing the arms of the Habsburgs, the Austrian dynasty who had taken over Spain in the sixteenth century. Turning it over, he could see the characteristic Greek cross with decorative finials quartering the arms of Castile and León, the two kingdoms that made up Habsburg Spain, the little castles and lions just visible in each quarter as he angled the coin into the torchlight.

He flipped it over again and peered closely at the worn metal to the left of the shield, rubbing the silver to remove the patina and checking for any irregularities. This was where he would expect to see the letters signifying the mint and the assayer, the man in charge of the mint. As he moved the torch slightly, he spotted them: the letters OMP vertically beside the shield. He knew that OM referred to the Mexico mint, the oldest and greatest mint of the Spanish Main, rivalled only by the fabled silver mountain of Potosi in Peru, and that P referred to an assayer who was in charge in the middle years of the seventeenth century, up to 1665. His excitement mounted as he realised what that was telling him.

The wreck they had been excavating dated from 1684, well within the circulation span of coins minted twenty or thirty years before. It was not conclusive proof that they had found the other part of the wreck, but it was enough to go on. All they needed now was a storm to blow away the sand over-burden around the cannon and then a spell of fine weather to allow them to carry out an excavation. This late in the season that would probably mean next year, but Jack had learned from experience to keep his frustration at bay by always having other projects on the go. Wreck archaeology in these waters was a waiting game, a matter of keeping a weather eye on the horizon and being ready to seize the chance at a moment's notice.

He clasped one hand around the coin and the other around the torch and Costas's tool, and waited for another lull so that he could crawl forward out of the pool into the cleft for the next wave to push him on after Costas. He held his breath and dropped down underwater, relishing the moment of calm and opening his hand to look at the coin once again. Something had been niggling him, something else that he had seen but not properly registered, and now in the half-gloom it was there before his eyes. Over the shield was the faint outline of another design, with straight lines like the cross on the reverse. At first it looked like the impression of a double strike, a common enough feature where the first strike had been too shallow, but in this case unlikely as it was a different design from the one underneath. And then he suddenly realised. It was a six-pointed star, a Star of David, a sign struck into the coin after it had been minted, perhaps years later. It was exactly the same as the sign they had found engraved into the lid of a small bronze box uncovered only days before in the excavation, a box that had been wrenched open during the wrecking, spilling what Jack now knew must once have included a treasure in silver bullion.

He punched the water with his clenched hand. His hunch had been correct. *They had found the other part of the wreck.*

He clasped the coin again, relishing the infusion of history he always felt when handling artefacts, his mind working overtime as his elation quickly turned into questions. If the chest contained the treasure of a merchant, why had he stamped his coins with the Star of David? Jack already knew that the ship they were excavating was an English vessel transporting equipment and people back from the failed colony of Tangier in present-day Morocco, on a route that would have had them sailing through waters off Spain and Portugal, where the Inquisition held sway. If the merchant was Jewish, why would he have openly revealed his faith at a time when to do so would have risked imprisonment or worse for him and his family?

Jack had already set Jeremy and Rebecca the task of research-ing the documentary evidence for the ship, of unearthing all possible material in the archives that might be of use to them, and this question would now go to the top of their list. As happened so often, one result, one discovery opened up a Pandora's box of further questions, leading to a path of discovery that Jack himself could never hope to navigate alone, knowing that it was always a team effort that drove the story forward.

He positioned himself to ride the next surge, hearing the water beginning to rush up behind him, and thought of Costas somewhere ahead in the light at the end of the tunnel.

He could hardly wait to show him what he had found.

2

Jack walked over the grassy headland above the cannon site and down the coastal footpath towards the beach. He had left Costas in their van beside the far cove after they had changed out of their wetsuits, having decided to return via the footpath to the expedition headquarters close to the excavation. To his left, the cliff dropped precipitously thirty metres or more, its course jagged and irregular where storms had gouged great chunks out of the rock and caused the land to slip down onto the foreshore. He veered right, avoiding a dangerous drop where erosion had undermined the path, and then passed an exposed section of cliff where a landslip earlier in the year had revealed the skeletons from a mass burial, soldiers whose uniforms still had their brass buttons attached, one of many places along the coast where the victims of shipwrecks had been laid to rest. Before the nineteenth century it had been the custom to bury unclaimed bodies close to where they had been cast ashore, without shrouds or coffins and often without ceremony. The Act of Parliament that ended the practice, the Burial of Drowned Persons Act 1808, had been a direct consequence of the wreck only a mile further up this coast of the frigate HMS *Anson*; a local solicitor who witnessed the tragedy had been so dismayed by the treatment of the bodies that he had drafted legislation. Today the location of those mass graves was marked only by the subsidence of the soil over the bodies as they had decayed, leaving depressions in the meadow and gorse at intervals all along the coast.

Jack paused for a moment, looking at the medieval church tucked behind the next headland on the other side of the beach, and contemplated the human cost that seemed at such odds with the tranquillity and beauty of the place on a day like this. The old records of the church showed that bodies from shipwrecks had washed up here with appalling regularity, most of them beyond any hope of recognition. Every few years a ship was wrecked within sight of the headland; during great storms, several might be wrecked on a single day. The cove lay on the western side of the Lizard peninsula, the most southerly point in England, and all ships entering and leaving the English Channel on this side would have had to make their way past the notorious reefs off the end of the peninsula. In the days of sail, many ships were blown by the prevailing westerlies into the shore, unable to tack and beat to windward or to hold anchor in the sandy seabed of the bay. And the coast had a siren-like quality, with captains lured to false hope by a long expanse of sand and shingle on the north-western shore of the peninsula, unaware that the surf concealed a lethal drop-off where the sea had piled up shingle just off-shore. Ships would broach to, swinging broadside-on against the shingle berm, and be pounded to pieces in a matter of hours, those on board doomed to perish in the churning undertow only a stone's throw from the local people watching helplessly from shore.

He continued on over the beach towards the church, skirting the surf, where he could see that the tide was just beginning to turn. The previous year the beach had been a hive of activity following their discovery of a Phoenician wreck less than three hundred metres offshore. It had been one of the highlights of Jack's career: not only the oldest shipwreck to have been excavated in British waters, but also the site that had led him and Costas on an extraordinary trail of discovery to the very furthest reaches of Phoenician exploration off the coast of Africa.

It was after they had returned from that quest in the autumn that Jack had snorkelled by himself one afternoon from the Phoenician wreck around the church headland into Jangye-ryn, the Cornish name for the rocky cove that lay beyond. Years before, as a boy, he had watched local divers raise a cannon from a wreck in the cove, something that had kindled his fascination with diving and archaeology. He had pored over the accounts of that wreck, determined one day to dive on the site himself and see the other cannon that were known to lie there. For decades it had remained no more than a dream, thwarted by a huge storm that had blown sand over the site and buried everything except the tops of the reefs that marked the perimeter of the wreck. The day of his snorkel had followed an unusual southerly gale, creating a rare longshore current that had swept sediment parallel to the coast rather than pushing it into the beach as happened with the prevailing westerlies. The current had dumped several metres of sand on the Phoenician site, fortunately after the last timbers had been raised, but it was just possible that it had shifted sand away from the cannon wreck in the adjacent cove. He had gone there with no expectations, but with a feeling that this time he might just be lucky.

What he had discovered had surpassed his wildest dreams. At first, swimming over the sand from the headland, he had barely been able to make out the bottom, the water still churned up and cloudy from the storm over the preceding days. Every time he had seen something dark he had dived down to investigate, only to find that it was a mass of kelp fragments broken off from the surrounding reefs and floating in clumps. There was still a great deal of sand everywhere, extending off in all directions, and as he swam further he resigned himself to another disappointment.

But then, as he neared the far side of the cove, he had seen another dark shape, and dived down again. It had intact fronds of kelp growing from it, so was solid, almost certainly a protruding section of reef. He had felt it and peered under the kelp, at first barely believing what he was seeing. He had surfaced, elated, then dived down again and again, pulling at the kelp roots embedded in the cannon, clearing them away for a better view. The breech was resting on an expanse of reef, swirling with kelp, and he decided to follow that in the direction of the shore. After a few metres he spotted another cannon, a smaller one this time, only the muzzle poking out of the sand. And then he had seen something that took his

31

breath away: a huge cannon at least three metres long, perched on a rocky ledge, the muzzle pointing out over the sand as if the gun were still sitting in its carriage. When he had finally come ashore after cleaning that gun too, he was as exhausted as he had ever been after a dive, and as excited. After all the years of discovery and adventure, he felt as if he had returned full circle, and finally realised the boyhood dream that had started it all.

Now he reached the end of the beach and began to climb up the rocks towards the church. The expedition camp lay in a small enclosed field behind the churchyard; beyond that lay the rocky beach of Jangye-ryn and the site of the cannon wreck. He stopped below the churchyard wall and looked back over the cove at the site of the Phoenician wreck, now devoid of boats and divers, as if nothing had ever disturbed the waters there. The last of the artefacts had been removed to the International Maritime University conservation labs on the other side of the peninsula almost a year ago, and some of them were already on display in the state-of-the-art museum that was due to open its doors to the world's press in only a few weeks' time.

No project was ever complete until all the artefacts were conserved, studied and published, a process that would take years in the case of the Phoenician wreck, and many of the students and staff of IMU who had dived on the site would make careers out of researching the finds. But when Jack had showed them the shaky video he had taken with his GoPro camera of the cannon wreck after his snorkel dive, there had been renewed excitement among the team. Conservation and research had its own ample rewards, but after months of diving and the daily adrenalin of discovery, the climb-down could be a difficult adjustment. Jack was not the only one who was fired up by the prospect of another excavation only a few hundred metres from the first, of a wreck much closer in historic time but no less rich as an archaeological site.

He reached into his pocket and took out the silver four-real piece, letting the sun catch the cross on the reverse. There would now be another focus for the excavation, at the new cannon site under the headland where they had found the coin, as well as at least another full season's work on the main site of the wreck. He carefully replaced the coin in his pocket and looked at his watch. Slack water at high tide, the best time to be on site, was in less than an hour, and he would need time to kit up and make the fifteen-minute swim out to the wreck from the nearest access point. Before that, he wanted to show the coin to Rebecca and Jeremy, as proof that their discovery of the new cannon site was even more important than they could have imagined. He took a deep breath, feeling the familiar excitement course through him, wondering what the dive on the wreck would reveal today. He could hardly wait to find out.

'Jack! I've got excellent news. The metrics on the cannon worked out.'

The words came from a burly figure hurrying down the lane towards him carrying a tablet computer. Andrew Cunningham was a former Royal Engineers major whose fascination with historic ordnance had led to a second career with the Royal Armouries, as well as an adjunct position with

IMU. He had given the team a detailed briefing on the cannons on the wreck, and Jack himself had accompanied him on Cunningham's first ever open-water dive, to the cannon opposite the cleft, which they had measured and photographed together. He stopped in front of Jack now, breathless and excited, and pointed at the tablet. 'It's exactly what you'll want to hear.'

'Walk with me back to the camp,' Jack said. 'Tell me on the way.'

As Cunningham came alongside him, he tapped the screen and brought up a succession of 3-D images. 'Your chap Lanowski has been incredibly helpful. He took the high-definition sonar scan and the data from our electronic measurement and produced these renditions. You'll recognise the two guns at the top as the four-pounders we know from the documentary sources that she was carrying as shipboard armament, as opposed to the other, larger guns, which were cargo, of course. Those two guns were identical, from the same Dutch foundry. We know she was carrying four of them, so unless they were salvaged somewhere, we'd expect to find the other two. Well, bingo. The gun you and I measured below the cliff was one of them. Same bore, same metrics, same foundry. It's beautiful.'

Jack paused, took the tablet and stared at it. 'Are you sure? It's not just a standard size of gun that another merchantman of the same period that might have been wrecked off the headland could have been carrying?'

Cunningham shook his head. 'That's where the metrics come into play. With the precision of our measurements, we can be certain that these guns were cast in the same foundry, by the same founder, at the same time.'

'Brilliant, Andrew. More proof that we're looking at the missing part of the same wreck. That clinches it.'

'You've got something else?'

'Follow me into the operations tent.'

They turned from the lane into the grassy compound beyond the churchyard. The IMU campus was less than ten miles away, off the Fal estuary on the other side of the peninsula, but it was essential that they have a base at the site, and Jack had enjoyed spending nights here camped with the rest of the team behind the headland. They walked past the equipment store into the large tent that served as headquarters. Standing over the chart table was James Macalister, captain of IMU's chief research vessel *Seaquest* and companion on many of Jack's adventures. With his white beard, blue Guernsey sweater and silk scarf, he looked the part, though he seemed out of place on dry land. Jack shook his hand warmly. 'How goes *Seaquest*?'

Macalister folded his arms, looking unhappy. 'I never like seeing her in dry dock. I don't like leaving her like that.'

'She's in good hands,' Jack said. 'If the Royal Navy trusts the yard to do their ships, then I trust it with ours. They must be pretty close to finishing her refit by now.'

Two other figures entered the tent, and Jack turned to greet them. Dr Jeremy Haverstock had been linked with IMU since first coming over from Stanford as a young graduate student ten years before, on the way getting his doctorate under the supervision of Jack's friend Maria de Montijo at the Oxford Palaeography Institute; since then he had become an indispensable part of the team as well as a close friend of

Jack's daughter Rebecca. She was there, too, looking tan-
ned and fit after spending much of the summer on site as dive
manager, having upgraded her diving qualifications to
advanced instructor level. She came over and kissed Jack on
the cheek. 'I gather you and Uncle Costas have been off on
one of your little jaunts together.'

'Word travels fast,' Jack said.

'I rang Costas after realising you two had been missing all
morning. You might perhaps have told someone what you
were doing. You know, safety backup and all that. Kind of
stuff they teach you in basic instructor training. Kind of thing
you guys might have learned after all those years diving
together.'

Jack coughed. 'Well, we weren't exactly diving.'

'What *were* you doing?'

'You don't want to know.'

'You were inside that cleft in the cliff, weren't you? I knew
you'd want to go in there after Jeremy and I spotted the
cannon.'

Jack pulled the coin out of his pocket. 'Check out what we
found.' He passed the coin to Rebecca, and the others crowded
around. 'Well I'll be damned,' she said.

'Where have I heard that expression before?' Macalister
said.

'Like father, like daughter,' Jeremy murmured. 'In so many
ways.'

Rebecca angled the coin into the sunlight. 'Dad, am I seeing
what I think I'm seeing? Unless I'm mistaken, that shield is
overstamped with a five-pointed star.'

Jack nodded. 'A Star of David. Just like the one on the lid of the bronze box from the wreck. What you and Jeremy call the treasure chest.'

'I've got to get a picture of this off to Maria,' Jeremy said, taking out his phone and photographing the coin. 'She was with me last week in the National Archives in Kew when I was working my way through the Admiralty Papers related to the wreck, the Samuel Pepys stuff. I've been racking my brains about that Star of David, and have shown it to as many colleagues as I can to try to get a parallel. This coin proves that the sign on the box is not just a one-off, that we're looking at something with definite meaning.'

'You and I are still set up to meet tomorrow morning in my office at the campus,' Jack said. 'We're going to brainstorm everything we've got.'

Macalister peered at the chart on the table. 'Before you arrived, Andrew was telling us about his identification of the gun. Taking that into account, and now the coin as well, it looks as if we have the missing part of the wreck. I'm guessing that you won't have time to get in any excavation there this season, but we can at least do a magnetometer survey.'

'My thoughts exactly,' Jack said. 'That should show us whether there are any other cannon buried in the sand, and if so, pinpoint the spot when we're able to put the water dredges onto it. We have to assume from the empty treasure chest that there are more coins to be found, at least in the hundreds given the size of the box. Our coin could represent a considerable scatter blown up into the cleft during the storm that wrecked the ship, but the main deposit could be on the seabed near that cannon. The mother lode.'

Rebecca eyed him. 'Wow, Dad. Mother lode. You really can

talk the talk. That's treasure-hunter speak. Never thought I'd hear the day.'

Jack grinned. 'Well, archaeology has its perks, but spend long enough recording potsherds and you see the light eventually. And there's a little boy in me, before the PhD and all that serious stuff, who would just love to find a treasure trove of Spanish pieces of eight.'

'Amen to that.' Costas came lurching through the entrance carrying a large black box that he dumped unceremoniously at Macalister's feet. 'There you go. One magnetometer transceiver, fully serviced and tuned.'

'Have you two been talking about this already?' Jack said.

'As soon as I got out of that cleft, I radioed James to let him know that we were on target,' Costas replied. 'I thought it would help; give him time to drive the boat round and get everything prepped. While he was doing that and you were having your post-discovery moment alone on the cliff, I nipped back to the campus to pick up the magnetometer and my newly modified metal detector. I designed the detector precisely thinking that we might want to use it to explore fissures and crevices in the cliff face, so it's got a specially adapted head that you can poke into cracks. While James drives up and down offshore with the mag, I'm going to get down on the rocks again on either side of that gully and see what I can find.'

'It'll have to be today,' Jack said. 'We've got Force 8 westerlies forecast for tomorrow, and a likely ten-foot swell.'

'Roger that.'

The tablet that Costas had been carrying in his shoulder bag suddenly sprang to life, talking and flashing colour. He took it out and propped it on the table. 'Oh my God,' Rebecca said. 'It's Lanowski, from the IMU campus. It's like he's become the computer. He's finally gone full cyber.'

A dishevelled face appeared on the screen, came too close and then moved back, trying to look into the camera. Jacob Lanowski's long, lank hair was strangely dishevelled, and his little round glasses were askew. He was holding something small and dark close to his chest and was having trouble controlling it. He looked like someone who had been handed a baby and had no idea what to do with it. 'Costas,' he said, his voice edged with panic. 'I need your help. And I need it now.'

Costas sighed. 'What is it, Jacob? I hope you haven't upset Little Joey.'

'Little Joey?' Jeremy said. 'I thought that was the robot you lost in the volcano.'

'Not lost,' Costas said. 'Sacrificed for the cause of archaeology. And this is Little Joey 4. A miniature sub-bottom excavator. A kind of underwater mole that burrows under the sediment, records everything in 3-D, then extracts artefacts and hands them to you.'

Lanowski became more agitated. The object he was holding began jumping and whirring, as if it were trying to get out of his hands. 'Costas, this is serious. I can't control him. I finished that adjustment to the control wiring, and he suddenly sprang to life. I realised I had no idea how to switch him off.'

'He?' Cunningham said, puzzled. 'Is it alive?'

'In some minds, yes,' Jeremy murmured.

Costas picked up the tablet with both hands, as if he were

holding Lanowski by the shoulders, steadying him. 'It's like one of those talking toys, Jacob. Squeeze its belly.'

'What?' Little Joey leapt out of Lanowski's hands and began spinning around in the air. He caught it just in time, fell backwards out of sight, then lurched towards the screen again, leaning over and fumbling. Suddenly the commotion stopped, and all they could hear was panting. Lanowski stood back, holding the robot in his hands. 'Okay. Phew. Thanks.'

'Crisis over?' Jack said.

Lanowski carefully put Little Joey out of sight, stepping away warily as if he thought it was about to spring back at him, and turned to the screen. He cleared his throat, swept back his hair and adjusted his glasses, then laughed nervously. 'Crisis over. Sorry about that. Back to the nanotechnology lab.'

'Just let Little Joey sleep,' Costas said. 'He's like a new puppy, remember. Not really house-trained yet. We can take him for a burrow this evening.' He tapped the screen, and Lanowski disappeared. 'Apologies for that.'

'A burrow?' Jeremy said.

'A dig,' Costas replied. 'He really likes to dig. It's his job, after all. And then when he's finished, he goes round and round in circles like a dog making a cosy nest. Something Lanowski programmed into him, I don't know why. I think that's what Little Joey was trying to do just now.'

Rebecca shook her head. 'You guys need to get out more often.'

'That's the plan,' Costas said enthusiastically. 'Next time Jack has an excavation. We were going to let Little Joey loose on the wreck here, but now it looks as if the weather is closing in.'

'Speaking of which,' Macalister said, tapping the magneto-meter. 'Costas, are you coming?'

'You bet.'

The two men lifted the box and struggled with it out of the tent, disappearing in the direction of the IMU truck parked in the lane outside. Rebecca handed the coin back to Jack and smiled at him. 'You're all just boys with toys, aren't you?'

'James is an old sea dog and gets restless when he's not on the bridge of *Seaquest*. Putting him in charge of a Zodiac boat with a useful job to do means he'll be right back in his element. Costas, well, you know Costas as well as I do. Give him equipment to test and he's as happy as a six-year-old with a box of Lego.'

'Speaking of Costas, I think I'd better go and give him a hand,' Rebecca said. 'I know he's as sure-footed as a mountain goat, but I don't like to think of him tottering along the cliff edge with more equipment than he can really carry.'

'What you're actually saying is that you'd like to find a coin too.'

'The thought did cross my mind.'

'Be careful on the rocks. Piece of eight, okay?'

'You're on.'

Rebecca picked up her hiking boots and phone and walked towards the entrance of the tent, Jeremy and Cunningham following. Jack suddenly remembered something. 'Before you go, Rebecca. While Costas and I were, ah, in that cleft and passing the time, he said something about a book you guys are planning, a kind of unauthorised biography. Anything you want to tell me about?'

The truck revved up and began to trundle over the potholes

down the lane. Rebecca looked back, her face expressionless. 'A book? Another one? Really? Got to go, Dad. Appreciate it if you'd look at my draft layout for the information board. Talk later.'

Jack started to reply, but then thought better of it. He picked up the coin from where Rebecca had left it on the table, put it in a clear plastic finds bag and then placed the bag in a tray labelled for immediate conservation. He went to the cool box, took out a bottle of water and drank from it, then walked over to the easel where Rebecca had been mocking up a public information board on the excavation to complement the one on the Phoenician wreck that was now permanently erected near the coastal footpath. In the centre of the board, between photos of divers on the site, she had pinned a facsimile of a letter dated 7 April 1684 from a local official to Lord Dartmouth, Admiral of the Fleet, about how the ship's captain had allowed his vessel to be driven ashore thinking he was on the coast of France, and how the justices and gentlemen of the county were extremely civil and saved what they could, and were 'very kind to the poor people'.

He read through the rest of Rebecca's text, scribbling a few comments on the board, then looked out of the open tent flap to the wreck site several hundred metres away across the cove, seeing two divers on the surface about to begin their shift. He thought about what Andrew Cunningham had said about her ordnance, about the 'Great Guns' that were the most prominent feature of the site. The fact that most of those guns were not ship's armament but cargo, packed muzzle to breech in two rows along the bottom of the hold, was one of many extraordinary aspects of the ship's story. She was called the

Schiedam, and was part of Lord Dartmouth's fleet carrying ordnance, tools, horses and people back from Tangier, the port in present-day Morocco which had been acquired by the English king Charles II as part of his dowry when he married the Portuguese princess Catherine of Braganza, but which was abandoned in 1684 in the face of Moorish threat.

The *Schiedam* was originally a Dutch merchantman that had been captured by Barbary pirates a few months earlier and was then captured again by a daring young Royal Navy captain, Cloudesley Shovell – who years later, as an admiral, was lost with his fleet in the Scilly Isles due to a navigational error, a catastrophe that precipitated the race to find a better way to establish longitude. Captain Shovell, in the *James Galley*, had escorted the *Schiedam* to Tangier, where she was entered into the books as a transport vessel. On her fateful return voyage she carried not only cannon and tools, some of them the private consignments of Tangier merchants, but also the workmen who had been employed to destroy the great mole in the harbour, the huge breakwater that had been laboriously constructed by the English to make Tangier a more viable port. The men had been paid off handsomely and dispatched home along with their wives and children and everything of value they could salvage from Tangier.

All of this meant that as an archaeological site the wreck was extraordinarily rich, a veritable porthole into life in the English colony at that time, manifest in artefacts ranging from the ordnance and small arms of the garrison to the personal items that people had been able to rescue in the face of the Moorish onslaught.

As if that history were not remarkable enough, no less a

person than the diarist Samuel Pepys now entered the picture; as an Admiralty official he was one of Lord Dartmouth's staff at Tangier, and much of his correspondence relating to the wreck of the *Schiedam* survived in the National Archives, where Jeremy had been working his way through it over the past couple of weeks. For Jack, the wreck gave a unique insight into an extraordinary and largely forgotten episode in British history, at a time when the direction of imperial expansion lay in the balance and the decision to abandon the North African colony saw greater focus on the 'Enterprise of the Indies', the drive to control India that was to dominate British maritime trade over the next two centuries.

He finished the water and put the bottle on the table. Later that day, before returning to the IMU campus he would draft a press release on the project, using Rebecca's text as the basis. The wreck was already a protected archaeological site under British law, and had attracted a great deal of attention in the media, both locally and nationally. Then he needed to ensure that the team dismantled and removed all the equipment currently underwater before the storm waves rolled in. But before that, he was due to carry out one last dive on the site, and he wanted to make the most of it. He glanced at his watch, his excitement mounting. It was time to kit up.

3

Half an hour later, Jack sat in his dive gear on the low stone wall that lined the path down to the beach, pulling at the D-rings on his shoulder straps to tighten his buoyancy compensator and scuba rig. He was beginning to feel uncomfortably warm in his drysuit, but with the water having cooled down after the summer he knew that a wetsuit would have left him cold by the end of his dive. He reached down for his hoses and pulled the pressure gauge for his tank around one side and his backup regulator around the other, clipping them to the bottom of his BC, then attached the inflator hose to the valve on the front of his drysuit and the other one to his BC hose. He jiggled sideways to make sure that his weight belt was in position on his hips below his harness, then strapped his dive computer and compass to his wrists. The final piece of equipment to attach was his camera, a compact, robust model in a plastic housing, which served him well for record shots and video underwater. He activated it to check the screen, then clipped the extendable leads on either side to the D-rings on his shoulders and tucked the camera under the BC strap across his chest. He shut his eyes and relaxed for a moment, enjoying the cool breeze. He was getting seriously hot now, and was looking forward to the first splash of seawater on his face.

'All right, Jack?' A diver already kitted up came down the path from the van parked in the lane at the top of the slope. Mike Trethowan had an extensive knowledge of wrecks along the coast of Cornwall, and a passion for discovery that matched Jack's own. The two men were about the same age, both had daughters, and they had hit it off as soon as they had met during a chance encounter diving off the same beach fifteen years before, when IMU was only on the planning table. Mike still ran the dive shop and training centre that he had operated then, but he was also IMU's chief diving officer and head of diver training. Many of the local divers who had trained with him were now stalwart members of the IMU team, complementing the students and academics who volunteered to join his projects from all over the world.

Mike leaned over Jack, untwisting one of his shoulder straps, and looked at his contents gauge, double-checking that his tank had the full 230-bar fill. Jack did the same for him, and then pulled on his thin neoprene gloves and pushed himself up, leaning over and pulling again at his harness straps for a final tightening. He picked up his fins, mask and snorkel and hood, and peered at Mike. 'Good to go?'

'I thought you only said that to Costas, Jack. I'm honoured.'

'Speaking of Costas, did you see the coin we found?'

'I just saw it in the finds tray. Brilliant. I knew there'd be something in that cleft.'

'Did you get a chance to show Andrew Cunningham your photos of that cylindrical iron object you found on the wreck?'

'He's very excited by it. He thinks it's either a really big mortar, with the breech section unscrewed and missing, or a segment from a bombard.'

'You mean like a medieval cannon?'

'Well, it's of wrought-iron construction, banded with loops of iron. That's where the word "barrel" comes from, as in gun barrel. The earliest big guns were built that way, with lengths of iron like barrel staves held in place with iron loops. He thinks that because of that early technique, it could be an obsolete cannon being brought back to England as scrap, something that might have been part of the defences of Tangier way back before the English arrived, even as early as the fifteenth century.'

'Very cool,' Jack said. 'Obsolete for them maybe, but historical treasure for us.'

'Exactly. While you're doing your excavation, I'm going to be just out of sight from you, digging out the bottom part of the cylinder from the sand so we can get a full profile view.'

'I'll have a break and come over and take a look. Give you a hand if you need it.'

'Cheers, Jack, but you need to get as much done in your sector as you can. I'm sure you've seen the weather forecast from tomorrow on. Today is probably our last day on site this season, and who knows how much sand there might be covering that reef next year. Anyway, John and Nadine from the previous dive shift are still out there, and if we get going, I should be able to use the remaining half-hour or so of their bottom time to have them dredging with me.'

'They've been great. Everyone has. A real team effort.'

'We owe a lot to Rebecca. She's been an excellent dive manager.'

'And to the girls in the café for the continuous supply of tea.'

'Essential.'

They walked down the ramp over the shingle to the beach, passing the line of kelp and debris left by the spring high tide a few days before. The cove was some five hundred metres wide, between the church headland and the cliffs to the north, but unlike the cove to the south, the sand here was crossed by irregular spines of rock that extended out from the shore, some of them carrying on as underwater reefs that separated wide sandy gullies. The shallow depth, the reefs and the exposure to westerlies meant that any ship driven in here during a storm would quickly have been ripped apart, but the excavation had shown that the sandy gullies were deep and contained undisturbed layers full of well-preserved artefacts. The weather that had played such a part in the wrecking and the dispersal of material was also an inhibiting factor in planning a dive operation, but Jack relished working on a site where there was such good preservation in shallow water, and where divers could go in for an hour and a half twice a day with minimal risk of nitrogen sickness.

He felt the sweat drip off his forehead and down his nose. They reached the surf line, ripples of water sparkling in the early-afternoon sun, the water beautifully clear as it extended off to the small Zodiac anchored as a safety tender above the site a hundred metres away. He dropped his fins and hood on the sand and walked out into the waves, swilling his mask and splashing water on his face, and then returned to finish kitting up. Mike turned to him, a familiar gleam in his eye. 'I meant to say, Jack. I think I might have found a very interesting new lead for us.'

'Oh oh,' Jack said, straining to bend down and pick up his hood. 'That happens every time you sit in front of your shipwreck database.'

'It was your coin. It made me think about Captain Avery's treasure.'

Jack peered at him. 'Pretty tired old ground, isn't it? A bit like the search for the Holy Grail. But like you, I'm one of life's optimists. And you do seem to have the Midas touch when it comes to finding new sites.'

'You just can't ignore it. There are so many references to that treasure around here that there must be a grain of truth in it. Avery was the King of Pirates, with seven chests of silver and one of gold, supposedly buried somewhere around here and never found. It's the same period, isn't it, the late seventeenth century. The evacuation of Tangier, the wreck of the *Schiedam*, the Spanish Main and the pirates of Port Royal; it's all interconnected.'

'You're looking at the bigger picture.'

'Well, one thing I don't buy is the burial story. About Avery's treasure, I mean. You're the most successful pirate ever, right? The only pirate ever really to hit the jackpot, scoring a treasure fleet in the Indian Ocean and then another one in the Caribbean, and virtually the only big-time pirate to escape capture. You retire to England, and then you spend the rest of your life in misery and obscurity. That's what the stories tell us. I just don't buy it.'

'Go on.'

'You don't bury treasure and then live in poverty. You spend it. He didn't bury it. He lost it in a shipwreck.'

Jack thought for a moment. 'That would certainly explain the misery and obscurity.'

'I dug up some notes that John took when he went to the county archives looking for unpublished parish accounts that might mention shipwrecks. You know, the Victorian craze among priests to write up the history of their parish and list all the wreck fatalities they knew about.'

'I think it was a bit of a guilt trip,' Jack said. 'A lot of those accounts came soon after the Act obliging the Church to bury unclaimed bodies from the sea in consecrated ground, and it always seems to me as if the priests were casting last rites over all who had gone before, all those buried along these cliffs.'

'Well, John did find the scrappy remains of a notebook written by one of those priests, for the parish at the southern tip of the peninsula, covering Kynance Cove. There's the usual ghoulish stuff, listing unclothed torsos and heads and other body parts – maybe, as you say, the guilt trip, to try to exonerate the Church for not having treated these remains as somehow fully human. Then there are a couple of pages of local legends, the usual monsters in caves and smuggling stories, and hints of treasure ships having foundered nearby. Nothing new in that, of course – you hear it everywhere along this coast – but I'd never heard the story that Henry Avery's treasure was lost in a wreck on the other side of the Devil's Bellows.'

'Bloody hell.'

'Could just be another Avery story. One of dozens.'

'Could be.' Jack thought for a moment, still holding his hood. 'Ever been through the Bellows?'

'Never. The old divers say it's a dangerous place at the best of times, that it can lure you in but then you get trapped by the alternating surge and current.'

'Sounds like our kind of place. Costas's, too.'

'One for the list.'

'Defo.'

Jack pulled on his hood and then his mask, ran his finger around the edge of the hood to ensure that the mask was sealed against his face and then picked up his fins and headed into the waves. Ten metres out, with the water at waist level, he put his snorkel in his mouth and dropped down to pull on his fins. He looked around to see Mike doing the same, then rolled over on his front and kicked out, at the same time pressing the button on his BC inflator to inject air into his jacket to keep himself afloat. Below him the sand was shimmering, the upper layer swept into suspension with the ebb and flow of the water, but further out it was more settled and he could see the ripples running out to the edge of his visibility, fifteen metres or more away. The reef to his right was smooth and free of marine growth in the turbulent waters of the inter-tidal zone, but below him was covered by patches of kelp that obscured much of the rock. A few minutes further out, he stopped and got his bearings, seeing the Zodiac less than fifty metres away near the edge of the cove. Below him, Mike was already swimming along the seabed, and Jack pulled out his trusty old Poseidon regulator from where he had wedged it under his BC hose, putting it in his mouth and hearing the satisfying hiss of the intake and flow of the exhaust as he took his first few breaths. He pulled the dump valve of his BC to empty it, then held the inflator valve ready to inject small bursts of air back in to bring him back to neutral buoyancy as he neared the seabed. He felt a rush of pleasure as he dropped beneath the surface: the joy of being underwater and on his way to a wreck site. He could hardly wait to get there.

Twenty minutes later, Jack was eight metres deep on the wreck, planning his next hour on the seabed. From below he had watched the two divers in the shift before him rise to the surface, check with the safety diver in the Zodiac and then drop down again to help Mike in his part of the site some fifteen metres away. He picked up the dredge that had been left for him and pulled it over to the edge of the rocky reef where he was due to excavate, making sure that the hose was floating well above the cannons that were exposed in the sand behind him. Then he let air out of his buoyancy compensator until he was floating just above the sand.

To his left lay the cannon that he had first seen when he had discovered the site the year before, its massive breech resting on the reef and the muzzle buried in the sand; seeing it again brought back the same rush of excitement he had experienced that day. He had known then that the few metres of reef next to the cannon contained other artefacts, some of them locked in concretion and others buried in fissures, and his task today was to uncover and record as many of them as possible. He had decided to begin next to the cannon and work his way along the edge of the reef to the right, dredging away the sand where it overlapped the patches of concretion and clearing any fissures that still contained sediment. He shifted the dredge into position and used the hammer hanging from it by a chain to tap the signal on the metal tube for the operator in the boat above to start up the pump. Moments later he heard a muffled chugging, and saw the sand around the nozzle of the dredge begin to disappear down the tube.

He lifted the tube so that the nozzle was just above the seabed, wedged it under his right arm and checked behind to make sure that the exhaust was not dropping sediment on the cannons in the gully. Then he aimed the dredge at the reef and began to work at the sand with his left hand, vigorously wafting deep patches until they were gone, and more sensitively working his way around features where the sediment was only a thin sheen. The concretion had spread over the reef like a solidified mass of tar, a result of the oxidisation of masses of iron objects that had fallen together on the seabed. Most of the lumps were unidentifiable, but he knew that inside them would be hollow casts left where tools and other objects had disintegrated, something that might only be revealed by breaking open the concretions or taking them to the lab to X-ray.

There were some objects, however, that were more clearly recognisable. An eroded fragment of shaped marble lay wedged into a cleft at the top of the concretion. It was the end of a small column, originally about ten centimetres across and a metre in length. Jack swam closer and peered at a fracture line, where he could see the grain of the stone. His suspicions were confirmed. It was *giallo antico*, 'ancient yellow', the distinctive honey-coloured marble from Tunisia that was quarried by the Romans. They had found other fragments on the wreck, part of the surrounds of an elaborate fireplace, but were certain that the stone had been reused from a Roman site somewhere near Tangier; *giallo antico* was not quarried after the Roman period, and the only source in the seventeenth century would have been one of the numerous ruins of ancient cities and buildings that dotted the north coast of Africa. He put his hand on the stone, feeling a wave of satisfaction course through him. He had dreamed for years of finding Roman artefacts off Cornwall, but never imagined that it might happen in this most unlikely of ways.

Below the stone, a well-preserved cannonball poked out of a mass of concretion that partly enveloped it, like the yolk of a fried egg. Further on were two long forms that he knew were musket barrels, the wooden stocks long gone but the brass trigger guard of one of them just visible. Andrew Cunningham had taken a group of them to test-fire a replica English musket of the period at the IMU campus the day before, and the lingering smell of black powder smoke had given an immediacy to the siege of Tangier – something that helped Jack to see the concretions in front of him for what they had once been: well-polished weapons in the hands of English soldiers desperately trying to hold off a besieging enemy more than three hundred years before.

Above one of the muskets a trickle of sand spilled from a fissure that ran down from the top of the reef, the lower metre or so still packed with sediment. He expected to find little in such a high-energy environment, on top of the reef where the sand and shingle might come and go with the storms, but he repositioned himself over the fissure and wafted the sediment into the nozzle of the dredge. To his amazement, he revealed a cluster of lead musket balls sitting on the smoothed surface of the bedrock below. He picked one of them up, weighing it in his hand, noticing the wear on its surface from centuries of movement underwater. In his mind's eye he saw the site as it must have looked just after the wrecking, a seething, tumultuous mass of smashed timber, sails and cordage, the cannons already having crashed to the seabed where they now lay, the smaller artefacts falling into gullies and fissures and working their way down in the sediment according to weight and density, a process of sorting and decay of which these musket balls were the final poignant residue.

He carefully put the musket ball back where he had found it, pushed off from the fissure and tapped the dredge with the hammer again, this time to signal for the pump to be switched off. As the chugging sound ceased, he surveyed the patch of concretion that he had cleared. It only amounted to a few square metres, but he had found far more than he had bargained for, and the rest of the dive would have to be devoted to the tasks that made this archaeology rather than salvage: photographing and sketching the finds, surveying them into the site grid using the innovative IMU sonic high-accuracy positioning system – something that only required a tap of the acoustic 'pencil' on the finds – and bagging and raising the musket balls, essential at this site, because to leave loose finds exposed for even one change of the tide could result in them being lost irretrievably in the ever-shifting sands.

He released his camera and took out a ten-centimetre scale

from his BC pocket, ready to photograph the musket balls, but then he saw something else that his wafting had exposed at the far end of the fissure. He tucked the camera back under the strap and dropped down again. A corroded iron sphere not much bigger than his fist was wedged into the rock. At first he thought it was a small cannonball, perhaps for one of the swivel guns that they knew had been mounted on the walls of Tangier, but then to his amazement he saw an accreted wooden plug sticking out of one end. *It was a grenade.* Andrew Cunningham in his prep talk on the ordnance had told them what to expect and what would be most exciting, and grenades were at the top of the list. He had explained that grenades had only become regular equipment among English regiments a few years before the siege, and that no examples had been found in archaeological sites dated as early as the *Schiedam*. Jack was thrilled to have made the discovery, something that would really help to put the wreck on the map for more than just its historical backstory.

He extracted his camera again, and the scale, and quickly took a series of photos, then put one hand on the grenade. This time it was not the turmoil of the wrecking that opened up before his eyes, but rather the final years of fighting by the English at Tangier as the Moors threatened to overwhelm them. Among the first-hand accounts he had read was one from 1680 of the English garrison in one of the towers holding out to the last man against the besieging force, using muskets and pikes and grenades, fighting at the end with their bare hands. In the blood-soaked arsenal of the tower the Moors had found boxes of unused grenades, a boost to their own armaments that gave them a greater tactical edge and eventually helped to persuade the English to abandon the colony rather than fight on. The grenade Jack had just found was thus a touchstone of history, an artefact that signified a shift in the course of events that had a profound effect on everything that followed. Had the English decided to retain Tangier, had they not instead transferred their focus and energies to India, the whole course of European and world history would have been different. For Jack, the artefacts he had found suddenly coalesced into something bigger, into a picture in his mind's eye that linked a single object to the wider flow of events. When that happened, when he felt that surge of adrenalin and insight, he was no longer just a dirt archaeologist; he was an explorer of history, and he was in his element.

He felt a tap on his shoulder, and turned to see the next pair of divers beside him with the acoustic pencil and a sketching slate. He gestured at the grenade and the musket balls, and they both made enthusiastic okay signs. The nearer diver then pointed at Jack, made a thumbs-up sign and opened her arms questioningly. Jack checked his air; he still had at least half an hour left. He pushed back, looking up at the underside of the boat and then back at the divers, and made an emphatic negative signal, sweeping his hands from side to side, then pointing at himself and the artefacts around him. He could have let them take over the recording, but that was not his way. He was diving on a shipwreck, immersed in the archae-ology and the thrill of discovery, fulfilling the dream he had first had as a boy exploring these very waters. Right now, he could not have wished to be in a better place.

4

Early the following morning, Jack sat on the doorstep of his study in the old Howard house above the IMU campus, sipping his coffee and watching the sun rise over the broad expanse of the estuary to the east. He checked his phone, making sure the message he had just written had been sent. Late the previous evening he had received a phone call from a man with a Spanish or Portuguese accent who had asked whether he had found any parallels for the Star of David symbol on the coin. His credentials had sounded plausible – a seminary in Lisbon – and Jack had assumed that he was one of the colleagues Jeremy had contacted at the National Archives, but he had looked him up as they were talking and had found no reference to the place or the man. When he had confronted him with it, the man had warned him to steer clear of researching the symbol and hung up. It was probably just a crank call, but Jack had messaged their security chief

Ben Kershaw to put him on alert. They had experienced the less pleasant end of this type of problem in the past, and it was always best to err on the side of caution.

He put the call from his mind and focused on the view. Leading down to the water's edge, he could see the engineering block where Costas and Lanowski would already be hard at work, and beyond that the dock that led to Carrick Roads and the open sea beyond. Several of IMU's research vessels were currently absent on projects, as well as one of the larger Zodiacs that Macalister had driven round to the site for the magnetometer survey the day before. The campus was in the grounds of the estate, land that had been in the Howard family for almost a millennium, and had begun to look less of an imposition on the landscape, with the architecture melding into the brick and stone of the old buildings and the newly planted trees beginning to reach the heights of those established more than two hundred years before.

He had to remind himself that IMU had been little more than a dream only twenty years ago, when he had inherited the estate and the mountainous debts that went with it. He had been working on a classical shipwreck off Turkey, contemplating the best course of action with his inheritance, when he had first met Costas, at that time on a short-service commission as an engineering officer with the US Navy at their Izmir base. Diving together on a shoestring budget, they had hatched the plan for IMU, and Jack had presented it to his old dive buddy Efram Jacobovich, by then a software tycoon with money to spare. The dream had become a reality, and within a few years the campus had departments ranging across the marine sciences, as well as one of the world's foremost centres for research on maritime and naval history. Efram's endowment gave IMU total financial independence and meant they could focus entirely on research and fieldwork rather than fund-raising. With a board of directors and a full academic faculty established, Jack had been able to take a back seat and concentrate on his role as archaeological director. It was a job that gave him a strong sense of continuity with his ancestors, at this place where generations of Howards had set off down the path to the sea, serving the Crown in war and conquest as well as embarking on their own ventures for exploration and profit.

He thought of the fine line between those motivations for seafaring as he drank his coffee and stared at the beautiful framed chart of west Cornwall that he had taken down from his study wall and propped in the sunlight for a better view. The chart dated from the 1680s, the time of the wreck of the *Schiedam*, and was by van Keulen, a famous Amsterdam cartographer who supplied charts to the Dutch East India Company. It was the nearest thing to a nautical chart that had existed for these waters at the time, with rhumb lines and compass roses out at sea, and a fair approximation of the coastline, though little detail inland.

Everything about navigation and seafaring that would be taken for granted in the following century – the professional Royal Navy, the scrupulous survey of coastlines that was to be its greatest achievement – was still a good way off in the seventeenth century. To be sure, there were naval captains who would have ranked in skill and daring alongside the frigate captains of the Napoleonic Wars, men such as Sir Cloudesley Shovell, but even for those men the lure of private venture might be greater. Pay was poor, the ethos of loyalty to the service not yet established, and to follow a letter of marque as a privateer was to some men as honourable a career as taking a King's commission, especially when the monarch had little knowledge of nautical affairs and the endless wars of the period were of dubious benefit to the navy or the nation.

Jack peered closely at the chart. He had brought it down to look at not only because of the *Schiedam* but also because of another extraordinary story of the same period, one that Mike had brought up before their dive yesterday. One of those men who had crossed the line between serving the King and serving himself, and then gone even further, was Henry Avery, an officer on board Shovell's ship HMS *James Galley* when the *Schiedam* had been captured from the Barbary corsairs, and later to become a notorious pirate. Quite what Avery was doing while the *Schiedam* was making her fateful final voyage was unknown, but he did not yet appear to have taken his decisive step over to the dark side.

During the evacuation from Tangier, a number of junior officers were seconded from naval ships to be temporary captains of transports and supply ships, especially those like *Schiedam* that were captured prizes with only skeleton crews. The man appointed captain of *Schiedam* was a master attendant of the naval stores named Gregory Fish, whose inexperience and incompetence probably led directly to the wrecking; he had imagined that the ship was off the coast of France, and he went to pieces when he was hauled from the wreck afterwards. But his appointment appeared to have been an aberration, probably forced on the authorities as the number of available commanders dwindled, and more capable and experienced officers such as Avery may well have been given other vessels to command, perhaps those with more challenging itineraries taking merchants and their goods off to diverse destinations in the Mediterranean and even across the Atlantic. Avery's possible involvement was something that Jack had asked Jeremy to look out for in the Admiralty papers, a small piece of the jigsaw puzzle that would help to fill out the historical backdrop.

He looked back through the doorway at another old framed document above the fireplace behind his desk, something that he still knew virtually by heart from when he had pored over it as a boy: a proclamation for apprehending Henry Avery and sundry other pirates, 'who may be probably known and discovered by the great quantities of Persian and Indian gold and silver which they have with them . . . Out of detestation to such a horrid villainy, and to the effect the same may not go unpunished . . . we do make offer and assure the payment of the sum of five hundred pounds sterling for the said Henry Avery.' The proclamation had been issued under William III in 1696, twelve years after the sinking of the *Schiedam*, by which time Avery had long been out of navy service and had transformed himself into the feared Long Ben, King of the Pirates.

Jack remembered what Mike had said about how everything they were dealing with from that period seemed to be interconnected, and another one of those links was between the Avery and Howard families. All the great seafaring families of this coast were closely tied, serving apprenticeships on each other's vessels, going into business together and intermarrying. The Averys were from nearby Plymouth, and as a boy, Henry had been taken on board the Howard ship *Seafire* to learn the Americas trade before service in the Royal Navy. Later he had embarked on a joint trading venture for American tobacco with Jack's ancestor John Howard, though his true intention had been to use the money to underwrite a slaving expedition to West Africa, a trade that the Howards abhorred.

That proclamation had been on the wall of this room since then, a reminder of unfinished business and a debt that had been remembered through the generations. If Mike was right and Avery's treasure ship really did lie beyond the Devil's Bellows in Kynance Cove, then some of that treasure would be payback that would go nicely into Jack's own charitable foundation, something he had used to fund humanitarian aid in Ghana and Sierra Leone since he and Costas had been involved in the salvage of a Second World War wreck off that coast the year before. The story that Mike had unearthed might be no more than a local vicar's pipe dream, but a trip to the cove when the weather allowed was now firmly on Jack's agenda.

He peered again at the chart, tracing the coast down from the site of the church headland and the wreck of the *Schiedam* to Kynance Cove, some four miles distant. The coastline was marked with numerous crosses that had been thought simply to be embellishments by the illustrator, but that might mark shipwrecks. Jack had wanted to look at the stretch of coast near the cove again, and he could see that there were several crosses in the right area. It was another wreck graveyard, like the church cove, and there was no telling which ships might be represented. But it was the nearest thing to a treasure map they had, and X might just mark the spot.

He took a picture with his phone and messaged it to Mike, then picked up the chart and replaced it on the wall beside the proclamation. Rebecca and Jeremy were due within the hour, and he needed to focus on another thread in his family history that might have a bearing on the wreck of the *Schiedam*, something that had arisen because of the Star of David symbol on the bronze chest and the coin. He turned to the mass of papers spread out on the old mahogany desk in front of him, quickly finished his coffee and began to read.

Half an hour later, Jack sat back in his chair with his hands folded behind his head, thought for a few moments, then leaned forward again. It was an incredible story, one that opened up the darkest chapter in European history prior to modern times. The wreck of the *Schiedam*, and the backstory of the evacuation of Tangier by the English, was more than just an archaeological fascination for him. It tied in to a thread in his own family history that had been passed down through the generations, and that he had researched extensively himself the previous year. An ancestor of his, Rebecca Brandon, also known as Rebecca Rodrigues Brandão, had been from a Sephardic Jewish family who had fled Portugal and settled in London in the eighteenth century. She married an English officer of the East India Company army and spent the rest of her life in far-off Purnea, in the foothills of the Himalayas, her Jewish faith remembered but not practised by her children and their descendants. But her own family had a rich Jewish history that went back to the period when the Jews of Iberia were persecuted by the Inquisition, a time of unimaginable horror and fear. Those who escaped had spread far and wide throughout the known world, from London and Amsterdam and France to the port cities of the Mediterranean and the New World. And one of them, João Rodrigues Brandão, had been a merchant in Tangier at the time of the English colony and the evacuation, before he too was caught up by the Inquisition.

Jack sifted the papers, finding a facsimile of a letter to the court of the Inquisition signed by João himself; amazingly, many of the *processo* documents detailing the tribunals of the Inquisition survived in the Portuguese National Archives. The decree expelling Jews from Portugal in 1496 had obliged those who wished to remain to reject their Jewish identity and adopt Christian practices and names. Many of those so-called 'New Christians', or *conversos* – among them João's ancestors – had secretly maintained their Jewish faith, and those suspected of doing so over the next generations were brought before the Inquisition to test the truth of their conversion. The persecution was fuelled by the same kind of resentment of Jewish wealth and success that led to their victimisation elsewhere in Europe; in the case of João and his family, they lived in Viseu, an inland town in northern Portugal, but he had his office and warehouses in the coastal city of Porto, where he exported tools and wine to the Portuguese colonists of Brazil and imported tobacco and other raw materials in return.

He picked up the copy of João's *processo* document. Like everything else about the Inquisition, it made chilling reading. João was accused of Judaism, heresy and apostasy, and was brought before the tribunal of the Inquisition a mere two weeks after his arrest. From one viewpoint, he was lucky:

most of those accused in Coimbra, the city where he was tried, languished in the cells for months or even years before they were brought to trial. There must have been some reason for the speed of his case, something that Jack would like to investigate further. João would have gone from the tribunal straight to his auto-da-fé, his act of penance, but whether that was a simple confession and promise of renewed Christian faith or something much worse was never recorded in the *processo* document, the decision usually only being read out to the condemned when they were standing in front of the pyres in the town square. The prospects would not have been good: the Inquisition had come back with a vengeance in Portugal after having been banned for several years by the Pope for its excesses, and in Coimbra alone more than three hundred Jews were burned at the stake; men, women and children, sometimes entire families together. It was a hideous outcome that even the priests watching must have viewed as a travesty of the teachings of Jesus, as if the Church were being pulled under by dark forces that wished to sever its connection entirely from the morality and humanity that had been its foundation.

It was Jack's friend Maria de Montijo who had collected together most of the documents that he had in front of him now, during a day in the archives in Lisbon when she was visiting family in her native Spain. She herself had said that there were loose ends still to follow up, and that more delving was needed to get the full story on João. His *processo* document seemed less complete than many of the others, more perfunctory, at odds with his wealth as a merchant and the interest that the Inquisition would normally have had in detailing his business and financial arrangements. Jack glanced again at the page of notes that Maria had given him along with the copy of the *processo*. The only financial detail was that João had sent 250 gold ducats to London; it had been the basis of one of the accusations levelled against him, as Jews were forbidden to send money abroad except strictly for business purposes. It was a substantial sum, the equivalent of about 4,500 Spanish reales, but that was a drop in the ocean of the Brandão family fortune.

Another document that Maria had found, listing property confiscated by the Inquisition, showed that João and his brothers had owned a tobacco mill in Lisbon valued at nearly 750,000 reales. Property in Portugal would always have been vulnerable to confiscation, and there was little they could have done about that; but liquid assets could easily have been secreted abroad – despite the ban – and a merchant such as João would have been doing that all his life, knowing that to fall foul of the Inquisition would mean losing his entire wealth if he had not already dispersed it elsewhere. With family and business partners not only in London but also in France and Holland and across the sea in the Caribbean, he would have had plenty of secure places to bank his money outside the reach of the Inquisition, providing the basis for his descendants to carry on the family business even if he himself failed to make it out of Portugal alive.

Jack knew that Maria was in Spain again this week. He wanted to know if there was any further evidence, perhaps in other sources, for João in Tangier, and to discover more about the family connections that would have led him to send his money abroad. The possibility that it was João who was represented by the Star of David on the coin from the wreck was tenuous at best, but it was a possibility that he had to explore as long as there was no evidence of other Jewish merchants dispatching goods from Tangier. With the wreck excavation almost certainly wrapped up for this season, he might even take a few days and see if he could meet up with Maria in Portugal himself, and they could visit the archives together.

He picked up his phone, scrolling for her number. Then he remembered the last time they had spoken, several months earlier, an awkward conversation when he had cancelled a dinner because he and Costas had had to fly off unexpectedly to Somalia. He had known Maria for ten years and had first gone out with her five years ago, but their projects always seemed to get in the way when they thought of spending more time together. Most recently the ball had been in his court, and promises had been made. He paused, and then put down the phone. This might take a bit more thought.

The door opened and Rebecca and Jeremy came in, Jeremy carrying his briefcase and a coffee and Rebecca with two mugs in one hand and a sheaf of papers in the other. 'Hi, Dad. I'm guessing you've been at it for a while. I thought this might be a two-coffee morning.'

'Just getting up to speed on our family history.'

'It's amazing how it feeds into your projects.'

'It's like an ever-expanding web, catching all kinds of episodes in history, endlessly intriguing. It's because we've got such a wealth of material about it, and because we come from a family with such a strong tradition of seafaring and exploration.'

'Which of course is why you're fascinated by the sea too, and why you do what you do. It's in the blood.'

'The circle of life.'

She leaned over and looked at the papers. 'You been researching my namesake again? You never did tell me whether you and Mama named me after her.'

'It was your mother who named you, remember? I didn't even know you were on the way when she left me to go back to Naples.' Jack paused, looking at the floor. Elizabeth had been on his mind again, and he had wanted to talk about her to Rebecca. Now was as good a time as any, even with Jeremy there, and he looked up at her. 'I just had no idea that her family were Camorra and had such a hold over her. All she ever wanted was to come to England to train as an archaeologist, and then go back to Naples to try to resolve the corruption in the archaeological service there. That turned out to be her undoing. I still can't believe that it was rogue elements in her own family – your family in Naples – that sealed her fate. I just wish she'd got back in touch and told me about you before it was too late. Maybe I could have intervened and brought her out of that mess. We never really split up, you know; she just left. That's why it's difficult for me with Maria, and before that with Katya.'

Rebecca reached out and touched his hand. 'I know, Dad. But don't worry about it. I was sent away to America for my own protection before I was old enough to know what was really going on, but I knew my mother well enough to know that she would never have walked away from her job. That place, Pompeii, Herculaneum, was her life, just like all of this here is yours. And she didn't want you involved in what was going on there in any way. There was nothing you could have done.'

Jack nodded. 'I know. But I just wanted you to hear it from me again. Anyway, enough of that. Back to your name. When your mother and I saw each other that final time in Herculaneum, just before she was taken, we talked about you, and she admitted that yes, she did name you after Rebecca Brandon, because she liked the name and knew how intrigued I was with her life story. So there's your answer.'

Rebecca settled back in her chair, looking round at the paintings of Howards on the walls. 'You don't have a portrait of her, do you?'

'I've never been able to find one. But she was said to have brought great beauty into the family at the period.'

'I find it very moving, actually,' Rebecca said. 'To think of her surviving and bringing up a family without fear of the Inquisition, after all those generations before her who had to endure torment and terror. I feel the same way when I see Jewish women in New York or Tel Aviv or Toronto: that they stand for all those girls and women who didn't make it through the Holocaust, showing that darkness *can* be overcome.'

'Yet that darkness is still lurking just beneath the surface,' Jeremy said. 'The Inquisition may be long gone, but there are still secret societies sworn to perpetuate its goals who are just as fanatical about stamping their authority on those who stand in their way. They are still thought to hold a lot of influence in church appointments and policy. Some of them are said to go back to the earliest days of the persecution of the Church in the Roman period.'

'We encountered some of that when we searched for the Jewish menorah,' Jack said. 'A fixation on holy relics shared only by the Nazis. A belief that to control the oldest relics of Christendom will somehow guarantee them ascendancy in the Church.'

'The horrible truth is, it probably would,' Jeremy said. 'The power of artefacts. You know all about that, Jack.'

'Indeed.'

Rebecca pushed Jack's coffee across the table towards him. He took it gratefully, drank half and then put it down while she and Jeremy drew their chairs up to the other side of the desk, Jeremy taking his laptop out as he did so. As he opened it up, Jack gave him a piercing look. 'Okay, down to business. Samuel Pepys and the wreck of the *Schiedam*. What have you got?'

5

Jack's phone flashed up a new message, and he picked it up, tapped the screen and opened the attached image. He looked at it for a moment, then passed it over the table. 'Excellent news from Macalister. They've just finished processing the magnetometer results and it looks as if they've come up trumps. In the image you can see the cannon that you guys found, and then another very similar pattern in the readings about five metres further out, under the sand. My guess is that the second reading is the missing four-pounder from the ship's armament, and that when we begin excavating there next season, we'll find other material from the ship's stern, the kind of artefacts that have been absent so far from the main excavation, such as personal belongings from the captain and officers' quarters. Everything seems to point to a scenario where the ship hit the reef where the main site lies and sank rapidly from the weight of the cannons in the cargo hold, but the stern section broke away and was blown inshore against that headland a few hundred metres to the south.'

Rebecca took a plastic finds bag out of her pocket and put it on the table. She opened it and carefully slipped out a blackened metal disc, which she passed over to Jack. 'Speaking of which, this is on its way to the conservation lab after we leave here. Costas and I found it in a fissure in the cliff face just outside your cleft, wedged in with a clump of at least three others that we couldn't get out. You remember what you told me to find?'

'Well I'll be damned,' Jack said. 'It's a piece of eight. That really clinches it. Brilliant.'

'Take a look at the obverse. It's more worn and patinated than your coin, but you can clearly see the mint mark, that T symbol with the S superimposed. I looked it up, and that's the mark for Potosí, the Spanish colonial mint in Bolivia.'

'Cerro Rico, the Silver Mountain,' Jack said, staring at the symbol. 'The largest industrial complex in the world at the time, and the nearest to a real-life El Dorado that the Spanish ever found.'

'El Dorado from hell, you mean,' Jeremy said. 'Worked by Inca slaves whose lungs turned to concrete with the dust, and whose women died of arsenic poisoning in the town's silver refineries.'

Jack peered at the surface of the coin beside the mint mark, where the shield design was just visible. 'It may be wishful thinking, but I can just make out the same overstamp here as on our coin.'

'That's what I really wanted you to see,' Rebecca said. 'Before coming here, we popped into the metrics lab and I put this under the ultra-high-frequency scanner, enhancing the surface depth. There's no doubt about it. It's the same Star of David symbol, from the same die punch.'

Jack stared at the coin. 'Bingo,' he said quietly. 'One of those stamps alone could have been an oddity, a previously unknown assay mark perhaps. But two of them means we're definitely on to something. I think we're looking at a merchant who uses his own die stamp to mark his money in a very particular way.' He passed the coin back to Rebecca, who bagged it and replaced it in her pocket. 'Okay, Jeremy. Now your turn. Our friend Samuel Pepys?'

A little over an hour later, Jeremy stopped talking and sat back, and Jack contemplated the scans and photocopies that had piled up in front of him as Jeremy had passed them across. They had examined in detail the material related to the *Schiedam* in the papers of Lord Dartmouth, Admiral of the Fleet, and in the Admiralty Papers in the National Archives, including all the references to the ship by Samuel Pepys in his capacity as Lord Dartmouth's assistant in Tangier and the King's secretary for the affairs of the Admiralty. They had seen Captain Shovell's account of his capture of the *Schiedam* from Moorish pirates, the stores lists in Tangier that had detailed her armaments, and Pepys's own urgent instructions for her employment in the evacuation of Tangier:

I have thought it very necessary for His Majesty's service that the *Schiedam*, taken from the Moors of Sally by His Majesty's Ship the *James Galley*, should be forthwith fitted for sea, manned and victualled and

appointed to carry to England the workmen, stores
and all other things belonging to and lately employed
in the works of the Mole here.

What Jack had found most striking was the attention that
Pepys had devoted months later to the salvage of the wreck
and the exoneration of her captain, Gregory Fish – the former
naval stores officer at Tangier who was described pathetically
in a letter after having been pulled from the sea, who 'lies
abed and cries instead of saving any of the wreck'. Pepys was
a scrupulous record-keeper in all his dealings, and by
concerning himself with the salvage, with 'such of the great
guns, bronze and iron, mortars and balls' and other ordnance
that could be saved, he was simply doing his job, but his
support for Fish – a man who would normally have received
the full force of his opprobrium for his evident incompetence
– was very unusual, not least his efforts to see the ship's
captain acquitted at court martial and to have his pay
continued. It almost seemed as if Pepys, who had been
responsible for Fish's appointment in the first place, was
attempting to exonerate himself, though Jeremy had suggested
another possibility: that he was trying to conceal something
else that might have been revealed had there been a full court
of inquiry.

Naval captains often took on private cargo for profit, and
even in the evacuation of Tangier, where the Crown was
ostensibly paying for everything, some of that private dealing
might have been going on as well, in particular payments by
merchants to captains for extra vigilance in the transport of
money and valuables. Such transport in Royal Navy ships was

strictly illegal, and for Pepys to have been shown to be involved in it in some way would have cast him in a damaging light, so it may have been in his best interests to pay off Fish after the wrecking in order to keep him quiet. A string of related questions came into Jack's mind. Was the private cargo in question the treasure in Spanish silver that they had now begun to find on the wreck? If so, did the overstamping with a Star of David suggest that the treasure belonged to a Jewish merchant? *Could that merchant have been none other than João Rodrigues Brandão?*

Jeremy picked up a book that Jack had already taken down from his library, a leather-bound volume from the Naval Records Society of 1935. 'This is the other great source on Pepys at the time, *The Tangier Papers of Samuel Pepys,*' he said. 'It contains an edited transcript of the diary that he wrote covering a large part of his time in Tangier in late 1683 and early 1684, as well as sundry other notes and records collated into the papers by various compilers and editors. As the editor of this latest edition makes clear, the diary is not complete, and not just because parts of it don't survive or Pepys himself edited them. It's also because later compilers chose to excise material. And that's where the real prize lies for us.'

'Go on,' Jack said.

'Pepys's more famous diary, the one he wrote when he was a young man in London in the 1660s, is best known for its candour and self-exploration, especially the salacious detail about his sex life. The Tangier diary is of a different tenor entirely, the work of an older, more careworn man, focusing on the task at hand and mainly recording his work interviewing claimants for recompense, assessing the value of property and arranging transport. But there are flashes of the old Pepys here and there, especially when he's found a bit of his former vigour and has had a night on the town. Knowing the contents of the earlier diary, the first editors of the Tangier diary in the Victorian period were highly sensitised to anything of that nature, and exercised a heavy hand. Instead of just deleting phrases and sentences, they cut entire diary entries when they saw Pepys veering back to his younger self.'

'How do you know this?' Rebecca asked.

'Because the editor of that 1935 edition flags the problem in his preface, saying that he went back to the original shorthand manuscript to find and reinstate material, but also that he continued to censor some of it himself. As a result, I decided that the only scholarly approach would be to go back to the original myself, in Pepys's papers in Oxford. As it happens, I know his particular shorthand well, because Maria uses it in her introductory palaeography course for new graduate students to show that the study of writing systems and manuscripts is not just about ancient languages, but also about deciphering coded and abbreviated scripts of more recent date.

'I was after three things. First, any reference to the *Schiedam*. Second, any reference to Henry Avery. And third, any mention of João Rodrigues Brandão.'

'Dad's and my ancestor, the merchant in Tangier,' Rebecca said.

'Right.' Jeremy put another sheet from his briefcase on the table, a facsimile of a manuscript page in Pepys's distinctive shorthand. 'In the 1935 edition of the Tangier diary, there are only two brief references to the *Schiedam*. On 15 November 1683, he notes that he sent fifty barrels of gunpowder ashore by Lord Dartmouth's orders, and "discharged a man to be mate of the *Schiedam Prize*, a flyboat". That's the first one.'

Jack picked up the page and looked at it. 'I take it that the gunpowder was part of the supply intended for the Moors, to pay them off for not attacking the town during the evacuation,' he said.

'Exactly. An odd-sounding arrangement, giving your enemy your gunpowder, but it mostly worked, except for the final few days, when the Moorish gunners got itchy. More on that in a few moments, because it comes into the story in a big way. She was called the *Schiedam Prize* because the word "prize" was often added to ships that had been captured, and a flyboat because she was a fluyt, a particular type of Dutch merchantman. The second reference, almost four months later, on 29 February 1684, lists the *Schiedam* among the ships in the fleet beating out of Tangier Roads during the evacuation but then ordered to divert to Gibraltar under duress of weather, and from there to rejoin the main fleet under convoy escort for England.'

Jack looked intently at Jeremy. 'So what else have you found?'

Jeremy looked at his computer screen. 'I worked my way through the entire original manuscript, finding a number of entries that had been deleted, but nothing relevant to us. And then I hit the jackpot with this deleted entry of 27 February 1684, the day before the fleet set sail. You have to imagine a pretty chaotic scene in Tangier, with the final charges being blown to destroy the harbour mole, masses of goods and belongings of all descriptions still being loaded onto transport vessels, people petitioning Pepys with last-minute claims for money, a massive thunderstorm lurking on the horizon and, for good measure, the Moors having decided to renege on their agreement and lobbing a stream of firebombs into the town. Altogether a fraught time, so for relief Pepys had allowed himself a few hours on the town the night before, liberally oiled with wine and brandy. This is what he writes the next day:

'"Did feel most abominable in the morning, with the old pains returning, and cold sweats withal. Did however the eve before liberally avail myself of Mrs ——, who did liberally dispose herself to me, and afterwards to the establishment of Madame ——, though only for carousing, for fear of the Pox, it being rampant in these parts, though of little moment to me, my own rampancy having been sated by Mrs —— most effectually. Did this morning find Booth's infernal sniffing most aggravating, and did upbraid him for it, though Booth still being privy to all my affairs, and essential. Received and confirmed Mr Fish to the command of the *Schiedam Prize*, he being previously store master to Lord Dartmouth on the docks and most inadequate to seafaring, but there being no others holding the King's commission who might be given the ship. Trusting that the mate and officers will make up for his deficiency. With Booth I am to accompany the *Schiedam* to Porto, there to conclude my business, and thence to rejoin Lord Dartmouth in his ship with the fleet standing off Portugal, and thence home, the *Schiedam* to sail in separate convoy when ready. Did eat some grapes, mighty fine, and drank several more glasses, and did begin to feel myself again, and now to conclude my business with the Moors."'

Jeremy looked up. 'Booth was his assistant, a man Pepys despised and relied upon in equal measure. He is never heard of again after this diary entry; he simply drops off the map. Perhaps he was fed up with Pepys and absconded during their trip home. His disappearance would have been a matter of anxiety for Pepys, as Booth knew all of his business, as he makes clear in this entry, presumably including sensitive Admiralty matters. At any rate, we may never know what happened to him. What we mainly learn here is that the *Schiedam* was for some reason diverted on her homeward trip, to Porto on the north coast of Portugal.'

'The home port of João Brandão,' Jack said.

Jeremy nodded. 'More on that in a moment as well.'

Jack looked at the diary, remembering his reading of it the previous year. 'Hadn't Pepys gone to Spain before from Tangier, on a kind of holiday?'

'Right, in December 1683. That's the way he portrays it in the diary, as a much-needed break, but it doesn't ring true. Pepys never went on holiday. And I discovered that he went to Portugal as well on that earlier trip, to Lisbon and then on to Porto. It was in another deleted entry, removed by the Victorian editor because of a lengthy description of a venereal problem that Pepys seems to have picked up in Seville.'

'Official business, or private?' Rebecca said.

'We can only guess. Pepys was assiduous in concluding his work for the merchants of Tangier, ensuring that their goods were shipped to the destination of their choice, but it would have been highly irregular for him to go himself to a foreign port for that purpose.'

'And what was his business with the Moors that he mentions in that diary entry?' Rebecca asked.

'That's another very interesting question. Pepys had gone on several secretive missions to meet with the Alcaïd of Alkazar, the local chieftain who was besieging Tangier, presumably to negotiate the deal whereby the Moors were to get gunpowder in return for a truce. But I think there was something else going on, a further fold in this story, something that may have been another official part of Pepys's mission in Tangier. That's as far as I've got with him.'

'And Henry Avery?' Jack asked. 'Your second research objective.'

'Ah yes. And so on to the final sentence of that diary entry. He appended it below the main entry, as a kind of footnote. "Henry Avery, acting junior master's mate of HMS *James Galley*, is appointed to take the *Black Swan* to Porto, and to meet us there, and thence to Port Royal in Jamaica, with all haste."'

'So that's what Avery was up to,' Jack exclaimed. 'Fascinating.'

'The *Black Swan* was another of the ships that Shovell had captured from the Barbary Corsairs, like the *Schiedam*,' Jeremy said. 'They were both originally Dutch fluyts, but unlike the *Schiedam*, which was designed only for European coastal waters, the *Black Swan* was an exceptionally well-built ocean-going ship that had been used as a fast packet for communication between London and the English Caribbean colonies. She was also unusually heavily armed, with the same firepower as a warship of equivalent size.'

'Well, well,' Jack said. 'Avery may still have been in the Royal Navy, but he gets his new career in the Caribbean off to a flying start.'

'At this stage, all those ships from Tangier were either transporting material and people back to England, like the *Schiedam*, or taking merchants and their produce to their other chosen destinations, fulfilling King Charles's promise that they would all be recompensed and relocated as they wished.'

'And that was Pepys's job,' Rebecca said. 'That's presumably why he mentioned Avery and the *Black Swan*. From what you say, Pepys was not a man to leave unfinished business. If the *Black Swan* was stopping off at Porto, then he may have needed to go there for some reason to facilitate her onward passage.'

Jack sat back, his hands behind his head. 'And that brings us to João Rodrigues Brandão,' he said.

'Nothing,' Jeremy replied, shaking his head. 'Not a single mention.'

Jack leaned forward. 'He should be there in Pepys's records, but he isn't. As far as we're aware, he's the only Jewish merchant in Tangier, and the only Tangier merchant from Porto. There were not that many Jews in Tangier, as a succession of governors had expelled them or made their lives difficult, the most recent one, Colonel Kirke, even insisting that Jewish merchants sleep outside the city walls, and only be allowed in during the day. Incredible. The English could be just as prone to anti-Semitism as anyone else, evidently. As a wealthy trader he would have been a prime applicant to Pepys for recompense and transport, and yet he's not mentioned.

It's like a black hole. It's what's missing that's telling the story.'

'Are there any other possible leads?' Rebecca asked.

Jack looked pensively at the papers. 'There is one other place: the records of the Inquisition in the Portuguese National Archives. The Inquisition was as assiduous about record-keeping as Pepys was. Maria didn't have time last year to dig out all the documents that might mention João, and there might be more to be found, some clue as to what he was up to before his arrest and why his tribunal was held so quickly. Pepys would have been in Portugal about that time as well.'

'Maria's out there now, you know,' Jeremy said, putting his papers into his briefcase. 'In Lisbon.'

'I knew she was in Spain, visiting family.'

'She hopped over the border to spend a couple more days at the archives. She's doing some research of her own, but she also wanted to tie up those loose ends about João. I wasn't supposed to tell you.'

'Pretty decent of her, if you ask me,' Rebecca said. 'Especially after you blew her out on that dinner date last year.'

Jack leaned forward. 'Costas and I had just found the last resting place of the Ark of the Covenant. I think she understood.' He turned to Jeremy. 'Anything else from the Pepys papers?'

'There is one final thing. I wanted to wait until we'd finished before showing you.' Jeremy took out another sheet from his briefcase. 'This is the same page of the diary that we've been looking at, with the deleted entry on Pepys's visit to Portugal, but it's digitally enhanced. I saw something in the margin and had Lanowski play with it to see if he could bring out the image more clearly.'

He passed it to Jack, who put it on the table so that Rebecca could see it as well. Just off the right-hand margin in the middle of the page was a small drawing, the image unmistakable. 'Fascinating,' Jack said. 'The four arms each extending out into two points, with the shallow V-shaped indent at the end of each arm. It's a Maltese cross.'

'He tried to erase it,' Jeremy said. 'That's why you can't see it so well on the original.'

'Could it already have been on the paper before he wrote on it?' Rebecca asked.

'Nope. I was allowed to take the original from the Bodleian Library in Oxford to the palaeography lab, to put it under the microscope. The scrape from the pen mark on the final shorthand symbol in the line extends into the nearest arm of the cross, showing that he made the drawing while he was writing.'

'A doodle?' she said.

'Pepys was a scribbler, but not a doodler. This has got to have some significance.'

'At that period it can only signify the Knights of Malta,' Jack said.

'So what were they up to in 1684?' Rebecca asked.

'Like virtually everyone else in the Mediterranean, being besieged by the Moors,' Jack said. 'At the time, they were thought of as the greatest bastion of Christianity in the region, the rock that would never fall. As a military order they took the fight to the enemy, meeting the Barbary corsairs on their own terms and inflicting many defeats on them. That is, until the corsairs captured the master of the order and his leading knights, causing those who were left in Malta to lose their nerve. It's thought that some of the greatest relics of Christendom, which had been entrusted to the Knights' care, were handed over to the corsairs to secure their freedom.'

Jeremy opened Pepys's diary. 'There's one mention of the Knights of Malta here, a strange one. On 17 February 1684 he writes: "Got a copy of the letter of thanks from the Knights of Malta to our king upon the redemption of some of them with the rest of the Christian slaves there." Clearly, in some way the English Crown was involved in the ransoming of captured knights, presumably the master and those others you mentioned, Jack. I can only imagine that Pepys acted as a middleman, as otherwise there would be no obvious reason for him to get a copy of the letter.'

'He certainly had his finger in a lot of pies,' Jack said. 'Clearly the King trusted him, to have sent him to Tangier to oversee the entire financial side of the evacuation. He would have been an obvious person to negotiate ransoms as well.'

'Pepys just couldn't stop himself from writing things down, could he?' Rebecca said. 'The inveterate diarist. He thinks he's keeping it private by writing it in his own special shorthand, but actually he's telling the world everything.'

'Not *quite* everything,' Jack said. 'But he is leaving us clues.'

The phone rang, an internal IMU number. It was Ben Kershaw, the security chief. Jack remembered the phone call the evening before from the man who had warned him to steer clear of researching the Star of David symbol. He turned to the other two. 'I've got to take this. But don't leave just yet. We might have some travel plans to discuss.'

6

Ten minutes later, Jack put down the phone and turned to Jeremy, who had been looking at the Henry Avery proclamation on the wall. 'You'll probably have gathered what that was about. Ben wanted to know who you've talked to about that Star of David symbol.'

Jeremy turned round and sat down again. 'I was in the National Archives when you sent the photo of the symbol on the bronze box to me. I showed it to the colleagues I was having lunch with, and it got flashed round another couple of tables. Maria has seen it as well, of course, and a couple of the research students at the Institute of Palaeography. And there's been a symposium this week in Oxford on Sephardic culture under the Inquisition: how Jews in Spain and Portugal covertly symbolised their faith under persecution in the same way that the early Christians did in Rome. It seemed a perfect venue to reach out for ideas.'

'Absolutely,' Jack said. 'It's just that I had a worrying phone call last night. A guy with an accent, maybe Portuguese or Spanish, purporting to be a professor at a seminary in Lisbon, wanting to know if we'd made any progress with the identification. While he was talking, I looked him up and he was bogus. I confronted him and he warned me to steer clear of researching the symbol further, then hung up. It was a mobile number, so I couldn't get his location.'

Jeremy pursed his lips. 'Probably anti-Semitic. Flash a Star of David around and they come out of the woodwork, even among some extremist academics.'

'Or it may show that we're really on to something,' Rebecca said. 'If somebody else is on the same trail.'

'Just be on your guard,' Jack said. 'If this guy was at the National Archives or at Oxford he'll know you were the one who put the image out, and if he's frustrated by my response he might decide to get back at you. And sometimes, of course, these people are not lone wolves but are part of anti-Semitic organisations. We've come across that kind of thing before. I've prepped Ben to be aware of anyone making similar enquiries showing up at the campus, and he'll be doing a group email to warn everyone against responding to calls like this. It may be an overreaction, but we can't be too careful.'

'Understood,' Jeremy said. 'You might want to mention the caller to Maria as well. Over the years she's had to field all kinds of nonsense from oddballs about supposedly ancient symbols, ranging from cranks to neo-Nazis. Running a place called the Institute of Palaeography, you kind of invite that. And remember she's also an expert on early Christian and Judaeo-Christian epigraphy, with her PhD being on the epigraphy and symbols from the Roman period inside the catacombs in Rome. She was the first person I emailed the symbol to and I'm sure she'll get back if there are any comparisons to be found.'

Jack thought for a moment. 'If I do go out to Portugal to see her, will you two come along as well? I'm thinking that I might be able to squeeze in a quick visit over the next two days, before I fly out to Jamaica.'

'Jamaica? What are you doing there?' Jeremy asked, closing his briefcase.

'You remember Jason da Silva?'

'Sure I remember Jason. He was in the year ahead of me in the archaeology internship programme at IMU. I'd just come from Stanford, and he was on secondment from the University of the West Indies.'

'Well then, you'll remember that his speciality is the English colonial period in Jamaica, and that he trained with us because he wanted to expand the underwater excavations off Port Royal. The earthquake there in July this year put the international spotlight back on the site, especially as it came very close to replicating the earthquake that destroyed much of the city in 1692.'

'The wickedest city on earth, that's what they called it, wasn't it?' Rebecca said. 'A bit like English Tangier.'

'There's quite a lot of similarity,' Jeremy said. 'I remember a graduate seminar where Jason gave a very vivid picture of the city in its heyday, and it sounds a lot like the Tangier we've been hearing about. Both colonial English outposts, both barely within the rule of law, both closely connected with the business of piracy.'

Jack nodded. 'And Port Royal is also the greatest trove of artefacts of day-to-day life in the seventeenth century other than from shipwrecks, and the nearest thing in recent historic archaeology to Pompeii and Herculaneum. Everything is lying there buried in the mud and sand, just as it was on that day when the town slid into the sea.'

'Didn't Jason do his PhD on the merchants' quarter?' Jeremy asked.

'That's why I'm thinking of him now,' Jack replied. 'I was his supervisor, remember. Jason's mainly of Afro-Caribbean origin, but his surname comes from the fact that his great-grandmother married into one of the old Jewish merchant families of Kingston and Port Royal. The da Silvas inter-married with the Brandons in the early nineteenth century, so he and I are actually very distant cousins. His dissertation was on Jewish material culture in early colonial Jamaica, looking at artefacts from Port Royal that could be attributed to Jewish merchants, so I'm thinking he might be able to help us with our Star of David.'

'Isn't Maurice Hiebermeyer out there with him now?' Jeremy asked.

Rebecca nodded. 'It's a bit tricky. He's supposed to be looking after their son to allow Aysha to take up her visiting fellowship at Oxford. A kind of payback for all the time Maurice was away doing his own thing in Egypt.'

'I thought he took Michael out to Port Royal with him.'

'I'm not sure that putting Michael to work as a site assistant is what Aysha had in mind. He's only four.'

Jack sat back, thinking about his old friend. He and Maurice went way back, further even than his friendship with Costas, to school and university. Since getting their doctorates under Professor Dillon at Cambridge, they had gone their separate ways, Jack underwater and Maurice very firmly on dry land, but over the last few years their paths had become closely intertwined again. Maurice's passion for Egypt had been dealt a huge blow when the new extremist regime had expelled all foreign archaeologists, and it had been Jack's remit to get him back on his feet again and apply his talents as a field archaeologist to IMU projects that he could regard as equally rewarding. He looked at Jeremy and grinned. 'I'm with Maurice on that one. The earlier you start them, the better. I'd have loved it at that age. Anyway, Port Royal is one giant sandpit.'

'It seems an odd place for Maurice to go,' Jeremy said. 'I mean, as an Egyptologist.'

'Same skill set, just a different period,' Jack said. 'It was one of the first bits of advice that Professor Dillon gave us at Cambridge. Leave your comfort zone, volunteer on sites outside your period and place. You'll be able to bring fresh perspectives on those excavations, and in turn take back new approaches and ideas to your own projects.'

'And there's the small matter of Egypt,' Rebecca said. 'The problem that for almost two years now it's been a no-go zone for archaeologists, with the regime showing no signs of faltering. Maurice and Aysha have simply had to refocus elsewhere. Aysha has been happy to return to her research on the early development of hieroglyphics, something she can do without having to be in Egypt, but for Maurice it would have to be something hands-on.'

'He'd go stir-crazy trapped in a library,' Jack agreed. 'It was always a problem when we were students. I had to lock him in his room to force him to get his essays done. He's a dirt archaeologist through and through. Any site, any period, as long as he's up to his neck in it.'

'Are we finally going to see him get his feet wet and put on diving gear?' Jeremy said.

'That would be the day,' Jack replied. 'The truth is, he's not just out there in Jamaica to get his archaeology fix. After the earthquake in July, when IMU agreed to fund part of the rescue excavation, we needed an experienced site director to lead our team. The idea was that Maurice would take over the land excavations, allowing Jason and his team of divers to focus on the newly exposed material on the seabed, especially organic artefacts in danger of disintegration or being washed away.'

'So you're definitely going out there to see them?' Rebecca asked.

Jack looked out of the window at the overcast sky. 'I was supposed to go last week, but I postponed when I saw that we might have a final brief spell of good weather on the site here. I'm flying into Kingston the day after tomorrow.'

'You diving?'

'That's the idea. It's pretty exciting. A whole new section of the merchants' quarter has been revealed, literally rising up out of the mud on the sea floor.'

'Is Costas going with you? Sounds like another place for you to get stuck down a hole together.'

'Depends how he gets on. He and Lanowski want to have Little Joey ready for a demo for the board of governors when they visit tomorrow. To convince them to fund it.'

'Surely a nod from Efram will see to that?'

'If IMU funded everything those two cooked up, we'd have a budget bigger than NASA. The Jacobovich Foundation has been incredibly generous, but it doesn't have pockets quite that deep.'

'You should get him to take Little Joey out to Port Royal for its trials. Lanowski spent two hours with his portable blackboard and a supply of chalk explaining the nanotechnology to me. It's a miniature sub-bottom excavator, a kind of underwater mole. Might be just the right thing for Port Royal.'

Jack nodded. 'I'll see how it looks when I get there and might suggest it. Jason tells me there may be intact cellars and storerooms, a real time capsule of seventeenth-century life.'

'Seventeenth-century life on the edge, you mean,' Jeremy said. 'Port Royal wasn't exactly a haven of civilisation, was it?'

'Pirate Central,' Rebecca added.

'All part of life's rich tapestry,' Jack said. 'And it fascinates me because the artefacts are going to complement those we've had from the *Schiedam*. They're all part of the maritime culture of the period.'

Rebecca eyed him wryly. 'There's more to it than that for you, isn't there?'

'What do you mean?'

'It's that look you have. Costas is always on about it. When there's something else driving you but you're not ready to let on. Something that's coming out of what we've just been talking through. The *Schiedam*, the Star of David, Pepys, the Jewish connection, that Maltese cross, Jamaica. You're on the trail of something, aren't you?'

Jack gave her a piercing look. 'As soon as I have anything to go on, I'll let you know. I promise.'

'You'd better. And if you need me to carry on with you from Portugal to Jamaica, I'm good with that.'

'It's a grand place for a honeymoon, I hear,' Jeremy said nonchalantly.

Rebecca and Jack stared at him. Jeremy raised his arms in defeat and picked up his briefcase. 'Okay, okay, I get it,' he said. 'Howards,' he muttered, shaking his head. At the door, he turned back and looked at Rebecca. 'Remember, we have a date tonight. You promised.'

'Yeah, in the archive room. If you want to burn some midnight oil together, that's where I'll be. I want to collate all the material you've got in that briefcase before we fly out, just in case we've missed any clues.'

Jack smiled at her. 'I'm really grateful. And to you too, Jeremy. Brilliant work on all the Pepys stuff. I'll get the Embraer put on standby to fly us out from RNAS Culdrose tomorrow afternoon. I'm going to call Maurice now.'

'And Maria?'

'And Maria.'

Jeremy hesitated, then turned back and took a blank sheet of paper from Jack's desk, quickly drawing on it and handing it to him. It showed a Star of David and a Maltese cross, followed by a blank space with a line under it. 'Maria would set us these exercises when I was a graduate student. She said that when you're sitting in front of a mass of evidence, when you know it's trying to speak to you yet you're not quite hearing it, you should distil it down to the essence. Stare at those few images for long enough, and you might just have that eureka moment.'

'Why the blank space?'

93

'Because if you need to do the exercise, then it means there's something missing. Something that provides the key to unlocking everything else.'

Jeremy picked up his briefcase again, and Jack watched him follow Rebecca out and shut the door behind him. He stared at the sheet for a moment, then looked up at another framed image on the wall in front of him, between the map of Cornwall and the Henry Avery proclamation. It was a print of English Tangier made in 1670 by Wenceslaus Hollar, something that Jack had acquired when they had begun the excavation of the *Schiedam* the year before. It showed the walls and towers of the old town, built by the Portuguese but refortified by the English, and within them the buildings of the administration and the garrison, the merchants' quarters and warehouses, the wharfside taverns, smoking dens and whorehouses, and beyond that the huge mole projecting out into the Mediterranean, the ships nestled within. Like Port Royal in Jamaica the town had become synonymous with iniquity and vice, and like Port Royal it had come to a dramatic end, not by natural catastrophe but by the stroke of a royal pen in London.

He picked up the copy of Pepys's Tangier diary and leafed through it, trying to transport himself back to those final few days of the evacuation in 1684, his mind racing. What was the true meaning of those symbols? How did a Portuguese Jewish merchant named João Rodriguez Brandão fit into the story? And what the hell had Samuel Pepys really been up to in Tangier?

Part 2

7

The English colony of Tangier, North Africa, 4 April 1684

Another mortar round came whistling in over the walls from the west, bursting nearby in a sheet of flame that lit up the room with a dull orange glow. The man in the wig and frock coat shifted in his chair uncomfortably, pressed the pieces of sea sponge deeper into his ears to block out the noise and blew the dust from the vibrations off the sheet in front of him, cursing under his breath as it got caught up in the wet ink. He picked up his quill and carried on writing hastily in his shorthand, leaning back to keep the cold sweat that was dripping off his nose from spoiling the paper. *Do intend to write a history of this whole lamentable business*, he wrote, *candid and disinterested, not in the style of panegyric or apology, which sort of writing seldom have any great authority or lasting reputation with posterity.* He lifted his pen to dip it in the ink, trying to stop his hand from shaking, and continued. *Myself pretty well having vomited this morning, did feel wonderful purged, yet then did the ague and the old pain return, and did reflect most heavily on the scourge of the Pox.*

He put down the pen and raised a trembling hand to his forehead, feeling the throb, still smelling the musty perfume of his companion of the night before, then reached out for the brimming glass of wine on the desk beside his papers. In the old days, a few hasty gulps would do the trick, but now, in his middle years, the hair of the dog could no longer keep at bay the remorse and grief that assailed him in the cold light of morning, remorse for having let himself down again, grief above all for having ill-used his late lamented wife by his absence and his fornication.

He stared at that last sentence in his diary, wondering whether to strike it out. To be frank and truthful, to be true to himself, his *unequalled* self, was to try to atone for the excesses of the night before, excesses that his younger self had indulged in freely but that his older self condemned in others, in those whose corruption and venality had made this place where he now resided such a den of vice. He took a deep breath and picked up the pen again, striking a line through the sentence. He was no longer that man, and had no time for such introspection. His diary now was about history, a history that he himself was making. All that mattered now was to record the detail, for therein lay the truth of history, and in so doing to reflect the care with which he, Samuel Pepys of the Admiralty, Fellow of the Royal Society, aspired to manage his own remaining span on God's earth, serving loyally His

Gracious Majesty King Charles, and above all his beloved Royal Navy.

The day had come at last, the day for the evacuation of Tangier, and he still had much to do. He took a slurp of wine, forcing it down against the bile, and then looked out at the early-morning light. The house they had requisitioned for his office was a former Portuguese merchant's dwelling near the top of the town, affording him a view out of the wide windows similar to the panoramas that his friend Wenceslaus Hollar had etched of this place shortly after the King had taken possession of it twenty years before, and that Pepys had studied on the ship before arriving. To his left lay the great sweep of the city walls, built first by the Portuguese when they had possessed this place, and then expanded at great cost by King Charles after he had inherited the town as a dowry with his Portuguese wife Catherine of Braganza. The walls were meant to keep out both the desert and the Moors, neither very effectually, Pepys found; he was continuously afflicted by the dust in the air when the wind blew from the south, and for the past few days the Moors had reneged on their treaty and lobbed mortar shells with increasing frequency over the walls, along with burning balls of naphtha that traced great arcs in the sky and splattered fire indiscriminately across the city. To the right, and even more costly to the King, ludicrously so, was the Mole in the harbour, built to keep out the winds of the Atlantic and make Tangier the greatest free port ever known, the key to trade with Africa and the East and the Indies, enriching the coffers of all who came to trade here, as well as those of the King.

And in the centre was the smouldering mass of the town, a

den of squalor and vice, where the lack of control from London meant that all who came here succumbed alike to the baleful miasma: administrators and officials, the soldiers of the garrison, the merchants who had flocked here to make their fortunes, drawing into their fold the worst of the low life of the Mediterranean and beyond. Pepys himself had predicted it when he had first been appointed to the Tangier Committee in 1666, but none had listened. The Civil War had been just over, the King newly reinstated, and the Age of Enlightenment had begun, in which the march of progress would sweep aside those human failings just as the prow of a mighty galleon cut through the tempestuous seas. Or so the King's advisers had believed, those with undue faith in human nature and optimism that the Kingdom of Heaven had somehow settled on the land in all its powdered and coiffeured splendour.

He remembered another night of vomiting five months earlier on the English Channel, after he had been abruptly and without explanation summoned to join the fleet off Spithead. It was only his third sea voyage, and the wind had been up; Secretary of the Navy he might be, but seaman he most decidedly was not. He had lurched into Lord Dartmouth's cabin, and had been given his commission with the Great Seal. He had the document pinned to his desk now, and read it again:

By order of Lord Dartmouth, Admiral of the Fleet for this expedition, and Captain-General and Governor of the city and territory of Tangier, and of all the forces there, horse and foot, the expedition is to remove from Tangier all of the inhabitants, their goods and effects, and then to destroy and demolish the city and Mole so as no pirates and enemies of the Christian faith may have any abode or retreat for the annoying these seas or coasts; to make and set fire to what *forneaus*, mines and other works he shall think fit for the total destruction of the city and Mole, so as to make the former uninhabitable and the latter unuseful for ever.

His own remit in this dismal enterprise was precise and exacting, utterly suited to his talents and inclinations: to see a true estimate and valuation taken of every man's property and interest in any house or tenement, in order for their reasonable satisfaction, with an assurance of the King's protection and gracious care of them, and to arrange and pay for transport to a destination of their choosing, within or without the King's dominions.

Secondly, he was to act as His Britannic Majesty's emissary to the King of the Moroccans and the Moorish princes who were besieging Tangier, to negotiate terms for the Moorish takeover, including an exchange of gunpowder for the ceasefire that was currently being so flagrantly breached. His ventures outside the city walls, accompanied by only a small retinue of unarmed men, had been his first forays into true danger since wandering the streets of London during the Great Fire of 1666, a lift in excitement that he had sustained too liberally and too often in the taverns and whorehouses of the harbour.

Thirdly, and most importantly, he had been handed a sealed letter from King Charles that not even Lord Dartmouth was to see, concerning a further exchange with the Moors for an artefact of priceless significance to Christendom. His plan for the conveyance of that treasure this afternoon out of Tangier had taxed him greatly, but needed to be put from his mind this morning until his work in this office was complete and he could depart for the last time to the port.

He finished his glass and poured himself another from the decanter on his desk. He drank that down too, more robustly this time, and cautiously fed himself a few grapes from the platter beside the decanter. The tide was definitely turning, and he ate some more. He was pleased with the analogy, fitting for a navy man, though he knew no more of tides than he did of spars and deadeyes, of mainstays and flying jibs. He shut his eyes for a moment, remembering his voyage here. After all those years managing the navy from his office in the Admiralty, seeing it grow under his constant lobbying and exertions into something approaching a professional service, thinking strategically always, looking ahead, he had been astonished to come aboard and find himself, when he was not paralysed by seasickness, mesmerised by the life of the moment, by the *emotional* response to being at sea, to the fact that there was little looking ahead and little looking behind, just a great and powerful living in the present. In his mind's eye, he had begun to see ships not as part of some vast enterprise, strategically planned and imagined in squadrons and fleets on a chart, but as individual slices through time, as microcosms of the moment, just as he had seen Tangier through the windows a few moments ago, and just as he had seen London when he had exulted in it and written about it almost twenty years ago.

He looked at the large leather-bound book on the right-hand side of his desk, on top of a pile of papers from the Royal Society on all manner of subjects that he had meant to catch up on while he was here, but had never quite managed to find the time. The book was John Bunyan's *The Pilgrim's Progress*, subtitled: *from This World to That Which is To Come, Delivered under the Similitude of a Dream*, given to him by Bunyan himself in gratitude for Pepys's help in getting it published. He had left it marked where he had been reading it the previous evening, before the lure of the tavern had proved irresistible, at the point where the narrator finished his journey from the City of Destruction to the Celestial City.

Pepys had ordered the book sent on to him in Tangier because it gave him some semblance of hope; not that Tangier itself would ever be resurrected, nor that there was a heavenly Celestial City to anticipate, but that there might somewhere on earth be a place where the vice and temptation that pulled men down from happiness might be expunged, and life reduced to its essentials. In his youth, even in those heady days in London, he had dreamed sometimes of joining the pilgrims on their quest to America, leaving the Old World behind in all its debauchery and starting afresh, seeking purity and light. Those feelings, at any rate, were ones he had when he was sober; the devil was in him when he had taken too much drink, and seen the flashes of lace and peachy skin that drew him back to those places of temptation again and again.

He looked at the unfinished page of his diary, stained now with a splatter of wine, and then at the hourglass on the other side of his desk, still more than half full. He *could* do it, after all; he had time. His mind was suddenly tumbling with ideas and images, of the fabled artefact that would soon be within his grasp, of *The Pilgrim's Progress* and the Celestial City, of being at sea, of seeing the myriad types and motivations among the applicants to his office for remuneration, of the meaning of that too. He took up his pen and stroked more lines through his previous entry, and then began to write feverishly, recharging his pen every few seconds and spilling droplets of ink on the paper, not caring:

> Artefacts, methinks, as with all human creations, like books and music and art, extend the span of our own compass, just as the navigator stretches his instrument over the chart to reach beyond the horizon. Artefacts are details of history, without which we tell stories that are utterly corruptible; knowing those details so intimately is no different from our everyday lives, filled as they are with our own artefacts, and artefacts thus serve to bring history before us. Acquisitiveness is in our nature, the need to find and take possessions, and present our discoveries to the world. Yet the artefacts with the greatest meaning are sometimes the most dangerous, and are best kept hidden until men learn to expel cruelty and venality and vice . . .

Nearly an hour later, Pepys stopped writing and turned his mind to the business of the morning. The most pressing last-minute concern for the Admiralty administration in Tangier, which meant him, was how to find officers to command the numerous transport ships that had been commissioned into the King's service to take people and goods back to England,

and to the numerous other destinations required. The problem was less of an issue for the requisitioned merchant-men, as they still for the most part had their masters and crews aboard, but it was acute for the many prizes captured by Royal Navy ships from the Barbary corsairs; most of those were previously merchantmen, whose crews had been murdered or sold into slavery and the pirate crews killed in the encounter or later executed. Those ships being essential for the transport arrangements, it had been necessary to winnow men from the Royal Navy squadron at Tangier to provide additional skeleton crews, and to promote lieutenants, midshipmen and even master's mates to temporary commands.

As the transport ships were now Royal Navy vessels, it was legally obligatory that their captains hold a King's commission, a ruling that Pepys himself had engineered several years before but that was now sorely tested by the lack of available manpower. There were no longer any officers to be spared among the squadron, with several of the captains openly professing rebellion should they be requested to weaken their fighting ability still further. For the two transport vessels that remained without captains, only one possible candidate from the squadron had been put forward, an officer who had been suspended under threat of court martial, and for the second of the vessels Pepys had been obliged to search among the supply officers of the port for those who held a King's commission, seeking so far without success one who had some measure of sea service before taking employment on land.

He had gone to see the two ships yesterday, both of them fluyts of Dutch origin, economically built from oak and pine, of three hundred and fifty to four hundred tons burden, their wide, deep-bellied holds well-suited to carry the armaments and other goods that had been progressively stacked up along the wharf-side over the past few weeks. One of them, the *Schiedam*, captured by Captain Shovell from pirates off Spain, had the more pear-shaped profile of the two, wide enough to carry two rows of cannon barrels laid side by side in her hull; he had watched the great guns from the city walls being laden into her, culverins and demi-culverins and falconets, as well as mortars, wall guns, boxes of muskets, cannonballs, and small barrels filled with grenades and musket and pistol shot, with space being left in the hull for horses and the workmen and their families who had also been allocated to the *Schiedam*.

The other ship, called the *Black Swan* after her distinctive figurehead, was the one he had earmarked for his secret mission; he knew enough of naval architecture to see that she would be the better sailor, so that whereas the slower *Schiedam* would need convoy protection by the Squadron for her voyage to England, the *Black Swan* would be able to chance it alone on her much longer voyage to the Caribbean, where she might need to outrun Spanish privateers as well as pirates. For that reason he had also ordered her armament boosted, so that instead of the paltry four-pounders usually carried by fluyts, she had six eight-pounders to each side, as well as a considerable supply of small arms. As far as anyone else knew, she was being armed in preparation for carrying those merchants of Tangier who wished for passage to the Caribbean and the New World, so there had been no need for him to reveal to anyone his true intentions for the ship. He needed the better captain for her as well, something he sorely hoped would resolve itself to his satisfaction after this morning's interviews.

The door opened, and his assistant Booth came in, carrying a handful of rolled plans and wearing his usual dapper clothes, looking more like a preacher destined for the New World than a junior official of His Majesty's Board of the Admiralty. 'Good morning to you, sir. A fine day for the evacuation.'

Pepys remembered that he still had his earplugs in, and took them out. Another fireball slammed into a street not far away, causing his glass to shake and the wine to slop onto his papers. He caught it just as it was about to topple over, and grunted, nodding curtly. Booth looked at him and then at the decanter, rather shrewishly, Pepys thought; he knew exactly what the other man was thinking. Booth was of overtly puritanical tendencies, a Cromwellian during the late war who had paid the price by never rising above his present lowly clerical rank within the Admiralty, though the more Pepys knew him, the more admirably he felt that he suited precisely that position. In small, sometimes not easily definable ways, he found Booth almost constantly irritating, and yet there was no question that he was an indispensable assistant. He was privy to so many sensitive affairs of the navy and the state that he was not a man who could sensibly be shunted aside; his and Pepys's lives were inextricably intertwined for the duration. Pepys knew this, he knew intellectually that he needed to accept Booth entirely into his confidence, and yet the sight of the man first thing on a fractious morning made his blood rise slightly and his stomach tighten.

He drained what was left of the wine in the glass and put it down with unnecessary force. 'What of this morning's business?'

Booth came up to the desk, passed over two documents and took the wine glass and decanter away, placing them out of reach on a table beneath one of the windows. 'The two officers remaining to be interviewed for commands, sir. These are their records.'

'Are they here?'

'They are waiting downstairs.'

'Well fetch them then.'

Booth left, and Pepys rose and retrieved the decanter, with two glasses this time, placing them on his desk just as a knock came on the door, Booth's always annoying rat-a-tat. 'All right,' Pepys bellowed irritably. 'I can hear you. Enter.'

The door opened and Booth ushered in a small, unremarkable-looking man wearing the blue uniform of an officer of the navy but without epaulettes.

'You are Mr Fish, I presume?' Pepys said, peering at the man and then at a document in front of him. 'Lord Dartmouth's Controller of Naval Stores for Tangier?'

'Yes indeed, sir, if you please,' Fish said, bowing a little too ingratiatingly, Pepys thought. 'I am accorded the rank equivalent of a lieutenant in the service, sir.'

'I can see that,' Pepys said, scanning the paper. 'The rank equivalent maybe, but neither the qualification, nor, I apprehend, the experience required for an officer's berth on a ship.' He peered at the man. 'Have you ever been to sea in any nautical capacity, Mr Fish?'

'Like you, sir, if I may suggest the comparison, I carry out a job of great value to the welfare and functioning of His

Majesty's Navy, but that employment requires, indeed obliges, me to remain with my feet firmly planted on the ground, except as required for passage between ports.'

'Firmly planted on the ground,' Pepys repeated scornfully, tossing the paper down and sighing. 'Unlike you, I do not wear the King's uniform, nor do I hold a commission, and it remains my heartfelt contention, presented to the Admiralty Board on many an occasion to much and continual frustration, that all who do so, regardless of where their feet are planted or the unquestioned importance of their employment, should have served a term under canvas as a seaman or midshipman, so as to display the minimum level of competence required should they be called upon as a commissioned officer, in precisely such an emergency as this, to exercise command of one of His Majesty's ships.' Pepys had felt his blood rise as he spoke, and he reached over and poured himself another glass, draining half of it and glaring at Fish. 'What say you to this?'

'Indeed, sir.' Fish looked flabbergasted, and a little crestfallen. 'Am I to be censured?'

'No, of course not,' Pepys replied, sighing again. 'Your job here is vital, and perforce you are carrying it out to the best of your abilities. There is much for you to do still in the docks, and little time. You may go.'

Fish bowed slightly, looking confused, replaced his hat, touched his fingers to it and hurried out of the door, closing it behind him. Booth, who had remained in the room for the interview, came hesitantly forward. 'Dare I say it, sir, that you were a little harsh on the poor man?'

'He is wholly inadequate to the task of commanding a ship, and weak of personality, I feel. He may be good at organising navvies on the docks, but he will go to pieces if anything veers wayward at sea. And I am the one who will shoulder the blame, for I cannot allow it to fall on my Lord Dartmouth, or indeed His Majesty the King.'

'He is for the *Schiedam*, then?'

Pepys grunted. 'Who is the next one?'

'By the name of Henry Avery, from Plymouth, aged twenty-five years, acting master's mate on board the *James Galley*.'

'Ah yes. Captain Shovell's henchman. Well, at least he is a seaman, unlike our previous offering. Is he waiting downstairs? Go and fetch him too, if you please.'

Pepys poured himself another glass of wine and sifted through the papers on his table, finding the document he wanted and quickly reading it as he drank. It was the action report by Cloudesley Shovell on the capture of the *Schiedam* from Barbary pirates off Cape Trafalgar in Spain two months ago, the event that had led to the ship being brought to Tangier and commissioned into the Royal Navy as a transport. Henry Avery, junior master's mate, had distinguished himself in the fray, not so much for his leadership as for a burst of single-minded ferocity that had seen not only most of the pirates butchered by his hand but also several of the innocent Dutch seamen captured by the pirates who happened to get in his way. The incident had been hushed up and the report had not gone beyond Pepys's desk, but it had given Avery an elevated status among the crew, respected by some and feared by others.

Shovell was already short-handed in the *James Galley* from having to release other officers for temporary commands, but he had been willing to relinquish Avery as well because he had been concerned that he was receiving too much adulation from certain wayward elements in his crew. After this temporary command, should Pepys deem him suitable, Shovell had suggested that Avery should not be found another ship but should be put ashore to await one, a circumstance that he would recognise as tantamount to dismissal; it might persuade him to turn his attention to the merchant service, where he could exercise his individuality without disrupting a rigid chain of command. That outcome was of little moment to Pepys at present, the pressing matter being the need to find captains for the evacuation, but he had wanted to see the man for himself; a propensity to violence in an officer could be a double-edged sword, one that could help or hinder equally, and he wanted to get the measure of the man before he made his decision.

Booth returned, followed by a man in naval uniform who doffed his hat as he entered. Pepys pointed to a chair opposite his desk. 'Mr Avery, I presume. Have a seat. Will you take a glass of wine with me?'

'If it please your lordship, I would rather remain standing, and be clear of head.'

'I'm not a lord, Avery, just a humble secretary of His Majesty the King, and you may stand at your ease, at least.'

Pepys picked up his own glass, taking another drink as he looked at the man. Avery had spoken with a pronounced West Country burr, very common among seamen. Among the officers, most West Country men Pepys had met had been of a highly agreeable disposition, cheerful and phlegmatic, continent rather than dominant: small, tough men with physiques that came from generations working at sea and under the ground. Avery, though, was from a different mould, much heavier-set, with a broad neck, wide-apart eyes and long arms, somewhat ape-like, Pepys thought. He could see what Captain Shovell had meant; this was not a man you would wish to see bearing down on you with ill intent.

'How may I be of service, sir?' Avery asked. 'Our ship the *James Galley* is fitting out for sea, and has no deck officer other than me. I will be sorely missed.'

Pepys always modelled his interviews on the examinations for lieutenant, beginning with a disarming question of moral intent. 'Sir, were I to ask you, would you take a ship to the Gambia for the slave trade? Take your time to answer.'

He looked at Avery shrewdly. The other letter in front of him was from his eyes and ears in Falmouth, the Admiralty agent who reported on the shipping in and out of Carrick Roads. One of the families operating from Falmouth was the Howards, heroes of the Armada battle the century before, royalists during the Civil War and therefore favoured by King Charles, and like many shipping families now with their eyes firmly fixed on the New World, on the lucrative possibility of trade with the English colonies to the north and the Caribbean islands, above all in tobacco and sugar. Like most shippers concerned with that trade, they had also cast their eye on the other apex of the triangle, the one that provided the slaves who worked the plantations, though they had rejected it. All who were involved in that trade were complicit in human trafficking, but the question in Pepys's mind was a personal one, his own moral threshold: whether a man would himself take that corner of the trade as his domain and profit from it. The question was beyond his remit as an Admiralty official, but it had always been a small luxury of his position to exercise his own moral judgement in selecting men to serve their king and country.

Avery remained bolt upright, staring ahead. 'Sir, as a midshipman on board His Majesty's Ship *Anne Prize*, following the bombardment of Algiers in the Year of Our Lord 1671, I did accompany Captain Trethewey down the coast of West Africa for the purpose of providing escort for vessels of the Royal Africa Company that were being harried by Barbary corsairs, and I did witness the Moorish traders bringing slaves on board those vessels.'

Pepys waved his hand impatiently. 'Yes, yes, I mean under your own volition, sir; were it your choice, not a necessity of your fealty to the service.'

'Sir, I remain and have always been a loyal officer of His Majesty's Navy, and while in that employ would never embark on private trade of any description.'

Pepys looked at him again. Avery would have been perfectly well aware of the opprobrium cast on captains who profited from the private transport of money while under the King's commission, and the concern in the Admiralty that the temptation might induce more junior officers to do likewise. Pepys himself had worked tooth and nail to try to reduce that temptation by increasing the pay for officers, and to extend their pay to the necessary periods ashore in times of peace, but his overtures had fallen on deaf ears among the more obdurate members of the Admiralty Board. So he sympathised with the officers' financial plight, but it was his duty to root out those who carried on the practice, to rein in those who had been tempted into dark waters.

He leaned over the letter on his desk, his hands pressed together as he peered at Avery. 'I have here a note from a reliable source concerning your presence in July last in the port of Mylor, near Falmouth, where you did meet with one Lowther Howard for the apparent purpose of jointly and severally sponsoring a venture on board Howard's ship *The White Rose* for the coast of the Gambia and Niger.'

Avery did not bat an eyelid. 'Sir, I was at that juncture unemployed, out of service with His Majesty's Navy, my previous ship, the *Bonaventure*, having been laid up, the war with the Dutch being over, and the crew all being paid off. I was at liberty to seek other employment at sea, and indeed did so out of necessity for my wife and two children, living as they still do in Plymouth, with no other means.'

'You are aware that Lowther Howard's venture was to explore the possibilities of the slave trade?'

'I had no occasion to pursue it, sir, as I was forthwith offered re-employment by His Majesty's Navy in my present ship, and have remained so since. But Lowther is my brother-in-law, and I know that misfortune befell him when his ship the *Nancy Galley* was taken by privateers off the Gambia and he and his crew were put up for ransom, thereby making the venture one I am sore pleased not to have entertained.'

Pepys grunted, took a sip of wine and tried to swallow the bile that suddenly rose up his gullet like a sword thrust from the belly. He picked up a handful of grapes, forcing them down. 'Would you go into the merchant trade happily otherwise?'

'Were there no longer to be employment for me in the

service, sir, should wars come to an end and the King see fit to decommission his navy, then I should like above all things to embark on a trading venture to the Indies East or West, one that would of necessity see me enter into an arrangement with another party, my own resources and savings as an officer of the navy being wholly inadequate to such an enterprise, with no other private means to my name.'

Avery was answering carefully; like most officers in the navy, he knew perfectly well of Pepys's abhorrence for the slave trade. There was nothing to be gained by prolonging the issue; this was not the Inquisition.

'Well, Avery, you will I hope remain in the service until you attain your own command by right, but meanwhile in this emergency we see fit to employ you with temporary rank in command of the *Black Swan*, a requisitioned Dutch fluyt commissioned as a Royal Navy transport, sound and seaworthy by all accounts, destined first for Porto in Portugal and then for Jamaica, the destinations both and severally of merchants of Tangier whom the King in his generosity has seen fit to recompense and resettle for their discomfiture during this evacuation, with me as his agent. She has twenty-odd crew remaining from her previous complement, and as for a master's mate, a bosun and others, you may temporarily promote them as you see fit, as is the right of a captain. I have discussed the matter with Captain Shovell, and he is in agreement. You will receive no censure for your action in the capture of the *Schiedam*. The *Black Swan* awaits you beside the Mole, and the fleet sails in a mere matter of hours. Now have a drink, man, to toast your new command.'

Avery remained upright, not taking the glass that Pepys had

poured him. 'Sir, I would rather not. I must remain clear of mind for the task ahead.'

Pepys shrugged. 'My assistant Mr Booth will follow you shortly down to the docks with the commissioning papers. You may go now.'

'Thank you, sir. I am much obliged.'

Avery turned and left, and Pepys listened to him clatter down the stairs and open and shut the door to the street. It was almost unheard of for an officer to refuse a glass of wine, especially on taking over his first command, but Avery was by all accounts a sober family man, and part of Pepys approved of the fact despite his own indulgence. More worrying was the ruthlessness and cruelty reported in his capture of the *Schiedam*, but that aspect of a man's character at sea, when his blood was up and a sword and pistol were in his hands, was something with which Pepys was, when it came to it, profoundly ill-acquainted; his concern was the administrative machinery that propelled otherwise sober men to unleash their inner demons on the King's enemies.

Whatever the concerns, Pepys reflected, Avery was a clear league above the hapless Fish. Avery would have the *Black Swan*, and Fish would have the *Schiedam*, where at least he would be sailing in convoy only to England, with competent crew among the surviving Dutchmen to rescue him from any calamity, God willing. He would need to get Booth to chase down Fish and tell him, which would have the doubly happy effect of clearing Booth out of the way for what Pepys had to do next.

Another missile came in, whistling down somewhere near the docks and detonating with a crash. Booth came in carrying a pottery jug he had brought up from downstairs. 'Juice of the mango fruit, sir, unadulterated by the poisonous water of this place, a most effectual cure, I am told by my Lord Dartmouth no less, for the morning delicacy.'

'I am too far gone in my own cure this day,' Pepys said, looking ruefully at the jug. 'Maybe next time.'

'Sir, I am mightily pleased and relieved to remind you that there will be no next time, since tonight we weigh anchor and depart this pestilential city, and that the next occasion you and I sit together will be in our office in Greenwich, where once again, God willing, you will fall into the sober and reflective habits of these dozen years past that so suit you.'

'It's Tangier, Booth,' Pepys replied, slumped down. 'It's this place. It casts a malignancy over men, one that afflicts us all. I have not been kind to you. Now I needs must send you to intercept Mr Fish – or shall I say Captain Fish, God help us – to inform him of his magical transformation. And get him some epaulettes, will you? He at least needs to look the part.'

Booth bowed slightly, took his stick and left. Pepys looked at the untouched wine, thought for a moment, then picked it up and drained it in one go, putting it down with a satisfied belch. That was better. *Far* better. And it was enough. He pulled open the drawer in front of him and took out a pair of small pistols, a new form of firelock with the cock and frizzen behind rather than beside the breech, less easily caught up in the pocket, and a screw barrel to allow quicker reloading. They had arrived only the day before, from his London gunsmith, who, knowing that Pepys was in Tangier, had thoughtfully added a small dagger blade that folded back against the barrel. The occupation of Tangier had seen a boom in the production of innovative weapons for gentlemen to carry concealed through narrow streets and alleys. Even at the best of times, in broad daylight, the city was a dangerous place, and where he was heading to now, he was going to have to be on his guard.

He carefully flipped back the frizzens, seeing that the priming powder was still in place, checked the safety latches behind the cocks and then pocketed the pistols, one on either side of his coat. He took a deep breath. It was time for his secret business.

8

Samuel Pepys stepped from the front door of the house, took a deep breath and looked out over Tangier, his last chance to do so from this commanding position beside the city wall before embarking on the *Schiedam* that evening. Below him the city was shrouded in smoke, a result of the Moorish mortars and the fires they had caused, but beyond it he could clearly make out the great arc of the harbour, the Mole on the west side and the smaller jetty to the east where the ships were still loading. Even from this distance the colossal engineering feat of the breakwater was apparent, but even more so its colossal futility, with the sappers having laid enormous gunpowder charges at intervals along its length in order to render it useless to the Moors and their Barbary allies whose ships would be entering the harbour within hours of the evacuation. The largest detonation would be saved for last, the fuse to be lit by the final sapper to leave, and was designed not only to breach the Mole but to be heard as far away as Spain and all along the Barbary shore, to tell the world that King Charles of England, Scotland and Ireland, but no longer of Tangier, had finished what he had set out to do.

It was a note of defiance that had a hollow ring to it, Pepys thought, but such displays were in the nature of kings, who in Pepys's extensive experience were inclined like disgruntled children to destroy their creations rather than see them fall into other hands, and to do it with the largest flourish and the least amount of grace possible. That, at any rate, was the King's desire; the work of actually pulling it off fell to others, to the army of officials and soldiers, sailors and engineers who were currently withdrawing like a closing sea anemone towards the harbour, most of them as vexed and bewildered by this enterprise as Pepys himself had been, and as earnestly looking forward to seeing the place disappear forever below the horizon.

He took out his little pocket telescope, extended it and aimed it at the jetty to the right, seeing the *Schiedam* and the *Black Swan* tied alongside and still taking on stores and cargo. The rest of the transports were either anchored in the harbour, awaiting the order to sail, or already standing offshore with the naval squadron, ready to form a convoy for England. At least he had satisfied his remit to the best of his abilities, and had done his best for the people and merchants of this place, reimbursing them for their forcibly abandoned property and seeing them on their way to their chosen destinations; all that mattered to him now was that his own belongings should be packed up and brought to the wharf, and that he should be able to conclude the last and most important of his tasks at Tangier, the one he was embarked upon now.

He pocketed the telescope and set off at a brisk pace down the steep cobbled street, crinkling his nose at the smell of gunpowder and naphtha as he passed through the layer of smoke. He had penned a hasty final diary entry just before he left, noting the appointments of Captain Fish and Captain Avery, as was his duty, that being the main purpose of his record; too hasty, though, as he now regretted it, for he had also unaccountably noted the purpose of his present expedition, and the onward voyage planned for the *Black Swan* to the New World. Unaccountably, or not so: for it was the wine that had made him incautious in his writing, or the yearning for it. He had nearly turned back to amend the entry, but then had thought to delay it, as none but Booth could read his shorthand, and in any case he would be back at the house when the present affair was done to pack up his belongings, at which time he could take up his quill and black out his doodles, infelicities and other irrelevances.

He passed four profusely sweating, half-naked black men with their naval taskmaster and his whip behind them, rolling two barrels marked 'gunpowder' up the street towards Henry Fort beyond the walls, part of the enterprise that he had engineered to placate the Alcaïd; presently to little avail, he reflected, as another burning missile seared the sky above him and plunged into the harbour, sending up a sizzle of steam like a red-hot skewer doused in a bucket. The coins in his pocket were jangling, and he quickly pulled off his cravat and stuffed it inside, muffling the noise. The last thing he wanted in the most lawless city on earth was to be walking along like a banker advertising his wares. He had grabbed the coins from the bowl on his table just before leaving his office, having remembered one of His Majesty's more sentimental edicts in his commission for Tangier:

By the King's Direction will be buried among the Ruins a considerable number of mill'd Crown Pieces of His Majestie's Coin, which Haply, many centuries Hence when other Memory of it shall be lost, may declare to succeeding Ages that this Place was once a Member of the British Empire.

It hardly seemed a priority in this rapidly eviscerating city, to satisfy the antiquarian whim of a king, but it was nevertheless a curiously affecting whim that tickled Pepys's fancy; and, perforce, he needs must put duty above all else, however ineffectual his efforts might be in the general scheme of things. Still, the sooner he dispersed coin or anything else from his person that might attract a knife in his back or a blow to his head, the better.

A cascade of slops splattered in front of him, and he veered to the other side of the street, narrowly avoiding a second bucketload from the balcony above. He hurried on, trying to focus on what lay ahead, feeling the effects of the wine a little more now that he was moving and his circulation was flowing. Note to self, he thought. What I would miss most if I were captured by the Moors? Wine, women and song. He put a hasty mental line through the last phrase, correcting it to: the exacting management of the affairs of His Majesty's Royal Navy. That was better. He lurched slightly around a corner, nearly slipping on some indescribable deposit on the cobbles.

The ground shook as another missile hit somewhere ahead, sending up a fountain of burning fragments that traced arcs in the sky like fireworks. He could no longer see the harbour, the upper storeys and balconies crowding the street ahead and obscuring his view.

A cart came clattering along the cobbles towards him, pulled by four burly men and overloaded with furniture and sundry other household items, precariously baled together with rope. He flattened against a wall to let it pass, and saw that it included the marble embellishments of a fireplace, small mottled-yellow columns that looked as if they had been lifted from one of the ruinous sites of the Romans or the Phoenicians that he had seen along this coast. People were taking everything, stripping their homes bare. The cart could only be destined for the *Schiedam*, the last ship still taking on private cargo. He wondered whether the hapless Fish would have the wherewithal to lade a vessel effectually, a matter about which Pepys knew precious little from a technical standpoint, though he had attempted to better himself on the subject, studying at his proudest foundation, the Royal Mathematical School for Naval Cadets at Christ's College, as well as with his friend Isaac Newton. All the abstract learning in the world, however, never equalled the arcane wisdom in these matters known only to those who actually went to sea. At any rate, the appointment of Fish had been his decision and was his responsibility, and there was nothing to be done about the matter now, except to pray that the man had some semblance of sea legs and a large dose of luck.

He turned the next corner into a street leading down to

the port, and took a deep breath. This would be his run of the gauntlet, as it always was, and he was going to have to steel himself against letting the wine draw him in. Every second door was a tavern or a whorehouse, leading to a conjoined nexus of rooms behind, drinking holes and smoking dens and sordid bedchambers, the air hung with the incense of the Orient and the seductive charm of the narcotic. He had been appalled by it when he had first arrived, and had pompously and self-righteously excoriated all those who indulged in it, but then this place had exerted its pull and he had found himself sucked into its delicious and free-floating ambience. On those mornings when he was hung-over and sober, when the cold sweat prickled his brow and his hands trembled, he was repelled by it, but a glass or two of the hair of the dog and the street took on an altogether rosier aspect.

Already the fishermen's carts were drawn up outside, bringing the oysters that were used to enhance the smell of ardour and subsume the odours of body and squalor that lay just beneath; and already the whores in the street were mingling with the sailors who had come up from the port for the last time, knowing that their next customers would be the soldiers of the desert who would come sweeping in as the last ship sailed out, men who followed a different creed but had the same carnal desires and the same weakness for pleasure that would forever be the lifeblood of places like this.

He struck out along the middle of the street, pushing through a knot of sailors and women, knowing that he was hardly an inconspicuous figure with his ample waistline and his finery, and that the whores would gravitate to him, as they always did, like flies to a light. He sensed eyes being turned in interest, but he kept his own rigidly ahead. He heard someone come up behind him, and felt a hand clutch his arm, pulling him. He tried to shake it off, and when he turned, he saw that it was the woman he had woken up next to with a pounding headache only hours before.

Even with the wine in his belly to soften his judgement, in the cold light of day she looked piteous, with smudged powder and sunken eyes, but instead of feeling repelled, he had a sense of the girl she had once been, and remembered that this was the last time he would ever see her. He reached into his pocket, fumbling for the coins, and pulled them out, spilling them into her upturned hands. It was not exactly the burial of coins among the ruins that King Charles had envisaged, but this was as good a way as any to ensure that they stayed in Tangier.

'A bientôt, Don Samuel, meu amor,' she said in the international argot of her profession, blowing him a kiss, and then she was off, linking arms with two sailors who had come up behind her.

Pepys turned again, making his way forward more resolutely, then stopped abruptly in his tracks, jumping sideways and pulling the brim of his hat over his eyes. Good Lord, he muttered to himself. Not now. It was the queen of the whores herself, Mrs Kirke, wife of the venal and dissolute governor, holding court like a Roman empress on the back of a cart, surrounded by the garish retinue whom she paid to dress up and float about her in a cloud of frippery and powder. Hazily he remembered that he had visited her the afternoon before, his reason overcome in the sultry heat of the day, and that there had been some fumbled carousing, over all too quickly in his excitement. She made him feel young again, as she did half the officialdom of Tangier.

The cart and its entourage trundled by, and after a decent interval Pepys raised his head and looked back. She was still there, a whirlwind of fans and brocades and sauciness, the last time, perforce, that he would see such a sight; though perhaps, just perhaps, he thought wistfully, she too would take passage on the *Schiedam*, and in the way of those on ships who always found a nook among the cramped indecency, he would have the opportunity for some attempt at rectification, of a duration to ensure more mutual satisfaction; that is, if he could make his way through her regiment of suitors and she were still inclined to remember who he was.

He hurried forward, turned a corner and exhaled forcefully, relieved that he was out of temptation's way. The place designated for the meeting was halfway along the alleyway ahead of him, a low, unassuming entrance that led down a passage to a room that had been the warehouse of a Portuguese Jewish merchant, João Rodrigues Brandão, whom Pepys had helped and befriended, taking him into his confidence when he had discovered that he had family connections in the Caribbean and would be able to facilitate the onward transport of the treasured artefact that Pepys was now, God willing, about to receive. João had been gone for three weeks, intent on concluding his business in Portugal and preparing to rendezvous with Pepys in the city of Porto when the fleet passed on its way back to England. Pepys had been worried for him; the Inquisition had eyes and ears everywhere, even in Tangier, and was always ready to pounce on anyone of João's faith. The *Schiedam* and the *Black Swan* were central to their enterprise, the reason why his priority this morning had been to find captains for them, to ensure that both vessels would be able to make their rendezvous off Porto in a week's time.

He turned to the wall beside him, undid his breeches and relieved himself. The burning sensation had lessened; the tincture of quicksilver prescribed by Lord Dartmouth's physician was working. That at least was something, and he felt heartened at last. Someone at the entrance to the alley suddenly shouted his name, and he turned back and stared, quickly hitching up his breeches. His heart sank; it was the inescapable Booth. 'What on earth do you want?' he exclaimed as the man came stumbling towards him. 'You will see that I resisted all temptation, if that is why you have followed me, so you need have no concerns on my account. And I told you to chase after Fish and Avery. You are not needed here.'

Booth reached him, and bent down with his hands on his knees, panting hard. Pepys could see that his face and hands were blackened like those of an artillery gunner, and one side of his coat appeared to have been scorched. 'Good God, man. What has happened to you?'

'One of the Moors' fireballs,' Booth said, straightening up. 'It bounced off the window and burst just outside. I fear our office is wrecked, and by now burned out.'

'Are you much injured?'

Booth rubbed his left ear. 'I can hear none too well on this side. But otherwise, fine. By great good fortune I was outside the room on the stairs, about to make my way to the harbour.'

Pepys suddenly felt faint. 'My papers,' he said anxiously. 'My diary. My books. All gone. This cannot be.'

'And it is not, sir, I am most pleased to report. I rescued what I could, including most that was on your desk, and have ordered it all to be taken along with such other of our belongings and papers that survived, to be embarked on the *Schiedam* forthwith.'

'I owe you thanks,' Pepys said, mightily relieved. 'My most profound gratitude indeed.'

Booth looked around. 'I had surmised that you might be here. Senhor Brandão's warehouse, is it not? He has been gone these three weeks past.'

'Can I keep nothing from you, Booth?'

The other man took out a handkerchief and wiped it across his face, blackening the cloth completely. 'Very little, I would hazard, sir. I could not do my job effectually otherwise.'

Pepys knew that he was now going to have to bring Booth in on the entire secret affair: on the reason for this meeting, on the association with Brandão and on the dangers that they might be about to face. In truth, cloak-and-dagger antics were not Pepys's forte, however much they gave him a certain frisson of excitement; going down a dark passage in the worst city on this side of the Atlantic, he would welcome a companion. It would mean that Booth would be privy to a secret that the King had entrusted to Pepys alone, and he would have to be sworn to silence. Yet it was possible that he might not prove a complete liability.

Pepys reached into his left pocket and pulled out one of the pistols. 'Can you shoot?'

'Indeed I can, sir. You showed me those very pistols when they arrived yesterday, you will recollect. Mr Pierrot, gunsmith, Drury Lane, a Protestant Frenchman, fled from

Orleans. His firelocks have a high reputation for the temper of their steel, for always sparking well with a fresh Dover flint.'

'For an avowed Puritan, you surprise me, Mr Booth.'

'You forget, sir, that though you see me this way now, and it is much my preferred course of life and belief, as a boy I served the Lord Protector Cromwell as a musketeer and pike man, and fought at Edgehill and Worcester.'

Pepys handed him the pistol. 'Then this is yours.' He pulled out his pocket watch, a beautiful silver repoussé piece by Patrick of London, and saw that it was still half an hour to ten o'clock, the time he had appointed for the meeting. The others were men of the desert, for whom time was told by the sun and the stars and all those other observations that sailors also made, but he knew from his past meetings with them that they would be on time; that they had an uncanny ability to match the hour told by his watch. He would have enough time to fill Booth in on the backstory, but only just. He put back the watch, pulled out his cravat from his other pocket and tied it back around his neck. 'And now I need a drink,' he said. 'But where to find one?'

Booth had been checking the safety latch and the springiness of the cock on the pistol, and feeling the sharpness and hold of the flint in the jaws. He put it on half-cock, engaged the safety and pocketed it, and then pulled out a pewter flask from inside his jacket. 'I have come prepared for just such an eventuality, sir.'

'Ah,' Pepys said, his saliva rising. 'The day brightens, even in these dark times.'

Booth unscrewed the top and passed it over. 'The juice of

the mango, sir. I assure you, it is truly most efficacious.'

Pepys gave Booth a wan look and sighed, then put the flask up and drained it, wiping his lips with the back of his hand and passing it back. 'I see a doorway opposite where we may be concealed, and I may talk. You will hear a tale that will astonish you. After that, we needs must enter the darkest pit of this place to conduct our transaction, and then, God willing, if still alive and uninjured, we will take our precious new cargo to the docks and depart this pestilential town once and for all.'

9

The air in the chamber was dank and heavy, still smelling of the tobacco that had once been stored in it, and the only light came from thin slits in the plaster near the ceiling, and through the entranceway. Pepys remembered how João had told him that he preferred to store his bales in humid conditions, and to dry the leaves just before milling; it kept in the flavour, and was why the Brandão tobacco had found such a ready market in Portugal, and for a while in Tangier too. He looked around, seeing if anyone was lurking in the corners, hoping that Booth was being vigilant outside in the alleyway. He spotted a coin in the dust and picked it up. It was a Spanish silver piece of eight, irregular and imperfectly impressed as they always were, but more satisfying as a crude piece of bullion than the milled coins of King Charles that he had given to the woman; those were somehow impersonal, whereas the Spanish coins spoke intimately of their history, of the slaves in the mines who brought up the ore, of those in the mints who cut up the planchets and hammered the dies and weighed the coins so precisely, and of the great galleons that sailed with them towards the Old World, running the gauntlet of privateers and pirates in the Caribbean and beyond.

He peered more closely at the coin, and saw that it had been overstamped with the Star of David mark of the Brandão family, a mark that he himself had seen João make on his coins with a special die and anvil in this very chamber. It was a clever way of ensuring that nobody in Portugal would steal them, or an unscrupulous banker winnow them, thinking that the absence of a few might go unnoticed; to be seen with a coin with such an overt symbol of Judaism would be to invite immediate arrest by the Inquisition, whereas João could secretly ship the coins abroad to pay for transactions within the family, who would then have the silver re-smelted and milled into local currencies. It was most unlike João to have mislaid even a single coin, and it made Pepys think of the haste with which his friend had departed, and to consider the risk attached to this enterprise that he himself, an emissary of the King of England and immune from the Inquisition, would never have to consider, but that laid João and his family bare to the worst form of persecution that humans had devised to inflict on one another.

He pulled out his pocket watch and glanced at it. As he did so, a person was suddenly there, having entered the room noiselessly; a man dressed in the cape and hood that made so many in the markets and back streets of Tangier indistinguishable of origin. He swept back the hood and Pepys saw that it was Ismail Ben Ali, son of Ali Ben Abdala, Alcaïd of

Alcazar, the local chieftain who had been deputed by the Sultan of Morocco to besiege the English at Tangier. Pepys had formed something of an acquaintance with Ismail and his brothers during his forays out of the city to meet the Alcaïd and negotiate the terms for the evacuation.

Ismail was delicately featured, rather beautiful in fact, with large dark eyes and a wispy beard, though with the fatalism of expression that Pepys had seen among men of the desert; for the Alcaïd's family were not Berber but were descendants of the Arabs who had swept across Africa a thousand years before, and retained both the outlook of the desert Arab and his extraordinary toughness. Most helpfully, Ismail had been schooled in his youth in Tangier by an excellent tutor in English; Pepys himself was no linguist and had scarcely grappled these past months with a word of Arabic or the local Berber tongue, other than for his needs on occasion in the markets, and, God forgive him, his nocturnal excursions.

Ismail said nothing, as was the custom of the Alcaïd until settled. He sat down on the floor, crossed his legs and opened his cape, revealing a bejewelled curved dagger on one side of his belt and on the other a long-barrelled gold-plated pistol, a distinctive type of firelock of Portuguese origin favoured by the Moors and made for them by the Ottoman gunsmiths of Albania and Greece.

'*As salaam alaykum*, Samuel Pepys,' he said at last. 'May peace be upon you.'

'And upon you, Ismail Ben Ali Ben Abdala.'

'I will pray first.'

'As you wish.'

Ismail closed his eyes and began quietly chanting.

Pepys felt he had come to know something of these men of the desert over the past few months. He knew them because there was something familiar about them, something they shared with the men of the sea. Both lived for the visible horizon, their worlds compassed only by what they saw, an endlessly shifting vista of sand or sea but always fundamentally the same. Where they differed was that the men of the sea could escape it; those so inclined could go below decks to their books and companions and ponder the wider compass of life, and the ordinary seamen could become the most domestic of creatures.

The men of the desert had no such luxury, nor inclination. For them, just as their God was everywhere around them, so they were inescapably part of that world of their experiences, one of extreme heat by day and cold at night, and of ceaseless struggle for water and food and survival. Their life suppressed all mundane emotions, and yet led to sudden explosions of elation or cruelty: a joyous outburst of song and dance or the flash of a knife through a throat, forgotten as suddenly as it had begun, something that Pepys had been shocked by at first but had learned to accommodate. And just as the experience of life for them was distilled to its essence, so their thoughts had expunged all doubt and ambiguity, so that there was only truth and untruth, belief and unbelief. They lived by instinct and intuition, in a world that did not pose them taxing questions about morality or meaning, in which life was life and death was no cause for grief.

This realisation had helped Pepys in his negotiations with the Moors on behalf of the Governor of Tangier and His Majesty King Charles of England. They had negotiated lines in the sand, exchanges of prisoners, access to water, gunpowder for ceasefires. As a fellow of the Royal Society, Pepys had existed in a world where the advancement of knowledge was built on doubt, where the best conclusion was often some shade of grey. To be thrust into negotiations that only allowed black and white had gone against all his instincts, and yet he had come to relish it, and to question whether those hours of heated debate on matters of propriety and morality in the coffee houses and taverns of London had too often been an excuse for indulgence, or mere sophistry. He had come to envy Mr Booth and the Puritans their similar starkness of belief, one in which the world was divided into sin and goodness, into cities where the devil held sway and those of light; indeed, the longer he spent in Tangier, the more he had come to believe that such extremes did truly exist.

Ismail opened his eyes. 'I am ready,' he said.

Pepys was aware of Booth having entered the room, standing in the shadows by the door, and he knew that Ismail would have seen him too. 'The Alcaïd has not kept to the terms of our ceasefire,' he said with admonishment. 'The firebombs have still been falling.'

'It was the action of my cousin, Abdullah-ibn-Ali ibn Hassn, who three days ago brought up his men and two Turkish siege mortars from Rabat, intent on sharing the spoils of Tangier. He needed to show his strength, and with the evacuation imminent he was fearful that he would not otherwise have the opportunity. Princes should show their strength. Your King Charles would understand.'

Pepys had a fleeting vision of the last time he had seen King Charles, dressed up in feathers and powder like one of Mrs

Kirke's retainers, heading off to yet another masked ball with his army of dandies and courtesans. 'Yes, indeed,' he said. 'The King himself has thought of coming to Tangier after the evacuation, not to land but to bombard the city after the Moorish army has lodged itself here, with each of his twenty ships mounting thirty-six guns to a broadside. He too would be showing his strength.'

Ismail was quiet for a moment. 'For now my cousin has run out of ammunition, but he will soon acquire more from the Turks.'

'English gunpowder is the finest in the world,' Booth said, coming forward from the shadows. 'Much better than Turkish powder. English powder is made with saltpetre harvested by the agents of the East India Company from the bat caves of eastern Bengal, far superior to the pigeon guano used by the Turks.'

'Who is this man?' Ismail said.

'Mr Booth, my assistant,' Pepys replied. 'I brought him along because he is highly knowledgeable in such matters.'

Ismail curled his lip. 'He does not look like a warrior to me.'

'He was a soldier in his youth, and has killed many with the musket and the pike; he is a man who would understand the way of the desert.'

Pepys's heart sank slightly as he watched what Ismail did next, though he had guessed what was coming. The younger man reached into a bag on the side of his belt and took out a hand grenade, its wooden fuse plug sticking out and a length of about two feet of wick extending from that. A year earlier, the Moors had liberated a large cache of grenades from the ordnance stores of Fort Charles, one of the outlying bastions of Tangier, which had been taken after a bloody fight, leaving not a single English soldier alive. King Charles himself had confided in Pepys that he could not bear to maintain Tangier knowing that the fort bearing his name – *his name* – had been captured and would forever be there under the Moorish flag as a taunt and a humiliation; but for the remaining English soldiers of the garrison, Pepys knew, far more difficult to bear was an enemy that was returning their own ordnance to them, fuses lit and with murderous intent.

For the sons of the Alcaïd and the other young bloods, the grenades had become playthings of chance, frequently with fatal results, and they had settled on them as a necessity of any parlay, extending the wick to allow a sufficiency of time for the participants to come to some meaningful conclusion, but keeping it short enough to restrict the sometimes endless sessions of their elders. Should the wick burn into the fuse, it would be the elders who would be least likely to run off in time, a further incentive to keep talks short. It had a certain charm to it, Pepys admitted to himself, but now was hardly the time for young men's games, even though he knew that he was going to have to go along with it.

Ismail took out a flint and steel and cupped his hands over the wick, lighting it with a spark. 'Five minutes by your timepiece, Mr Pepys, if you are lucky.'

'You have the artefact with you?'

Ismail reached into a pouch on the other side of his belt and took out a swaddled package about the size of a large cup. The leather looked very old indeed, and Pepys could see on it faded lettering that looked as if it might be Latin. He had sworn to João that if it came into his hands he would not open it; but João had also told him the sign to look for to prove its authenticity, according to a tradition passed down from the earliest Christian Jews, who had protected it at the time of the Roman emperors. He leaned forward, peering at it, and then motioned with his hand for Ismail to turn it. And there it was: the unmistakable sign of the fish, the symbol that the early Christians had used for their faith, with the Greek letters alpha and omega on either side of it.

He breathed out slowly, hardly daring to believe it. 'And what would the Alcaïd your father have in return?' he asked, anxiously watching the wick, now already a quarter-way advanced.

Ismail placed the package in his lap, and put his hands on his thighs. 'The corsairs of Sale acquired this from the Knights of Malta in return for freeing some of their number who had become hostage. This grieved and angered the Sultan, as the Knights are the only Christian forces who dare oppose us at sea, and to return them to the fray seemed the height of folly. Seeing the Sultan's displeasure, the Bey of Sale sent this package to him, thinking that he might use it to trade something in return from the Christians, and the Sultan thought of Tangier and sent it to the Alcaïd. To us, what is in here is only of as much value as its ability to hold water, for that is how we would use it. We are not people of material possessions, nor do we need symbols of our faith. God is everywhere, within and around us. But knowing it has value for you, our price is high.'

Pepys pursed his lips, glancing at Booth, and then nodded, mainly in assurance to himself that there was no turning back now. 'You know that I was authorised by the governor and the Lord High Admiral, my Lord Dartmouth, to offer the Alcaïd all the remaining gunpowder of the garrison in Tangier in return for the cessation of artillery bombardment, and also to promise a lessening of the destruction by our sappers of the main fortifications of the city, though not of the Mole. This has been done, and the gunpowder is being delivered as we speak, to be left in barrels outside Henry Fort before we depart the port.'

'And what in addition for this object?' Ismail said, eyeing Pepys coolly.

Pepys hesitated, and then took a deep breath. 'Unbeknownst to the Alcaïd, a larger than necessary amount of the powder was to be used in the final destruction of the Mole, to effect a decisive breach but also to limit the amount left for you. It was not to be in breach of the agreement, but was not a ploy made in good faith, I hazard. Hearing of this, I made my way to the Mole yesterday afternoon and obliged the chief engineer to portion out one third of the powder in the main charge, which I presently have stored under lock and key in another warehouse of Senhor Brandão, near the eastern wharf. It amounts to thirty-two barrels, enough to fill the magazine of Alcazar and make the Alcaïd and his sons the envy of the Barbary shore. I hold the key to the storeroom on my person. Hand me that package, and we shall exchange; do not, and that store too will be blown sky high as we depart Tangier. The decision is yours.'

Pepys felt as if a burden had been lifted from him, one that had plagued him since he had put it in process, that had darkened his mind and led him to the previous evening's debauch; and yet what he had done was an act tantamount to high treason, which should see him condemned and beheaded in the Tower. He glanced at Booth with some trepidation, but the other man did not bat an eyelid, and then he recalled that, of course, Booth knew everything he did, and had probably even followed him down to the Mole.

The wick was now well over halfway burned. Pepys looked at Ismail, awaiting a response. Suddenly there was a commotion at the entrance and two men strode in, both holding pistols, one aimed at Pepys and the other at Booth. Pepys's heart was hammering, but he tried to keep his composure. 'Who, pray, are you? And I would favour you to hold those pistols away, if you please, gentlemen.'

The nearest man continued to aim at his head. 'We are the Altamanus, the Black Hand, and we work for the Inquisition of the Holy See in Portugal. Our mission is to retrieve for the Church of Rome what is rightfully ours; to take it from the hands of heathens and apostates and those who do not follow the True Cross. We have been on the trail of the heretic Brandão for some time, and our source among the Knights of Malta has led us here. And you have been most easy to follow, Mr Pepys. You are not cut out for intrigue.'

Pepys stared at the man, astonished. João had mentioned these people, the name, their special mark, their infiltration of the priesthood of the Inquisition, the spread of their tentacles as far as the Portuguese colony of Brazil and even beyond that. It had hardly seemed credible when he had heard it, but now, with the muzzle of a pistol in his face, it was another matter.

Booth turned to the man, his face serious. 'If, sir, you mean those who follow the Church of England, or the Protestant faith, then you are sore mistook if you think that we do not as well follow the True Cross, as the Lord Jesus Christ is our witness.'

Pepys drew himself up. 'Furthermore, know you that I am an emissary of His Britannic Majesty King Charles the Second of England, Scotland and Ireland, and as such am immune from the edicts of the Inquisition or any of their sundry affiliations, as is my assistant Mr Booth.'

The man gave a humourless smile. 'It is a pretty plea, Mr Pepys, but in this chamber there is nobody to hear it except these four walls, and this barbarous Moor.'

'What is it that you want, pray?'

'Do not play the fool with us, Mr Pepys; it ill suits you. We want what the Moor is holding.'

Pepys glanced at Ismail, who was motionless, sitting upright, staring at the other man. Pepys knew that Ismail's pistol was cocked, as it always was; for the men of the desert, there was no half-cock, no middle ground. He had seen Ismail and his brothers shoot in competition, when they drew with lightning speed, but it was in parlay with other chieftains that they were most likely to have to show their skill, to shoot the other man before he could shoot them, when negotiation failed and white suddenly turned to black. Ismail's hands were still resting on his thighs. He was ready, like a lion about to pounce.

Pepys's mind raced. He needed a pretext, something that would cause a distraction, however momentary. Then he remembered again what João had told him about the Altamanus, about their mark. He turned to the man. 'Pray, sir, show me your hands.'

141

'Why do you wish this?' the man replied, looking at him scornfully.

'Because I know about the mark of the Altamanus. When I see it, I will believe you and I will know that we are defeated. Show it to me, both of you, and what you want will be yours.'

The man glanced at his companion and grunted. They both turned their hands palms outwards, still holding their pistols but dangling them, showing the distinctive tattoo of a black hand. At that moment, Ismail's gun cracked deafeningly and the first man went down, falling backwards and hitting his head on the floor. As he did so, his pistol discharged, and Ismail fell back, shot through the chest. Booth raised his own weapon at the other man and fired, the puff of smoke from the primer followed by a jet of flame from the muzzle. The man staggered back, a spreading patch of red on his chest, but then lurched forward again. Booth clicked out the blade on the barrel, leapt on the man and drove it into the side of his neck, twisting and turning it as they crashed to the floor. He pulled out the blade and pushed back to his knees as the man frothed and gargled, blood splattering from his mouth, and then went still, his eyes wide open.

Another gun discharged, and Pepys saw that the man on the floor had raised a second pistol and levelled it at Booth, who dropped to the ground clutching his leg. Pepys took his own pistol from his pocket, fumbled with the safety lever and then aimed it at the man, pulling the trigger. The flint snapped against the steel, but there were no sparks. *A misfire.* The face of the steel must somehow have got damp in his pocket, from the perspiration on his hand, perhaps. He pulled back the cock and frantically wiped the steel dry with his shirtsleeve, his hands shaking. The man lurched upright, dropped his pistol and came for him, reaching out just as Pepys pulled the trigger again. This time the gun fired, the ball going through the man's stomach and out of his back, impacting on the wall behind in a spray of blood and bile.

The man staggered back, his chest soaked red from Ismail's bullet, holding the second wound in his stomach, the blood pulsing out between his fingers. Pepys realised that none of them any longer had a charged weapon. He looked at the blade on his own pistol barrel, but felt frozen, unable to open it. Pulling a trigger was one thing; doing what Booth had done was another. But the man of the Altamanus was in no fit condition to fight any further, and he knew it. He staggered to the entrance, where he turned, pointing a bloodied hand at Booth, swaying as he spoke.

'You,' he snarled, spitting blood. 'We will find you, and you will pay for this.' He turned to Pepys, pointing at the package. 'And you. Don't think that we will give up. We have been searching for that for a thousand years, and we will have it.' He made the sign of the cross on his chest, dripping blood as he did so, and then was gone, leaving a room filled with gore and bodies, with Pepys the only man left standing.

He suddenly remembered the grenade. To his horror, he saw that the wick had disappeared into the fuse and sparks were flying out of the hole. He looked around, desperately searching for water, a bottle of wine, anything to douse it with, but there was nothing. They had only seconds to spare. He lurched over, slapped Booth hard on the face to waken him and grabbed him by the shoulders, dragging him towards the entrance. Booth, coming round groggily, saw what was happening and crawled the remainder of the way himself, his bleeding leg dragging behind him.

At the last moment, Pepys remembered something else, something crucial. *The package.* He lurched back to Ismail, lifting it from his lap. Ismail's head was lolling, his face deathly pale, but he opened his eyes and looked at Pepys. 'It is my time,' he whispered, blood tricking from his mouth. 'Allah calls me. Go.'

Pepys staggered back to the entrance, falling through it just as the grenade detonated behind him with an immense crack, sending shards of red-hot metal into the wall opposite and covering him in a cloud of sulphurous smoke. He picked himself up, his ears ringing, then pulled Booth to his feet and helped him out of the smoke and debris, looking around to see if there was any sign of the man who had escaped, but seeing nothing. Out in the alley, he tucked the precious package into the inside pocket of his coat, coughing and blinking away the smoke as he tried to see ahead.

He had a sudden thought. If those men had known to come to João's warehouse in Tangier, they would know to look for him in Portugal. If the wounded man somehow made it out of here, if he passed on word of what had happened, then João would be in mortal danger. Pepys could only pray that he would remain free until the fleet arrived off Porto, when they could carry out their plan to send the package away and he could spirit the merchant and his family out of Portugal and the clutches of the Inquisition.

He turned to Booth. 'We have no time to lose,' he said, his voice hoarse from the smoke. 'We must get to the *Schiedam*. Now.'

10

Coimbra, Portugal, the Court of the Inquisition,
25 April 1684

A scream rent the air, a hollow, piercing sound that reverberated off the walls of the audience chamber, rising from the dungeons below as if from the fires of hell itself. The man in the soiled robe stood motionless, waiting for the screaming to stop, as indifferent by now to the sounds of suffering as were the priests who sat in judgement in front of him. It ended as abruptly as it had started, and for a few moments all he could hear was the cooing and flapping of a dove that had made its way into the chamber from the courtyard outside. He stared up, straining against the weight of the chains that shackled his legs, and spotted the bird far above, a flickering phantasm of white against the metal grille that was the only source of light in the chamber. The symbolism seemed lost on the priests, or they were ignoring it, but to the man it was as if Christ Himself had come to cast judgement on the priests, to witness the torment they were inflicting in his name, in this place that seemed as far from God as it was possible to get. The man looked back at the row of cassocked figures in front of him. He would tell them nothing of his secret, even if they took him to the rack and tore him limb from limb. He might not be of their faith, he might not believe in their Saviour, but his God was their God and he would not let this abomination of divine will snatch from humanity all shreds of succour and hope, take from those who most needed it the greatest lost treasure of Christendom itself.

The priest who acted as president of the court raised his spectacles on their handle and peered at the codex on the lectern in front of him. He was clean-shaven, gaunt and austere, like the others of the tribunal, in contrast to the prisoners who came before them, with their bedraggled beards and filthy rags. 'The Conselho Geral do Santo Oficio, the General Council of the Holy Office of the Inquisition, calls forth João Rodrigues Brandão, of Viseu and Porto.'

The man in the robe remained still for a moment, staring at the Grand Seal of the Inquisition that hung down in front of the lectern, at the image of the wooden cross with the olive branch on one side and the sword on the other. The priest had spoken in Portuguese rather than Latin, the language of the Church, the language in which he had delivered judgement on the emaciated, pitiful wretch who had just been dragged outside to undergo his auto-da-fé, his act of penance. None

146

who came before the Inquisition for their *processo*, their trial, knew whether they were to live or to die, whether the auto-da-fé was to be a mere public confession or an execution, but the smell of burning that seeped in from the courtyard showed that the fires had been stoked and that today was not to be a day of mercy.

The man shuffled forward to the designated spot, the chains clanking heavily around his ankles, and stood in the shaft of sunlight that came from the grille in the tower above. 'I am João Rodrigues Brandão, of Viseu and Porto.'

The priest lowered his spectacles and stared at him with rheumy eyes. 'What is your occupation?'

'I am a merchant, as were my father and grandfather and great-grandfather before me. I import tobacco from the Portuguese estates in Brazil, and in turn export wine and other goods to the colonists.'

'It is a family affair?'

'My brothers and uncles and cousins are part of the trade.'

'You bear a Portuguese name, and yet your brothers and uncles and cousins when they depart this realm to live abroad choose to change their forenames to those of their Jewish ancestors. Francisco becomes Abraham, João becomes Joshua, Luisa becomes Esther, Eleanor becomes Rebecca. They only retain the Portuguese surname Brandão because it is well known and good for business. Is that correct?'

'You know we are *conversos*. When our Jewish ancestors were expelled from Spain by Isabella and Ferdinand, we came to Portugal and became New Christians, according to the law. That is how we have lived now for eight generations. But those who choose to go beyond this realm are not bound by the rules of this court or of the Kingdom of Portugal, and may choose to revert to the names of their ancestors.'

'They did not leave Portugal legally. *Conversos* do not have the right to travel abroad. They fled the Inquisition.'

'*Hereticos*,' one of the other priests muttered, pointing a crooked finger.

'I am not responsible for the actions of my brothers and uncles and cousins,' João said.

'Have you sent money abroad?' the first priest asked. 'Do you too plan to flee Portugal?'

'I only send money abroad to pay for trade goods.'

The priest shuffled the papers in front of him, raised his spectacles and peered down. 'Two hundred and fifty gold ducats, three weeks ago, on a Portuguese merchant ship bound for Amsterdam, confiscated from the ship before it left Lisbon. The banker who managed the transaction denounced you.'

João stared at the seal again, trying to keep his expression impassive. It had only been two weeks since they had come for him, seeking him first in his home in the hills at Viseu, the town in northern Portugal where his family had lived since their arrival in the country as refugees almost two hundred years before, and then at his warehouse near the mouth of the river Douro at Porto, the harbour city north of Lisbon where he carried out his business. He should have waited to consign the gold to one of the English navy vessels in the port rather than to a Portuguese ship. The English captains supplemented their meagre pay by transporting money and specie at extortionate rates, but their ships were vessels of war, able to fight off Barbary corsairs, and were not subject to harbour inspections in Portuguese waters.

He had been lax, but his attention had been on another cargo that day, a cargo of extraordinary secrecy, and only once he had seen that dispatched safely in a ship bound for the Caribbean had he felt a sudden urgency about safeguarding his own wealth, allowing himself to accept an offer from a captain of any nationality. He had been too hasty, and was paying the price for it now. The banker was a distant cousin on his wife's side, another *converso* with whom he had always done business but who had evidently succumbed to the threats of the Inquisition and been willing to denounce his clients. The tentacles of the Inquisition spread far and wide, and nobody could any longer be trusted, even those of his own faith and family.

The priest muttered something to the man by his side, then turned and conferred with the others on the bench behind him. João felt light-headed, weak from days with barely any food, but he had to keep the trial going for as long as possible to buy time. At least his payment for the secret cargo was safe from the clutches of the Inquisition, the silver pieces of eight overstamped with his own trade mark of a Star of David to keep others from being tempted to make off with them, and then dispatched in an English naval transport direct from the English colony of Tangier in North Africa to his brother in London. With that money on its way, he had made arrangements for his wife and children to flee Portugal on another ship. Despite the loss of the 250 ducats, he had the solace of knowing that when his family arrived in London they would not be penniless and destitute like so many other refugees from the Inquisition; his brother would see to that.

He cleared his throat and tried to hold himself upright. 'Of what am I accused?'

The priest turned back towards him, and placed his hands on the lectern. The others followed his gaze, crossing their arms over their cassocks and staring at some distant point beyond. 'You are accused of Judaism, heresy and apostasy,' the priest said. 'Judaism, because you have never renounced that faith. Heresy, because it is heretical not to believe in the sacred tenets of the Church of the Holy See. Apostasy, because having professed to be a Christian, you were clearly no such thing. How do you answer on each of these counts?'

João glanced up at the tower, blinking hard in the dusty shaft of sunlight, trying to spot the dove, and then looked back at the priest. To be a *converso* arraigned before the Inquisition at Coimbra was almost inevitably to be accused in these terms, and to be certain of being condemned. And yet he experienced a wash of relief that his true purpose in the docks at Porto had not been discovered and that he had not been brought here to reveal that secret cargo, and he felt emboldened in his reply. With only one outcome possible no matter how he responded, there seemed nothing to lose. He stared defiantly at the priest. 'I am accused, and therefore in the eyes of the tribunal I am guilty.'

The priest looked at him sternly. 'Confess, and the court may show you mercy. If the auto-da-fé is to be execution, we have the discretion to order the executioner to strangle you before your body is tied to the stake.'

'I wish for no special treatment.'

'Do you have anything further to say?'

'I have this to say. I am placed in a cell five feet by eleven, with five others, where the only light comes from a narrow opening in the ceiling, where the chamber pot is emptied only once a week, and where all spiritual consolation is denied. The Holy Office of Portugal is a tribunal that serves only to deprive men of their fortunes, their honour and their lives. It is unable to discriminate between guilt and innocence, and is holy in name only. Its works are cruelty and injustice. It is unworthy of rational beings, and unworthy of the God it professes to serve.'

There was a sudden tension in the chamber. Those among the priests who had seemed impassive now stared at him with shock and contempt; the one with the crooked finger seemed apoplectic, unable even to point. João had repeated the words of Father António Vieira, the Jesuit priest and friend of the *conversos*, whose report on his own imprisonment had led the Pope to suspend the Portuguese Inquisition for seven years. Three years ago, when it had been reinstated, Father Vieira had fled to Brazil, knowing that the Papal Bull exempting him from prosecution was worth little more than the paper it was written on, and that there would be agents of the Inquisition who would hunt him down to the far corners of the earth. He had set himself up as head of a community deep in the rainforest, protected by *conversos* who had once served as soldiers of the Portuguese king, and by others, English, Dutch and Germans among them, who had gone to the New World in search not of gold and silver but of a different kind of treasure, of enlightenment and toleration far removed from the cruelty that the Inquisition and age-old prejudices had inflicted on the Old World.

By repeating the words of Father Vieira, João knew that he was sealing his own fate, but it was hardly as if it had hung in the balance; the Inquisition had returned with a vengeance after its suspension, using the overheard conversations of those relaxed years as evidence of heresy almost as if they had planned it, and many *conversos* who would previously have been let off with a penance were now going straight to the stake. He knew now that his dream of one day joining Father Vieira was over, but he took solace in the covenant he had made with his brother in London to use that silver to buy passage for his wife and children to their cousins in Port Royal in Jamaica, and thence to seek a safe route away from prying eyes across to Brazil and to the chosen place. He remembered, too, the promise he had made to Father Vieira when he had first heard of the treasure that he was to dispatch to safety: that one day that too would reach the promised land, that it would make the place so holy that the power of those who would seek it would fall away like storm waves battering an island fortress, spent and impotent.

The smell of burning from the auto-da-fé was stronger, and he imagined invisible wisps of smoke encircling him like a coil of snakes, drawing the flames in after them. He remembered as a boy being dragged by the priest from his schoolroom to the *quemadero*, the place of burning in the square outside, to watch his grandfather's auto-da-fé. The priest had pinched him by the ear until he cried, and had told him that his grandfather was being shown mercy, that it was better to burn quickly on earth than eternally in hell.

But they had not burned him quickly; they had lashed him

naked to a stake and placed a ring of glowing coals around him, a fiery ring that they pushed ever closer until he was roasted alive. It was the same fate that had been suffered in the Roman Colosseum by Laurentius, one of their own community who had felt the call of Christ and gone to Rome at the time of the emperors, and was now revered as a saint for his martyrdom. Watching with horror his grandfather's fate, it had seemed to João that history had collapsed in on itself, that all those generations since Laurentius had been swept away and he himself was standing on the blood-soaked ground of the Colosseum, the agents of darkness who had brought about Laurentius's death now on his own trail as well.

He felt his palms go clammy, his breathing shorten, and he shivered in spite of the heat of the chamber. The next walk he took would be his last, following the condemned man before him, whose last bodily exhalations had now returned to wreathe the chamber. He must try not to show his fear, try to keep his dignity in front of the crowd outside, to show those who had been forced to attend the auto-da-fé that he was still able to stand on his own two feet, that the Inquisition had not broken him.

Suddenly, without a word, the president rose, followed by the rest of the tribunal, and they filed silently out. João knew that this could only be a brief reprieve, part of the theatre of the court. He stared again at the cross on the seal below the lectern, trying to keep his mind focused, to keep his thoughts strong against what lay ahead. The cross was the same shape he had seen countless times on the pieces of eight that had fuelled his life as a merchant, made from the silver ore that had been the greatest source of wealth from the New World once the gold of the Aztecs and the Maya and the Inca had run out. He had been there himself when he was young, to the great silver mines of the mountains, travelling from Port Royal in Jamaica to Mexico and then south to the viceroyalty of Peru, inland by llama to the high Andes.

At Potosi he had seen the mountain of riches, the Cerro Rico, where wealth seemed to flow like burning lava and yet which seemed to suck men into it, not only those whose greed became too much but also the countless Inca who died from their toil, their lungs choked by dust. Every planchet of silver, every rough-cut piece of eight, all of them stamped with the arms of Castile and Leon, represented a terrible human cost. Each year millions were minted, and thousands died. For weeks after his visit he could still smell the molten arsenic used to refine the silver, the reek of the underworld itself. For João, the cross stamped on each coin had come to represent the bars of a prison, locking away a grim truth on the other side of the world where the avarice of a few had condemned so many to a living hell.

He shut his eyes, running again over his business dealings as he had done every day since his arrest, reassuring himself that he had left his affairs in good order. Months earlier, he had dispatched 800 gold escudos to Port Royal in Jamaica, where, God willing, it would remain in the safe hands of his cousin until his wife and children should arrive. Port Royal had been good to the Brandão family, a place well suited to their way of doing business. They had offered brokerage to the buccaneers of the Spanish Main, men with letters of marque from the Governor of Jamaica to attack Spanish ships carrying silver and gold from Mexico and Peru, and all manner of goods for the settlers in the other direction. Buccaneers with plunder not in bullion or specie brought their goods to the wharves of Port Royal for a quick sale, and were usually satisfied with a few reales to spend on the whores and taverns of the port; those goods in turn went for a healthy premium to the Portuguese colonists of Brazil, creating a circle of trade that kept everyone happy: the pirates, the merchants, the governor of Jamaica, even the Portuguese customs officials of Brazil who took their cut, to the discomfort only of the Spanish Crown.

And then there had been the business of Tangier. João's father had jumped at the chance when the English had taken over the city from the Portuguese and made it a free port, encouraging Portuguese merchants already there to remain and expand their dealings. They had watched the dissipation and corruption of the English colonists, just as they had done in Port Royal. Dissipation and corruption could be good for business, providing the goods and money continued to flow. In Jamaica the source of wealth was the Spanish Main; in Tangier, it was to have been the treasures of the East, with the city a halfway house for the plunder of the Indies. But Jamaica was in an ocean where the English navy held sway, whereas Tangier was hemmed in on three sides by the besieging army of the Moors, a force that proved too much for an English garrison enfeebled by drink and disease. The English had their hands full at home, with the seemingly endless conflicts with the Dutch and in Ireland and the threat of a religious civil war, and holding on to the failing colony had proved just too much.

João remembered the portly, bewigged Englishman from the Admiralty who had sought him out in Tangier three months before, always jotting down notes in his curious shorthand, his Portuguese halting and imprecise. The English Crown had decided to appease foreign merchants in Tangier who might be of future use by offering them generous compensation and resettlement, even allowing them to buy surplus equipment and stores at a token price. But these arrangements were not the main reason why the Englishman, Samuel Pepys, had befriended him. In Tangier, the Jewish *conversos* had been free to follow their old religion, but few had done so openly, many of them still having interests in Portugal and unwilling to risk arrest by the Inquisition should they have to return home; as it transpired, the English decision to leave Tangier and repatriate the merchants had shown their caution to be wise. Pepys had sought him out because the Brandão family were known for their discretion and care, both in keeping their faith to themselves and in their business dealings; they could continue to conduct business in Portugal more safely than *converso* merchants who had been less careful, something that had been critical to the proposition that he had come to discuss.

The Englishman had known something else: that João came from a family of Jews sympathetic to Christianity who had fled Judaea after the Roman conquest and gone to live in Spain, and then after the expulsion had settled not only in Portugal but also in a wide diaspora including England, Holland and the islands of the Caribbean. He had come not only because of the Brandão reputation, to drive a bargain for freightage to the New World with one of the most reliable firms operating out of Tangier, but also because of that history; to deal with a family who for over a thousand years had provided safe haven and succour in their mountain fastness to refugees from the persecutions of those elements in the Church who would eventually form the basis of the Inquisition. The Englishman had wanted discretion and reliability, but also to deal with those to whom he could reveal the nature of his cargo and who would share his passion for its safe arrival somewhere far away from those elements, in a place akin to the haven that the Spanish Jewish community had once provided to refugees from Roman persecution but which now would need to be in a place of security somewhere beyond the fringes of a far wider world.

João had wept with joy and relief when the Englishman had revealed the nature of his cargo. For over a thousand years, that very treasure had been protected by the Brandão family, ever since it had been brought from Rome by a Christian legionary escaping persecution by the emperors. The Brandão family themselves were descended from the legionary, a man called Proselius who had married a Jewish girl. They had protected it through the centuries, through the collapse of empires and the ravages of lawlessness and war, telling nobody but their own children, generation after generation, until they were uprooted by the eviction of the Jews from Spain and decided in fear for its safety on their long trek west to pass it on to the castle fastness of the Knights of Malta.

There it should have remained, secure until the time for its revelation, but then the worst had happened. The master of the order was captured and enslaved by Barbary pirates, and in desperation those knights who remained, weakened in body and resolve, had chosen to offer up the treasure as ransom. It had passed from the pirates to their Moorish overlords, and then to the Sultan of Morocco. The Sultan's eye had been fixed on Tangier, obsessively, an all-consuming passion, and he too had used the treasure as a bargaining chip, to secure as much as he could of the gunpowder and artillery and fortifications of the town from the English, in return for allowing them to depart unmolested.

It had been the Englishman, Samuel Pepys, an official sent by Charles II to wrap up his affairs at Tangier, whom the Sultan's emissary had approached for the negotiations. As soon as Pepys had seen what was on offer, he had agreed to the terms but sworn the Sultan to secrecy. The treasure could not return to the English Crown, to Charles II, where it might become a pawn in the religious war that seemed about to erupt, a conflict between Catholic and Protestant. Instead, Pepys would find a way for it to be spirited off to a new place of safety. That had led him to seek out João in Tangier, to strike a bargain, and then to find him again in secrecy at his warehouse at Porto three weeks ago in order to pass him the package and the silver that was to be used to pay the captain of the chosen ship – Henry Avery of the *Black Swan*, though Avery was not to know the true nature of the package he was to transport – for its safe passage to the New World.

João had taken a huge gamble on his return from Tangier to wait on in Portugal for that rendezvous, and now he was paying the price. With the Inquisition closing in on all *converso* merchants who had returned, even those like him who had not openly professed Judaism while they had been away, every day that he had lingered had been a day of increasing anxiety. It was made worse by his decision to dispatch the package to Port Royal in the care of his eldest son Lopo, who might thus escape the immediate clutches of the Inquisition himself but who would be sailing into uncertainty and danger. For a son to disappear would not in itself attract interest – a common enough occurrence in a family with overseas business interests, and easily explained away – but for João's wife and other children also to disappear would attract immediate suspicion.

He had needed to play a very careful game, one that had stretched his nerves to the limit. Once a man was arrested by the Inquisition, the arrest of his wife and children would inevitably follow. As long as he continued to be at liberty, then so would they, but with every passing day the risk of discovery and denunciation grew greater. He had planned to remain in Porto for as long as he judged possible after his son's departure in order to maintain an image of normality, to allow the ship a good head start and to make the arrangements for his family's departure. He had ordered them from Viseu to the waiting ship only when he knew that his own arrest was imminent, in the knowledge that their absence would be reported to the Inquisition by the town priests the next day but that his attempts at explanation might buy them the critical hours they would need to escape.

Even after he had been dragged to the cells, every day that passed, every day that he had survived deprivation and anxiety before his *processo*, was one more day's sailing from the clutches of these people, from those who would take the greatest symbol of Christendom and use it in their crusade against any who refused to bow before them, Christian,

Jew and Moor alike. If holding out against confessing meant that he bought more time, even a matter of a few hours, then he could endure further gnawing, crushing uncertainty about his family, and the remorse he knew would follow should he find out that they had not escaped in time. All he could do now was stand firm and say nothing, knowing that to refuse to confess would aggravate the tribunal and seal his fate, but that in so doing he would be keeping faith with those who had gone before him and sacrificed their lives in order to prevent the greatest treasure of Christendom from falling into malign hands.

The door to the chamber suddenly swung open. He felt a rush of hot air from outside, and tasted the tang of burning in his throat. He took a deep breath, and steeled himself. He knew that his time had come.

11

A man came forward from the door of the audience chamber and stood in front of the lectern on the edge of the shaft of light. The door clanged shut, shaking the dust in the air, and they were alone. The man was tall, thin, with a hooked nose and a bald head, his face cadaverous and pale. He wore the tight-fitting black robe of a Jesuit, and hanging by a golden chain from his neck was the Grand Seal of the Inquisition, something that not even the president of the court had worn. João stared at him and felt a cold stab in the pit of his stomach. He had seen this man before, officiating at an auto-da-fé in Lisboã, a spectacular affair where the King himself had been present; never at a provincial court such as Coimbra or at a straightforward case of heresy. He swallowed hard, trying to keep his composure. *Something had gone wrong.*

'You know who I am,' the man said.

'Cardinal Diego da Silva, Bishop of Ceuta and confessor to the King.'

'And Grand Inquisitor of Portugal.'

João's mouth was dry. 'Why are you here? Your court is at Lisboã, not Coimbra. I am a mere *converso,* one of thousands. I am of no special interest to you.'

'You know that is not true.'

'I know only of what I am accused.'

The cardinal opened a scroll he had been carrying. 'Do you have business dealings in Jamaica?'

'It is common knowledge. A branch of my family has lived at Port Royal for several generations, ever since the English took over the island from the Spanish.'

'Your cousins provide brokerage for the English pirates who prey on the Spanish treasure ships, converting their stolen goods for a profit. It is how the Jews of Port Royal have grown rich.'

'And those goods we sell on to the Portuguese colonists in Brazil, benefiting the coffers of the King through the cut he takes on the sale of all imports into the colony. Dealing with the English in Port Royal is hardly a crime against the Church, or against the King of Portugal. And we are surely not beholden to the Spanish.'

'And what are your dealings with the former English colony of Tangier in North Africa?'

João felt his heart pounding, but he held the other man's gaze. 'You know full well that I had warehouses there until the English King Charles decided late last year to abandon the colony. My family had business interests there from the time when Tangier was ruled by the Portuguese. As the English had intended, I and the other Portuguese merchants there hoped to use the free port to increase our trade with the East, in my case to broker the shipment of fine textiles from India and include them in my consignments to the Portuguese colonists in Brazil, also to the benefit of the coffers of the Portuguese king. When that trade failed to materialise, when the Moors besieged Tangier and the English decided to leave, I closed my office and departed.'

The cardinal looked at the scroll. 'Not before receiving a generous settlement from the English Admiralty official sent out to Tangier to pay reparation to those being dispossessed, a Don Samuel Pepys.'

'The English king paid foreign merchants the value of their property in Tangier, and the cost of shipping them to their chosen destination. You doubtless have had the documents before you. Don Pepys was a scrupulous record-keeper. I received no more or less than the others.'

The cardinal rolled up the scroll and stared at João, his eyes steely and merciless. 'Then why did Don Pepys visit you in secret when he came to Portugal from Tangier three weeks ago?'

João felt dizzy, and swayed. He had not eaten more than a few mouthfuls of prison gruel for days, and the water they had been given had been too foul to drink. He had been sustained by thinking that he had done everything possible to conceal his activities, but there were informers everywhere. All he could do now was to bluff for as long as possible. He took a deep breath.

'I have told you that the English settlement with the merchants of Tangier was to arrange shipment of their goods and belongings to any port they desired. Don Pepys came to Portugal to facilitate the onward shipment of some of my trade stock to London, and that of other merchants who had also been inconvenienced. I had bought a large lot of surplus tools that had been used by the English engineers to destroy the great mole at Tangier, to render the harbour useless to the Moors. The tools had come on a Portuguese ship from Tangier to Porto, where Don Pepys arranged for them to be transferred to an English vessel bound for London. From there, I had intended to place them in a cargo destined for the Portuguese settlers in Brazil. I have traded in tools in this manner many times before, often with the English. Their iron is superior to our own, and the tools are much prized by the tree-cutters of the Amazon forest. You can easily verify the details. The name of the English ship is the *Schiedam Prize*. She was also carrying armaments taken from the city defences, long guns and mortars, and many small arms. She departed Porto on her final return voyage to England on the day of my arrest two weeks ago.'

'We know of this ship,' the cardinal replied, waving his hand dismissively. 'And we know that she also carried silver coin stamped with your sign. That is of no interest to us. But there was another ship that you contracted from Porto, was there not? One destined not for England but for the New World. One in which you and Don Pepys had placed a cargo of far greater value than a few boxes of cast-off tools and your own paltry savings in bullion and specie.'

João felt his resolve disappear. Fighting the Inquisition was always a losing battle. Once you stepped into the audience chamber you were guilty, and they always had proof. His words when they came out sounded distant, barely audible. 'How do you know this?'

'Because we have eyes and ears everywhere. Because your cousin the *converso* banker who transacted your gold, the gold that we intercepted when you put it on a Portuguese ship, knew that you had secretly passed another package to another English ship sailing out of Porto. He is a brave man, your cousin, evidently remorseful at informing us of your gold shipment, and it has taken us all this time with the rack and the thumbscrew to extract the full story of what he knows, enough for us to delay your *processo* for two weeks but enough for me to come here now. Yesterday, after we put his wife on the rack before his eyes, he finally confessed and said that he had seen a package with a leather case inside stamped with the arms of the Knights of Malta. A package that had been passed to you by Don Pepys.'

João felt like retching. *So they knew*. He tried to stand firm, but felt himself swaying. 'And what of it?'

The cardinal stared at him. 'We know what the Knights of Malta gave to the Moors in return for the freedom from slavery of their Grand Master after he was captured by Barbary pirates. And we know what the Sultan of the Moors gave to the English in Tangier in return for their gunpowder, and for not demolishing the main part of the city. Don Pepys had a most trustworthy secretary who came with him to Portugal but disappeared mysteriously, a man named Booth, who proved most compliant when we pulled out his fingernails, gouged open a recent wound that had been healing on his leg, and started to disembowel him, a process that his confession did nothing to halt.'

165

'What do you want from me?'

The cardinal leaned forward slightly. 'We want the name of the ship, and its destination.'

João shook his head. 'I will take what I know with me to the stake. I have nothing to gain by talking.'

'You have your family. Your wife and children.'

'You cannot threaten me with that. By now they are safe in another English ship, two weeks out from Porto on their way to London. They are beyond the reach of the Inquisition.'

The cardinal snapped his fingers and gestured towards the doorway. João turned, straining his eyes in the gloom. He could make out several figures being pushed into the chamber, a woman and four children, pale, emaciated, in rags, but instantly recognisable. His eldest son Lopo, whom he had sent to Port Royal, was not there, a small mercy.

He tried to speak, but no words came out, and he fell heavily to his knees, his chains clanking around him. Even before they had begun to interrogate him, the priests of the Inquisition had known exactly how to break a man like him; had known that physical torture was as nothing compared to the mental torment they could inflict on a father who had seen with his own eyes other women and children being led out and burned at the stake, suffocating in the smoke of their own roasting flesh. He looked up imploringly at the man towering over him, his eyes welling up. 'Have mercy on them,' he said, his voice choked. 'I beg you, have mercy on them.'

The cardinal stared down at him. 'It is not the job of the Inquisition to show mercy. That is in the hands of the Lord. But tell me what I want to know, and I give you my word that they will not burn.'

João stared at the man's cassock, trying to think straight. The ship bound for Port Royal had been gone for two weeks now, since the day of his arrest, having left Porto on the same day as the *Schiedam Prize*; with a fair wind it could already be halfway to its destination. Even if the cardinal sent ships after it, they would be too far behind and would be outrun and outgunned by the English vessel, whose crew and weapons would be superior to anything the Inquisition would be likely to hire for the pursuit. He remembered the captain whom Pepys had introduced to him, a tough, no-nonsense man he felt he could entrust not only with the package but also with his son. Drawing on his last reserve of strength, he struggled to his feet, wiping his face, and stood before the cardinal.

'You swear by God,' he said hoarsely, swaying again. The cardinal nodded, almost imperceptibly, and João wiped his mouth again. 'Her name is the *Black Swan*,' he said. 'Her captain is an officer of the English navy named Henry Avery. Others will attest that the *Black Swan* lay off Porto two weeks ago. Don Pepys arranged it. She is bound for Port Royal in Jamaica.'

The cardinal stared at him a moment longer, as if making up his mind, and then nodded more emphatically, not at João but at two others, who came up behind and roughly took his arms, pinning them against his back and binding his wrists together. João arched his neck around towards the doorway, looking for his wife and children, but they were gone. For a moment he wondered whether they had been a phantasm, whether this was all a dream. 'You gave your word,' he said, his voice hoarse and wavering. 'Your word that they will be spared.'

The cardinal leaned forward, his face only inches from João's right ear, so close that he could smell his breath. 'Do not think that what you sent away in that ship will ever be safe,' he hissed. 'We will chase your treasure to the ends of the earth and the end of time, if needs be. We have a long memory.'

He stood back, made the sign of the cross over his chest and raised his hands in a brief gesture of prayer. In that instant, João saw it, the black mark on the palm of his right hand: the shape of a cross. It was the sign of the Altamanus. *So it was true.* He had only ever heard of it in legend, a story of darkness and evil that had kept him awake at night as a boy, that had kept them all vigilant in their task as guardians of the treasure, generation after generation. The Altamanus, the Black Hand, the emperor's chosen henchmen, had chased Proselius from Rome, across mountain and sea, to the far reaches of the Empire and beyond, until they had lost his trail in the wilds of Spain. It was the Altamanus who had been most feared in 1492, when the expulsion of the Jews from Spain might make the guardians of the treasure visible again, exposed to malign eyes, those who were forever watching and hunting, a fear that led them to pass their precious legacy to the safety of the Knights of Malta. And now all that stood between the Altamanus and their goal was a boy at sea, his safety tenuous and his ultimate destination in the folds of legend itself, protected only by the bulwark that João had provided, each minute of his *processo* buying precious time for that ship somewhere out on the Atlantic on its perilous voyage into the unknown.

The cardinal turned abruptly and left, making the sign of

the cross again as he passed by the Great Seal of the Inquisition on the lectern. The priests of the tribunal filed silently back in and sat down, followed by the president of the court. High above them, the dove cooed and fluttered, disturbed by the commotion below, and then swooped down through the open door towards the courtyard and the sky beyond. João felt glad that it had escaped, that it had found a way out of this place of condemnation, but at the same time it was as if his last hope of reprieve, of surviving the judgement that was about to be passed on him, had disappeared.

He closed his eyes, and thought of what Father Vieira had said in his final secret meeting with his followers before he had left for the New World: 'We are what we do; what we don't do doesn't exist, and we only exist on days when we do. On the days when we don't do, we simply endure.' Now João knew what he had meant. What João had done, what had come to define his existence, had been set in motion the moment he had taken that package from Pepys and stowed it on board the *Black Swan*. Since then, since his arrest, he had simply been enduring, in a shadowland on the fringes of existence. And now he knew that the next steps he took could lead only to one place, to the place where cruelty and wretchedness and pain would be expunged, where all he would know would be the light that Father Vieira had seen in the furthest reaches of the New World, a light of purity in a place untainted by prejudice and persecution.

He remembered that Father Vieira had called that place El Dorado, the Place of Gold, the same term the Conquistadors had used for the fabled fount of riches that had obsessed them since their arrival in the Americas almost two centuries ago, a place beyond the lands they had ravaged and pillaged in their unquenchable thirst for gold. Father Vieira's El Dorado was another kind of fount, a place where the treasure that João had sent them would glow in the light of the sun, where a simple cup touched by the lips of their Messiah would take its rightful place as a greater treasure than any amount of gold and silver that the Conquistadors could have imagined.

The president of the court put on his spectacles, positioned the scroll he had been carrying on the lectern and nodded curtly at the men holding João. They dragged him forward into the dusty shaft of light, the chains tearing and digging into his ankles. In that moment of pain, João knew that this was no dream. As they positioned him and held him blinking in the light, he smelled the lingering waft of burning on their tunics, and saw the white flecks of ash. He realised that his legs were like jelly, and that it was not just from exhaustion. For the first time, he felt a cold shiver of fear, not for his family now, but for what lay ahead for him.

The priest opened the scroll, found his place and began to read. '"This tribunal, with the authority invested in it by the General Council of the Holy Office of the Inquisition in Portugal, finds you, João Rodrigues Brandão of Viseu and Porto, merchant, guilty of the crimes of Judaism, heresy and apostasy, and commits you forthwith to make your penance before the priests and people of Coimbra, and to suffer the auto-da-fé. May God have mercy on your soul."' He rolled the scroll up and looked at the men on either side of João. 'The work of the tribunal is done. Now it is your job to carry out the sentence of the Inquisition. Let him burn.'

Part 3

Part 3

12

Santo Cristo del Tesoro, Caribbean Sea, present day

The door to the antechamber swung shut, blocking out the sounds of the sea and the helicopter that was powering down outside. The man who had just arrived smoothed back his hair where it had been ruffled by the wind and walked towards a second door at the end of the passageway ahead, past pyramidal stacks of black-painted cannonballs that had been there since the days of the pirates. Beside him a ramp led to the upper revetments, the embrasures encased now in glass but the cannons still thrusting their muzzles out to sea. He looked up at the massive lintel above the door, a slab of austere white marble brought all the way from the shores of the Mediterranean, and saw the date carved into it: *Anno Domini MDCLXXX* – the Year of Our Lord 1680. Below that was the Seal of the Inquisition, the gnarled cross with the sword on one side and the olive branch on the other, and on either side of that a hand carved in jet with three fingers curled and the forefinger pointing to heaven, the same symbol that he and the others he would meet here had tattooed on the palms of their hands, as had their predecessors for countless generations before that.

He crossed himself and pushed open the heavy metal door, hearing it clang shut behind him as he carried on into the audience chamber. It was high-ceilinged like the great hall of a medieval castle, modelled on the chamber of the Patio da Inquisicão at Coimbra in Portugal. Above him were slits near the top of the walls for the sunlight to shine through, their angle concentrating the beams on a raised dais in the middle of the floor, with channels cut into the masonry surrounding it that dropped into a drain. At Coimbra they had the benefit of a courtyard outside, a place where the auto-da-fé had been conducted in full view of the heavens; here they had no such luxury, with the buffeting of the wind making fires impossible; instead the builders had opted for an interior design where the sentence of the court could be carried out swiftly and cleanly in front of the eyes of the tribunal.

Beyond the dais was a long oak table with chairs behind it where the priests had once sat. Today they were occupied by the five other men of the Altamanus. His arrival had made their number complete, a number that had been fixed since the days of the Roman Empire. The man in the centre gestured towards an empty chair at the end.

'Professor Salvador,' he said, speaking English with an eastern European accent. 'We hope you had an uneventful flight.'

'To Colombia from London was restful, but the helicopter ride to the island was less easy. There is a storm brewing on the horizon.'

'Yes indeed.' The man leaned forward. 'A storm in more ways than one, a storm from heaven itself. For more than three hundred years the Altamanus has been waiting for this day. For more than a thousand years before that we stalwartly served our Lord, strengthening the Church as we once strengthened the emperors. And now at last we are close to the time for exaltation. We await your news eagerly.'

Salvador eased himself onto his chair and leaned forward, nodding at the others around the table. He pulled a small felt-lined box from his jacket pocket and opened it, taking out a shiny silver coin and holding it out for the others to see.

'In May of 1684,' he began, 'a ship arrived in Jamaica from Portugal, an English naval transport named the *Black Swan*. She was destined to become the personal vessel of one of the most notorious pirates of the day, Henry Avery. But for our purpose now, all that matters is that she was carrying on board Lopo Rodriguez Brandão, a Jewish *converso* fleeing the Inquisition in Portugal with a supply of coin from his father João. That itself would have been enough for the Inquisition to send the Altamanus in pursuit, but our intention was not to apprehend a heretic. Our intention was to take something the boy had with him, a package containing the greatest lost treasure of Christendom: the Holy Chalice. Three hundred and thirty years ago, we failed in our endeavour. But now the trail has opened up for us once again.'

The man beside Salvador spoke, his English strongly

accented. 'But we did capture the boy and bring him here. And he did confess.'

Salvador nodded. 'By the time we had extracted a confession from his father at Coimbra, the *Black Swan* was too far ahead for our ships to catch up with it. But our spies had already been following João for months, watching his movements in his adopted city of Tangier, waiting for him to return to Portugal where we could take him. His family was part of the Christian Jewish community who had sheltered the Roman Proselius and hidden the Chalice in the mountains of Spain, but we knew that it had gone to the Knights of Malta when the Jews were expelled from Spain. The Knights then had more strength than us, and we could not contrive a way to break into their fortress. But when we got wind that the English in Tangier had been offered an extraordinary treasure by the Moors, and that the Knights had some time earlier given up the Chalice in return for the freedom of hostages, we convened a meeting just such as this one. And when we learned that the Englishman responsible for negotiating with the Moors had been in secret discussions with João Brandão, and that together they had devised a scheme for secreting the Chalice away in a new hiding place, one far beyond the bounds of the Old World, we sent out our men. It was only a chance betrayal that prevented us from snatching the treasure there and then.'

'It was no betrayal,' the man beside him said, looking around the table for agreement. 'When our men confronted the Englishmen, our men were both killed, one outright and the other dying soon afterwards, but not before he was able to send word on to Portugal. We must acknowledge our failures and not seek excuses. Only that way shall we grow in strength.'

Salvador eyed him. 'I stand corrected. You are right, Don Pedro.' He turned back to the others. 'We were too late to catch up with the treasure before it left Tangier and then Portugal, but from the father's confession we knew where it was going: to Port Royal in Jamaica, where he had brothers and cousins. We did not reach the island in time to prevent the boy from dispatching the package on the next stage of its journey, but that did not save the boy from our men. We brought him here, and under torture he broke. The Chalice had been sent to the heretic Father António Vieira deep in the Amazon of Brazil, where he was establishing his community of the like-minded, all of them enemies of the Church and in the sights of the Inquisition.'

'Whom then we destroyed.'

'We were only six, then as now, but just as we do today, we recruited others to do our bidding. We organised an expedition among the pirates of Port Royal, paying them enough to make it more worthwhile than any voyage of plunder they might have undertaken themselves. After months of searching, after half had died of disease and exhaustion, they discovered the place and ravaged it, killing everyone they could find and burning the buildings to the ground. But Father Vieira and a few chosen companions had managed to escape. The Chalice had disappeared back into history.'

'And the boy?'

'He was a heretic, like his father, and deserved the same fate. But as long as Vieira was still at large, there was a chance that he might try to make contact with his followers among the Jews of Port Royal. We let the boy go, but kept our eyes on him constantly for the rest of his life. In return for leaving his family alone, he paid us half of his profits from brokering plunder for the pirates, allowing us to fill our coffers and refortify this island. We have been watching and waiting ever since.'

'And now?' the man at the centre of the table said. 'Are you able to tell us of progress?'

Salvador turned the coin round, showing the obverse. 'This is one of the coins that the boy had with him when he was captured. It carries the trademark of the Brandão family, the Star of David. It was the discovery of another such coin three weeks ago on a shipwreck off England that led me to call this meeting.'

'Go on, Professor.'

'As you know, for years I have made the study of early Christian and Judaeo-Christian symbols my speciality, something that was encouraged when I was first presented as a novitiate to the Altamanus by my father. By the time a place became vacant for me among the six at this table, I had already completed my doctorate and had taken up my position at the seminary. For years I have searched for any further evidence that might help us in our quest for the Chalice, but to no avail. And then last week I was attending a conference at Oxford when one of my more junior colleagues flashed around an image of an identical symbol that had just been found underwater, wondering if any of us had seen anything like it. Naturally, I kept quiet, but I immediately called on our friend Dr Henriques to make some discreet enquiries of the director of the excavation team, Dr Jack Howard.'

'The man who searched for the Jewish Menorah,' one of the others murmured. 'We well remember that.'

'Indeed. It was that story that particularly raised my interest. That search also took Howard to the Caribbean, to the Yucatán, about as unlikely a place to find the Menorah as South America is to find the Holy Chalice. It revealed Howard's knack for following many disparate, apparently disconnected threads over a wide geographical area and then tying them together. The search for the Holy Chalice will be a similar process, and I already know of the existence of several such threads. Not only did Howard find one of these coins, and then more of them, but the coins came from the wreck of the *Schiedam*, the ship that sailed with the *Black Swan* to Portugal when Tangier was abandoned. That could only pique his interest. And then, after a little delving, I discovered that Howard's own background includes being descended from none other than João Rodrigues Brandão. Where there is a connection of that nature, you can be certain that Howard will be sniffing out the trail.'

'And you have now reached a point where we can act; the justification for calling a meeting?'

'There are others searching with him, in Portugal, in the National Archives there. A colleague of mine named Dr Maria de Montijo is one of them. She and I were graduate students together working on the epigraphy of the catacombs in Rome, and we continue to maintain cordial relations. I knew she was the one who researched the Brandão family in the Inquisition archives for Howard because she put a history of the family online. I called her last week and she told me that she is again in Lisbon for more research. A few further enquiries revealed that Howard is there with her as we speak.'

'Have they made the connection with Vieira and South America?'

Salvador leaned forward, looking at the other man intently. 'I don't know. But I think it is likely. Howard is travelling on to Jamaica tomorrow, for a scheduled visit to a project at Port Royal funded by his university. But I would be astonished if he was not also going there in search of the Brandão connection. And as for Maria de Montijo, I remembered something from our encounters in Rome when we were students. On one occasion she was flying off to Bolivia because she was volunteering for a remote mission community somewhere in the mountains beyond Potosi. She told me that her family had done it for generations, and that it was because of her Sephardic Jewish roots. The mission was founded by a Jesuit in the late seventeenth century. She would not say more.'

'A Jesuit?' the man beside him said. 'Could that be the heretic Vieira, where he went after fleeing our attack?'

The man in the centre of the table turned to one of the others. 'Hernandes, we need to find someone from that community we can interrogate.'

'As soon as we leave, I will be on to it.'

He turned to the man on his left. 'And Howard? Jamaica is your territory.'

'I can arrange for him to visit us here,' the man said. 'I have already been to Port Royal to try to find out more, after Professor Salvador contacted me several days ago. And we have a boat that monitors activity there every day.'

'Do not pick him up until he has had time to visit the site.

It is possible that he will find further clues there that will be useful to us.'

'Understood.'

The man stood up, and the others shifted back their chairs and did the same, all of them bowing briefly and crossing themselves. Salvador put the coin back in the box and looked around him. He had only been here once before, when he had been inducted into the Altamanus, and he had not yet properly studied the place. He knew that nothing had been removed since it had been the secret Casa for the Portuguese Inquisition in the Caribbean, and that even after the Inquisition had been formally abolished in 1821 it had continued to serve its original purpose, only this time solely in the hands of the Altamanus. Many had died here; few brought to this place had left it alive. In contrast to the days of the Inquisition, no records had been kept of more recent tribunals, and there was no cemetery to mark their numbers; the bodies were simply fed to the sharks.

He looked around the walls, seeing leg irons and chains, gibbets and nooses, hooks and shears, as well as a rack, the companion of one that he had been shown in the torture chamber below them. That one, still in use, had smelled of blood and fear, and seeing it had given him a strange sense, as if he understood what had driven the men of the Inquisition over the centuries, and what drew him and the others to it now. It was not so much about the Church, about some higher spiritual good; rather it was about control, about keeping order in a world of chaos, about chaining men's minds for their own good, about cleansing their thoughts and making them see the true light.

The man who had convened the meeting picked up his briefcase and walked towards the shaft of light, where he turned to face them. 'We will find this man Howard,' he said, his voice echoing in the lofty chamber. 'But we have left too many loose ends in the past, had too many failures. This time, it will be different. We will bring him here, and he will tell us what we want to know. And then we will destroy him.'

13

Pátio da Inquisição, Coimbra, Portugal

Jack Howard walked round the corner into the square in the centre of Coimbra, with Rebecca and Jeremy close behind. A flock of pigeons erupted from the patio, disturbed by a group of students going between classes in the old buildings of the university that surrounded the square. It was a brilliant day, sunny and warm, the buildings white and stark against the blue of the sky, and Jack felt refreshed after their quick coffee in a bar on the way. He glanced at his watch, then saw a familiar figure with her arm raised hurrying through from a large colonnaded building to the right.

Maria had dark hair and eyes, features of her Mediterranean background that she shared with Rebecca, and was wearing jeans and a loose top. She came up to Jack and embraced him, and waved at Rebecca and Jeremy. 'How nice to see you all. I hope the last-minute change from Lisbon to Coimbra for our meeting wasn't too much of a problem. I'd finished at the archive, and wanted you to see this place. It's part of our shared history, Jack, and yours too, Rebecca.'

Jack smiled, very pleased to see her for the first time in several months. 'We've got a car picking us up in three hours to take us back to Porto to catch our flight to Jamaica. I thought that should give us enough time. Not enough for dinner, though.'

'Huh. You owe me, you know.'

'I promise. When this is all over.'

'When have we heard that before?' Rebecca said, eyeing them. 'You two really should get your act together.'

Maria smiled at Jack, and then linked her arm through his. 'One day you should listen to your daughter. Meanwhile, let's have a little tour before we settle down. The rector of the university is an old friend of mine and I've managed to arrange for us to be alone inside, outside normal tourist hours. Come on.'

For the next half an hour Maria took them through the rooms and passages within the colonnade, the Casa of the Inquisition in Coimbra from the sixteenth to the eighteenth century, and now part of the university. 'So,' she said, as they came back into the audience chamber, a cavernous space with a tower on top. 'This was where your Brandão ancestors were brought to trial, and my grandmother's ancestors too, and Jason da Silva's, and countless others around the world who are descended from Sephardic Jews. We've seen the cells where they were held, the probable torture chamber, the audience chamber here for the tribunals, and outside in that pretty square the place where the burnings took place.' She turned to Jack. 'There's something I have to tell you. I looked everywhere in the Archives for further records of your ancestor João. There's nothing beyond his basic *processo* record, either in the Inquisition archive or elsewhere. If he'd been reprieved at his auto-da-fé, there'd be some record of him somewhere, given that he was such a prominent merchant. I'm afraid it points to only one conclusion. There was no homecoming.'

Jack nodded. 'I'd suspected as much.' He looked around, trying to imagine what it must have been like for João on that day, walking out into the courtyard and seeing the pyres already stoked up and smouldering, quite conceivably with the remains of a previous victim burning within. Jack had a vivid historical imagination, but this time it failed and he shook his head. 'The horror of it is hard to take in.'

'How often did that happen?' Rebecca asked, her voice subdued. 'I mean, the burnings?'

Maria glanced at the brochure she had been carrying. 'At Coimbra over the years of the Inquisition there were two hundred and seventy-seven autos-da-fé, resulting in three hundred and thirteen people being burned at the stake, most of them Jews, men, women and children.' She lowered the brochure. 'Coimbra was not the only court of the Inquisition; overall the figure for burnings in Portugal is well over a thousand. And that's only part of the story. The number who were penanced – that is, condemned but at the last minute reprieved, usually while they were standing in front of the pyres thinking they were about to be burned – was over thirty thousand. All those people had been in these cells, sometimes for years, whole families living under the shadow of the terrible end that might await them, smelling the burning flesh from the pyres, hearing the sounds of the torture chamber, enduring the anguish and screams of those in the cells around them who could take it no more. It hardly bears thinking about, and all of that in a beautiful place such as Coimbra.'

A dove flew through the chamber, and Jack looked up, watching it flap around before finding its way back out into the courtyard. The view above could have changed little since the seventeenth century, and it gave him a fleeting sensation of João at that moment when he too had stood here, but it still gave him no sense of what he might have endured in the cells or how he had dealt with what lay ahead of him. He put his hand on one of the stones of the wall beside him, pressing against it to try to feel the history, and then pushed off, looking at Maria. 'Is there somewhere we can sit and talk?'

She gestured towards a small room off to the side. 'The curator has kindly allowed us to use her office. We have an hour before the custodian locks the place up. I have something I need to tell you, something you will hardly believe, but before that, I want to hear where you have got with the evidence from the *Schiedam* and from Tangier.'

Almost an hour later, Jack finished talking and poured himself another coffee from the espresso machine that Maria had put on the table in front of them. He had filled her in as fully as possible on the finds from the wreck, on the story of Pepys in Tangier and on everything else that had led them to the stage they were at now.

Jeremy's phone vibrated and he took out his tablet, calling

up something on the screen. He stared at it, tapped it a few times, then lowered it, evidently still pondering what they had just been discussing. 'About Pepys,' he said. 'It makes me wonder whether securing this treasure was the main reason he was sent to Tangier. I mean,' he said, putting down the tablet and leaning forward, 'his trip to Tangier was at very short notice, right? One day he was happily writing up ledgers at the Admiralty in London, and the next he was with a naval squadron in the middle of the English Channel. He wasn't even told their destination and the plan for evacuating Tangier until they were well away at sea. I get that it was all incredibly hush-hush, very sensitive, because King Charles didn't want his own people or his enemies to get wind of a backdown. The evacuation could only be presented as a fait accompli, done and dusted, when it was all over. But maybe, just maybe, all that cloaked an even more secret mission for Pepys himself, something that even he didn't feel able to write about.'

'Pepys did wear another hat as a negotiator,' Rebecca said. 'He had the skill to pull something like this off.'

'It's an intriguing idea,' Jack said. 'In those final few months while Tangier was still English, it would have been essential to maintain a posture of strength to keep the Moors from overwhelming the place. For King Charles to have suffered a military defeat of that magnitude would have been humiliating and damaging, especially at a time when he was facing the possibility of war and religious strife closer to home. The besieging army of the Moroccan sultan had already over-whelmed the outlying forts and defences of Tangier, and both sides would have known perfectly well which way the pendulum would swing and how quickly it would happen were there to be an all-out Moorish assault. On the other hand, the appearance of a negotiated settlement, an arrangement for a transfer of power, would allow the English to leave with their arms intact and their heads held high, and to present the evacuation to the world as a decision based solely on the failure of the colony to attract sufficient trade.'

'I think something odd was going on in addition to that,' Jeremy said. 'On one occasion in his diary Pepys lets slip that he's preparing for a night-time mission to meet a Moorish prince in the desert, but then we hear nothing more about it.'

'Maybe there *was* yet another layer to all this,' Rebecca said. 'Maybe the Knights of Malta really did give up a great treasure to the Moors, and King Charles had come to know of it. Maybe Pepys was sent from England to negotiate for it, offering some concession, perhaps a curtailment in the English plans to demolish the fortifications.'

'It's possible,' Jeremy said. 'We know that the English handed over large quantities of their remaining gunpowder to the Moors, in return for the Moors backing off and not attempting to take the city before the evacuation was completed. Those negotiations were very hush-hush, as a deal of that nature would not have gone down well with the people at home at a time when Barbary corsairs were raiding the south coast of England and enslaving people taken from the towns and ports there. So with all of that negotiation already going on, what I'm suggesting is that Pepys was in pole position to pull off some other secret deal as well, without being unduly noticed.'

Jack took out a handwritten sheet from a folder in his bag.

'I wanted to wait until now before reading this out. Before leaving for the flight this morning, I was going through my material on the Brandão family. As well as the contemporary documentation from the Inquisition archives, there's this sheet written by my great-grandmother shortly before she died. It had been several generations since any of her ancestors had called themselves Jews, but her memory of that tradition was still strong. Here's what she wrote:

'"My great-grandmother, Rebecca Rodrigues Brandão, was from a Portuguese Jewish family who fled to London at the time of the Inquisition. Originally her ancestors had lived in Spain, but they had fled to Portugal following the expulsion of the Jews from Spain by Ferdinand and Isabella. They were so-called Christian Jews, the descendants of Jews who had fled Judaea at the time of the Roman conquest, who maintained their Jewish faith but were sympathetic to Christian teachings. In the early years in their mountain villages in the Pyrenees they provided safe haven for Christians fleeing the persecution of the Roman emperors, and later for other Christians persecuted by the Roman church itself. It was said that they also guarded the greatest relic of Christ, and that they passed that on to the Knights of Malta for safe keeping when the Jews were forced to flee to Portugal. That relic was the Holy Chalice, the cup used by Christ at the Last Supper."'

Jack put the paper down and sat back. 'So there you have it. A family story, told hundreds of years after the events it describes, by an old person herself generations beyond a time when her ancestors even called themselves Jews.'

'Amazing,' Rebecca said, picking up the paper and scanning

it. 'The Holy Chalice. The greatest lost treasure of Christendom. Do you believe this?'

'All I can say for sure is that if the cup existed, it did not make its way back to King Charles in England or we'd surely have known all about it. For a king facing a divisive religious war, to have the Holy Chalice raised above his head might have given him more strength than the greatest army, at least in his own eyes.'

'The Inquisition would have loved to get their hands on it too,' Jeremy said. 'Just spiriting it out past the agents of the Inquisition in Tangier and Portugal would have been challenging enough. That's consistent with a picture of extreme secrecy, and also with Pepys using a merchant such as Brandão, who came from one of the families that had safeguarded the treasure in the first place. As for its disappearance, Pepys might have been an unswervingly loyal servant of the Crown, but on a personal level he would have been appalled by the idea of King Charles using such a relic for his own nefarious purposes. If you read his Tangier diary, you get the sense that the older Pepys, a few stages beyond the bon viveur of his youth, was inclining more towards the ideals of the Puritans, to a vision of purity and sanctuary that many sought in the New World. Perhaps he conspired to get the relic to a new place of safety a long way away, where it would remain out of the clutches of anyone in Europe, even his sworn liege King Charles.'

'This is all speculation,' Jack said. 'It could be one of the most incredible stories we've ever uncovered, but there just aren't enough hard facts to go on. Stories of the Holy Chalice abound, and at the moment we have to think that my great-grandmother's account is another one of those.' He pointed to the tablet in front of Jeremy. 'Was there something you wanted to show us?'

'Ah, yes.' Jeremy picked the tablet up again. 'Do you remember how Pepys drew that Maltese cross sign on the page of the diary that I found in the Oxford archive? We looked at it in your office in Cornwall before coming out here.'

'Absolutely. Go on.'

'Well, just out of interest, I had the sheet put through phase-contrast X-ray imaging at the Institute of Palaeography, the same machine we used to reveal faded writing on the Roman scrolls from the Villa of the Papyri in Herculaneum, you remember? I had to call in a favour from the Curator of Manuscripts at the Bodleian Library to let me do it, but judging by the result just sent to me, it looks as if it might have been worth it. I think old Sam Pepys was in a bit of a state the morning he wrote about the pox and all that, and really regretted it later on and tried to erase it. What I'm looking at here might be nothing, but as we said when we talked about this before, he didn't usually doodle, and if he had – in a momentary lapse of judgement – drawn something of significance to do with the Chalice, he might accidentally have left us a clue. I mean, looking at that symbol and those letters, I'm pretty sure of it. Those are ancient Roman and Greek.'

'Jeremy, I think we'd like to see it?' Rebecca said.

'Oh. Yes. Of course.' He turned the tablet round and passed it to Jack, who angled it so that Rebecca could see it too. Magnified in the middle of the screen was the sign of the fish, as used by early Christians in Rome, flanked by an alpha and omega in capital letters. 'Fascinating,' Jack said. 'Maria, this is right up your street.'

She took the tablet and stared at it. '*Dios mío*,' she said quietly. 'Then it is true, and no longer speculation.'

'You said you had something to tell us,' Jack said. 'Is now the time?'

She nodded slowly, putting the tablet back on the table. 'Especially now that I have seen this. But before then, I need to go outside where I can get cell reception and make a call. I won't be long.'

Ten minutes later, Maria returned and sat down, taking a deep breath and holding it, as if she were bracing herself. Then she exhaled forcibly and looked at Jack. 'Okay. Are we ready?'

'Fire away.'

She took a quick gulp of her coffee and began. 'Unlike your Sephardic ancestry, which is so far back that a Jewish tradition disappeared generations ago, mine is much closer, with my grandmother having been a practising Jew. As a result, I know a lot about my Sephardic background from oral transmission, and I have a very particular connection with this story. Just like your Brandão ancestors, back at the time of the Roman Empire my ancestors were Christian Jews as well, living in north-east Spain. The story of the Holy Chalice, of how the community hid it and it then ended up with the Knights of Malta, was part of my grandmother's family tradition too, passed down through the generations.'

'Did they know where it went after that?' Jack said.

She paused, looking intently at him. 'What I am about to tell you was a sworn secret in my family for generations. Since my teenage years I have volunteered at a remote community in the High Andes of south-eastern Bolivia. I help tend the animals, repair walls and buildings, do domestic chores. The reason I go there, and why my mother and grandmother went there before me, is that the people in the community are my distant cousins. We are all descended from a small number of people who escaped the destruction of a similar community in the Amazon forest of Brazil in 1685. The community had been set up by Father António Vieira, a Jesuit who had helped the Jews of Portugal and who was himself persecuted by the Inquisition. Father Vieira survived, and with those few others re-established his community in Bolivia, where it has remained free from persecution ever since. Those who destroyed his original community were an organisation called the Altamanus, also known as the Black Hand, who traced themselves back to the Praetorian Guard of the Roman emperors, and who had been seeking the Holy Chalice ever since. They are the people I believe are on your trail now.'

'Wait a minute,' Jeremy said. 'Are you saying that Father Vieira had the Chalice?'

'According to the tradition of our community, it was brought in secret to Port Royal by João's son Lopo Brandão, who then sent it to Father Vieira's care in Brazil. After the community there was destroyed, and fearful that the Altamanus might catch up with him again, Vieira decided to conceal it somewhere away from his new community in a place where outsiders would not dare to go. According to tradition, he had it placed deep in the mountain of Cerro

Rico, the silver mine of Potosi, about three hours by llama from the new site of his community, the place where I go to visit. He had ministered to the Inca boys who worked as tied labourers in the mine, and they knew a deep place in some abandoned workings. Only they and Father Vieira would know its whereabouts. That sign of the fish, Jeremy, was a marker, carved secretly in the tunnels to show the way. It was also the sign said to have been on the leather bag holding the Holy Chalice, with those Greek letters too. Brandão must have told this to Pepys so that he knew the package was genuine, and Pepys then idly doodled it in his diary.'

'Good God,' Jack said. 'How long have you known all this?'

Maria paused. 'I was sworn to secrecy about this too, but I just called the present head of the community, Father Pereira, and he agreed that you should be told. With the Altamanus almost certainly on your trail, and the possibility that they might find enough clues to search for the community themselves, he wants the Chalice found and removed so that it can be taken to a new place of hiding, one known to fewer people. He is fearful that the Potosi story might be known by too many descendants of the community and reach other ears.'

Jack leaned forward. 'Can you get us there?'

'Father Pereira will set up a contact for you at Potosi. Someone will take you into the mountain.'

'Do you know who any of the Altamanus are?' Jack said.

Maria nodded. 'One of them. I'd suspected it for years, but then I saw the tattoo of the black hand on his palm the last time we met. That's their sign, something we've known about and feared since the time of the Romans. He teaches at a seminary in Spain, but always shows up at conferences and seminars. His name is Fernando Salvador.'

'You mean Professor Salvador?' Jeremy exclaimed. 'He was at the Oxford conference last week. He gave that paper on images of the Last Supper in the early Christian catacombs of Rome, the one paper you couldn't attend. It was a bit tedious, for such interesting subject matter.'

'Don't underestimate him,' Maria said. 'But I didn't attend for a reason: I can't stand the man. He happened to be a graduate student working in Rome at the same time as me, in the Catacombs of Callixtus. He was focused on the paintings, while I was doing the epigraphy. I got to know that place so well because of playing an endless game of cat-and-mouse with him, trying to avoid working in the same passageways. I made a discovery there, something that unfortunately he saw and wanted: a cross made from two Roman pilum spear points fused together, shoved into a pile of plaster fragments in an empty burial niche, the remains of a painting of the Last Supper above it. Tradition has it that the Roman soldier Proselius gave a gravely wounded Christian woman a cross just like that when he realised that he couldn't save her, and this might have been the very one. Father Pereira has it now, but at the time of its discovery it was a physical struggle to get Salvador off me. I threatened to scream and call the police, and eventually he backed off.

'I'd already begun to realise that he had a kind of pathological obsession with early Church relics, as if that were the real reason he was researching in the catacombs, to find some list of treasures that he thought had been concealed there at the time the Holy Chalice was spirited away. I told him to read

Church tradition, and to understand that when Proselius's boss Laurentius talked about treasures, he was explicitly referring to the people of his congregation and not to some stash of holy relics. He then made a kind of pass at me, which was pretty revolting given that he'd had his hands at my throat not long before, and later got drunk at a dinner party at the Spanish School of Archaeology and started spouting some serious anti-Semitic rant at me and my friends. But having said that, from an archaeological viewpoint he knows his stuff, and if there were any parallel to that Star of David symbol to be found, he'd know about it.'

'He must be the one who called me at IMU,' Jack said. 'Not a very adept spy.'

'He's an unpleasant piece of goods, but he's not the one you've got to worry about. The Altamanus always recruits from a wide range of backgrounds: academics, soldiers, police, some big business names, all sharing a passion for their cause and for the objectives and methods of the Inquisition. There's some big-time control dysfunction going on there, as well as the sadism. The current head of the six men who form the organisation is thought to be a former high-ranking Stasi officer from East Berlin in Cold War days, when the Stasi ran their own equivalent of the Inquisition.'

'So these people really are hands-on, not just a bunch of fantasists,' Jeremy said.

'Absolutely,' Maria replied. 'By the 1680s, they had infiltrated the highest ranks of the Inquisition in Portugal, and were responsible for a dramatic increase in the number of so-called heretics being hunted down and burned at the stake. The Inquisition gave them a focus they had not had since the days of the Roman Empire, a cause they had yearned for over the centuries when neither the Church nor the state provided what they wanted. When the Inquisition came along, they took to it with a vengeance, and it became their sworn creed in just the same way that their Praetorian Guard ancestors had sworn blood loyalty to the emperors. Without the Altamanus, the Inquisition would not have lasted as long as it did, into the early nineteenth century. And it is the Altamanus that has kept the idea of the Inquisition alive, because they have been unwilling to relinquish something that gave them such a powerful *raison d'être*.'

'How are they funded?' Rebecca asked.

'In the late seventeenth century they extorted the Jewish merchants of Port Royal, promising them immunity from the Inquisition if they agreed to pay over a portion of the earnings they had made by acting as brokers for the pirates. The Altamanus had a symbiotic relationship with the pirates, feeding them information about Spanish treasure ships in return for a cut, and then creaming further profits from brokerage when the captured ships were brought in. And they employed the pirates for their dirty work, just as today they call on the low-life fallout from drugs crime across South America and the Caribbean.

'By 1680, only twenty-five years after the rise of Port Royal, the Altamanus had enough money to build a stronghold of their own on an island they called Santo Cristo del Tesoro, Christ of the Treasure. It was meant to be where they would house the greatest treasures of Christendom when they found them, with the Holy Chalice as the centrepiece. But it was more than just a stronghold and a repository. It also included a scaled-down replica of the audience chamber next door to us now, and a torture chamber. The island was under no jurisdiction, and they could operate with impunity, under the aegis of the Inquisition but in reality acting on their own. It was another dark chapter in the history of the Caribbean at that period, alongside piracy and slavery and all the cruelties of colonisation. Countless people disappeared on that island, some who had been branded as heretics and others people whom the Inquisition wanted disposed of for other reasons but could not arrest because they were on foreign soil. Even after the Inquisition officially ended in 1821, those in power where the Inquisition had once held sway continued to employ the Altamanus to snatch people and take them to the island, never to be heard of again.'

'It all sounds horribly familiar,' Rebecca said. 'Like a seventeenth-century version of the CIA's secret offshore torture sites.'

'Do we know where this island is?' Jack said.

Maria shook her head. 'It's tiny, a dot in the ocean. Nobody has ever been able to get near it, or wanted to.'

'Could be something to ask Jason da Silva about,' Jeremy said, looking at Jack.

'I'm going to have to get him up to speed on all of this.' Jack's phone vibrated, and he looked at it. 'Excuse me. I have to take this.'

He got up and went outside for better reception, returning after a brief conversation. 'That was Captain Macalister. The site of the *Schiedam* is shut down for the duration, with twenty-foot waves forecast this evening. He's just driven Costas and Lanowski with Little Joey to RNAS Culdrose, where the Embraer is waiting, having returned to pick them up. It's due in Porto in three hours, and after refuelling will go on with us to Jamaica. The pilot doesn't want to delay because the same weather system that's battering Cornwall is stoking up hurricane-force winds in the west Atlantic. We should pack up here and get to Porto to wait for them.'

Jeremy turned to him. 'With what we've got now, we could always call a rain-check on Port Royal and head directly to Potosi. We might not find any better clues than we've got already. And time is not on our side.'

'Dad would never do that,' Rebecca said. 'No way.'

Jack gave Jeremy a steely look. 'There's a whole team out there waiting for us, wanting to show us what they've found. In my philosophy, it's one for all, not all for one. It's the team that drives the exploration forward, not just Jack Howard.'

'There's that other thing too, isn't there, Dad?' Rebecca said, collecting her things together. 'About the voyage being as rewarding as the destination.'

Jack slipped his phone into his pocket and slung his bag on his shoulder. 'Sometimes the strands all tie together and point in one direction early on, and other times they lead to different places, all equally fascinating. I know that by the time I get off the plane at Potosi on our next leg, my mind will be focused completely on that quest, and everything else will be stripped away. But I'm not there yet, and there's another equally powerful strand of this story that's leading straight to Port Royal. I want to see in my mind's eye what that place was like when the *Black Swan* arrived there that day in 1684, and I want to really touch that history.'

'You're saying you want a Jack Howard moment,' Rebecca said.

'And you want to get back in the water,' Jeremy added.

Jack smiled and put a hand on his shoulder. 'You've seen through me. Truth is, I can't wait to meet up with Jason and for the two of you to see the site. It's an incredible place.'

'And you're looking forward to seeing your old friend Maurice.'

'That too.'

'All right,' Maria said, leaning up and kissing Jack on the cheek. 'Just don't spend too long over it. A day at the most. Father Pereira is going to feel vulnerable as soon as I tell him what you know, and I'm worried that the Altamanus will already suspect where you're heading. And this time, when it's all over, come back to me and let's do dinner, right? Be careful, all of you.'

14

The following morning Jack sat in the front cabin of the IMU Embraer, having left Portugal at dawn, with Rebecca, Jeremy, Costas and Lanowski as the only other passengers. They had been scheduled to arrive in Jamaica by now, but had been advised to divert around the leading edge of a cyclonic system that was building up in the mid-Atlantic and pushing hurricane-force winds towards the Caribbean. Jack himself had been taking a spell piloting the aircraft when the call came through, and had skirted the mountainous wall of black clouds shot through with flashes of lightning, as awesome a display of the power of nature as he had ever seen. The course predicted for the storm took it to the south of Jamaica and over the basin to the west of Panama, but even so he knew that Jason and the others at Port Royal would be anxiously watching the weather reports. The divers could easily get out of the water in advance of bad weather, but it was the site itself that was at risk, in shallow depths where storm winds could rip up and destroy the fragile archaeological remains exposed by the earthquake three months earlier. He knew that a hurricane was Jason's worst nightmare, and that was one reason why IMU had agreed to provide emergency funding for a rescue excavation within days of his call to Jack with a plea for more equipment and specialised personnel.

Jack looked once again at the papers and charts that had preoccupied him for most of the flight, then at his laptop screen. He had used the time to get up to speed on the archaeology of Port Royal, and had spent the last four hours immersed in the minutiae of day-to-day life in the late seventeenth century, at a place that represented much that was beguiling and much that was bad about the first period of European settlement in the Caribbean. There were some remarkable similarities with Tangier, a matter of coincidence that he had reflected on a good deal as he also cast his mind back to the wreck of the *Schiedam* and her incredible backstory. Both cities were taken over by the English from the Spanish or the Portuguese, and both were gateways, one to Africa and the East, the other to the Caribbean and the mainland of the Americas. Both had sunk into vice and debauchery, and both had come to abrupt ends within a decade of each other, the one through abandonment and the other through natural calamity. Where they differed was in their nature as archaeological sites; almost all evidence of English Tangier had been subsumed beneath the modern city, whereas Port Royal remained largely abandoned, the archaeology just beneath the surface and still astonishingly rich.

He felt the aircraft descending, and looked out of the

window to see the south coast of Jamaica coming into focus, with the spit of land that defined Kingston Harbour just visible in the foreground. Viewed from here, the spit seemed a mere tendril of sand, hanging in the haze like a mirage, a ripple in the fabric of reality that would surely close up and disappear as they came closer. That thought made him sense the fragility of Port Royal in space and time, a town built on land that could turn to quicksand in the blink of an eye, where the bustle and energy of those few short years in the seventeenth century, the brick and masonry houses and the conspicuous consumption, seemed almost in defiance of its tenuous foundations. It was a place that had been on the edge in many ways, where the only sensible lifestyle was to live for the day, entirely in keeping with the nature of the people who were drawn to it. For the English who had come to colonise these lands it was their first port of call, and yet for many it would have seemed the antithesis of the Celestial City that had attracted the more pious of them to the New World, as if to get there they were first to be tested by temptation in a place where the devil so clearly held sway.

He glanced back at the others. Rebecca and Jeremy were also glued to the view, each occupying a separate window seat. He was glad that Rebecca had come along; for some time she had expressed an interest in the archaeology of the New World, and this would be a fascinating toehold for her. Jeremy had become her inseparable companion over the two years since she had finished school, and it was hard to imagine them without each other. Jack thought again of her mother Elizabeth, of the last time he had seen her, when she had explained to him why she had left England all those years before without telling him that she was pregnant, of the life she had been forced to lead under the control of her Mafia family in Naples; and then he remembered first meeting Rebecca after Elizabeth's murder, when her guardians in New York had brought her to see him. It all seemed so long ago now, almost ten years. He felt a wave of regret, a stab of sadness. He hoped he had done right by Elizabeth, that he had brought Rebecca up to be a reflection of her mother as well as her father, that all the care and love she had received from Jack's friends had gone some way to making up for the loss that she had experienced so early in her life.

He looked across at the other two occupants of the cabin, Costas and Lanowski, leaning towards each other fast asleep and snoring, with the case containing Little Joey strapped into the seat between them. They were like proud parents, exhausted after a first flight with their new offspring. He smiled and turned back to the view. He remembered Maria's warning to be on his guard in the days ahead, but he tried for these final minutes of the flight to put that from his mind. He was looking forward to seeing Maurice Hiebermeyer, his close friend since they had been boys together at boarding school; they fuelled each other as archaeologists just as he and Costas did as divers. And he was looking forward to getting his teeth into some archaeology again. He had received a message from Jason before they had taken off suggesting a breakthrough in the search for parallels for the Star of David symbol. He watched the Embraer line up for its final approach, the landing lights of the runway flickering ahead. It was going to be an exciting afternoon.

★ ★ ★

Less than an hour after landing at Norman Manley airport at Kingston, they were in an SUV racing towards the site of Port Royal along the Palisadoes, the old Portuguese name for the spit of sand that formed the southern reach of Kingston Harbour and was also the site of the airport. Jason da Silva had met them off the plane, and had facilitated the clearance of their equipment through customs; Little Joey had raised a few eyebrows but fortunately was dormant, and the equipment they would need for the dive that afternoon was already on site, part of the store that had been shipped over from IMU after the earthquake in July. Jack was in the front, sitting next to Jason, a fit, serious man of mixed Jamaican background in his early thirties, and a distant cousin of Jack's through their shared strand of Portuguese Jewish ancestry; it was the first time Jack had seen him since examining Jason's doctoral dissertation almost two years before.

'So, Jason, how have you been getting on with my old friend Maurice?'

'He's a dude. Best land archaeologist I've ever worked with.'

'That would be the first time anyone has called him a *dude*,' Rebecca said. 'He'd probably secretly love it.'

'And his shorts?' Jeremy said.

'Somehow always flying at half-mast. Don't know how, but they always stay up.'

'That's Uncle Hiemy,' Rebecca said. 'If he's got those shorts on and a trowel in his hand, then you know he's happy.'

Lanowski was sitting in the rear cargo compartment, tinkering with Little Joey and seemingly oblivious to the world around him, but Costas was between Rebecca and Jeremy in the back seat, and he leaned forward. 'So, can someone give me the lowdown on this place? Port Royal for dummies, in five minutes?'

'You got it,' Jason said, pulling the vehicle up by the foreshore. 'Now's as good a time as any. The site's only a mile away from the airport, and we're pretty well there already.'

'I think I can see what must be the former Royal Navy Dockyard buildings ahead of us,' Jeremy said.

'Correct,' Jason replied. 'The buildings included a careening wharf for cleaning hulls, a victualling store, a hospital and in the nineteenth century a coaling station. But that was Port Royal's second guise, well after the period we're interested in. A naval presence continues with the Jamaica Defence Force base at the very end of the spit, but the town today is just a sleepy fishing village. It's what lies under it that we're after, the most important English settlement in the Caribbean in the seventeenth century.'

'"The wickedest city in the world",' Costas said, reading from a tourist brochure he had picked up in the airport. '"A latter-day Sodom, struck down for its debauchery and vice."'

Jason smiled. 'The tourists are a little disappointed when they come here and all they see is the old fortifications and cannons and a few bumps in the ground. But there's certainly an element of truth to that image. After the English captured Jamaica from the Spanish in 1655, this place grew so rapidly that by the time of its destruction in 1692 it covered at least fifty acres and had seven thousand inhabitants, a large town for the time. Everyone knows the story of the pirates and how they ruled this place, but what's of more interest to me is the merchants. You remember my dissertation, Jack? I called Port Royal an emporium, one of those places where cultures interface, where trade between the nations on either side flows in and out but neither side holds sway, so the only law is made up by the merchants themselves.'

'But this was an emporium with a catch,' Jack said. 'Instead of an interface between two nations, on the one side you've got civilisation, and on the other side piracy.'

'Exactly,' Jason said. 'That's where the vice and debauchery comes in. The English Crown notionally held the strings, but they didn't have enough troops to protect the place from the Spanish, so they ended up employing the pirates to police themselves. Not hard to see where that might lead.'

'But it was the merchants who really ruled the roost,' Jeremy said. 'I remember your seminar at IMU when you said that all the imports to the Caribbean from England had to come through this place, and that all the pirate loot ended up being brokered here too. Any halfway-competent merchant who set himself up here had it made.'

'Not only that, but nearly all the gold and silver bullion that made it to England and on to English ships came through here, almost certainly including those coins from the Mexico and Potosi mints that you found on the wreck of the *Schiedam*. And there's another, less savoury fact, given the state of undeclared war between the English and the Spanish at the time: the merchants were also covertly supplying goods to the Spanish, who were short of many commodities because of piracy and the English blockade. Maurice has been finding out about one aspect of that trade in his excavation, something that's difficult for me with my African roots to confront, but that is part of the reality of this place.'

'I think I can guess what it is,' Jack said.

'I'll let Maurice fill you in. We'll be seeing him in a few minutes.'

Costas pulled out an apple and began munching. 'So what about Port Royal sinking under the sea?'

Jason nodded. 'Eleven forty-three a.m. on 7 June 1692. We know the exact time of day from a pocket watch that was found underwater. A massive earthquake hit the place, followed by a tsunami. Everything here is built on sand, in places more than twenty metres thick, all of it waterlogged below sea level. The earthquake liquefied the sand, causing buildings to be swallowed up and the northern and eastern parts of the town to slide under the sea. More than thirty acres were inundated, hundreds of buildings gone, over a thousand people dead, to be joined by several thousand more over the following weeks and months, succumbing to disease as they tried to exist in a wasteland of corpses and ruins and decay. Every attempt to resurrect the town to its former glory basically failed. Fire, hurricane, cholera, more earthquakes . . . it's as if the place was cursed.'

'But the most recent earthquake has been a boon for you,' Jack said.

Jason turned to him, his look intense. 'This place is truly incredible. It's an underwater Pompeii. You won't believe what we've found. But now we've got a hell of a lot to do in a very short space of time, because the hurricane is due to hit within the next twenty-four hours. I hope you're all ready to pitch in.'

'You bet,' Jeremy said, and the others murmured in agreement.

Jason gunned the vehicle forward, and a few moments later

they came to a halt beside a large excavation on one side of a fortification wall. Jason directed Costas and Lanowski into a low building where they could get Little Joey ready for the dive, and then he took Jack and the other two across a planked boardwalk to a familiar figure lying completely prostrate on the ground, excavating something with minute precision inches from his face, apparently oblivious to their arrival.

Rebecca turned to Jack, whispering, 'Dad, it seems a shame to disturb him.'

Jack had seen Hiebermeyer like this before, often, and he knew that the best thing was to give him a few moments, not to break his concentration. They carried on watching, and then Hiebermeyer got up on his knees and bent forward, his shirt barely covering his posterior. After a few muttered words in German, he suddenly said, 'Eureka!' and raised an exquisite miniature glass inkpot into the air, letting the light shine through it and dance on his face. He turned, spotted them, and scrambled to his feet, his trowel sticking out of his back pocket. 'Jack. Rebecca. Jeremy. How delightful to see you.'

'What have you got, Maurice?' Jack said.

'It's amazing, Jack. The destruction debris is just below the surface. Jason thought there was less chance of finding intact material here on land than underwater, but there you go.' He leaned over and handed Rebecca the pot. 'One for the conservation lab.'

'Thanks, Uncle Hiemy. Aysha sends her love, by the way.'

'Show them your big find, Maurice,' Jason said.

Hiebermeyer peered at them, his eyes gleaming with excitement, evidently too preoccupied with the site to think of Aysha's love or anything like that. He took off his little round glasses and wiped them on his shirt, then lifted his sombrero, running his hand through his thinning hair. 'All right,' he said, putting the glasses and hat back on. 'Where we are now, where I found that pot, is a pretty lavish house, a merchant's dwelling no doubt. So,' he said, walking as he spoke, 'I cross the street here, I go up this brick revetment, and then I step over this stone threshold into this very substantial courtyard.' He strode quickly in a straight line parallel to the boardwalk back in the direction they had come, turned left and walked another ten metres or so, and then did the same again, describing three sides of a square. 'There are holes about five metres in, undoubtedly once containing wooden posts that held up a sloping roof, and here in the centre, we find a raised stone plinth over a metre high.' He clambered up the plinth, and stood in the middle. 'Any ideas?'

'Some kind of peristyle courtyard?' Rebecca said. 'An exercise ground?'

'In Port Royal? The only exercise that was done here was in the taverns and the whorehouses. No other ideas? Well, when I first started uncovering this, it reminded me of a simple predynastic temple complex that Aysha and I excavated near Karnak in Egypt, with a central raised platform for a statue of the god and a covered courtyard around it for worshippers.'

'But you're not in predynastic Egypt,' Rebecca said. 'You're in seventeenth-century Port Royal.'

'Indeed. As I keep having to remind myself. And then, as we excavated further, I found this.' He reached down under a protective wooden cover and pulled up a mass of rusted chain, with shackles hanging from it. 'This shackle is for the neck, these ones for the ankles and these ones the wrists. By ratcheting it at the back, you could tighten them so they drew together, undoubtedly causing the victim excruciating pain. There are apertures for shackles to be chained to the rock at seven further points around this plinth, allowing eight people to be held together here at one time.' He put down the chains and gestured around. 'This was the slave market of the Royal Africa Company, and this plinth is where people in chains were inspected like cattle and auctioned off.'

'Good God,' Jeremy said. 'I had no idea that went on here as well.'

Jason stepped down into the courtyard and walked across to join Hiebermeyer. 'This was one of the lucrative sidelines for the merchants of Port Royal that I was talking about. The Royal Africa Company wasn't allowed to sell slaves directly to the Spanish, but the merchants could buy them and then sell them on themselves covertly at a profit, paying the pirates to ship them to rendezvous points off the coast of Spanish America, where they would be met by the buyers. Some of the slaves sold here would have ended up in the silver mines in what is now Bolivia, just about the nearest thing to hell that existed on earth at that time.'

'Those slaves could have been your ancestors, Jason,' Rebecca said quietly, her arms crossed and her voice wavering. 'This must be hard for you.'

'So Port Royal wasn't the pirate theme park of the tourist brochures after all,' Jeremy murmured.

'Most decidedly not,' Hiebermeyer said. 'And even after the city was lost to the sea and the pirates were outlawed, this was where the English authorities brought those they captured to be executed, leaving them hanging in gibbets on the spit until all that was left was their bones. These less pleasant truths of history are what stripping away the surface has revealed to us.'

'That's archaeology for you,' Jeremy said. 'The good, the bad and the ugly. We can't shirk from it.'

'There's nothing else I'd rather be doing,' Hiebermeyer said. 'But this time I'm glad Aysha isn't with me. Egyptian mummies are one thing, but finding the shackles used on slaves only a few hundred years ago is another.'

Jack watched Jason reach down and pick up the chains. His own Howard ancestors had been complicit in the slave trade, not as slavers themselves but as tobacco and sugar merchants, part of the triangle of trade between England, Africa and the Americas that was dependent on slavery. The Howard fortune, the money that had paid for the old manor house at the IMU campus where Jack had his office, was built on the Howard success in that trade. Rebecca knew that too, and he could see that confronting the stark reality of what had gone on here was upsetting her.

Jason weighed the chains in his hands and bowed his head for a moment. Then he cast them down, took a deep breath and walked back towards the others. 'Okay. Let's get over to the finds shed. Rebecca and Jeremy, if you don't mind, there's a big job bubble-wrapping some of the more delicate items and stowing them in the cellars of the old naval buildings where we keep our equipment. Jack, we need to get Costas and Dr Lanowski to boot their robot up and come down with us to the foreshore for our dive. The tanks should be filled in half an hour or so, and with this weather system now looking even more likely to hit us, I want to be in the water as soon as possible after that. Let's go.'

* * *

A few minutes later, Jack and Jason were walking down towards the foreshore, passing the line of the old defensive walls with their rusted cannon, and then the huts that served as the finds conservation lab. Jack had taken a few moments to look at the extraordinary range of intact artefacts brought up from underwater, including pottery vessels, glass, pewter, silver cutlery, and silver and gold coins of all possible denominations and origins for the period, but dominated by gold escudos and silver pieces of eight from the Spanish Main. Jason peeled off, talking quickly to a lab-coated assistant at the entrance to the conservation lab, and then hurried back alongside Jack. 'We need to batten down the hatches before the hurricane hits. There are outdoor fresh-water storage tanks that need to be sealed over.'

'Remember, we're all here to help. That includes me.'

'Thanks. We'll need every pair of hands we can get.'

Out in the channel, a steady procession of fishing vessels, yachts and pleasure cruisers were making their way towards Kingston Harbour, moving from the open ocean into more protected waters in advance of the bad weather. Jack scanned them, and turned to Jason. 'Do you ever get prying eyes? I mean, from out in the harbour?'

'There are always one or two watching the excavation. Over the past few days we've noticed one big cruiser that's come by repeatedly, slowing down with binoculars trained. Probably some rich guy with time on his hands, but we do kind of ask for it, as we issue press releases when we find anything, and there's a lot of local interest.'

'What about at the site, on land?'

'Only one incident I can think of. We had a guy volunteering in the finds hut a couple of weeks ago. We have an outreach programme to get local people involved, helping with washing and cataloguing pottery finds. He was educated, not a local, and was asking a lot of questions about you, though that's not uncommon when people who've read your books see that we've got the IMU logo all over our equipment. He became agitated when I couldn't give him the time he wanted, and we had to get our security guards to remove him. I remember he claimed to be some kind of seminarian, from Portugal. Why do you ask?'

Jack pursed his lips. 'Do you get the IMU security emails?'

'I'm not on the grid. I wasn't sure whether I was meant to be. I'm only a research associate.'

'That was an oversight. I'm fixing it now.' Jack pulled out his phone and tapped a message to Ben at IMU security. 'And you've just become an adjunct professor. That's one appointment I can make without having to go through the board of directors.'

'Much appreciated, Jack. That'll give me a bit more clout here in Jamaica. So do you have a security concern?'

Jack described the call he had received about the Star of David from the bogus Portuguese professor, and then Maria's account of the background to the Altamanus. 'So you can see we're not the only ones on the trail. What we don't know yet is how seriously to take it as a threat.'

'The security guards here are a bit more attentive as a result of our altercation with the volunteer. And of course there's the Jamaica Defence Force base, which keeps crime here at zero. But the fishing hamlet at Port Royal is a sleepy place, and without something more definitive, I don't think we could excite much interest among the local police.'

Jack stopped and turned to him. 'There is one thing Maria mentioned that I wanted to run by you. Have you ever heard of an island called Santo Cristo del Tesoro?'

Jason paused. 'Yes, I have. But it's a bit of a mystery. It crops up several times in the pirate documents in the Jamaica archives, among those I found when I was researching Henry Avery for you. Supposedly it was a secret place established by the Inquisition when the Portuguese ruled in the Caribbean in the sixteenth century. It was heavily fortified, but the pirates were cautious of it for another reason too, with rumours of torture chambers and execution, of nobody who strayed there coming out alive. Even during the heyday of the pirates the Inquisition was still regarded with fear, probably a result of the Jews such as the Brandão family coming here having escaped its clutches, and telling stories of torture and interrogation and burnings at the stake.'

'Do you believe in it? The island?'

'Supposedly it wasn't far off the coast of present-day Colombia, and was surrounded by treacherous currents. That much rings true, because the clockwise Caribbean Current and the anticlockwise Colombia-Panama Gyre coincide about thirty miles off the Colombian shore, not a place you'd want to be sailing if you could avoid it. The abyssal plain in that basin is more than three thousand metres deep until close inshore, but there are volcanic outcrops that might break the surface, and one of them could have formed a small islet that has escaped all the surveys. That part of the Caribbean is surprisingly poorly known. You can't see it on Google Maps because that was the route drug traffickers took to fly cocaine out of Colombia, and the DEA and the CIA restricted satellite coverage.'

'But the pirates knew where it was?'

'The name means Christ of the Treasure, and supposedly refers to some great treasure of the Church that they stored there. Henry Avery was intrigued and scouted the place out, but took one look at the fortifications and stayed away.'

'They would have found it empty of treasure, as it wasn't what they stored there that gave the island its name, but what they *hoped* to store there,' Jack said.

'It sounds as if you know something I don't.'

'How much time have we got?'

'About fifteen minutes until the tanks are filled.'

'When we were with Maria, we didn't just talk about the Brandão connection. What do you know about the Holy Grail?'

'The Holy Grail? Only the King Arthur stuff. The medieval fantasy.'

'Okay. We'd better sit down.' They had reached a wooden bench beside the foreshore. Jack filled Jason in on the story that Maria had told him, describing the ancient background to the cup, the extraordinary saga of its voyage to Tangier and Porto and then across the Caribbean, Father Vieira and his refuge in the High Andes, the Altamanus and Maria's worry about their ruthlessness and power even today, and finally Father Pereira and his community. Jason listened intently, occasionally interjecting, and when Jack had finished, he got up, raising an arm in acknowledgement to the team members who had just offloaded their breathing gear from the back of a truck.

Then he turned back to Jack, his expression serious. 'So you and Costas are really going to Bolivia?'

'Tomorrow, on the IMU Embraer. Everyone else is staying here to help you, including Rebecca and Jeremy.'

'It's reassuring that you're not taking them along too. Potosí is a bad place. A *really* bad place. If there's one town where you can still get a sense of what it was like in Port Royal during the colonial era, it's that one. There's something about that mountain. It exerts a huge allure, but it destroys the lungs of everyone who works in it and seems to cast a dark shadow over the place, turning good men to bad. The Spanish knew it, and it remains the same today. You're going to have to be on your guard.'

'Father Pereira is sending one of his people to guide us.'

'Just do what you have to do and get out of there as quickly as you can. And take some breathing gear if you're intending on spending any time inside the mountain.'

'Thanks for the advice.'

'It looks like we're good to go.'

Jack turned and saw Costas coming down the slope with Little Joey perched on his shoulder, Lanowski beside him carrying his laptop and a virtual reality headset. They looked like a pair of teenagers about to try out their latest radio-controlled toy. Beside them the team members had laid out three e-suits, the all-weather Kevlar-reinforced drysuits that were IMU's signature equipment, allowing Jack and Costas to penetrate places of extreme cold and heat where conventional diving gear would not have worked. The water here was warm and the depth shallow, but there were many reasons for using the e-suits: the full face-mask helmet and visor allowed them to talk via intercom, the computer-controlled buoyancy system would keep them from sinking into the silt and stirring up the visibility, and the oxygen rebreather rigs they would be using today also meant that they would not be producing any bubbles, something that was potentially damaging to a fragile overhead environment and dangerous to those beneath it.

Jack turned and looked out at the site. Extending beyond the foreshore was a jetty and dive platform that would allow them to enter the water without having to slog through the mud. The surface of the water was a reflective sheen, slowly undulating, belying the wonders that lay beneath and also the storm that was set to sweep through in a matter of hours.

Jason turned to him. 'When Costas gets here, I'll give you both a briefing on what we're about to see. I told you in my message before you got here that we'd found something underwater that will answer your question about that Star of David symbol and the Brandão family. I promise you, Jack, this is going to be one of the dives of your life.'

15

Jack adjusted the tilt of his e-suit visor, optimising the refraction of light through the lens to give him the most realistic view of the seabed outside. He dropped several metres below the surface, following a yellow baseline that had been staked into the sea floor as it gradually sloped away out of sight into the bay. At first all he could make out of sunken Port Royal was a haze of green-brown silt, but then he started to pick out features: a course of bricks sticking out of the silt to the right, and to the left the low masonry foundation of a wall. It was the familiar image from the first photographs by divers in the 1960s, showing what was left after the buildings close inshore had been salvaged by survivors of the 1692 earthquake, and then had been degraded by natural decay and erosion. Further offshore the ruins survived to a greater height, and as he reached the fifty-metre mark on the baseline, now at a depth of eight metres, he began to see more substantial remains around him, walls of brick and masonry that rose for several courses above the seabed, shrouded in silt. Ahead of him a large sector was visible where the outlines of rooms and passageways could be made out; it looked like an open-area excavation on land, left to fill naturally with sediment after the recording had been completed.

Jason's voice came through the intercom. 'That's where we were working before the earthquake struck in July,' he said, finning alongside Jack. 'Most of the buildings here had wooden upper structures, so very little of that survives. What we're looking at is a street-front tavern and probably a place where prostitutes worked; not organised enough to call it a brothel but really quite similar to what you'd see at Roman Pompeii, for example. The big difference here was that Port Royal was more like a Wild West frontier town, with dirt streets and fairly hasty structures that were probably originally envisaged as temporary, but that had been expanded into larger complexes by the time of the earthquake.'

'That's one reason why the destruction was so extensive.'

'Both on land and underwater,' Jason replied. 'We think most of the buildings were shaken to pieces even before the land subsided, and that the initial salvage would have been a bit like picking up debris from a shipwreck, retrieving timber and other flotsam from the surface and the shoreline. The exception was the merchants' quarter we're heading towards now. There, a fault line running parallel to the shore caused a whole block of buildings on the seafront to drop out of sight intact before the earthquake had a chance to shake them up. It must have been horrifying for the people, most of whom can't have made it out alive. Then in the earthquake this July, another fault line opened up at ninety degrees to that one and revealed it all to us. I can still barely believe what I saw when I first dived there after all the silt had settled. You and Costas have found a lot of amazing stuff in your career, but this has got to be up there with the best of them. Prepare to be amazed.'

Jack turned to check that Costas was following behind them, seeing his headlamp in the haze and beside it the miniature form of Little Joey hovering in the water. He turned back and followed Jason further down the baseline, heading towards the point where the seventeenth-century wharf and shoreline was located. Jason had come to a halt in front of a wide dark patch in the seabed, a sudden drop-off. As Jack approached, he could see that it was a rectangular pit at least ten metres wide extending out into the channel, with lights shining into it from a gantry partway along. He reached the edge and stared down, taking in as much as he could in the gloom and the silt. Jason had been right about their discoveries in the past, but nothing he had seen before could have prepared him for this. It was an astonishing sight.

The earthquake in July had literally split open the seabed, leaving a fault line running from shore as far out as the eye could see. The pit was perhaps eight metres deep, and had been reinforced inside with closely spaced scaffolding. He could now understand why Jason had been so anxious about the path of the hurricane forecast for the next day. Not only would the storm tear up the scaffolding at this shallow depth, but it would also destroy the mass of airlift tubes and hoses that were trailing down into the pit, connected to the bank of pumps they had seen on the shore opposite the site. Pulling those hoses out and stowing them safely away would be a daunting task for the next team of divers. Jack remembered the image on the meteorology chart, and glanced at his computer. Time was not going to be on their side. They would need to keep this dive brief and to the point if they were to make way for the work that would need to go on for the remainder of the afternoon and into the evening.

The corrugated tube nearest to him bucked and strained as it sucked sediment out of the pit and took it away to the anchored buoys a hundred metres to the east, where the outflow ejected it down-current away from the site. Around the edges of the pit the silt was continuously trickling in from the surrounding seabed, and he could see how even a slight increase in the current might defeat them, making the job of clearance impossible. He turned, seeing Jason come out of the murk beside him and float above the edge of the pit. Costas's voice crackled through the intercom. 'I'm just catching you guys up. Little Joey has gone walkabout.'

'Can't Jacob send him a treat, some kind of electronic biscuit?' Jack said.

'That's the plan.'

There was a whirring in the water in front of him and suddenly a pair of eyes appeared out of the gloom only inches from his face, blinking and staring at him, miniature water jets pulsing on either side. Jack reached out, and Little Joey came forward, nuzzling his hand. It was hard to tell which was most disconcerting, that or the alarmingly lifelike blinking. 'I've got him,' Jack said. 'Are we good to go?'

Costas came up alongside them. 'Give a dog a bone, and he's yours.'

'What do you mean?'

'You were the first person Joey saw after Jacob sent him the biscuit. He thinks you're the provider. He's bonded to you for this dive.'

Little Joey shot round the other side of Jack, peering defensively at Costas, blinking hard. 'Just what I needed,' Jack said. 'Jacob, are you there?'

The intercom crackled again. 'Roger that.'

'Are you fully in control of Little Joey?'

'Roger that.' There was a pause. 'Well, mostly. Just look on it like taking a dog for a walk. He'll strain at the leash when he senses anything interesting. He's been programmed for this dive to react to any features that seem too regular to be natural, brick and masonry especially. Also he might jump up and try to lick your face.'

'Great. I thought that was supposed to be Costas.'

'You were in the right place at the right time. He's yours now.'

Jack turned to Jason. 'Okay. Are we ready to move?'

'We need to drop down in single file,' Jason replied. 'This is going to be an exercise in careful buoyancy control. Hit the side of the pit, and you'll cause an explosion of silt that will reduce visibility to zero for the rest of the dive. Our egress point is the entrance of a buried warehouse, about twenty metres ahead.'

Jason swam forward over the pit, activated his helmet lights and slowly descended below the level of the seabed. Jack followed suit, with Little Joey hovering at his shoulder, and Costas came behind. The silt suspended in the water reflected the light from his headlamp, but even so he began to make out brick and masonry protruding from the walls on either side, substantial sections intact for a metre or more in height. Most excitingly, between the courses of brick he saw wooden planking, preserved for more than three centuries in the anaerobic sediment, evidently part of the cladding of a wall. A window frame loomed into view, surrounded by brick and packed with fine sediment that oozed out of the room beyond.

'It's incredible,' Jack said. 'I've only ever seen anything like this in towns buried by volcanic fallout, at Herculaneum and Pompeii and at the Bronze Age site of Akrotiri in the Aegean.'

'Okay,' Jason said. 'We're nearly at the bottom now, so it's time to activate your virtual screen.'

Jack settled into the space beside Jason, pressing a control on his computer to override the automated buoyancy system and inject an extra blast of air into his suit to keep him well above the silt in the bottom of the pit. One of the airlifts had been anchored just ahead, about a metre above the seabed, and he could see the silt being drawn towards it, clearing the water for a few metres around. The readout inside his helmet flashed up a yellow warning sign, a routine feature when the system was overridden, and he waited for it to reconfigure, watching as Little Joey scampered ahead through the water out of sight and then came hurtling back, halting in front of Jack as he had done before, blinking expectantly. 'Jacob, I think he wants another treat,' Jack said. 'He must have found something he knows I'd like.'

'Oh yes,' Lanowski replied, his voice edged with excitement. 'I'm seeing what he saw, and you are going to like it *very* much.'

'Jack, are you seeing what I'm seeing?' Costas said.

'I'm just waiting for a system check to finish. Activating now.' Jack pressed the control on his helmet for the virtual screen. He watched the yellow lattice appear before his eyes and take on the shape of the pit, and then saw it begin to show three-dimensional features on either side. As it stabilised, an astonishing scene met his eyes, a breathtaking image like nothing he had ever seen before underwater. He already had some sense of the extraordinary preservation of the buildings on either side of him; now he was looking at a ship, almost intact up to the stumps of its masts, lying with its stern facing them and heeled over slightly to port. He swam towards it, wanting to see it with his own eyes, and out of the gloom began to make out lines of hull planking and then the architecture of the stern, the rudder askew but still hanging off one of its pintles. 'A reinforced iron-clad rudder,' he murmured, feeling it with his glove. 'Iron pintles, rather than the usual bronze. Fascinating.'

He reached out and placed his hand on the hull planking, seeing the old barnacle encrustations, and Jason came alongside him, his voice crackling on the intercom. 'We think that all the other ships that must have sunk during the earthquake were salvaged from the shallow waters, but that this one was driven over the wharf by the tsunami and came to rest where the earth then opened up and swallowed it along with these buildings. We haven't penetrated the hull yet, but the deck hatches are open, suggesting that it was tied alongside and unloading cargo when the earthquake struck.'

Jack swam back for a wider view, staring at the shape of the stern. 'Are we looking at a fluyt?'

'You've got it. It's just like the *Schiedam*, which was wrecked only twelve years earlier. We think from the wear and evidence of repairs that this was an older vessel, so she could well have been contemporary with the *Schiedam*, even perhaps from the same Dutch yard. You can see the pear-shaped profile, the narrow deck, the wide cargo hold, the shallow draft. It gives you a brilliant image of how the *Schiedam* would have looked.'

'And begs the question of what a Dutch merchant ship was doing in the Caribbean.'

'I've thought about that too. The Dutch and the English were allies by 1692, so it would have been possible for a ship of the Dutch West Indies Company to dock at Port Royal, though it seems unlikely that they would have been doing trade here; mostly the WIC was concerned with the slave trade from West Africa and the Dutch colonies of the Caribbean, with Port Royal being mainly an English pirate den by this date.'

'What's her armament?'

'That's another fascinating thing. The guns are in disarray and several are missing, presumably as a result of the tsunami, but she was far more heavily armed than the usual fluyt, with six eight-pounders on either side. The one gun we've been able to see so far with our probe has the Portuguese coat of arms on the breech and the stamped mark of the British Board of Ordnance above that, with the letter T for the Tangier garrison.'

'Tangier?' Jack said. 'That's amazing. Are you certain?'

'I messaged the image just before you arrived to Andrew Cunningham, knowing that he's been your ordnance expert for the *Schiedam*. He said that old Portuguese guns from Tangier taken over by the English but not wanted by the Royal Navy could have found their way on to merchant ships all over the place, with many of them, such as those carried by the *Schiedam*, being destined for sale or scrap. He also pointed out that *Schiedam* was not the only fluyt known to have been at Tangier, and that our ship here could even have been equipped with her extra guns while she was under Royal Navy control. A lot of merchant ships of this period have complex histories, when you factor in the number that were captured by North African pirates, rebranded and even commissioned into naval service as transports, as happened to many vessels during the evacuation of Tangier.'

'To me, it's all pointing in one direction,' Jack said. 'This may have been a fluyt fitted out in Tangier, but the only good explanation for it being here in Port Royal is that it was captured again, and yet again rebranded. If I'm right, you've made one of the most incredible discoveries ever in marine archaeology.'

Costas came alongside. 'You mean it's a pirate ship. I could have told you that.'

'Care to enlighten us?'

Costas pointed up. 'Check out Little Joey. He's just cleared the silt from the carved wood above the stern window.' They all looked up, seeing Little Joey hovering in the water gazing down at them expectantly. Astonishingly, he had revealed a relief carving of the laurel wreath around a coat of arms, and within it the unmistakable shape of a skull and crossbones. 'I couldn't believe it when I saw it,' Costas said. 'I thought that was just Hollywood.'

Jason had risen in the water and was peering at the carving. 'The skull and crossbones, otherwise known as the Jolly Roger, was definitely used by Caribbean pirates on flags during the decade following the earthquake, but this is the earliest known example. Fantastic.'

'Well I'll be damned,' Jack said. 'Jacob, are you getting this? Little Joey deserves another treat, big-time.'

'Done,' Lanowski said, his voice crackling on the intercom. 'I didn't even have to tell him what to do next. He's gone off of his own volition to do a high-resolution multi-beam scan. It's coming online as we speak.'

'It's actually quite moving for me,' Jack said. 'When I was a boy, my father made up a story about a pirate ship full of treasure being found by explorers on a lost Caribbean island, having been hauled up a creek but then abandoned after the pirates had been killed, the hull still intact but overgrown by mangroves and vines. I used to dream about what it would be like to go on board, to find Henry Avery's brace of pistols still sitting in the captain's cabin, to see pieces of eight spilling out of treasure chests. As I grew up, I realised that this would be impossible, that the timbers would have disintegrated long ago, but now it feels as if I've come full circle. It's tantalising to think what might lie inside that ship. This could be a most incredible time capsule of pirate life.'

Jason sank down again beside them. 'She may have been a pirate ship, but she would have been a bit of a wallower with that wide hull. My guess is that she was a kind of mother ship, the one in which the more nimble vessels of the flotilla would dump their loot before going after other victims. That scenario would fit in well with her offloading at the wharf. It makes me itch to see what's inside her too.'

'Pieces of eight,' Costas crowed, parrot-fashion. 'Pieces of eight.'

'If that's the case, we'll have them coming out of our ears.'

'What do you mean?'

'Wait till you see what I've got in store for you next,' Jason said. 'Our ship when it blew ashore wedged itself exactly along the line of the street, crushing the fronts of the buildings to our left but leaving those on the right side intact. We need Little Joey to leave the ship and vacuum out the hole in the wall ahead of us. Jacob?'

'Right.' They could hear Lanowski fumbling with something. 'Position fixed, feeding in new coordinates now. I'm taking over and going in manually.' Little Joey shot away from the timbers towards the hole, vibrating and spinning in the water as if trying to shake something off. 'Small behavioural issue,' Lanowski said, sounding agitated. 'He doesn't like to be put on a leash. Okay, powering off and restarting now. We're good to go.'

Little Joey advanced towards the hole, his strobe lights playing across the wall. As they swam closer, Jack could see that the hole had been bored into the silt between the wooden posts and lintel of a doorway, with brick facing visible on either side and a step up from the level of the street. 'This is a warehouse, a relatively well-built structure, the headquarters of a merchant,' Jason said. 'We've only managed to get into one room so far, but it's the strongroom at the back, so it's particularly interesting. Because the material filling the other rooms is soft silt, your scanners should pick up their dimensions as we go by, giving you an idea of the overall layout of the place.'

Jack followed Jason into the hole, his headlamps modulating automatically to suit the conditions, and Costas came behind. A baseline had been laid through to the point where Little Joey was entering a further room about eight metres ahead, visible only as a smudge of light. Along the line, safety tanks had been placed at intervals, as well as the hoses of two surface-demand hookah regulators that connected to pumps on the surface. 'The biggest danger in here is roof collapse, so we've shored up what we can with scaffolding and wood,' Jason said. 'But we don't want any discharge of bubbles rising into it, so double-check that your systems are in full rebreather mode.' Jack finned cautiously on, watching his buoyancy, taking extra care not to disrupt the silt on the floor. To his right, just before the entrance to the rear chamber, he saw a large opening filled with the ghostly shapes of sacks and barrels. 'Do you have any idea of the contents?' he said. 'That's an incredible sight.'

'The barrels are filled with the residue of wine, madeira and port from Portugal. We've had it analysed, and the mineral signature most closely matches the Porto region to the north.'

'Where the Brandão family were based.'

'And the sacks contain tobacco.'

'João was a tobacco merchant first and foremost.'

'Wait until you see what we've found in the strongroom.'

Jason swam through the hole at the end of the passage, the other two following. It was a gloomy, windowless chamber, about five by three metres across, with barely enough room for the three of them to fit inside, Little Joey floating above.

The only contents was a bronze chest about a metre across and half a metre deep, set against one wall, the lid prised back. 'It was open,' Jason said. 'At the moment of the earthquake the merchant who worked here was accessing his money, and didn't have time to lock up before fleeing.'

'Maybe he needed the money to pay for the loot being offloaded from that ship outside,' Costas said. 'That's what they were, brokers for the pirates, weren't they?'

Little Joey began shaking and whirring, flashing his strobe and pointing his miniature arm toward the chest. 'Jacob, he's doing it again,' Jack said.

'No,' Costas said. 'This time it means he's excited. He wants you to see something he knows you'll like. He knows you like treasure, because we told him.'

Little Joey gestured again, and then turned to Jack, making what could only be described as a thumbs-up sign.

'Don't tell me you programmed that into him.'

'He's just trying to encourage you,' Lanowski said. 'To go and have a look at what he's seen.'

'Sometimes I worry about you guys. Too many late nights in the engineering lab.'

'Don't diss Little Joey. After all he's done for you.'

'I've got to hand it to him. He is a robot after my own heart.'

They finned forward and peered inside. At the bottom was a smattering of perhaps a hundred coins, all of them silver pieces of eight, patinated after being underwater for so long. 'There was also a small box of gold escudos, but we've removed those,' Jason said. 'There was probably never much more in this chest than was strictly needed for transactions. Port Royal was not a place to store large supplies of money, even in a strongroom like this. The Brandão family and the other well-to-do merchants would have banked their wealth elsewhere.'

'Fantastic,' Jack said, floating back from the box and looking around, Little Joey blinking at his shoulder. 'Is this what you wanted to show us?'

'It's not everything. Have a look on the left side of that chest.'

Jack swam forward and peered over. Beside the chest was a small anvil, with a coin-shaped depression in the top, and on top of it a copper-alloy cylinder about ten centimetres long. 'It's a die punch,' Jack said. 'For milling coins.'

'Turn it over.'

Jack did so, staring at the base of the punch, while Little Joey helpfully came alongside and jetted a small stream of water at it, clearing away the silt. Jack stared again, hardly believing his eyes. 'Well I'll be damned,' he said.

'What is it?' Costas asked.

Jack pointed the end at him. 'Check it out. The Star of David.'

'There's a hammer on the floor,' Jason said. 'This is what the guy was doing here at the moment the earthquake struck: putting the stamp of his family firm on these coins. It wasn't João, because we know he was long gone by this point, but it was a member of the family who were here carrying on the business.'

'His son Lopo,' Jack said, staring. 'The young man who brought the treasure to Port Royal from Portugal in the *Black Swan*.'

'Now have a close look at one of those coins.'

Costas reached down and picked one out. It was covered in a black patina, but the shape of the Star of David overstamp was unmistakable. It was the same mark they had found on the coins from the *Schiedam*, the mark that Jack was now certain was the merchant stamp of the Brandão family, the mark that had opened up the trail they were embarked on to find the greatest lost treasure of Christendom. Costas turned, his face creased in a smile behind his mask, and handed it over. 'Here you go, Jack. Bingo.'

That evening, Jack walked back along the spit between the site of Port Royal and the international airport, intending to meet the car there that Jason was going to send after him to go on to their hotel. He had wanted half an hour alone to reflect on their discoveries and plan ahead for their trip to Bolivia the next day. Finding the Brandão warehouse had suddenly brought everything into sharp focus, solidifying what had until then been just speculation. The next step was a leap into the unknown, taking Maria's revelations and going to the Cerro Rico, the Mountain of Riches, the main source of silver in the Spanish colonial period, including the coins that they had found on the shipwreck site in Cornwall and now at Port Royal itself. He was excited at the prospect, and also apprehensive. The mountain did not give up its silver lightly, and if the treasure they were seeking was also there, discovering it might present formidable challenges. And all the time they knew that agents of the Altamanus were on their trail, men such as the one Jason had encountered among the volunteers at Port Royal. It was essential that they keep their travel as secret as possible. When he and Costas flew out tomorrow, it would be in the IMU Embraer, and there would be no easy way for anyone without access to specialised equipment to monitor their route or work out their final destination.

Ahead of him he could hear helicopters at the airport revving up, ready to take off before the storm rolled in. A distant flash of lightning streaked the sky to the east, and he felt the first drops of rain on his face. Perhaps delaying that car ride had not been such a great idea after all. Behind him he could see the flickering lights of the excavation, and the derrick on the barge that they had brought over the trench to pull out the airlifts and the other equipment. Jason had planned to leave the scaffolding in place, but he fully expected the trench to be filled by sediment if the storm swept over it. It would frustrate their plans to complete the excavation of that part of the site this season, but the infill of sediment would ensure that his extraordinary discoveries would remain protected and intact for the next year.

With Little Joey's video footage of the wreck, Jack was certain that he would be able to persuade the board of directors to allocate more resources and make it one of IMU's flagship projects for the next season. Maurice had already been mapping out an excavation strategy for the site on land, and Jeremy and Rebecca had been talking at length with Jason about the most practical way to expose and raise the wreck. It promised to be a hugely exciting project, a complement to their work on the wreck off Cornwall, allowing Jack to look ahead in his own schedule and plan the next year in a way that had rarely been possible at this stage in a quest.

He glanced back along the coastal road. They should all be coming along in the car, minus Costas and Jacob, who were planning to stay with Jason to help store away the electronic equipment and then hole up for the duration of the storm in a secure Second World War coastal defence bunker near the end of the spit. He turned back, the rain now driving in harder from the east, and saw the ominous blackness that marked the leading edge of the hurricane. Two men hunched over under their hoods walked by in the opposite direction, the only people he had seen since leaving the site, and then his phone chirped. He took it out, saw that Costas was messaging him and tapped it to respond, putting it on loudspeaker. 'Costas? Can you hear me? What is it?'

'Jack. The weather's coming in, so I've only got a minute. You remember I put Little Joey back in to have a ferret around at the bow of the wreck?'

'Any luck?'

'Take a look at the video. See you tomorrow at the airport for the flight.'

Jack clicked on the video link, turning his back to the rain. At first he saw only a black screen, the timer and data just visible at the top. Then Little Joey appeared, looking at him, blinking rapidly. He remembered that Lanowski had programmed a selfie shot into the robotic video sequence, just to make sure everyone knew who was taking it. The scene swiftly reverted to black again, with a scatter of white where the light was reflected by the silt in the water, and then the extraordinary image of the ship's hull appeared behind that, a section of planking leading up to a longitudinal timber that marked the edge of the lower deck. Jack could clearly see the tumblehome of the hull, and the planks curving inward towards the bow. Suddenly Little Joey was in a maelstrom of silt, burrowing forward, only the nozzle of the water jet visible in the screen. Then, as he reversed the process and sucked away the silt, the massive oak stem post came into view, and above that something irregular and dark extending into the sediment. He repeated the jetting and vacuuming, then reversed the camera again, blinking suggestively and pointing with his pincer. The camera reverted to front view, and Jack saw what had been revealed.

He could hardly believe his eyes. It was a figurehead in the shape of a swan, tarred black. The *Black Swan*. They had found Henry Avery's ship. He froze the image and stared at the screen, shielding the phone from the rain, his mind racing. Avery had sailed the *Black Swan* from Tangier to Jamaica in 1684, and then she had disappeared, presumably into the hands of pirates. When he conducted his most infamous piratical adventures a decade later, it was in his ship the *Fancy*, but the *Black Swan* could have been used exactly as Jason had suggested, as a mother ship, and was fated to be off Port Royal on the day the earthquake struck.

He pocketed the phone and walked quickly towards the airport, now visible only as lights in the darkness, his head hunched over. It was a truly astonishing find, a remarkable confluence of archaeology and history, and another piece of hard data on the trail they had been on since leaving Cornwall. He hoped Lanowski had given Little Joey an extra-large electronic biscuit. He would forward the video to Maria when he got out of the rain. He could hardly wait, and stepped up his pace.

He had been too preoccupied with the screen to notice that the two men who had passed him had turned around and were now closing in on him from behind. The blow to his neck when it came caused instant numbness, and he fell heavily to his knees, toppling forward and hitting his forehead hard on the pavement. For a few moments he remained conscious, just enough to see the blood join the rivulets of rainwater in front of his eyes; then there was only blackness.

16

J ack awoke with a start, as he had done innumerable times
since being hauled into this place, his head having lolled
forward until the pain had become too much. The throbbing
from having been knocked out the evening before had eased,
but he still had no certainty how long he had been out cold or
where he was. All he could tell from his hunger and thirst and
from the sounds outside was that it had been a considerable
time and that he was beside the sea. It was night, probably
close to dawn, but with the full moon shining through the
bars in the door, he had been able to get some sense of his
surroundings. He eased himself into a better position, taking
the weight of his body off his wrists, which were chained to
the wall above his head, and feeling the circulation slowly
return to his hands.

For hours now he had endured this position, chained just
low enough that he could squat on the cold flagstones, but

high enough that he was continuously jolted awake by the pain in his wrists. He pressed his hands against the wall. The stone was damp, mildewed, and there was a smell of mould, as well as of blood. It might have been his own from the beating he had taken while being dragged in here, but at the moment he did not care. He was chilled and thirsty, but those feelings were subsumed by the constant need to shift his body, to avoid the aching, shooting pains that eventually made any position agony and rendered more than a few moments of sleep impossible. Whoever had positioned those chains knew exactly what they were doing.

He heard movement outside, the jangling of keys, and suddenly the door creaked open. The man who stood silhouetted in the moonlight struck a match. 'No electricity in here, of course,' he said, apparently to Jack. 'Only candles, as always. We have no need to update to the methods of today, or to tamper with history. You of all people should appreciate that, yes? It is good to start on convivial terms, on terms of mutual appreciation. I know that you will be in agreement.'

He went around the chamber lighting candles in holders on the walls, and then blew out the match and tossed it on the floor. Jack knew what was happening. The friendly voice, conspiratorial even, the disarming familiarity were tools of the trade for the experienced interrogator. He could see him more clearly now, a dapper, bearded man wearing a dark jacket and an open-necked shirt. Jack knew that even that was part of the ruse, that he needed to marshal all his remaining strength to be on his guard.

'What do you want?' he said, gritting his teeth against the pain. 'And get me out of these chains.'

'Of course,' the man said. Jack could hear that he had a slight accent, Spanish or Portuguese. '*Of course*. We just need to go through some formalities.'

'The only formality here is for you to release me,' Jack said. 'And if you don't, others who are searching for me will come and do it for you.'

'You mean your friends? I rather think not.'

'Where am I?'

'There is no harm in you knowing; it may amuse you. A small island between Jamaica and the South American mainland. Privately owned, of course, and under no jurisdiction but our own, as it has been for hundreds of years. This building was constructed during the period of Portuguese rule in the seventeenth century. More precisely, it was built under the orders of the Inquisition. You came here by helicopter.'

'So who the hell are you?' Jack exclaimed, wincing from the pain in his neck. 'The Grand Inquisitor?'

'Don't affect ignorance, Dr Howard, or be flippant. It does not become you. We know about Dr Jeremy Haversham in Oxford and Dr Maria de Montijo in Lisbon, about their prying and digging. We are the Altamanus, the Black Hand. We are the oldest soldiers of the Church, older even than the Knights of Malta or Jerusalem, or those who guard the Holy See in the Vatican. It is our sworn duty to recover the lost treasures of Christendom and bring them back within the fold of our order, where they belong. By any means necessary.'

Jack shut his eyes for a moment. *So it was true.* He remembered Jason's story of the semi-mythical offshore island, the one that even the pirates had feared. 'So what is this place?' he asked. 'A seventeenth-century version of a War on Terror rendition black site, only you're the ones doing the terror?'

'You are partly correct. In the early part of that century we allied ourselves with the Portuguese Inquisition, and infiltrated its ranks. Our greatest interest had always been the so-called Christian Jews of Spain, in what they might have concealed of the holy antiquities of Judaea, so after they had been expelled from Spain in 1492 and most had gone to Portugal, that became our main area of operations. But unlike the Inquisition, we were not anti-Semitic. We despised the Inquisition for perpetuating the weakness of the Church, for maintaining its continuous need to build on fear, to persecute those who did not follow its dogma. For the Altamanus, strength comes from recovering all that once made Chrisendom great, the symbols of power that will allow us to rebuild the Church as it was in the time of the first Christian emperors.'

'You mean when the emperors hijacked the Church to make it serve their own needs,' Jack said. 'When the Praetorian Guard became the so-called Altamanus, changed in name but unchanged in their allegiance to cruelty and despotism. Your objective is to militarise the Church.'

'It is the will of God. We are the soldiers of the Lord.'

'It's a little hard to see any of that in the teachings of Jesus. To see a justification for what you are doing to me now.'

'You asked about this place. In the middle of the seventeenth century, the Inquisition weakened. A Portuguese priest who had been imprisoned for heresy, Father António Vieira, a sympathiser with the Christian Jews, had reported on the conditions of the prisons to the Holy See, and in 1674 the Pope suspended the tribunals. We redoubled our efforts, putting new men in place and ensuring that when the Inquisition returned seven years later, it was ruthless in its methods. But we also took matters into our own hands. If the courts in Portugal could be shut down at the whim of the Pope, then we would set up our own, somewhere on the far side of the world where no edict could impede our work.'

'By court, I take it you mean torture chamber.' Jack had begun to identify the shapes he had been looking at in the flickering candlelight, various implements hanging from the walls, and beside the man a large wooden frame with cogged ratchets at either end. 'What is all this, a film set, some kind of joke?'

'It was no joke to the first prisoner we brought here, a *converso* Jewish boy called Lopo Rodrigues Brandão. In April of 1684, he had been sent on a secret mission by his father from Portugal to Port Royal in Jamaica. He was carrying money for their family, who lived in Port Royal, and a far more precious cargo that his father had brought from Tangier, something that had been in the possession of the Knights of Malta. The money was stolen by the English captain of the ship on which the boy had taken passage, the future pirate Henry Avery. The precious object was destined for a secret community in the Andes led by Father Vieira, who had become a kind of messianic figure for the Portuguese Jews and offered them a promised land.'

'How do you know all this?' Jack asked.

'Because the boy was taken from Port Royal just as you have been, and he told us.'

'You mean he was tortured.'

'He was persuaded.'

'What happened to him?'

'Our methods were cruder then, less refined. We were still learning our way. But he was released, and continued to live as a merchant in Port Royal, thanking us for our mercy by giving us a share of his profits.'

Jack nodded towards the apparatus in front of him. 'So is that what you have in mind for me as well?'

The man smiled, opening his arms expansively. 'Come, Dr Howard. We are friends. Would I do that to you? Of course, there are those of my colleagues who would, ratcheting it up, seeing which of the tendons in your hips or your shoulders would go first. Perhaps they will have their chance, if you do not cooperate with me. But as long as you and I are friends, I will keep them away. And anyway, for a man like you, what would be the point? We could break you on the rack or pull out your fingernails, and still you wouldn't talk. You've faced death too many times to be afraid of that.'

Jack shifted sideways, relieving the pressure on his hips. 'This is getting tiresome. I need water.'

'We know that physical torture is not the answer,' the man continued. 'That is because we know how to break a man like you. We know where your weakness lies.' He took out his phone, tapped at it and showed it to Jack. 'Your weakness is that you are a father.'

Jack squinted at the screen. It showed Rebecca kitting up by the seafront at Port Royal. It had been taken from out at sea, evidently with a telephoto lens. He remembered the boats they had seen navigating the channel on the way to and from

Kingston Harbour, some of them fishing vessels, others cruisers and yachts. It had been impossible to carry out their diving unobserved, not that there had been any reason to do so. He felt his anger rise. 'Enough games. Nobody threatens my daughter.'

The man waved the phone. 'My dear Dr Howard, or may I call you Jack? Nobody *is* threatening your daughter. Not yet.'

'I've asked you already. What do you want?'

'You know exactly what we want. Three hundred and thirty years ago, we went up into the mountains and found Father Vieira's followers. They called the place El Dorado, but all we saw was deprivation and hardship. We were like the Conquistadors again, like the Praetorian Guard. When we could not find Father Vieira or the treasure, we put them all to the sword and burned the place to the ground. We knew the boy could not have been lying, after what we put him through, so Father Vieira must have taken the treasure and concealed it in another place.'

'And you expect me to tell you where?'

The man lifted Jack's head by the chin and forced it back against the wall, in the process revealing a tattoo of a black hand on his palm. He spoke close to Jack's ear. 'In the days of the Inquisition, all those in the condemned cells knew that we were not in the business of empty threats; they had all seen women and children as well as men tied to the stake in the town square, suffocating in the smoke of their own burning flesh, only losing consciousness after they had endured unimaginable pain and anguish. Think of that when you think of your daughter. Rebecca, isn't it? I will return in one hour.'

He released his grip, and Jack felt an excruciating pain in his neck. The man turned and walked towards the door. Jack shifted his body again. 'I don't know your name,' he said. 'Friends should know each other by name.'

The man turned. 'It is of no consequence. But you know me as Dr Hernandes, of the Lisbon St Christopher Seminary.'

'Then we *are* old friends,' Jack said. 'I thought I recognised your voice. You called me at the IMU campus three days ago to warn me against carrying out further research on the coin.'

'Old friends indeed. We knew the Star of David had been stamped on the coins that Lopo had taken to Port Royal for his father. We were on the trail ourselves and did not want you to carry out your own investigations, but then we realised that our best course of action was to let you lead us there. After all, you are the experts, and we have patience, having waited over three hundred years. And we never give up.'

Jack tried to take a deep breath, feeling the pain searing across his chest. He was beginning to understand what it felt like to be crucified. He also knew that his only chance of escape would be to appear to comply. 'All right,' he said, wincing again. 'But here are my conditions. I won't tell you where the treasure is now, but I will lead you to it. In return, I want food and water and warm clothes, and for you to get me out of these chains. *Now.*'

17

Jack stumbled out onto the old stone jetty just as the sun was beginning to rise above the eastern horizon. Behind him, set into the rock, he could see where he had spent the night, a low grey structure that looked like one of the concentric forts built during the sixteenth century on the southern coast of England, the curtain walls still armed with cannon that poked out of embrasures facing the sea. The island itself was a bleak coral outcrop only a few hundred metres across and surrounded by open ocean, with no other land visible as far as the eye could see. It was an image that could have come straight out of the age of the pirates, except for the very modern boat that he was heading towards now, a substantial deep-sea fishing vessel with trawl derricks and a mass of netting against the stern railing.

One of the men who had taken him out of the torture chamber pushed him up the gangplank, and they stood on the stern deck waiting for the others coming behind them to board. Jack looked down instinctively at his wrist, checking the time, then remembered that they had taken his watch. He felt as if every muscle and tendon in his body had been stretched to the limit by his night in chains, and his wrists were already chafing from his hands being tied behind his back. But he knew that if he were to stand any chance of escape, he would need to put that ordeal behind him, and focus on what lay ahead.

The wind was already up, a bad sign this early in the morning, and the waves were licking the side of the hull, even though the boat was in the lee of the jetty. He looked out to the west, seeing lines of whitecaps on the horizon, and realised that the gloom in the sky beyond that was not the receding night but a looming storm, its leading edge already reaching far over them and beginning to blot out the sun. A far-off flicker of lightning lit up the sea, and a few moments later he heard the distant rumble of thunder. He remembered the forecast that Jason had shown them at Port Royal the day before. It looked as if he were about to exchange one form of darkness for another, moving from a seventeenth-century Inquisition torture chamber into the teeth of a hurricane.

A diver appeared up the stern ladder, tossed a wrench on the deck and quickly removed his tank and regulator, strapping it to the railing. He made a thumbs-up sign to the deckhouse, and the engine coughed to life, spewing out clouds of diesel exhaust over the sea. The two men who had escorted Jack aboard, both of them carrying MP40 sub-machine guns slung over their shoulders, were joined up the gangplank by the man who called himself Hernandes. Two crewmen cast the boat off from bow and stern, and the captain let her drift off the jetty with the wind, keeping the engine in idle.

The boat bobbed uncomfortably from side to side, and Jack struggled to keep his balance. He was not looking forward to this; the last thing he needed now was for his old seasickness to return. He remained in the same spot while one of the armed men took the bags that had also been brought aboard down the hatch in front of him, returning a few moments later with a large strip of black cloth in his hands. Jack knew what was coming, and took a step towards Hernandes. He needed to stall for time before he was blind-folded, to see everything he could that might hint at their course and position. The other armed man saw him move and immediately grabbed him by his wrist binding and jerked his arms up, pulling him back to his original position. Jack doubled over in pain, his shoulders still tender from being suspended in chains the night before, but the man pulled him up roughly and held his head while the other approached with the blindfold.

Hernandes had seen the commotion, and signalled for the men to wait. 'Dr Howard. I trust you had a restful few hours after I left you last night?'

'Your thug here took his time coming to unchain me.'

'Ah yes. My apologies. We needed to focus our attention on tracking your daughter in Jamaica. But he did bring you food and water?'

'It was a little difficult to eat with my arms chained to the wall.'

Hernandes turned to the man with the blindfold, a scarred thug who looked at Jack with piggy eyes, and they exchanged a few words in Spanish. Hernandes turned back to Jack. 'I apologise for my men. They did not know that you had become our friend. He will give you water once you are settled in the hold.'

'I'm no friend of theirs, and no friend of yours.'

'You should learn to get on with them. They will be your constant companions until you bring us to our destination.'

Jack nodded up at the sky, feeling the first drops of rain on his face. 'It looks to me as if that could take longer than you might have envisaged. If we're going out into a hurricane, this could be a one-way trip to Davy Jones's Locker.'

Hernandes raised his voice against the wind that was now whipping past them. 'We are in good hands. We hire this vessel for a reason. The captain knows what he is doing. We will skirt the leading edge of the storm, and actually get where we're going a little faster. In Colombia we will meet up with my colleagues, who will escort us onwards. You are hungry, yes? This evening we will celebrate our new friendship at a beachfront villa I own while you reveal to us our travel plans. The kind of place you would love to take your daughter. My colleagues in Jamaica will invite her along too if there are any hitches in our little expedition, except that she and her awkward boyfriend will not make it further than this island. If you do not cooperate, then here they will stay, permanently. Bon voyage, Dr Howard.'

He clicked his fingers, and the man with the blindfold came forward. At that moment the captain put the boat into gear and gunned it forward, expertly avoiding the reef that formed one side of the harbour entrance and steering directly into the waves, towards the lightning that was now visible all along the horizon ahead. The boat crashed and juddered into the first big wave it hit on the open sea, rising high on the crest and then dropping into the trough, the engine screaming and vibrating as the screw broke water. The second wave covered them with spray, and the man with the blindfold slipped and fell, rolling into the scuppers. He picked himself up, cursing and adjusting the gun on his back, just as the captain executed a ninety-degree turn to port and brought the boat around, with the wind now on her starboard quarter, steering diagonally across the waves. Jack just had time to see the far side of the island shoot by to their left before he was roughly blindfolded, the sheet tied painfully around his eyes. The man who had been behind him held him by the wrists and pushed him forward until he reached the stairs at the top of the hatch, then pushed his head down as they went below decks. Jack gritted his teeth, smelling the diesel and feeling his stomach rise and fall with the swell. This was not going to be pleasant.

A seemingly interminable time later, Jack braced himself with his elbows against yet another crash as the boat ploughed and shuddered through the waves, rising so high at the bow that he felt as if he were being brought upright and then falling equally precipitously in the other direction. With the blindfold still on, he had no way of gauging how long it had been since they had left the island, but he guessed three, maybe four hours. The blindfold did have the advantage of covering his ears and protecting him from the worst of the noise, but the roar of the diesel engine only inches from his head sent a continuous tremor through his body, setting his teeth on edge. He had long ago ceased to smell the fumes, but he knew that his headache and nausea were not caused just by seasickness. In every sense this had turned out to be a voyage from hell, exactly as he had anticipated when he had seen the fury of the storm as they left the island.

He shifted again as the boat lurched through a trough, trying to cushion the worst of it against a wet rag he had found in the scuppers, flexing his limbs to keep the circulation going and to stop his hands from becoming numb where they were tied at the wrists. Remembering to keep moving had kept his mind off the nausea; being able to spring into action was crucial to his plan. He focused on his calculations, running through them yet again. If he was correct about the island, that it was the one that Jason had described, then it was some thirty nautical miles south from the island to the nearest point on the South American mainland, on the coast of Colombia. From the position of the sun when he had fleetingly seen it before being blindfolded, he knew that they had set off on a bearing almost due south; there had been no perceptible change in their course since then. With a boat of this type being able to make seven, maybe eight knots, and with the wind behind them, they might now be within a few miles of the shore of Colombia. They would be beyond the reach of the Caribbean Current, sweeping north towards the Gulf of Mexico, and within the anticlockwise motion of the Colombia-Panama Gyre, the surface current that flowed eastward off Colombia. It was conceivable that someone floating in the water now might be able to make it alive to that shore, swept in by the wind and the current from the grip of the hurricane and into less mountainous seas. *If his calculations were correct.*

He remembered in the Embraer flying into Port Royal seeing the radar image of the meteorology showing the storm circling clockwise in the same direction as the Caribbean Current, its eye heading slowly past Jamaica. According to that pattern the leading edge should be about where they were now, with calmer waters beyond it to the south. Jack's plan depended on his egress still being within the ambit of the storm, where the ship would have no chance of chasing and recovering him. By now, as they headed towards its outer edge, the wind should be abating, but something was not right. Over the last twenty minutes or so, he had noticed the rise and fall of the boat increasing, and the shrieking and battering of the wind outside the hatch becoming even louder. He guessed that the captain's plan was going awry, that they were no longer abreast of the storm but were being drawn back into it, unable to make adequate headway as they slipped back down each wave. For Jack, the urgency now was not just a matter of escape but of survival. If the boat was failing to climb the waves, there was a greater risk that each following wave might overwhelm it and drive it under. Blindfolded and with his hands tied, there would be no chance of escape. He needed to act now.

He braced himself against another judder, swallowing his impulse to throw up. He could not let himself succumb to seasickness, something that he knew would instantly debilitate him. He rolled over so that his back was facing the propeller shaft that ran down the length of the keelson beside him. He grabbed the rag he had used as cushioning, and then shifted as close as possible to the point where the shaft came out of the engine cowling. The water and oil in the bilge sloshed back and forth, drenching him. He blinked hard, feeling the water get under his blindfold and into his eyes, but tried to keep steady. What he was about to do would only increase the risk of the vessel being swamped, but it was the only way of attracting the attention he wanted.

He took a deep breath, braced himself against the hull frames and with the next lurch pushed the rag into the shaft, narrowly avoiding being drawn into its gyrations himself. He slipped, hitting the small of his back and convulsing in agony, trying to convince himself that the pain was good, that it would keep him focused. He listened for a change in the tempo of the engine, hoping and praying. At first nothing happened, and then there was a deep groaning and screeching sound and the throbbing ceased. The rag had caught around the shaft, seizing it up. *It had worked.*

He rolled aside, waiting. Seconds later, he heard a huge shrieking of wind as the hatch swung open, and then the clattering and cursing of someone coming down the ladder. A light switched on, just perceptible through his blindfold, and the man stumbled against him, kicking him hard in the abdomen. Jack had already tensed himself in anticipation, but even so, the pain took his breath away. The man dropped down heavily as the vessel lurched again, then Jack heard panting and more cursing. The man must have seen the rag wrapped round the shaft, and would be desperately trying to cut it away. Now was Jack's chance.

He kicked out as hard as he could, catching the man in the legs. The man slipped back, bellowing with rage, and cracked his head somewhere on the engine, falling heavily into the scuppers. Jack pushed frantically with his feet until he and the man were back to back, then wriggled along so that his hands were positioned behind the man's neck. A thunderous crash shook the boat as a wave broke overhead, and Jack waited, expecting the boat to be swamped and to plummet down. The man moaned, and then began moving. Jack raised his hands over the man's head and down to his neck, wedging his lower back against the back of the man's head so that the cord tying his hands would act as a garrotte. He pulled hard against the man's windpipe, holding tight while the boat lurched again. The man made a terrible noise as his neck gave way, and he slumped limply.

Jack extricated himself and rolled the body against the propeller shaft, feeling blindly in the scuppers for the knife that the man must have been using to cut the rag, praying that it had not slipped down the keelson out of reach. He felt something sharp, and pulled out a large fisherman's knife with a serrated edge. Holding it behind his back, he began sawing awkwardly at the cord, bracing himself to stop from falling sideways or accidentally plunging the knife into his own back. Suddenly his hands were free, and he dropped the knife, flexed his wrists and ripped off his blindfold, blinking hard and shielding his eyes against the light.

With the blindfold gone, his ears were exposed and the grinding noise of the engine as it tried to re-engage the shaft was deafening. Beside him, the body of the man was rolling to and fro, his eyes open and bulging, with blood running out of them, and his mouth open. The rag on the shaft was barely holding on by a thread, and suddenly it whipped away and the shaft began spinning again, the propeller biting into the water and bringing the boat back on track. Jack crawled across the hull frames towards the base of the ladder, looking up through the open hatch and seeing the storm clouds racing overhead. He had felt nothing while killing the man, just adrenalin. All that mattered now was survival. He picked up the knife, shoved it in his pocket and began climbing the ladder, knowing that his own life now hung by a thread, that every step might be his last.

He came out on deck, stumbling and reeling, into a scene of biblical proportions. The waves were mountainous, dwarfing the boat each time it dropped into a trough. The sky was black, but sheet lightning lit it up every few seconds, the crash of thunder distorted into an ear-piercing howl by the wind. Through the spray he could just make out the light in the wheelhouse, and crouched figures silhouetted inside. The captain would know that his only hope now was to drive the vessel forward at full throttle, and to keep the wind dead astern. If the boat wallowed too long in a trough, if the engine faltered again or they got caught in the water slipping back off the crest of the wave ahead, the next wave could swamp them, driving them under with the huge weight bearing down from above. There would be no warning, no chance of escape, just a terrifying maelstrom of struggling and screaming and burst eardrums as the boat hurled down into darkness and oblivion hundreds of metres below.

A derrick broke loose and whooshed off like a broken helicopter blade into the sea behind, hitting the water but being held there by a cable that was still attached to the stanchion that had anchored the derrick to the deck. Jack jumped back as the cable swept from side to side over the deck, the rope taut against the stern rail as the boat rode up the next wave, then slack and wavering as they slipped into the trough. He knew the derrick would act like a sheet anchor, potentially creating enough drag to hold the boat in the trough for that critical second too long. He had to carry out his plan when the line was taut, when he could slide down the deck without the risk of being swept aside and could reach the diving cylinder that was strapped down beside the fishing net inside the stern rail of the boat.

He waited until the boat started up from the trough and the line went taut, but then hesitated. The wind shrieked around him, tearing at his face, and all he could see was the mountainous wall of water of the next wave bearing down on them. He knew that his decision to jump into that might be his last conscious act. But if he were to go, if this really was time-up, he preferred it to be of his own volition and to be enveloped by the sea alone, rather than trapped in the boat with those who had kidnapped him, who had threatened his daughter and all that mattered to him. He would see them vanquished by the sea and dead, but he would not die alongside them.

Something smashed into the deck beside him, kicking up a spray of splinters. He heard the crack of the next round above the shrieking of the wind, and quickly squatted down against the stanchion, looking back at the wheelhouse. One of the men had smashed the rear glass and was firing his MP5 down the deck. The captain must have felt the drag and realised that the derrick had gone. They were trying to shoot away the cable, probably having decided that it would be too dangerous to come out on deck and try to chop it away with an axe.

Bullets ricocheted off the metal of the stanchion only inches from him, but Jack remained still, hoping they had not seen him. And then the boat lurched sideways as the derrick was dragged off to port by a wayward current, and he felt the rudder turned hard right, the captain desperately trying to compensate to keep from wallowing and coming broadside-on to the waves. Another magazine's worth of bullets sprayed around him, and suddenly the cable parted with an enormous crack, coiling and whipping off as it followed the derrick out of sight behind them. The boat lurched back, and as it did so, Jack was thrown sideways and on to his feet, in full view of the deckhouse. He could see the man with the gun looking at him, and reloading. They would have realised that he was not the man they had sent below to fix the engine. This time, he would be the target.

More bullets splattered around him, gouging into the wood. As the boat rode up another wave, he let go of the stanchion and slid down the deck, tumbling into the fishing net. Kicking and pushing at it to extricate himself, he pulled himself over to the scuba tank, snapping open the cam on the belt that held it to the railing and pulling it towards the opening over the stern ladder. It was a steel tank, twelve litres, and only had a regulator attached, no buoyancy compensator or pressure gauge.

The boat was reaching the top of the wave, angled now at almost forty-five degrees, and he held the tank against his chest with one hand and the railing with the other – the only thing stopping him from falling off into the sea. A bullet pinged deafeningly off the shoulder of the tank, ricocheting away a hair's breadth from his face. He stared into the raging tumult below him. There was no time to think, no time for prayer, only time for action. He let go.

18

Jack entered the water as if in slow motion, his senses heightened and acute to every change in the sea around him. The wave had broken just as he had jumped, and it was as if the interface between air and water was no longer sharply defined but was one of increment, the spray becoming suspended globules that coalesced into the mass of water behind. He was completely immersed before he realised it, his eyes shut tight at first but then open to the blur underwater, seeing the surface above him illuminated by flashes of lightning and sensing the yawning darkness below, an abyss he knew from the Caribbean bathymetry charts to be at least four thousand metres deep. He clung on to the tank with both arms, not yet risking reaching for the regulator, fearful that the tank would be swept out of his grip if he relinquished his hold. Because the tank was steel he knew that it would make him sink, but he was still buoyed up by the surge near the crest of the wave, an immense force that he knew would keep him near the surface until he was able to slide down into the next trough and plunge beneath the oscillation of the waves.

He broke the surface, gasping for air, and for an extraordinary few moments he could see the boat below him, wallowing in a trough while he rode the crest of the wave behind it. Through the spray he glimpsed a man hacking frantically at something near the stern rail, then giving up and crawling back towards the deckhouse. Jack braced himself, thinking that this was the wave that was finally going to swamp the boat; that it was going to curl over and throw him back down onto the deck before forcing the vessel under. But then he saw the boat power up the slope of the next wave, and felt himself drop down below its level into the trough. He shut his eyes against the stinging of the spray, and took a deep breath, expecting it to be his last before going under. He could hold his breath in these conditions for a minute and a half, maybe more, enough for him to sink the ten metres or so below the wave oscillation into calmer water that would allow him to let go of the tank with one hand and reach for the regulator. He had no way of knowing whether there was air left in the tank, or whether the valve was open. But it was his only chance of survival.

Something suddenly jerked at his feet, pulling him violently down and then back up, almost completely out of the water. To his horror he realised that his feet were still tangled up in the fishing net, that he must have taken it out with him as he jumped. That was what the crewman had been desperately trying to hack away: the line where the net was still attached to the boat. Like the derrick, the net would be acting as a sheet anchor, except that this time Jack was part of it. He knew that he only had seconds to try to disentangle himself before the boat went under, taking him with it.

He gasped for air again, keeping a tight grip on the tank. He could do nothing while the boat was rising up the wave and the line was taut, but after it crested and the line went slack, he might be able to free himself. A blinding flash of lightning lit the scene, followed almost immediately by an immense crack of thunder, and he felt a jolt of current in the water. He breathed deeply, deliberately hyperventilating while he could, preparing for what was to come. As he followed the boat up the crest of the next wave, he saw the tangle of netting spread out around him like the tendrils of a giant jellyfish. The boat ploughed on, the lines of the net pulled taut behind it, like some sea stallion drawing a chariot over the waves. Jack slipped back behind the crest and was suddenly underwater, the sea ahead of him a blur of bubbles and current. The rope pulled him forward with a force he had not felt before. Instead of relenting with the next trough, the pull continued, and rather than breaking the surface again, he continued to descend. He realised what had happened. The net had finally pulled the boat under, and it was not going to rise out of the waves again. It was on a one-way trip to the sea floor several thousand metres beneath him, and unless he did something about it very soon, he would be going along with it.

He kicked his right foot free of the net, but his other ankle was caught in a loop of rope that acted as a self-tightening knot. The more he tried to shake it free, the tighter the knot became. They were dropping deeper now, below the level of the wave oscillation, and he could see the hazy form of the boat sinking at horrifying speed into the inky abyss below. Suddenly he remembered the knife that he had put in his pocket before leaving the hold. He released one hand from the tank and reached around, feeling for his thigh pocket. The knife was still there, caught in the webbing. He pulled it out, strained forward with all his strength and began sawing with the serrated edge at the rope, holding the tank by its valve with his other hand.

The fibres of the rope were incredibly hard, oiled and solidified by years of use, and at first he could make no progress. Then the knife severed one strand, and another, and eventually the rope gave way, snapping where it had been taut and going slack in the water. Jack kicked it away with his feet, then watched it draw together and follow the boat as it sank out of sight below. For a moment, even in this maelstrom, he remembered what he had said to Hernandes: *Nobody threatens my daughter*. As far as Jack knew, Hernandes had been in the cabin of the boat. By chance, Jack had engineered his own payback, of the most horrifying sort.

He must have been holding his breath now for more than two minutes, and his lungs were beginning to convulse. He dropped the knife and frantically reached for the regulator hose, putting the second stage in his mouth and pressing the purge button. *Nothing*. He grabbed the pillar valve on the tank, trying to turn it anticlockwise to open it. Still nothing. The valve appeared to be fully open, and the tank bled out. His mind raced. It did not make sense. The diver he had seen using this rig before they left the harbour had still been breathing from the regulator as he came up the ladder, and to empty it entirely he would have had to suck on it strenuously in a way that Jack had not seen him do. Perhaps the valve was jammed closed, rather than fully open.

He wrapped both hands around it, swinging the tank up in the water and using its weight to give his twist of the handle more bite. Suddenly it cracked open, and he quickly took one hand away to press the purge valve again on the regulator second stage, this time blasting air through the mouthpiece to clear it of water. He breathed deep and fast, shuddering with relief, before forcing himself to slow down. He could feel resistance, and he opened the valve fully. The resistance was still there, a tightness at the end of each breath. That at least answered the question of how much air was left in the tank. Resistance meant that he was well below the reserve threshold of fifty bar, and almost certainly within the final few atmospheres of pressure. Regardless of any efforts to slow his breathing now and make it last, there was no getting around the reality of his situation. Within a few minutes he would have sucked the tank dry.

He was caught in a terrifying conundrum. By continuing to hold on to the tank, he was heading inexorably deeper, dragged down by its weight. He needed the tank to survive right now, but very soon the air would be gone and he would have to abandon it and try to surface. He was already stretching the envelope for a free ascent, close to the critical depth where he would not have enough oxygen in his system to ascend without a buoyancy aid. His current oxygen level would already be severely depleted by having held his breath until only a few moments ago; it would be suicidal to attempt an ascent before that level had normalised. To make matters worse, there was not enough air in the tank to allow him to saturate his system with oxygen as rapidly as he would have liked. Taking deep breaths would anyway only waste unabsorbed oxygen through exhalation, and feeling the resistance that deep breaths would bring, knowing that the tank was emptying, might trip him over into the first stages of panic, something that would only increase his metabolism and oxygen consumption. He needed to stay calm, to take shallow breaths, to be in the best state of mind to make a judgement call on the time to ascend before the point of no return was reached.

He passed through the thermocline, a sudden drop of several degrees in the ocean temperature and his first certain indication of depth. In this part of the Caribbean he knew the thermocline was at about sixty metres. It was a crunch point for his survival; beyond that depth without a buoyancy aid, he would have little hope of making it to the surface after ditching the tank. He tried to relax, to quell the instinct to breathe hard and maximise his oxygen intake, and instead allowed being underwater to have the effect it usually had on him, slowing his heart rate and his breathing. For a few moments, holding the tank and sinking into darkness, he felt suffused by serenity, as if he were levitating in the ocean, becoming one with something that had been his passion all his life. Then he snapped out of it, realising that he had allowed his mind to prepare his body for shutdown, for the end he had always known might be the price he would have to pay for that passion. This was not the right time, or the right place. He remembered what Costas had once said when they were a hair's breadth from oblivion. *Don't think. Just act.*

He took as many short, quick breaths as he could, feeling the resistance as the tank finally emptied, and then spat out the regulator and pushed the tank away, seeing it disappear into the depths. He had taken short breaths rather than one deep one in order to saturate his bloodstream with oxygen, but without having to hold the air in his lungs; that would only have wasted oxygen, as he would have needed to expel the air as he ascended in order to keep his lungs from rupturing. He began to swim up, not kicking, but using a more energy-efficient frog-stroke, at the same time pulling down with his arms, keeping his movements controlled and measured. He passed back through the thermocline, avoiding looking up at the daunting distance to the surface but instead focusing on the horizon he could see between the shallower water that was penetrated by sunlight and the inky blackness below. He tried not to work too hard, to increase his tempo in a way that could lead to panic.

At about thirty metres, he did look up, seeing an undulating mass like storm clouds, shot through with white smudges where lightning was hitting the surface. He knew that this was going to be the most trying part; most freediving blackouts occurred only a few metres from the surface. He began to retch, to feel the ache of oxygen starvation, and tried to suppress the urge to open his mouth and breathe.

He suddenly lost that urge, and his legs felt leaden, warning signs that he was seconds away from blackout. He tried to pull himself up further, running on empty, and then his arms gave way too and he hung motionless in the water. He could not understand why he had not blacked out; it must have been some extra will inside him. He felt movement, and then saw that the lower reach of the wave oscillation was only a few metres above, a point where the surge might take him the final ten metres or so to the surface. He summoned up some extra hidden reserve and pulled himself up, feeling the current draw him in just as he lost consciousness.

All movement and pain was gone, and he seemed to be in a place of light, hearing only the soft sounds of the sea and a breeze that gently brushed his face. There were figures on the foreshore, and he realised that they were all there, Rebecca and Costas and the others, beckoning him on, waving for him to come across and join them. Then the scene fragmented and he was back in reality, coughing and taking in great gulps of air on the surface of the sea, riding a gigantic wave to its crest and dropping down into a trough below. He lay on his back as the waves carried him forward, doing nothing more than was needed to keep his head above water, trying to conserve his energy for what might lie ahead.

A burst of rain swept over him, and he opened his mouth to catch the drops, grateful for a taste of fresh water. He came upright, trying to see beyond the raging waters around him, peering above the crest of the next wave. There was something ahead, a brightness in the sky, perhaps marking the edge of the storm. At the crest of the next wave, he could see it more clearly. The wind was still whipping spindrift off the top of the waves, but ahead of him there seemed to be a dramatic lessening of the seas, and even a hint of blue in the sky above. Far in the distance he could make out a white surf line, and beyond it a hazy dark shape receding into the background. *It was land.* He still had a long way to go, but the sight gave him a burst of adrenalin that he knew could see him through. He

remembered his vision in those few moments of uncon-
sciousness before hitting the surface. He owed it to them, to
those who mattered most. There was no way he was giving up
now.

Several hours later, he was floating off a long sandy beach,
with people visible under parasols, and huts and houses set
among groves of palms behind it. The sun had been blazing
down fiercely for at least an hour, and the storm was no more
than a distant darkness on the horizon, swirling away to the
north. With the wind and waves having tailed off, he knew
that he was being taken inshore by the Colombia-Panama
Gyre, but some time back the current had swerved east to run
parallel to the shore, potentially taking him out to sea again in
the direction of the Atlantic. For half an hour or so he had
been swimming as hard as he could, diagonally from the
current, still using its force behind him but trying to edge
closer to the surf line, where he should be able to break free
and make landfall. He had swept past dangerous outcrops of
reef and rock, trying to find a place to strike inshore, and
finally here it was, a beach that continued out of sight to the
east as far as he could see.

The final obstacle was the surf itself, a rolling succession of
waves that broke and crashed on the beach, surging forward
almost to the parasols and falling back in a vicious undertow
that dragged the sand and shingle along in a thunderous
cacophony. It was a last legacy of the storm, a result of a swell
created by the maelstrom to the north that had been
imperceptible to Jack in the deeper water but had risen up as
he approached the shallows. The beach was only a few

hundred metres away, but the obstacle was still considerable. He swam up one wave and tried to bodysurf from its crest, but slid back as it rolled ahead of him against the shore.

In the trough of the next wave, he scraped his left thigh hard against something, and spotted a black mass of reef running parallel to the shore. Tendrils of blood filled the water around him, but he felt no pain. He knew that to be thrown against the reef again could kill him; all he could do now was judge the best wave to ride over it. He let the next two go, treading water as they broke over him, coming perilously close to the reef each time, then rolled onto his front, arms and legs splayed, and surfed the next one into shore, riding just beyond the crest until it deposited him on the sand ahead of the surf. He knew he had to get further to avoid being sucked back by the undertow, and he crawled forward, inch by inch, eventually reaching the tideline and safety.

He stood up, swaying and feeling faint, and looked at his shredded trousers and the bloody wound in his left thigh. The coral had scraped off the skin over a large area and gouged a deep runnel down the middle, where fragments remained embedded. It was not good, but he was alive. *He had made it.*

He was desperately thirsty, and he needed medical attention. But before that, there was something he urgently needed to do. He used his last remaining reserves to stagger up the beach towards a palm-roofed bar, one hand pressed against his thigh, the blood oozing out between his fingers. He reached the counter, and stood there panting, oblivious to the stares of those around him. A woman rushed up with a handful of table napkins and lifted his hand aside, pressing them against the gaping wound in his leg. 'Doctor, doctor!' she shouted, looking around at the other people in the bar.

Jack saw a lifeguard running over, carrying a yellow medical bag. The barman gave him a glass of water, and he drank it in great gulps, his hand shaking and his teeth rattling against the glass. He put it down, and the barman poured another, but Jack reached out and grasped his arm.

'*Por favor*,' he said, his voice rasping, barely audible. 'I need to use a phone.'

Part 4

19

Near Potosi, Bolivia, the High Andes

Jack braced himself as the four-wheel drive engaged and the driver of the truck negotiated another hairpin bend on the side of the mountain, the single faulty headlight barely illuminating the rocky track ahead. It had been less than twenty-four hours since he had escaped from the sea on the coast of Colombia, and twelve hours since he had signed himself out of hospital and met up with Costas on the tarmac at Bogotá airport. He had been dead to the world for almost the entire flight to Bolivia, but had been woken up for an on-board shower, food, a change of clothes and kitting-out for what lay ahead, before they had landed at La Paz and he and Costas had met up with their driver for the long trip into the mountains.

It had been midnight when they had left the Embraer at the

airport, and it was now nearly four a.m., still pitch dark but with a smudge of dawn beyond the ridges to the east. The road, which had started out tarmac, had soon become gravel and then little more than a track, pocked with holes, blasted crudely out of the side of the mountain, becoming even more tenuous as they wound their way higher. His GPS wrist computer included an altimeter, and he had watched it pass the four-thousand-metre mark more than an hour before. The plan had been to use this back route in order not to draw attention to themselves by driving through Potosi itself. It had seemed like a good idea at the time, but after four bone-rattling hours, he was not so sure; he had begun to dream of flat roads and of finding some way to relieve the ache in his neck.

He shifted his legs to a new position, feeling the pain in his thigh where he had impacted with the reef. It had taken twenty stitches to close up the wound and two further hours for the doctor to pick out the fragments of coral from the surrounding graze, but now it was just a matter of antiseptic and bandaging. The local anaesthetic had worn off long ago, but he was reluctant to take one of the codeine pills the doctor had given him; he needed to keep his head as clear as possible over the next few hours.

When he had called them from the beach, he had kept the extent of his injury from Costas and Rebecca, but had impressed on them the need to make arrangements immediately for him and Costas to meet up with Maria's contact at Potosi before any of the Altamanus realised that he had survived the storm. His first call, though, had been not to them, but to IMU security; Ben and an armed team had already landed at Kingston airport and taken everyone from the Port Royal site away to a secure location in central Jamaica for the duration. Jack was prepared to take another risk with his own life to see this through, but not to risk the lives of his daughter or his friends, and knowing that they were in safe hands had been his one precondition for the plane taking off for Bolivia the night before.

He felt dehydrated, but did not feel like drinking. He knew that it was an effect of the altitude, and he forced himself to sip from one of the little plastic bottles that had been wedged below the dashboard. He looked back at Costas, who was leaning half asleep on a pile of woven blankets in the back seat, his fleece done up to his neck and wearing a multicoloured woollen hat with flaps over his ears. Costas had suffered unexpectedly from altitude sickness an hour earlier, and they had stopped while he threw up. The driver had insisted that he chew a wedge of coca leaves, and that had put Costas into something of a trance. Already, Jack thought, being at this place had taken its toll, and they had not even reached the mountain yet.

The truck jumped, and came down with a bone-crunching crash. Costas lolled awake, and Jack thrust an open bottle of water into his hand, watching while he blearily drank. The driver, a small, swarthy Incan with a cheekful of leaves, gave him a cheerful nod, gestured outside and switched off the engine. As it shuddered to a halt, Jack felt an overwhelming sense of relief. He pulled down the latch of the door, kicked it open and dropped out, feeling the throb in his leg and then quickly leaning back to avoid falling further down the vertiginous drop below.

He made his way around to the front of the vehicle, stretching his arms and arching his back. The sky was a brilliant speckle of stars, just about the clearest he had ever seen, with the Milky Way cutting a dense swathe overhead, and near the horizon the seven stars of the Pleiades, the constellation that the Inca associated with harvest and regeneration. He had not realised how cold it was outside, and he rubbed his hands together, walking back to the rear door to get out his bag with his gloves and other gear.

Costas came out groggily from the side, staggered slightly and then bent down with his hands on his knees, spitting into the darkness. 'Those leaves definitely help,' he said. 'But right now what I need is a big drink of water and a couple of hours' proper shut-eye.'

'Amen to that,' Jack said, pulling out both of their bags. 'By the look of it, this is our stop.'

The driver came back from where he had disappeared up the road, made a sleeping gesture with his hands and pointed to a low building just visible in the gloom ahead. Jack put his hand under Costas's shoulder and raised him up, and they both trudged behind the man, passing a llama munching unconcernedly at some scrub.

Inside the building, the man switched on a torch, pointed to a table with bottles of water and some bread and then at a room with two mattresses and sleeping bags on the floor. Jack opened a bottle and passed it to Costas, then opened another one himself, drinking as much as he could. He went into the other room, slung their bags on the floor, dropped down onto one of the mattresses and rolled over, instantly and dreamlessly asleep.

★ ★ ★

He awoke before Costas did, feeling the cold, and pulled the sleeping bag up for more warmth, but then realised that there was little point; with the light of dawn already shining through, they were going to be woken up shortly anyway. He heaved himself up, gave Costas a shake and then went into the next room, smelling coffee and pouring himself a cup from the flask on the table. Costas followed him, half asleep, and did the same, and they both sat down and ate some bread. Jack looked at Costas's weather-beaten face, stubbly and lined beneath his hat. 'You look really great,' he said.

Costas peered at him. 'You don't look so good yourself. You look like you've been through a wind tunnel.'

'I did have a little swim in the Caribbean.'

'How's your leg?' Costas said, swallowing his bread and draining his coffee.

'Okay. How's your head?'

'Bad. I'm going to take some more of those leaves. They can't make me feel worse. Before that, I need to find the men's room.'

Jack pointed to the open door. 'Welcome to the Andes.'

The view when they got outside was stunning, something that had been impossible to appreciate the night before. Five hundred metres below them in the valley, the city of Potosi lay spread out over undulating hills, its colonial-period streets and alleys following the natural contours of the land. Jack could see the main church, and the cluster of courtyard buildings that he knew was the site of the mint that three hundred years ago had made this place one of the economic engines of the world.

The horizon all around was marked by the jagged line of the Cordillera de Potosi, the local range of the Andes, but what dominated the scene was the peak directly in front of them: Cerro Rico, the Mountain of Riches, the end of a continuous slope that rose some eight hundred metres from the nearest point in the city, broken only by the plateau they were on now. It was like a volcano, blasted and lifeless, the rock grey-blue below and red-brown above, the plateau and the slopes strewn with the spoil and tailings of almost five hundred years of mining. Jack knew that the mountain was riddled with tunnels and shafts, some extending a thousand metres deep and more; somehow he and Costas were going to get in there, into one of the deepest shafts, and get out with the extraordinary treasure they had come this far to find, a prospect that in the cold light of dawn seemed as daunting as anything they had ever undertaken.

He followed Costas to the edge of the slope, then went back and splashed water from one of the bottles over his hands and face, thinking about the history of this place, once the heart of the Spanish viceroyalty of Peru. More than half the silver that was mined in the world before modern times had come from here, along with huge quantities of tin and zinc. He also knew that millions of people were estimated to have died working this mine in the centuries following its discovery by the Spanish in the mid sixteenth century, with upwards of fifty thousand Inca and African slaves toiling here at any one time. This truly was El Dorado, the fabled fount of riches that the Conquistadors had sought, a place where the ore could yield fifty per cent silver and millions of ounces could be refined every year – yet also where the dark side of European exploitation of the New World was visible like nowhere else, a hell on earth where it had been estimated that every hundred wheelbarrow-loads of ore had cost a human life.

A battered truck came bouncing over the potholes on the road behind, coming to a halt in a cloud of dust beside Jack. The door opened and a tall young man wearing a down jacket and baseball cap and sunglasses got out, chewing gum. He spat the gum out beside the road, then saw Jack watching and walked over, his hand outstretched. 'Apologies for that,' he said, his accent American. 'I'm trying to kick the coca leaf habit, and chewing gum helps. I'm Marco Henley, from the mission. Father Pereira sent me. I'm a good friend of your friend Maria. You're Jack Howard, and you must be Costas. Welcome to Cerro Rico.'

They all shook hands, and Marco pointed to the mine entrance ahead of them. 'I'm going to give you a quick tour before we get down to business. I trust the driver we sent was okay for you? You need to meet the boy who's going to take you into the mine. I want to get that done now, at the start of the day, so that we can avoid prying eyes later on. I know the backstory and I know about the Altamanus. But there are a lot of people here keeping a watch on our behalf, too.'

'Where are you from?' Costas asked, as they walked along towards the mine entrance. 'I'm Greek, but I grew up mainly in Brooklyn.'

'Yeah? I'm half-Colombian, but I grew up mainly in Rhode Island. I was one of those privileged kids whose parents had a colonial clapboard on the seafront. Went to NYU, majored in architecture, got bored with planning skyscrapers for tycoons, joined the Marines, two tours in Afghanistan. After that, I came down here looking for something to do, figuring that since my mother is Colombian and I can speak the lingo, I might be of some use. I met Maria while I was hanging out in Potosi thinking of becoming an artist, and after she found out about my background she invited me to meet Father Pereira, who eventually invited me up to the mission. That was four years ago, and I've been there ever since. The place was in a bit of a state, and I've put my building skills to some use. Also, though they were pretty well on the ball about the Altamanus and that whole history, their security arrangements needed a little tweaking. Basically I provide that. I remember reading about you; you were in the navy, right?'

'A long time ago,' Costas said. 'Engineering, submersibles, pretty technological, but I did see some active service in the Gulf. Jack was a diver with UK Special Forces.'

'I read that too.'

They reached a large dusty plateau in front of the entrance, a gaping rocky hole reducing to a narrow shaft that descended out of sight. The slope of the mountain reared high above that, covered with scree from which rocks of all sizes had tumbled onto the plateau, some of them then rolled by miners into rough walls to form sleeping and cooking places for their families. 'One of the many hazards of this place,' Marco said, putting his hand on a boulder as they walked by. 'Every once in a while someone gets crushed by a falling boulder, or hit on the head and killed by something as small as your fist. But you won't see anyone wearing hard hats here. It wouldn't make a difference, and they would just see it as tempting fate.'

The plateau was teeming with people, perhaps two hundred

of them, all shrouded in dust and engaged in some form of labour. A line of boys pushed wheelbarrows of ore out of the entrance, dumping their contents in a pile by the road, where others were shovelling it into the back of a battered old dump truck. Several men carried a crate labelled DYNAMITE off the back of a pickup truck, and women stood behind rickety stalls along the path of the barrow boys with jugs of water and piles of flatbreads on the tables in front of them. 'Those are their mothers and sisters,' Marco said. 'I want you to meet Juan, who's going to be taking you down the shaft tonight.'

A teenage boy had detached himself from the group around the dump truck and walked hesitantly towards them, a younger boy following. He was taller than most, with dark eyes and high cheekbones, more Inca than Spanish in origin. His nose and mouth were caked in dust, and he quickly wiped them with the back of his hand as he came up to them, waving at the other boy to stay back.

'Juan, this is Jack and Costas,' Marco said, then tapped his watch. '*Medianoche, correcto?*'

Jack smiled at him. '*Habla usted Inglés, Juan?*'

'A little, señor.'

'Call me Jack. We'll see you inside the mine entrance at midnight, right?'

The boy nodded, and hurried back to the barrows. 'He's a good boy, intelligent,' Marco said. 'He wants to be a doctor, so he can tend to his older brother, who is slowly dying from silicosis. But it's very hard for him. They live with their mother in that cavern by the entrance. And you can already see the look in his eyes that they get when they've breathed in too much dust, when the mountain has taken them over.'

'How old are they, the younger ones?' Costas asked. 'Looks like child labour to me.'

'They start as young as eight,' Marco said. 'They work five-hour shifts, usually at night so they can go to school during the day, pushing out thirty or forty wheelbarrow-loads on each shift. The dust means that they'll all eventually suffer from silicosis, where the lungs basically turn to rock. It debilitates most of them by the time they're in their twenties. The doctors chart their decline, and it's not uncommon to see lung capacity dropping below fifty per cent by the time they're eighteen. In addition to that, they suffer from *mal de miner*, headaches and weakness of the legs caused by breathing in the toxic gases that linger in the tunnels after dynamite has exploded. Whole sections of the mine, especially the deep parts, are fragile honeycombs of passageways, and can collapse at any moment. About twenty people a month die in accidents. The average life expectancy is less than forty. It's no wonder they call the place *la montaña que come a los hombres* – the mountain that eats men.'

'That eats boys, more like,' Costas said, coughing and spitting on the ground, and then taking out a few more of the coca leaves that the driver had given him. 'Thank God we brought our breathing masks with us.'

'You can go ahead and thank God here outside the mine, but make sure you don't mention him in there. God doesn't hold much sway in that mountain.'

Just before the entrance lay a pit about eight metres long by three metres wide, and covered by a line of dust-caked planks. As he passed by, Jack looked into the cracks between the planks, then stopped, stunned. 'Am I seeing human skeletons?'

'Correct,' Marco said. Costas joined Jack and stared open-mouthed into the hole. It was filled with a dense jumble of human bones, some of them articulated skeletons, others crushed and jammed together, with hundreds of skulls packed at one end. 'There are lots of these mass burials around, but this one was uncovered when a boy with a barrow fell into it. An anthropologist came up from the university in La Paz and determined that they were all African slaves. The Inca were favoured for underground work, because of their small stature and their stamina, just like their descendants here today, but the Africans with their larger size and musculature were put to work in the mint, pushing around the stone mills that ground the ore. They even had a name for them: *acémilas humanas*, human donkeys. They rarely lasted more than a few months, but there were always more to be had in the slave markets of Port Royal and elsewhere in the Caribbean.'

Jack stared at the skulls, remembering Maurice only two days before on the stone dais of the courtyard at Port Royal, chains and shackles in hand, explaining in sombre terms what he had uncovered. Jack had found it difficult then to populate the image in his mind's eye with the human traffic that had filled that place, but now the reality of it was laid out starkly before his eyes, and it filled him with horror. He looked up at the mountain and hesitated, suddenly filled with revulsion for this place, wishing he was not here. But then he looked at the line of boys who trundled beside him, covered in sweat and dust. He had to go on; he could not give up now. He took a deep breath, and followed Costas and Marco the final few steps to the entrance.

'You'll see under the dust that the rock is smeared with

blood,' Marco said. 'They sacrifice a llama here every week to propitiate the god of the mountain, and use the meat to feed the boys. At this point we are literally standing on the border between the Christian world and something dark and forbidding beyond, as if this were the entrance to the underworld. Father Pereira will go no further than this when he visits here to minister to the boys.'

He walked through the cavern and stooped as the tunnel lowered, the way ahead lit dimly by wobbling electric bulbs attached to the ceiling, powered by a generator outside. 'Those finish pretty soon,' he said, his voice muffled. 'After that, it's headlamps and torches. We won't go further than that.'

Jack coughed, feeling the dust catch in his throat. Ahead, it was like mist, billowing around the jagged rocks where the tunnel had been crudely hacked out of the mountainside. Costas suddenly sprang back, clutching at the rock. 'What the hell is *that*?' Jack came up behind him and saw what he had seen. Leaning against the side of the tunnel was a lurid life-sized idol made of papier mâché and cloth, with horns on its head and eyes made of marbles. It was dressed in multicoloured paper streamers, and had burned-out cigarettes and cigars in its mouth and opened cans and bottles in its hands.

'That's El Tío, the Uncle,' Marco said. 'The Lord of the Underworld, a devil-like spirit that the miners worship, leaving him gifts of coca leaves and tobacco and alcohol. Once you get deeper into these tunnels, you'll see more of them, and they get more frightening. Years ago the missionaries tried to turn the miners from El Tío, but to no avail. The ominous thing is that he's a god of both protection and destruction. The miners know perfectly well that no amount of placating will save them from what the mountain has ordained for them, so they accept that El Tío may only be bent on their destruction. It's a kind of fatalism that allows them to go deep into the mine every day without breathing protection, despite seeing what silicosis has done to virtually everyone who works here.'

The ground shook, and a rumble came up from the depths, followed by a dull glow and a waft of hot dust. They all began coughing, and quickly moved back to the entrance, shifting aside to let a line of boys with wheelbarrows get through. 'Jesus,' Costas said. 'That really is like the exhalation of the devil.'

Marco led them out into the sunlight again, and Jack saw that the puff of dust from the explosion had covered them in a sheen of white. The boys around them looked like an army of ghosts, as if they were preparing for some voodoo ritual in front of their god. Marco caught his gaze, and led them further out. 'You'll find very few places in the world where people, especially children, are so constantly on the edge between life and death, and where the shadow of death hangs over them night and day. For the local Inca it has been this way for countless generations, since even before the Spanish came along, when the local chieftains began to work the mountain. It's as if they're enslaved to it, with no hope of reprieve. All we can do is try to improve their chances of a better life through education. But it's an unrewarding task, with no other employer within hundreds of miles.'

'So what do we do now?' Jack said.

Marco turned to them, his face serious. 'Father Pereira has decided that it's too risky for me to go to the town and be seen with you. If the Altamanus are here and see us together, they'll know that I must have come from the mission. He's fearful that they will then try to capture me and use their techniques to find out its location. Instead I'm to give you the details of a place in Potosi that you can use as a safe house before you venture into the mine tonight. You have to wait until then because the area of the mine that you will need to penetrate is currently being dynamited, and a way through will need to be reopened and shored up by the boys when that finishes this afternoon. You'll stay up here for the remainder of the day, resting in the place where you've just slept, and then make your way down to the town under cover of darkness once evening falls. There's a tunnel leading from the safe house all the way under the entrance of the mine; once there, you'll meet up with Juan. From now on, until you get back to the mine, you're on your own.'

'What is this safe house?' Jack asked.

Marco passed him a slip of paper. 'Memorise this location. It's an entrance in an alleyway behind the Casa de la Moneda, the buildings of the mint. A woman who will recognise you will meet you there at nine p.m. In the nineteenth century, an earthquake opened up a chamber beneath the mint that had been sealed up since the late seventeenth century. The passageway leading to it from the mountain was dug to allow the chamber to be a secret smelting and minting establishment, right under the noses of the official mint. A maverick assayer had the idea of setting up his own illegal mint rather than just creaming bullion from the official output, which was the usual way but risky – the assayers were constantly investigated and if caught were immediately garrotted. As it happens, he wasn't so lucky and was arrested for other reasons, but the chamber remained undiscovered and was sealed up with the minting equipment still inside, exactly as it had been when it was last used in 1686. After it was revealed by the earthquake, those who found it decided not to tell the authorities but to keep it as a safe house, at a time when there was much revolutionary disruption in Bolivia and such a place was useful for harbouring refugees from the various military regimes. The mission has known about it since then and used it for the same purpose when it has been necessary for someone to go to ground.'

'How will we contact you or Father Pereira when this is all over?'

'We will know how to find you. We have many friends among the boys of the mine.' Marco turned and shook hands with both of them. 'One other thing. Are you armed?'

Jack patted his bag. 'Beretta 9 mm with three mags. Both of us.'

'Good.' Marco squinted as the sun broke through a cloud, then gestured back at the opening into the mountain behind him. 'Out here, the miners are Christians. Inside, they worship the devil. When you go in there, you are going to have to do all you can to keep out of the clutches of the devil as well. Go now, and get some rest. Keep out of sight until dusk. God be with you.'

20

An hour after dusk that evening, Jack and Costas moved carefully into the lower reaches of the town, trying to be as inconspicuous as possible as they made their way towards the address that Marco had written on the scrap of paper. There were enough other Europeans in the town, priests and municipal officials and mining engineers, for them to pass without undue notice, but even so Jack was concerned that they should find the alley behind the Casa de la Moneda before too many eyes followed them from windows and cafés and they attracted the inevitable trail of children.

As they entered the alley, a woman who had clearly been waiting hurried up to them, gesturing for them to follow her down a stepped passageway. She stopped at a door, looked around, then opened it with a key, ushering them in and locking it behind her. They followed her down another flight of stairs, through a succession of low barrel-vaulted cellars to a far room with a stack of wooden beams beside one wall. She moved these aside, revealing a low door. She unlocked that too, ushered them inside, and then left without saying a word, locking the door again behind her. She had completed her task, and Jack knew that she would have wanted to minimise communication with those she was helping in case she were to be captured and made to talk.

They walked cautiously into the chamber. It was like a church crypt, lit by candles, and was constructed from blocks of the grey-green rock they had seen on the mountain. At one end of it Jack could see a grille that he knew must mark the entrance to the tunnel that Marco had talked about, their access point to the shaft under the mountain some two kilometres away. But for the moment it was what lay in the centre of the room that drew his attention: a succession of tables and anvils set into the masonry, with tools on the floor and walls all around. 'Well I'll be damned,' he said. 'I see what Marco meant. It's an intact seventeenth-century mint, with all the equipment and tools still *in situ*. Fascinating.'

'Always good to get a little more archaeology in when you're under duress.'

'My thoughts exactly.'

'Talk me through it, Jack.'

Jack pointed to the grille in the far corner. 'I assume that the ore came in by sack through the tunnel. It's hard to imagine it being carried more than two kilometres from the seams under the mountain, but there it is. Somewhere nearby there must have been a smelting factory, presumably in some other part of this complex that's maybe yet to be uncovered. The hot liquid silver would have been cast into thin bars that would then have been pounded and rolled into thin strips, to the thickness of the coin denomination required. Those strips are what would have arrived in this room for the actual minting process. They were called cobs, hence the name Spanish colonial hammered coins are often known by today.'

'So this room is where the silver was made into coins.'

'That's right. The first thing was to make planchets, what we would call flans or blanks. Those heavy table shears like manual paper-cutters would have been used to do that, requiring the workmen to put their full strength into cutting the metal. Then, once you have the planchets roughly sized, you hold them in tongs and use these other shears and the hammers and chisels to snip and cut them to the exact weight required. You then give the planchets an acid bath to clean them, probably in that vat over there, and you're ready for the final part of the process.'

'The hammer and the anvil.'

Jack picked up a rusted cylinder beside the anvil, the base showing an incised obverse design of the Habsburg coat of arms of Spain. 'The next stage is the fun bit, where all the idiosyncrasy of the final product comes in. You anchor one die in the anvil, the obverse, you place the planchet on top of that, you hold the other die in a pair of tongs over it and your assistant whacks the whole thing as hard as he can with a heavy metal mallet. If you're lucky, you'll get a reasonable coverage of both designs on the coin. If you're a bit sloppy or tired, the designs might only partially appear. But it doesn't matter, because it's the weight that counts, and providing you can see the assayer and mint marks you've got your piece of eight.'

'And then if you're a Portuguese Jewish merchant named João Rodrigues Brandão, when you get your coins you go one step further and stamp in your own distinctive mark of a Star of David to make them really yours.'

'Exactly.'

'So we've nearly got the full story. We start with finding those coins on the wreck of the *Schiedam*, we go to Port Royal where the coins were taken after being robbed from the treasure ships, and then we come here to the place where they were minted. Next step, the mountain where the ore was mined.'

'Let's hope that closes the story in more ways than one.'

'Speaking of which, it's time to do our equipment check,' Costas said. 'Three hours to go until zero hour at midnight, and I want to get some rest.'

'Roger that.'

They opened up their packs and checked the contents systematically, laying them out and putting back the items they would not need immediately. They had side-mounted hydration units, one water flask in each side pocket, with hoses that clipped on the shoulder straps of the packs beside their necks; in their first-aid kits they also carried rehydration sachets and water purification tablets should they need to take water from the mine, and Costas had a water-purifier pump. For food they carried energy bars and quick-burst energy gels used by athletes, all they expected to need given that they only planned to be inside the mountain for a short time. Costas pulled out his breathing helmet, a sealed full-face unit developed at IMU that had a Kevlar helmet, a mask to protect the eyes and a double-filter breathing unit, with a quick-fit attachment for a miniature air cylinder in the event that they had to go underwater. He checked the fittings, and waved it at Jack. 'They may believe in the protective powers of their voodoo god, but I wasn't overly impressed by that one we saw. With all those butts in its mouth, it looked like an advertisement for lung disease, not something to ward it off. I'll take my chances with one of these.'

'I'm with you on that,' Jack said. 'We've each got a backup, too, so Juan can have one if he wants.'

They tested the headlamps on their helmets and the 1000-lumen diver hand torches that they also carry with them, and then the spare batteries. Lastly, they both took out the holsters containing the Beretta 92F pistols that had been issued to them by the captain of the Embraer from the on-board armoury, not the first time they had needed to be armed on an archaeological quest. They checked that the magazines were full, loaded a magazine into each pistol and then strapped the holsters over their shoulders. Jack checked that his sheath knife was securely on his belt, and then tied his bag up and clicked the flap shut.

'Okay,' Costas said, shutting his own bag. 'Any final thoughts?'

'I'm glad I stopped Rebecca from trying to come with us. She wasn't happy with me, and I feel bad about laying down the law. But there was no way I was having her involved in this.'

'You did the right thing.'

'And you?'

'Final thoughts? When will this headache go, and when can I have my next gin and tonic from my favourite poolside bar in Mauritius? Will it be this week, or next? That's all that matters. And making sure Lanowski puts Little Joey to sleep properly for the flight back from Port Royal. I should have given them a call, really.' He put his pack on the floor to use as a pillow, and then lay down with his hands clasped over his front. 'Time for some shut-eye. My alarm is set for midnight.'

He was asleep almost immediately, snoring gently. Jack lay down too, knowing that he still needed to rebuild his strength after his injury and that the altitude would be taking a toll on him as well. But he was only able to doze fitfully, woken by a dream of rushing water and darkness, of being sucked back down again by the boat, unable to disentangle himself. He lay awake after that thinking not of ancient relics, but of the people who had enriched his life, the people he loved: Rebecca and Costas, Maria and Maurice, all the others. He remembered the words of the Roman Laurentius when he had been challenged to produce the wealth of the Church and had declared that the true treasure was in the people, in the congregation. Perhaps that was the lesson of the Holy Chalice, Jack thought, now as it had been then: that it was not the artefacts that mattered but the people, that the hunt for lost treasures was really about giving meaning and measure to the lives of those who had embarked on the quest.

There was a sudden clattering from the direction of the stairs, and the sound of the door closing. Jack reached for his Beretta, keeping it concealed under his pack with his finger on the safety. Someone came into the room, and he could see it was the woman who had brought them in here. She was clearly distraught, and came towards them quickly. '*Dios mío, Dios mío*,' she said, fanning her face with her hand.

Costas had got up, and held her by the wrists, calming her down. 'What is it? Tell us.'

She stared into his eyes, taking deep breaths. 'I was sent here by Marco to tell you. *They* have arrived. He said you would know who I meant. They have been to the mine, questioning everyone there, and they have taken the boy. Not Juan, but his little friend.' She put her hand over her mouth, trying to control her emotions. 'My nephew Pedro. They took him into the mine.'

'Okay,' Jack said, putting a hand on her shoulder. 'It's okay. We'll find him. I need you to go to Marco and tell him that this changes nothing. *This changes nothing.* Can you do that?'

She sniffed, wiping her eyes, and nodded. '*Sí*, I will do that now. Please be careful. And bring back my nephew.'

She turned and hurried back towards the door, closing it behind her. Jack turned to Costas. 'We need to go now. Once our message reaches Juan, he'll be looking out for us. We'll just have to hope that he managed to evade capture too.'

'And that Pedro hasn't given the game away. The boys must all have seen those fish symbols carved into the walls, even if they couldn't know their significance. Miners are often superstitious, and they'd be used to the idea of symbols to ward off bad luck, including those from hundreds of years earlier whose meaning might be lost.'

'All I'm thinking about is that boy. If we hadn't come to Potosí, he might not have been taken. He's our responsibility.'

'If they have gone deep and we're following them, we might have the upper hand. There may be no other way out for them than to get past us.'

Jack took a deep breath, steeling himself for what lay ahead.

He remembered his discussion with Maria and Rebecca and Jeremy just before they had left Portugal for Jamaica. Then, he had wanted to follow all the strands, to go to Port Royal first, to see where that would lead him. He had not yet felt that narrowing of focus, that intense drive to put all his energies into one objective that he had known would come when the time was right. Now, though, that time had come. Being hung in chains on the island, being taken to his limit in the sea had stripped him to the basics, and focused him on what had got him into those predicaments in the first place. The passage that lay ahead of them into the mountain was constricting his focus further. And there was no going back now; once in there, there could be no deviation, and there was no other reason for entering that place where no human being rightly belonged. He just prayed that they would be the first to the secret place, and that they could reach the boy before it was too late.

Costas took out his Beretta, pulled back the slide to chamber a round and replaced the gun in its holster. Jack did the same with his, then they both took out their breathing masks, hooked them round their necks and over their heads, and pulled the straps tight. They put on their backpacks and activated their head torches, switching on the lights and angling them to see a few metres in front of them as they were walking.

Jack led the way to the entrance to the tunnel, pulled open the grille and played his beam along the rough-cut rock walls. It seemed incredibly narrow, just wide enough for a small Inca to carry a sack of ore, and it was hard to believe that it extended more than two kilometres before it joined one of the shafts from the mine entrance. He was going to have to be hunched down all the way, and would have to marshal all his reserves to battle the claustrophobia that this place seemed designed to bring on. He half turned his head so that he could see Costas's beam. 'This is it, then. You good to go?'

'I'm behind you, Jack. Good to go.'

21

Almost an hour later, Jack went down on all fours to ease the pain in his back, scraping his shoulders against the jagged rock of the tunnel wall as he did so. It was the most constricted space he had ever tried to negotiate for this length of time, and every step had become agonising. For each brief spell of a few metres where they could walk, hunched over and squeezed between the walls, there were long stretches where they could only crawl, and then sections where even crawling was impossible because of the protrusions on the floor. The only advantage of the appalling constriction was that he had long ago ceased to concern himself with claustro-phobia, as all his thoughts and energy had been focused on the physical struggle. Where the tunnel had widened for a few metres he had moved aside to let Costas squeeze ahead of him, but now Costas had stopped too, lying on his back on a flat section of rock. This was far harder going than either of them had imagined, and Jack was seriously beginning to wonder whether they would make it in time for their rendez-vous with the boy, in a little less than half an hour now.

He rolled over and sat upright in a gap, hitting his helmet against the rock as he did so, then activated his wrist computer to check the air quality, seeing that it was still within acceptable parameters. Before entering the tunnel, they had observed a slight but vital movement of the air, crucial for their survival; the difference in altitude between the chamber where they had entered and the mine entrance where they would exit meant a difference in pressure, one that drew in air from the shaft ahead and in turn from outside. As a result, the air was cleaner here than they had experienced with Marco at the mine entrance, and during their halts they had lifted their visors several times to take quick bites of the energy bars that they had brought along with them.

Jack raised his visor again now, sucking at the tube from his hydration unit, and switched to the altimeter on his computer. It showed 4,398 metres above sea level, about four hundred metres below the summit of the mountain and the same elevation above the town. They were only two hundred metres below the reading for the mine entrance that he had cached when they had been with Marco; that difference had been decreasing as the tunnel gradually gained in elevation, an encouraging sign of progress. What they could not measure, because their GPS did not work underground, was how far they had come, and how far they still needed to go. They had been forced to rely on old-fashioned dead reckoning, but after Jack had counted the first five hundred steps, something he had started doing to stave off the claustrophobia, he had given up. He knew they must be within a few hundred metres of the shaft, but even that was a daunting prospect. He desperately needed to stand up, to feel his bones fall into position again and to ease the incessant throbbing of the wound in his leg.

He saw Costas turn over and continue to struggle on, and he resealed his visor and followed. He could see streaks of blue-grey ore in the rock, something he had started to notice a few hundred metres back, a sign that they were coming close to the mountain and its rich seams of ore-bearing rock. A minute or so later, Costas turned back, his head torch flashing blindingly, and Jack saw him looking up.

'We've made it, Jack. We're at the shaft.'

'Thank God for that.'

'I thought we were supposed to thank that chain-smoking devil of the deep.'

'Not yet. He only holds sway in the mine itself.'

Jack staggered out of the fissure and was at last able to stand upright, feeling a rush of relief as he stretched his limbs properly for the first time in more than an hour. Above them was one of the mine's typical stepped shafts, a series of slightly offset circular wells about eight metres high dug one on top of the other, with a narrow ledge at the top of each section to allow another ladder to be perched against a revetment below the next ledge, and so on upwards. It allowed miners to climb hundreds of metres using small ladders, while still being able to raise and lower buckets of ore through the central space. It was also extremely dangerous, as the ladders were precarious wooden affairs with slats that looked hardly thicker than Jack's thumb, and the yawning hole of the shaft beside them became deeper and more deadly as the miners climbed higher. Jack exhaled, peering up at the smudge of light above. Nothing about this mountain was easy.

He glanced again at his altimeter. 'One hundred and forty metres to the mine entrance above us,' he said. 'Are you ready?'

'This place is like playing real-life snakes-and-ladders,' Costas said. 'Let's hope this one really is a ladder, and not a snake.'

'I'm going first. Only one of us on a ladder at any one time, okay?' Jack stepped onto the lower rung of the ladder, feeling it nearly buckle under his weight. The rungs were only wide enough for one of his feet, and he had to remind himself that the ladders had been designed for men who were commonly a foot and a half shorter than he was and less than half his weight. The ladder sagged horribly as he reached the middle rungs, and then he was at the top, standing on an irregular rock-cut ledge perhaps half a metre wide contemplating the next ladder and looking down at Costas as he creaked his way up. This was going to be a hair-raising exercise, but there was no alternative.

He repeated the procedure five times, and then ten, and then twenty, trying not to look down, and then he was one segment away from the top, the roof of the tunnel less than twenty metres above. He waited for Costas to join him, and they went up the final rise together, this time a series of rock-cut steps that brought them out just behind the El Tío god they had seen with Marco that morning. The light had come from the line of dim bulbs stretching in from the entrance; outside it was pitch dark, and peering through the tunnel Jack could see the brilliance of the stars as he had the night before. He snapped up his visor and breathed in the night air, relieved beyond measure to have finished that ordeal, but knowing that he could not relax yet with the biggest challenge still ahead of them.

He glanced at his watch: 12.20 p.m., only twenty minutes late. Juan suddenly appeared beside them, his face beset with anxiety. '*Mi amigo Pedro,*' he said. 'Have you heard?'

Jack nodded, putting his hand on Juan's arm. 'Marco sent word to us. How many men?'

'Three,' Juan said, holding up his fingers. 'One older, two ugly men, bad people.'

'Armed?' Jack said, lifting his fleece and showing the holster beneath.

'*Sí,*' Juan said. 'Like that.'

'How long ago?'

Juan glanced outside at the stars. 'Three hours, when I hid from them and they took Pedro, and I sent word to Marco.'

Costas looked at Jack. 'So they've been down there three hours?' He turned to Juan, pointing at the tunnel. 'How long will it take us to get there, to where we want to go?'

Juan pointed at Jack's watch. 'Thirty minutes, not long.'

Costas looked at Jack again. 'If that's the case, then they haven't found the package, otherwise they'd be back up here by now.' He turned back to Juan. 'What does Pedro know?'

Juan became agitated. 'Pedro knows nothing, *nothing.* He knows only the signs, the fish, he will take them there. But he does not know what I know, where to go at the bottom. They will hurt him, but he can tell them nothing. I am very afraid for him. They are bad men, they will kill him.'

'Okay,' Jack said. 'The sooner we get down there, the better. They'll know we're on our way, and being down there for three hours can only mean they're waiting for us. They took the wrong boy to tell them what they want, but they'll know we're bringing the right one.'

'Is there anyone else here?' Costas asked Juan. 'Any other miners?'

'It is the Festival of Quyllurit'i,' he said. 'The Inca festival of the stars. No miners today.'

Jack unslung his pack, opened it and offered Juan a helmet and breathing mask. Juan turned away, shaking his head, glanced at the El Tío idol and put a wedge of coca leaves into his mouth. Jack shrugged, pursing his lips. 'I tried.'

Juan picked up a wooden stake with cloth soaked in some bituminous substance tightly wrapped around one end. 'Oxygen,' he said, pointing at it.

Jack understood what he meant; he and Costas could test the air quality inside the mountain on their wrist computers, but for the miners it was done the old-fashioned way, with a flame. He wondered how the miners would gauge when to turn back. Normally when a flame flickered out, the oxygen level was already dangerously low, enough to cause blackout. If a miner fainted and remained unconscious for more than a few minutes in such conditions, he would die. They must have some sixth sense, something that told them to go no further. Jack remembered the El Tío figures, and wondered whether they had a practical function as well. If you could not light a cigarette to give as an offering, it was telling you to go no further. If you did go further, you were propitiating a god no longer of protection but of destruction, a god who had told you that the passageway ahead only spelled death. It would have been an age-old wisdom that the boys would have known to ignore at their peril.

Costas unzipped the inside pocket of his trousers and pulled something out, handing it to Jack. It was a small plastic sleeve, inside it a heavily patinated piece of eight that Jack recognised as the one found by Rebecca when she and Costas had gone metal-detecting near the cleft in the rock at the *Schiedam* site. 'Rebecca wanted me to give you this. She wasn't sure whether you'd be happy with me bringing it here, but she felt you might like to have it in the place where it was made, taking it back to its source. She didn't say this, but I think she thought it might bring you good luck.'

Jack took the coin out of the sleeve, weighed it in his hand and remembered his last conversation with Rebecca, wishing it had been different. He clasped his hand round the coin, then put it in his pocket, staring grimly down the passageway ahead. 'Okay. If that's good luck, it's good luck for all three of us. Let's get the job done.'

Twenty minutes later, they were standing beside the third fish symbol that Juan had found, carved into an old stone surface in the side of the passageway. All the miners knew about them, Juan had said, but they left them undamaged out of superstition, and none of the others knew what they meant or where they led.

Jack had suspected that the end of this trail was not going to be straightforward, and Juan's evident apprehension had not eased his mind. Juan had said that the centre of the mountain was so much in danger of collapse that it had been declared a no-go zone, but still the dynamite men went there, risking everything for a few more barrow-loads of ore, risking the lives too of the procession of dust-shrouded boys who took it

301

up the tunnels. Tonight the mine was quiet because of the festival outside, but the dust and gas from the blasting the day before was still there, along with ore in the passageway where the boys had stockpiled it on the way up. The only other people in the mine, somewhere ahead of them, were the three men of the Altamanus and Pedro, but there was little they could do about that now other than to keep as quiet as possible and hope that they saw them first rather than the other way around.

They turned a corner and confronted another El Tío figure, sitting against the wall in front of them at a point where the passage divided. This one was more sinister than the one at the entrance, its face almost entirely devoid of recognisable human features, its body coloured black and deep red, the horns on its head curved upwards and inwards like those of a bull. It had none of the embellishments or offerings of the others, and looked far older. Juan knelt down in front of it, took a knife from his pocket and slashed the blade across his forearm, drawing blood. He pressed his dripping arm against the statue, smearing blood over the torso, and then picked up a handful of dust and rubbed it in the wound to staunch it. Jack realised that the dark and red on the statue was all blood, some of it recently congealed, other parts years old, and that what he had just witnessed was a form of human sacrifice.

Costas stood beside him, his head torch playing on the figure. 'As if they didn't give enough of themselves to this mountain already,' he muttered. 'So, which way now?'

Juan got up and pointed to the right. There was nothing else to indicate that this was the correct direction, no fish carving visible in the wall. Jack realised that the bifurcation in the passage must date from later than the seventeenth century, and that this could happen ahead as well. When those who had brought the treasure down here marked their route with their signs, this had been the sole passageway and they had only needed to make their mark at regular intervals; now, though, after much more tunnelling, the lengths between the marks would include points such as this one where later workings had added other tunnels going off to either side. It meant that they were now utterly reliant on Juan to know which was the correct route, and to lead them forward. What happened when Juan decided that he could go no further, when the god of the underworld finally stopped him in his tracks, was something that had not yet entered Jack's calculus.

He suddenly felt faint, and swayed slightly, clutching at the wall. It passed as quickly as it had come, but it was a warning sign. He checked the air quality reading on his computer. An oxygen-deficient atmosphere was considered anything below 19.5 per cent, and his computer was flashing an amber warning. Combined with the reduced pressure at altitude, meaning that there was less gas overall, they would already be within the danger zone, and he also had to factor in his own reduced performance as a result of blood loss and exhaustion from the events of two days ago. He reached into the left pocket of his trousers, pulled out one of the sachets of energy gel that he had put there and tore it open, quickly raising his visor and squeezing it into his mouth. The visor had only been open momentarily, but it had been enough for him to take a suffocating lungful of the dust outside, and he coughed and retched as he struggled to swallow the gel. He leaned back against the side of the tunnel, swallowing hard to get rid of the cloying taste of the dust, and pushed one of the hydration tubes forward through his helmet so that he could drink from it. He tried to relax, to control his breathing, to keep from hyperventilating. He knew that from now on he was going to have to be extra careful.

They rounded a corner, and Costas stopped beside a small wooden crate covered in dust lying against the side of the passageway. He knelt down and opened it, revealing a stack of red sticks and coils of fuse. 'Dynamite,' he said, taking out one of the sticks and holding it up. 'Good old-fashioned dynamite. No electronic fuses, no fancy timers, just a wick and a match.'

'Now is *not* the time to be playing with explosives,' Jack said. 'The last time you did that, you finally used up our nine lives. Yours, and mine.'

Costas thought for a moment, then took out two more sticks and shoved them into his trouser pocket. 'I just have a gut feeling that these might come in useful. Trouble is, the one bit of kit I don't have is a lighter.'

'Juan will have one. To light the cigarettes for El Tío.'

Costas looked at Juan, held up the stick of dynamite and made the motion of a lighter under the wick. 'Juan, can I borrow your lighter, *por favor?*'

Juan looked at him in consternation, the flame of his torch flickering perilously close to the crate, Jack thought. Then he glanced down the passageway and up it again, and made a sideways motion with his hand, shaking his head. 'No, no, señor, it is too dangerous. The dynamite men ran away and left these here because the mountain is falling in ahead of us. It is *too* dangerous.'

Costas put out his hand. 'It's for your friend Pedro. To rescue him, to frighten the men. They will be scared of dynamite.'

Juan pursed his lips, shaking his head, but he reached into his pocket, handing over a Zippo lighter. '*Gracias*,' Costas said, slipping the lighter in his other pocket. 'I'll return it.'

'I'm with Juan on that one,' Jack said. 'I think we've come to the part of the mountain where the honeycomb of tunnels is halfway to collapse. Throwing a stick of dynamite into that could be bringing down the roof on our heads big-time.'

'Let's hope it doesn't come to that,' Costas said.

They crouched through another steep section of passageway into a completely different, cavernous space, dropping down over a rocky scree at least twenty metres to the bottom, where Jack saw his beam reflect off a pool of water. The cavern had clearly been formed from the collapse of numerous tunnels in the bedrock above, revealing rich seams of blue-grey ore all around. He could see why the dynamite men had come down here, the seduction of the place for them, but he could also see the danger. On the far side of the chamber above the pool was an extraordinary image of El Tío, this time not a model made of papier mâché but a huge bas-relief carved in the rock, showing only the horns and the rough outline of the face. It looked old, perhaps as old as the first Inca who had come to mine here before the Spanish arrived, and was surely the origin of the El Tío cult, a banshee of the depths standing sentinel at the mouth of hell itself. It must have terrified the first Spanish who saw it, and made them feel as they mined and blasted the mountain that they were constantly knocking on the door of the devil himself, tempting fate with every new seam they opened up. Juan must have seen it many times as he pushed barrows of ore up from this place, but it was horrifying him now, and he stood back against the wall of the passage, eyes wide and skin ashen beneath the pall of dust.

Jack's heart sank as he panned his torch around the cavern. The collapse of the tunnels and the blasting had obscured the passage they had been following and revealed numerous alternatives, tunnels whose shattered entrances could be seen extending into the rock all around the edges of the cavern. The water at the bottom meant that what they were looking for must surely be here somewhere; those who had concealed the package in the seventeenth century would not have been able to take it beneath the water table. With the mass of rubble filling the base of the cavern, it could be buried beneath tons of rock. They might have reached the end of the road, and yet there was still no sign of the three men and the little boy who they knew were down here somewhere.

There was a low rumble in the mountain, and the ground shook, sending small cascades of rock from the ceiling and a shimmer through the dust in the air. 'Not dynamite,' Costas said quietly, keeping stock still as he waited for more. 'Natural forces.'

'El Tío,' Juan said, his voice wavering. '*El Tío.*' His torch spluttered and nearly went out, and he lurched forward, swaying slightly. He turned and began to make his way back up the passageway, his face contorted with fear, shoving a fresh wedge of leaves into his mouth and chewing frantically. He squeezed past Costas, and made his way towards Jack. The torch spluttered again, and Jack slipped and nearly fell, cursing. His exhaustion was catching up with him, and in a flash his frustration boiled over. He grabbed Juan by the shoulders, pressing him against the side of the tunnel.

'Where is it?' he said. *'Dónde está?'*

For a moment he remained there, his body taut, and then he fell back against the opposite side of the tunnel, shocked at what he had done. Juan stared at him impassively, as if resigned to his fate, the same look that his ancestors must have given the Europeans who drove them mercilessly day after day to extract and carry the ore from these tunnels. Jack had treated him no differently. For a moment he felt like taking out the piece of eight that Costas had given him and tossing it into the bowels of the mountain, then turning back to follow Juan and leave this place forever.

The boy spat out a stream of coca juice, wiped his mouth with the back of his hand, then picked up the torch from where he had dropped it. Jack held out his hand. 'I'm sorry. *Lo siento. Gracias.*' His voice sounded hoarse, hollow. The boy looked at the proffered hand in silence, then pointed down the rock-strewn passage in front of them, to the place where the water was visible below the carved image. He made a gesture of someone diving and coming up again, and pointed down at the water. Then he turned and scrambled up the tunnel out of sight.

Costas had been edging ahead and turned round to see what was going on, looking at Jack. 'You okay?'

Jack put his hands on his knees, leaning back against the rock. 'Just give me a moment.' He shut his eyes, and tried to steady his breathing. Since heading for this mountain, he had nearly lost his cool with his daughter, the person he loved more than anyone else in the world, and now he had frightened a teenage boy. 'We've lost Juan. He's taken off back up the tunnel. I don't think we'll see him again, and I don't blame him.'

'Maybe I shouldn't have taken his lighter. Maybe he needed it to placate the god.'

'I know where the treasure is. He showed me just now.'

'I didn't hear him say anything.'

'He pointed and gestured. I'm sure he meant in the water, and out the other side. It must be a sump.'

Costas aimed his torch at the water, seeing the reflection of the carved image above it. 'Looks like the entrance to the underworld.'

'Thought you didn't believe in that stuff.'

'Down here, I don't know what to believe any more.'

Jack caught up with him and they both edged forward, making their way around boulders and jumbles of rock, listening intently for any further signs of imminent collapse. Jack felt as if they were walking through a latticework of rock stretched across a giant sinkhole, liable to be swept down and crushed at any moment. They were only metres away from the pool, and it looked like liquid jet, its surface impenetrable to light. Across the pool to the left was another sump, possibly part of the same underwater cavern, but it was definitely the one ahead of them that Juan had pointed towards. Jack eased off his backpack, sensing another presence. *Something was not right.*

Suddenly there was a violent commotion beside him. An arm wrapped around his throat and he felt a muzzle pressed against his neck, then a voice snarled into his ear, one from his nightmares, of chains and torture and the rushing fall into the abyss.

'Jack Howard. We meet again.'

22

Jack stared at the man who had spoken, astonished. 'Hernandes,' he said. 'How the hell can you be here? You went down with that boat in the Caribbean.'

The man affected a smile, took off his gloves and pulled up the dust mask that had been dangling from his neck. The two men who were with him remained as they were, one with his pistol against Jack's neck and the other behind Costas. 'You are forgiven for not being observant. You were, after all, wearing a blindfold at the time, and trussed up in the hold of the vessel. I took a Zodiac back to the island soon after the boat left. A pressing matter had come up, and I arranged for you to be looked after on your arrival in Colombia by these two colleagues of mine. As it happened, the weather proved more of an adversary than our captain had imagined. Much more extraordinary is that you survived.'

'Nothing extraordinary about it,' Costas said, pushing back

against the man holding a pistol to his head. 'You don't know Jack Howard.'

'Oh, but I do. I know he has a daughter, Rebecca, whom he adores. And friends such as you that he unaccountably admires. Jack Howard has his weaknesses.'

Hernandes nodded, and the two men who were holding them pulled off their backpacks and holsters and began to frisk them, the one behind Costas producing the dynamite from his pocket and tossing it aside. 'Planning to start a small war, were we?' Hernandes sneered.

'Seeing you, I don't think any weapons will be needed at all,' Costas said.

Hernandes nodded again, and the man behind Costas punched him hard in the kidneys, pulling his arms back as he doubled over and putting a cable tie around his wrists. 'I think we have little need of you, other than as a hostage. It is Dr Howard I want to talk to.'

'Where is the boy?' Jack said. 'You and I have nothing to talk about until you show him to me.'

'He has proved most helpful,' Hernandes said. 'You are probably wondering how I come to be here. It was easy enough picking up your trail once we realised that you had somehow survived the storm. Your Embraer jet flying from Jamaica to Colombia was the first clue, and monitoring air-traffic control told us that your destination from there was Bolivia. Once you had arrived and set off on the road from the airport, and we could then see your route into the moun-tains, I knew that there could only be one plausible destination, one that would have been obvious for someone seeking to hide something in the seventeenth century as well. Where better to conceal what he was carrying than in the place where it might confront evil itself, at one of the entrances to the underworld. We had followed your Embraer to Bolivia by private aircraft, and then took a helicopter to Potosi to be here ahead of you, arriving late yesterday. Our contact here had already located a boy who might take us into the mine, who knew it intimately. And here we are.'

Hernandes nodded again, and the man holding the pistol to Jack's neck reached out with his other hand and pulled Pedro from behind a rock. He was badly bruised around one eye, and had clearly been crying. Jack tried to keep his cool, knowing that he had to play for time, to seek the best opportunity to strike back. He turned to Hernandes. 'Release the boy, and I'll give you what you want.'

'And what would that be?'

'The greatest lost treasure of Christendom. The Holy Chalice, the relic sought by your organisation since the time of the Roman Empire. A treasure that I know lies within metres of us now, but that you will need me to find.'

'And how is that?'

Jack gestured towards the pool. 'Because only I have the equipment and the skill to reach it.'

Hernandes said nothing for a moment, then nodded slowly. 'The boy can go. But if you don't surface from that water holding what I want, my man here will blow a very large hole in your friend Costas's head.'

'Let me talk to the boy.'

Hernandes nodded again, and Jack crouched down in front of him. 'Pedro, do you understand English?'

'*Sí, señor.*'

311

'You must go to your friend Juan, who is waiting for you outside the mine. You must go with him far away, running as fast as you can, away from this mountain. Do you understand?'

'*Sí, señor.* I understand. Juan and I must go as far as we can, running away.'

'Good. Go now.'

Pedro hurried up the passageway out of sight, and Jack turned to confront Hernandes again. 'All right. I have a miniature air cylinder for this helmet in my backpack. You will need to let me get at it.'

Hernandes stepped back, and Jack leaned over his backpack, extracted the cylinder and screwed the valve into the aperture below the visor. The helmet had a built-in regulator, and the cylinder would allow perhaps ten minutes of air, no more. He opened the valve to test it, hearing it hiss as he sucked on the mouthpiece. He looked over at Hernandes. 'I'll need the other one too, the one my friend is carrying in his pack. This one alone will not give me enough air.'

Hernandes grunted, and the man holding Costas kicked the pack forward. As Jack reached over towards Costas, their eyes made momentary contact and he nodded almost imperceptibly to the right, towards the far side of the pool, hoping that Costas would catch his meaning. Jack had noticed that there might be another exit point from the sump on that side, one that he might conceivably reach out of sight once he had gone in and then use to surface back in the cavern unexpectedly. Costas would have guessed that Jack didn't want the second cylinder because he was planning a longer dive. A few weeks earlier, Jack had watched him use the miniature cylinder to demonstrate to a class at IMU the effect of cracking open a diving tank when full, showing how shockingly loud it could be. And Costas had lightning-quick reflexes, the ability to respond to a diversion faster than anyone else Jack had come across. He just prayed that after all these years he knew his friend well enough to gauge what he was thinking, that they were both fine-tuned to the smallest signs in each other's demeanour and behaviour, an intimacy of knowledge that came from being divers together and depending on each other for survival.

Jack shoved the second cylinder into his side pocket and walked down to the water's edge, looking into it but seeing only the reflection of the carving of the god, and his own image. He stepped in, advancing carefully as the bottom sloped down, and then switched his torch to high beam, panning it round as he slipped under the surface. Close to the bottom he could see rocks, a continuation of the path that had once been the final few metres of the tunnel they had been following from the mine entrance. The water was filled with a dark haze that he realised must be minerals that had leached out from the surrounding ore. He was swimming in silver, literally immersed in the essence of the place, in what had driven so many to come here and work themselves to death. It was a peculiar, unnerving sensation, not something that made him feel good. He just wanted to find what they had come for, and to make it with Costas out of the mountain alive.

His regulator hissed and the bubbles from the exhaust rose over the front of his visor. The system had been designed for exactly this purpose, to allow IMU teams exploring caves a few minutes of air to get through a sump; he just had to hope that he had interpreted Juan's gesture correctly and that the passage came up abruptly on the other side. Reaching his arms ahead, he felt an overhang and pulled himself under it. Whoever had come through here with that precious package three hundred and thirty years ago had been small and lithe, better able to get through the opening than him.

He was completely under the overhang now, but there was no clear way forward. The passage had been blocked; that same person had sealed it up with stones after coming back out. He felt along it and realised that he might be able to prise them out. He began pulling at one in the centre, loosening it and dragging it away, and then the others came away more easily. He realised that he had been breathing hard and would be depleting his air supply. His plan depended on the other cylinder remaining unused, having the full force of its pressure available for when he resurfaced. He prayed that this was it, that the place he was seeking was just beyond.

He pulled himself through, breaking surface moments later. Beyond the sump there was no continuation of the tunnel, only a solid wall of rock. The miners who had come this far had clearly reached the end of the seam, and had abandoned the place without widening the passage any further. With that image of the god outside putting off all who ventured into the cavern from trying to go any further, this would have been a perfect place to hide a treasure. He could see how the miners to whom Father Vieira ministered might have led him here, and helped him seal up a treasure that would be doubly secure under the dreaded gaze of their god.

And then he saw it. Sitting in a hacked-out niche was an ancient leather bag, looking almost fossilised, the folds in the leather cracked and blackened. He put down his torch and picked up the bag, feeling the weight, seeing the shape. There was only one thing he wanted now, the confirmation, and he saw it as soon as he turned the bag around: the outline of a Christian fish incised on the leather with the letters alpha and omega on either side. *He had found it.* He thought of where this package had been, of the Roman soldier Proselius in the catacombs, of Samuel Pepys in Tangier, of Port Royal, and of the baleful shadow of the Inquisition hanging over it, something that today he would do everything he could to see extinguished once and for all.

He had no time to ponder any more, just to act. He had to hope that the overhang that had been blocked up at this end would be open at the other side of the cavern, that he would be able to get through while he still had some air left. He panned his torch in that direction, getting a sense of the route, and then left it wedged in a cleft beneath the niche, hoping that Hernandes would see the smudge of light through the water and assume that he was still there. He took the leather bag with him, holding it close to his chest with one hand while he felt his way forward with the other. The torch was still giving enough light to see the rock around him, and when he reached the far side of the cavern he dropped down, praying that he had been right. He saw light coming through, a glow that could only come from the torches of the men in the cavern. He dropped down further, seeing that he would have no trouble getting through. *This could work.*

He quickly found a place to leave the bag, moving some stones around to keep it secure, and then hovered under the overhang, making sure that his exhaust bubbles rose out of sight of the chamber. He was only about three metres deep, but it was still enough for an ascent with full lungs to cause an embolism, so he would need to expel as much air as he could before doing so. He would need to do that under the overhang, and hope that the residual volume still in his lungs would give him enough time to swim underwater to the edge of the pool without blacking out, holding the second cylinder in his hands ready to crack once he hit the surface. After that, it was in the lap of the gods. He just hoped that Costas would be able to react in time. This would be their only chance, and what happened in those first few seconds would be critical to whether they lived or died.

He calmed himself as much as he could, taking slow breaths, already sensing the cylinder emptying. He brought out the second cylinder, holding it ready in his left hand, and then took five deep breaths before exhaling hard and spitting out the mouthpiece. He swam forward slowly from under the overhang, using rocks on the bottom to pull himself along, taking care not to move too quickly and cause ripples. The reflection of lights on the surface of the water helped him to see the bottom more clearly. After about a minute he reached a point where it began to slope up, and he looked to the surface, seeing that he was in standing depth. He needed to be as close as possible to the edge of the pool, and yet not risk being seen. He was feeling the need to breathe now, an urgency that normally he would have tolerated for longer but that now, in his depleted state from inhaling the poor air in the mine, might push him quickly to blackout. He saw a cleft in the rock, and drew his feet slowly up to it, giving him a secure hold for when he made his move. He held the cylinder tightly with his left hand and clasped his right hand around the knob of the valve, staring at it, his mind blank. It was now or never.

He erupted to the surface, twisted the knob hard anti-clockwise and threw the cylinder into the chamber towards the men, flinching at the deafening shriek as the air escaped. The next few seconds seemed to happen in slow motion. Costas slammed his elbow into the man behind him, and then slipped down to reach the pistol that fell from his hand. He fired blindly, his hands still tied behind him, but his first round hit the man in the head and took him down immediately, and one of the others hit the second man in the shoulder and knocked him back into the rocks. At the same time, Jack surged out of the water and leapt on Hernandes, bringing him to the floor just as the man in the rocks fired in his direction. He reached for the holster containing Hernandes's Beretta and fired as fast as he could in the direction of the man, seeing eruptions of blood as the bullets found their mark. Then he thrust the muzzle into Hernandes's throat, putting his other arm in a half-nelson around the man's neck.

He looked over at Costas, who was on the ground, pushing his helmet back into place, but not visibly harmed. 'You okay?'

'Roger that,' Costas replied. 'Apart from a slight ringing in the ears. Nice one, by the way. Your little diversion.'

'Our two friends?'

'Both down. Permanently.'

'Is your binding off?'

'Just done it. Some good sharp rocks in this place. Jack, we need to get out of here. That little fireworks display will have shaken this place up a bit and might not go down too well with old Smokey the Bandit. I think he might be about to wreak his vengeance. Who knows how much more it will take for the mine to collapse.'

As if on cue, an ominous rumble came up from the depths of the mountain. Suddenly the ground shook violently and Hernandes leapt up, catching Jack off guard but also losing his balance, slipping and falling into the scree beside the path. A massive slab of rock disengaged from the roof and plummeted down, shattering into boulder-sized chunks as it hit the ground. One of them fell with a sickening crash on Hernandes's legs, and he howled in pain. 'My legs!' he screamed, his arms flailing. 'Get me out of here!'

Jack ignored him, and went back to the edge of the water. 'I've got to get something.'

'Make it quick, Jack,' Costas said. 'That isn't the last we'll hear from Smokey. I've got a bad feeling about this place.'

Jack slid into the water, his headlamp still on and swam back towards the overhang. He held his breath and dived down, seeing the bag where he had left it among the rocks, mesmerised by the image of it in the light, thinking of the countless adventurers and romantics who had dreamed of such a moment. He thought too of where such artefacts should be, and how sometimes they were best left undisturbed. This time, though, was different. The evil in this mountain could not be allowed to cast a shadow on it any more; not some supernatural evil, but the evil that men do, the evil that was the real monster lurking in the darkness of such places where human endeavour had gone so badly wrong.

Moments later he was out of the water, and the package was securely in his bag. Hernandes was delirious with pain, and

Jack had no interest in showing him what he had found. He had no wish to exult in the discovery, or show that he had won the day. He wanted the man and everything he represented extinguished as soon as possible, but not before he had told him why. He put on his backpack, and watched Costas do the same and then pick up the three sticks of dynamite.

'Good to go, Jack?'

Jack swivelled around to show him the new bulge in his own backpack. 'Got what we came for. We're done here.'

Costas took out the lighter he had borrowed from Juan. 'I think it might be time to light this place up.'

Jack nodded grimly. 'And to finish the job I thought I'd finished in the Caribbean Sea two days ago.'

'You will never destroy the Altamanus,' Hernandes snarled. 'We will come back, always.'

'Right now, I don't care about that,' Jack said. 'What I do care about is ridding the world of anyone who kidnaps and tortures children. All the high ideals of your organisation are bogus. The Inquisition was no more than a front for sadists and psychopaths. And I haven't forgotten that you threatened my daughter and my friends. Nobody gets away with that.' He turned to Costas. 'Over to you.'

Costas lit all three sticks of dynamite at once, and tossed them into the rocks out of reach of Hernandes, who shouted with rage, flailing his arms about and trying to reach them, to no avail. Costas looked at Jack. 'Time to go.'

'Roger that.'

They ran up the passageway, out of the cavern and past the blood-soaked El Tío, then as fast as they could towards the entrance to the mine. The detonations when they came were like a bellow from the god himself, resonating through the tunnels and making the ground shake. Seconds later, they were enveloped in the dust cloud that came up the passageway, but they kept moving, knowing that they were only minutes from the entrance. Then Jack felt something else: not the vibration of a blast, but a deeper shuddering, as if the whole mountain were shaking. The sound when it came was not a bellow, but a roar.

They passed out of the entrance and on to the plateau just in time to avoid the second surge, a huge eruption of dust that burst out as the centre of the mountain collapsed in on itself. They continued to run until they were out of the danger zone, and then Jack turned back to watch, trying to catch his breath, feeling the precious package safe in his bag. Nobody would be going into that place ever again, neither he and Costas nor Juan and Pedro, nor any of the countless others whose lives had been blighted by serving the insatiable greed that had first drawn men to the mountain.

Costas came alongside him, and they stripped off their gear together, panting hard, saying nothing. Jack put his hand on Costas's shoulder and felt an enormous wave of relief course through him. It was over.

They were free.

23

Two days later, in the early morning, Jack stood on a grassy patch beside a high mountain pass that led from Potosi into the Bolivian Andes. The boy who had guided him sat beside his llama, chewing on coca leaves while he fed grain to the animal from a small sack. Jack did not feel thirsty or hungry, a side effect he knew of the altitude, but he also felt that in this rarefied place he was beyond the need to cater for bodily needs, that there was something else giving him the strength to press on. He knew the thin air would be playing tricks with his senses, heightening the sound of the llama's hooves on the stones, the smell of thyme on the mountain slopes, the biting cold of the wind, but to Jack that seemed right, as if here at the top of the world it was the senses rather than intellect that should shape his thoughts.

He pulled the woven Inca cape he was wearing closer around him, and stared down at the yawning chasm of the valley and the jagged peaks beyond, a snow-capped fringe that seemed to reach up beyond the atmosphere itself. He could see why this place had been so detested by the Conquistadors, intent only on gold and silver that was not to be found here, but was so beguiling to those who had come to the New World to find purity and light, men such as Father Vieira of Portugal, who had led his small flock from the clutches of the Inquisition to found a place where the persecution that they and their ancestors had endured might become a thing of the past.

The boy got up, gesturing for them to move on, and Jack slung his trusty old khaki bag over his shoulder and continued trudging up the narrow path behind the llama. He felt like a penitent, wounded and scarred from his trials of the last few days, on a pilgrimage to a place of healing. They passed above a thin veil of mist into the clouds, and he was no longer able to see the valley below. The path narrowed even further, skirting a precipitous rocky slope to the left and a drop-off to the right, and then they rounded a corner and entered a wide space of meadows and cultivated terraces set back into the mountainside. In the centre was a cluster of low-roofed buildings of stone and mud brick surrounded by paddocks and byres filled with stacks of straw. The boy gestured towards the larger of the buildings, and then led his llama off to join others in one of the paddocks, waving at another boy who was tending them.

Jack paused for a moment, taking in the view, then crossed a mountain stream that ran through the terraces and made his way towards the buildings, passing several other people working the crops and taking straw to the byres. There were

Inca among them, but one woman looked more European than Andean, with striking blue eyes and a complexion that could have been Mediterranean, possibly Spanish or Portuguese. She smiled as he passed, pointing up towards the main building, and Jack nodded in acknowledgement. He knew that he was expected; the boy whom Marco had sent earlier with the message was probably the other one tending the flock.

He reached the entrance to the largest building, a single-storey farmstead of several rooms with a wide patio in front. The air was filled with the smell of llamas and coffee, of woodsmoke and cooking. Before Jack could knock, a man came out, smiling, and offered him a mug of steaming coffee.

'Jack. Very good to see you. Have this before we talk.'

Jack was not at all disarmed by the familiarity, despite the man being someone he had never seen before, and he accepted the drink gratefully, shaking the proffered hand as he did so. The man was of medium height, with a beard and cropped dark hair, and wore a distinctive metal cross over his sweater. Like the woman, he was clearly of European origin, though he seemed completely at one with this place. He gestured at Jack to sit down on a simple wooden bench under the patio. Jack did so, taking off his bag and placing it beside him, and the man sat down as well. Together they looked out over the valley while Jack drank his coffee. It tasted of this place, of the animals and the smell of the air, and he felt instantly refreshed. 'Thank you,' he said. 'That was much needed.'

'We always add a little something, a herbal infusion to help with the altitude. The same that your guide will have been chewing.'

'I'm grateful to you for sending him. I'd never have found this place otherwise.'

'I should introduce myself. Father Francisco Pereira. But you know who I am, of course. I'm the current head of this community.'

Jack put his hand on the mud-brick wall behind him. 'These buildings are old,' he said. 'Eighteenth, perhaps early nineteenth century?'

Father Pereira nodded. 'The mud brick has been renewed many times, but the stone foundations date from the time when the children and grandchildren of Father Vieira's followers founded this place in 1743. They had been wandering through these mountains for years, the survivors of the massacre of the original community by the soldiers of the Inquisition, seeking a place where they could be self-sufficient and safe. We've been here ever since, the descendants of those original few, all of us the result of many generations of intermarriage with the local Inca.'

'Hence your toleration of the altitude,' Jack said.

'And our ability to survive on very little, on the basics of life.'

Jack gestured at the building again. 'You have no church?'

Father Pereira opened his arms expansively at the view. 'When you have all this, who has need of a church?'

Jack nodded at the cross on his chest, a crude conjoining of two ancient metal spear points. 'I've heard about that.'

'From Maria de Montijo? It is another great treasure, the cross she found in the catacombs that we believe is the original made by the Roman legionary Proselius. The story of Proselius giving his cross to the Christian woman whom he could not save has been passed down through the generations since he arrived among our ancestors in Spain in the third century. He had made it from two broken spears on the battlefield where he had his first vision of God. Maria brought this to us when she began to fear that the Altamanus were on her trail, and now it will be worn by the head of our community always.'

Jack peered closely at it. 'Those are Roman pilum points, undoubtedly. And of the right period.' He sat back again. 'I know that Maria feels very much a part of your community.'

'Everyone is part of this community who is descended from the Christian Jews who gave protection to Proselius and his precious cargo. That includes you, Jack.'

'I am honoured.'

'The honour is ours. You have carried on the legacy of those countless generations, and have saved the greatest treasure of Christendom from the forces of darkness.'

'What do you think will become of the Altamanus?'

Father Pereira pursed his lips. 'They will not go away. You have cut off one head of the monster, but there are more. The monster may lie dormant for a while, licking its wounds, perhaps even for generations. We are used to it. We have been confronting the Altamanus since the time of the Roman Empire. With their greatest prize now so far from their grasp, their power will diminish. But we will always be on our guard.'

Jack opened his bag and took out the swaddled package inside. 'My bag went through a world war before I owned it and since then has carried some pretty amazing artefacts, but I think this one takes the cake.' He handed the package over

325

to Father Pereira, who took it reverentially and placed it on his lap. The leather had solidified with age, but in so doing it preserved the shape of what lay inside. 'Will you open it?' Jack asked quietly.

Father Pereira was suddenly overcome by emotion, and staunched his tears with the back of one hand. 'No,' he said eventually, clearing his throat. 'No. This is the wrapping put on by Proselius himself, and we are sworn not to remove it until peace reigns on earth.'

'Well,' Jack said, leaning forward and giving him a piercing look. 'I've cast my archaeologist's eye over it and I can give you a few hints. What's inside is definitely pottery, not metal or glass. It's obvious from the weight. So we can get rid once and for all of the idea that the Holy Grail was some kind of chalice. From the likely shape, I'd say this is the kind of basic pottery drinking bowl that you'd expect to see in a modest Jerusalem household of the early Roman Imperial period. When I realised that after I first picked it up in the mine shaft, I became convinced that it could be genuine. You can see many examples of these simple cups from Judaea in archaeo-logical museums around the world. This is the drinking cup of the common people at the time of Jesus.'

'As it should be,' Father Pereira said. 'The idea of the chalice was a medieval fantasy. That is what makes this an even greater treasure.' He lifted the object in his hands, and then turned to Jack. 'Why are you doing this? Why are you entrusting this cup to us? It could be the centrepiece of your museum, and the greatest story of archaeological discovery ever told. It would assure your name and that of your team of the highest place in the annals of archaeology.'

Jack pondered his response, looking at the scene of tranquillity in front of him, at the llamas jangling their bells in the distance and the women carrying baskets in from the terraces. 'The truth is, some artefacts are best not displayed in museums, and some stories of discovery are best left untold,' he replied at last. 'You yourself said it. The darkness that drove the Inquisition is still there. To reveal the treasure now would provide a beacon of hope for many, yes, but it could also unleash dark forces on both sides, those who would use it as the Crusaders used the cross to prosecute holy war, and others who would start wars of their own to see it destroyed. The Inquisition of the seventeenth century may never rise again, but even worse has happened in recent time than the horrors of those years. The history of the last century has shown that.'

'It will assuredly be safe here,' Father Pereira said, pointing up at the jagged snow-capped peak behind him. 'For the Inca this mountain is an *apu*, a protective spirit. It is one reason why our community is immune from any outside interference; the mountain spirit is seen as protecting us, and we in turn are its guardians. No government troops have ever come here, and the guerrillas steer well clear. At the top of the mountain is a sacred cave where the *apu* resides, a place that the Inca call the gateway to heaven. This package will go there, and will be safe until the time is right to reveal it.'

Jack smiled. 'I'm glad to hear it. I couldn't think of a better outcome. It's been fantastic to reach the end of the trail, but sometimes it's best for the world if the mystery remains.'

Father Pereira looked at him quizzically. 'You are a dreamer, Jack. Most of us dream only at night, and our dreams are as dust in the mornings. But those who dream during the day live out their dreams as reality: the visionaries and the romantics, the poets and the explorers. You are one of those, and we're grateful to you for it.'

Jack got up, slung his bag over his shoulder and reached out to shake Father Pereira's hand. He stepped off the patio, and then turned back. 'One final question,' he said. 'Did Father Vieira ever find his promised land?'

The other man smiled. 'Does Jack Howard ever find the treasure at the end of his quest?'

Jack thought for a moment, then gestured at the swaddled shape in Father Pereira's hands. 'Not always,' he said. 'Often the treasure is in the quest itself, in the companionship and the revelation, in the danger and the adventure. But sometimes, just sometimes, he does.'

He turned down the path, waving at the boy with the llama who was coming up to join him. This place was as close to El Dorado as Father Vieira could ever have envisaged, and Jack felt for a moment like casting his bag aside and lying down in the meadow, soaking up the place, allowing his dreams to find their final resolution far above the yearnings that drove men to seek new horizons and new treasures in the world below. But he was not ready for that yet, and his own home awaited him, his friends and his family. It was time to go.

Epilogue

Three days later, Jack stood near the cliff edge above Kynance Cove in Cornwall, contemplating the broad sweep of the bay from Lizard Point to the craggy headland of the Rill to the north-west. It was a beautiful day, as near to dead calm as they could hope for in October, perfect for the dive they had planned to do beneath the waters of the cove below him. He could see as far as Land's End some eighteen nautical miles to the west, and beyond that to the open ocean that continued uninterrupted for over three thousand miles to the Caribbean and the coast of South America.

It was the same vista he had contemplated only two weeks before from the cleft in the rock above the cannon site, holding the silver Spanish coin that had sparked their extraordinary quest. Yet here it was different, less constricted. Numerous ships had been wrecked in the cove below and still more on the jagged rocks beyond the end of the peninsula, but the ripples of the tidal stream that he could see off the point would always have given some hope, some possibility for ships blown in from the west of rounding the peninsula and finding safe haven. And here, instead of just seeing storm and wreck, he also saw ships striking out west, close-hauled and beating out to sea or with the full force of an easterly behind them, among them the ships of his own ancestors that had swept round the point with the ebbing tide, sailing off towards the horizon for duty and glory and fortune.

As he continued staring, time seemed to contract. A seagull swept by, circling and holding in the breeze as it eyed him for food, and then dropped down to join the others on the rocks that rose from the waters below. Further offshore, a seal popped up, scanning the cove, and a brightly coloured fishing boat stopped to haul in a crab pot, flashing and sparkling as it bobbed in the sea. In his mind's eye, Jack saw the successive waves of history that had passed over these waters, flashing by as if in fast motion: the simple rowed boats of prehistory, the broad-beamed, square-rigged ships of the Phoenicians and the Romans, the high-sterned carracks and galleons of the Age of Discovery, and the ships of the seventeenth century that had so gripped them over the past weeks: the *Schiedam* with her cargo of guns and tools and people from far-off Tangier, and from even further away, from the Indies West and East, the pirate ship that might lie below them today, carrying an unimaginable treasure out of the mists of legend into real history, into the present day.

He picked up his mask and fins and shifted his weight belt on his shoulder. He had already made one trip down the steep path to the cove carrying his scuba rig, and now he would be joining the others with the remainder of his equipment. His wetsuit was only half on, keeping his upper body cool in the breeze, but even so he was warming up and looking forward to getting in the water. He reached the final flight of rock-cut steps and then was beside the sea, negotiating the rocks on the foreshore and walking out across the sand.

The rock in the cove was serpentine, a beautiful variety unique to the Lizard peninsula, maroon and green and grey, run through with contrasting seams. He paused to touch an outcrop, the rock silky smooth where it had been polished by the sea, the streaks of red deep and vibrant where it was still wet. When he had first brought Rebecca here nearly ten years before, she had called it Utopia, and she had been right. Kynance Cove was a kind of dream land, an elemental place of rock and sea and sand, and as he followed the sand through a passage in the rock to the further beach, he felt as if he were entering a more elevated place, one where life was distilled to its essence. This was his El Dorado, his Mountain of Silver, where all that mattered to him now were the people ahead of him preparing to dive and the quest that had drawn them all to this place.

The headland that divided the two beaches was itself split off from a further jagged outcrop called Asparagus Island, the space in between forming the second beach; it was intertidal, inundated and swept clean by the sea twice a day. Stepping through the shallow lagoon between the beaches, Jack understood what Rebecca had sensed as a girl, the feeling of entering a place that was pristine and untouched. To his right, the serpentine of the headland was marked by great caves, gouged out by the sea over the millennia, and to his left the huge slab of Asparagus Island was itself split by a fracture line that he could see running at an angle from the cliff to a sheltered corner of the sea below. He walked in that direction, following the line of footprints in the sand, rising over the hump in the middle of the beach and seeing the water in the little cove beyond. Tucked under the lee of the island was their entry point, at the base of the fracture line, and he could see the others there, in various stages of kitting up and preparation for their dive.

He slung his weight belt on the sand and dropped his mask and fins beside his tank. Rebecca and Jeremy were already in the shallows, sitting down to put their fins on, and Costas was sitting on a rock in the tattered remains of his boiler suit, the dismembered elements of a regulator second stage spread out over his lap. 'Got an equipment problem?' Jack said, pulling on the arms of his wetsuit. 'You can always buddy-breathe with me.'

'Nope,' Costas replied, pulling a wrench from his tool belt. 'It's a new bit of kit they finished at the engineering lab while we were away, with a piston bypass to give a greater volume of air. I'm just seeing how it works.'

Jack smiled, shaking his head, and then walked down to the water's edge, seeing that Mike Trethowan was already in the sea some ten metres away, in the shadow of the island, where the fault line went underwater. Jack waved, catching his attention. 'Costas and I won't be long. I can't wait.'

'It's looking good, Jack,' Mike shouted back. 'The vis is great, and there's only a bit of slurp through the tunnel. We should be okay.'

Jack stared at the dark patch that he could see underwater at

the base of the cliff beside Mike, the entrance to the tunnel
that went through to the far side of the island and the open
sea. Above the entrance was an opening, visible now at low
tide, where the water that surged through the tunnel came
out in a blowhole, the 'Devil's Bellows' of local legend. He
remembered the words of a Victorian traveller who had seen
it in full vent: 'an immense chasm, into which, as the tide
rises, the sea rushes with such impetuosity as to force the
water out at an opening above, and the accompanying noise
resembles that of thunder'.

Jack himself had stood on the headland overlooking the
island during heavy seas and experienced the bellows in full
fury, a stupendous sucking and draining sound followed by a
geyser of water that exploded out of the blowhole, spraying
him with flecks of foam and water even though he was more
than fifty metres away. For a diver to venture into the
blowhole in anything other than conditions of dead calm
could spell death, through being thrown against the walls and
crushed by the surge and suck of the current, or being trapped
in the middle, unable to get out either way as the water surged
in and out, a kind of living purgatory that could only end in
drowning. It had happened before, and for many years divers
had shunned the place, knowing that even when the surface
of the sea appeared calm, there might still be enough swell to
create a lethal surge inside the tunnel. To dive there was only
viable after several days of dead calm, which was what had led
Mike to call Jack on the day of his return from Bolivia and
suggest that they organise a dive as soon as possible. It was
exactly what Jack had needed after all they had been through,
and he had relished the chance to return to this place of

cleansing that so encapsulated his love for the sea and for diving.

He pulled up the back zipper of his suit and watched Mike drop underwater with his camera to film the entrance to the tunnel, Jeremy and Rebecca now snorkelling overhead. From here the black maw of the cavern looked like the entrance to the underworld, like the cleft in the lava that he and Costas had explored in the Phlegraean Fields near Naples several years before; for a moment he imagined that the soft slurping of the blowhole was the music of the sirens, or the lyre of Orpheus, as if the god of the underworld were tempting him to leave the paradise of the cove and plunge into his clutches. Today, though, the devil was slumbering, and he knew that they would conquer his lair.

He remembered Mike's excitement on the phone the day before when he had suggested the dive. Mike had been speaking to an old local diver, one of the few remaining from the first generation to explore this coast when aqualungs had become available after the Second World War. The diver had been down the tunnel, the first ever to do so, and had seen a cannon and a pewter plate concreted to the rock, and then had explored the ledges in the cove beyond and discovered a smattering of potsherds, blue-and-white Delftware from Holland of the late seventeenth century. That had convinced Mike that they were on the right track, that the story of the pirate Henry Avery's ship being wrecked in Kynance Cove could only refer to this site; even the pottery fitted, if the stories were true that Avery's last ship in the Caribbean had been a commandeered Dutch vessel.

All they had to hope for now was that the storm of the last

week that had blown them off the *Schiedam* excavation and had been battering this coast all the time they had been away might have shifted the sand from the seabed on the far side of the island, and that as they swam through the tunnel they would see before them the king's ransom in gold and silver from the Mughal fleet and the treasure ships of the Spanish Main that Avery had plundered during his career as a pirate. Jack knew that it would probably remain no more than a dream, a dream of treasure that had sparkled before him all his life, but he also knew that he would be thrilled enough to find a few more pieces of pottery and to see with his own eyes that a wreck really was there. It would open up another page of history for him, and that was all the treasure he needed to keep alive the quest for adventure and discovery that had driven him forward since he had first dived beneath these waters as a boy.

He turned to Costas, smiling as he saw the familiar figure in his boiler suit festooned with tools, the regulator put back together again and hanging from his scuba rig in front of his chest. Jack put on his weight belt and donned his own tank, kneeling on the sand to shift it into position and tighten the straps, and then took Costas's hand to help heave himself back up again. He clipped his hoses into place, and after he and Costas had checked each other's air, they walked towards the water's edge carrying their fins and masks. Moments later, Jack was in the sea, feeling the immense sense of release he always experienced as the water cushioned and enveloped him.

They finned on the surface towards the other three, coming to a stop just as the sand dropped away towards the dark hole that yawned beneath the rock face. Mike had risen to the surface, and filmed them as he spoke. 'Everything looks fine down there. I'll be just behind you.'

'You should go through first,' Jack said. 'This should be your discovery.'

'We don't know if it's just going to be sand yet,' Mike replied. 'Anyway, I want to turn around and film Rebecca and Jeremy entering the tunnel. Don't worry, if there's gold to be seen, I'll be there like a shot.'

'Okay.' Jack turned to Costas. 'You ready for another dark hole in the sea?'

'I'll dive with you anywhere, Jack. You know that. Dark holes and light.'

Jack held his regulator ready. 'Good to go?'

'Good to go.'

They dropped down together, coming to a halt four metres deep at the base of the sandy slope that marked the beginning of the tunnel. Above them the lip of the cavern was fringed with kelp, vivid green in the sunlight, the fronds wafting to and fro with the current. The bellows proper, the aperture for the water spout, could be seen above that, part of the fault line that rose from the tunnel. In front of them, all Jack could see was blackness, a forbidding hole that he knew carried on for another sixty metres or so until it came out at the other side. He took out his torch and switched it on, seeing Costas do the same, and they played the beams around the stark rock walls, smoothed and swept clean of growth by the water that raged through here for much of the time.

He glanced behind, seeing that the other three were underwater too and watching through the cavern entrance, and then he began to swim slowly forward, sensing the darkness closing in behind him. He felt the current push him back, but he finned steadily, knowing that the surge would soon return in the opposite direction. It was easy to see how the tunnel could be a death trap, but he knew they would be safe today. He sank down on the sand, Costas behind him, and then looked up and saw that a crack of light had appeared along the top of the tunnel, showing where the fault in the rock was beginning to open out towards the far side. Ahead of him he saw the light at the end of the tunnel, an opaque glimmer that became clearer as he rose off the sand with the next surge and moved forward again. He no longer needed his torch, and he switched it off, stowing it in his BC pocket. The tunnel had become more like one of the caves in the headland, a sinuous, expanding cavern that opened out into sunlight, and he began to see the first sparkles of light on the water above.

So far he had spotted little evidence that the level of the sand had dropped. But as he rounded the last corner, it fell away dramatically, leaving outcrops of rock and boulders on the seabed exposed. And then he saw it, something that made his heart pound with excitement. Wedged between two boulders was a highly eroded cannon, with another one concreted into a rocky cleft beyond. In the fissures below he could make out blue and white sherds, the same type of pottery that the old diver had described, and further on a large patch of concretion. All of it was devoid of marine life, and had clearly been buried for years. He swam further, beyond the rock walls of the tunnel, and came to the apex of the little cove that formed the far side of the island, a gully some twenty metres across with rock ledges on either side and in the centre a sandy plain that sloped off in the direction of the open sea.

He paused, waiting for Costas and Mike to come alongside. He was elated by the discovery, and because a tunnel that had seemed so forbidding had led them to another place of great beauty, surpassing even the cove they had left behind them. He looked up, squinting against the rays of the sun, and then down again, watching a spider crab shimmy across the gully. The sand was sparkling in the sunlight, but there were no rocks or cannon sticking out of it. He turned round, looking for Rebecca and Jeremy, knowing that archaeological riches could await them in the cracks and crannies of the seabed around the cannon. But as he did so, out of the corner of his eye he saw Mike gesturing from where he had swum ahead on to the sand. Costas grabbed Jack's shoulder, turning him back round, and they both swam forward, dropping down beside Mike to see what he had found.

And then, extraordinarily, it all opened out before them. What had seemed like sunlight sparkling off sand was a mass of coins, thousands of them, covering the seabed as far as Jack could see. The storm had stripped away the mobile sand and exposed a more compacted layer, one that had cushioned the coins on its surface and prevented them from working their way deeper into the sediment.

It was an incredible sight, like nothing Jack had ever seen before. He reached down and scooped up a handful of coins, feeling their weight. The silver coins were discoloured and patinated, but the gold ones were immaculate, most of them as sharp as they had been the day they were minted. They included Mughal issues of the Indian emperor Aurangzeb –

exactly what Henry Avery and his gang had plundered from the Mughal fleet in the Indian Ocean – but Jack could also see Spanish cobs, hundreds of them, both silver pieces of eight and gold escudos. He caught Mike's attention, but an okay sign seemed wholly inadequate, and they stared at each other in numb incomprehension before both dropping to the seabed again and trying to grasp the enormity of their discovery. Costas had gone off on his own to the edge of the gully, trying to trace the perimeter of the deposit, and Rebecca and Jeremy had arrived over the sand, swimming slowly off in different directions with their masks glued to the seabed, clearly in the same state of disbelief that Jack himself had experienced a few moments ago.

He sifted through the coins, picking up one of the silver pieces of eight. It had the same cross and shield design as the piece of four he and Costas had found in the cleft near the *Schiedam* site. But like Rebecca's coin find at the same place, this one was not from the Mexico mint, but from Potosi. With a jolt, it took Jack back again to that place, somewhere he had put from his mind since arriving at the cove. He held the coin up, thinking of everything he now knew had gone into creating these coins, the toil and the misery and the human cost. And then, just as he was about to replace it and look at another coin, he saw what it had on the reverse.

It was stamped with a Star of David design.

He reeled back, breathing hard on his regulator. And then he remembered Henry Avery's history of larceny. It was not only the Howard family that he had done out of money. He had also absconded with the coins that he had taken on board in Portugal that day in 1684, the money that João Rodrigues

Brandão had intended for his family in Jamaica, along with a far more precious cargo. To Avery, that symbol that João had stamped on his coins to keep others from using them would have been of no consequence, silver being silver to a pirate and the weight being all that mattered in the taverns and whorehouses of Port Royal.

Jack stared at the coin, feeling that he had come full circle. He looked at the others as they swam over the seabed, reaching down to pick things up, and then he glanced up at the surface, where the sparkling water seemed a reflection of what lay below. He swam back towards the edge of the island and rose up the side of the rock face, seeing it continue above him in wavering distortion, and then he broke surface, took out his regulator and injected air into his buoyancy compensator, rolling onto his back and floating head-first into a niche in the rock. He remained there, barely breathing, letting the swell gently rock him, hearing the exhaust bubbles of the others erupt gently on the surface and then dissipate. All he could see through his mask was sun, sea and rock, a view even more elemental than his vision on the beach before, as if in this place all ambiguity had gone. He thought of what lay beneath the surface, of what he would see if he dipped his mask down, but he dared not do it, in case it should turn out to have been a phantasm. He thought of Rebecca, of her life ahead, of the only wisdom that he could impart. There were few certainties, mostly just surmises, and the prize would always be dangling somewhere ahead. But if enough coalesced, if you kept a weather eye on the horizon, then sometimes, just sometimes, the treasure might turn out to be real.

He held the coin up to the sun, seeing the cross glinting on one side and the coat of arms on the other, the Star of David faintly visible above that. More than three hundred years ago, Henry Avery, former naval officer and apparently reliable merchant, had sailed off with Howard money intended to finance a joint trading venture, but had instead used it to seed-fund the greatest and most rapacious career of plunder ever to be seen on the high seas. For three centuries, the Howards had not forgotten. Now Jack considered the debt to have been repaid.

He flicked the coin out of his hand, watching it sail high in the air and then fall into the sea, the concentric ripples joining the exhaust bubbles of the divers below.

They had hit the jackpot at last. He thought of what Costas would say.

Bingo.

Author's Note

While I was writing this novel, I had beside me the actual coin that Jack finds in the first chapter, a Spanish silver piece of four minted in Mexico in the middle years of the seventeenth century; you can see that coin on the cover of this book, alongside a photo of me diving on a wreck, taken by my brother Alan. In a fascinating connection with this story, that coin was found on the wreck of HMS *Association*, the flagship of Admiral Sir Cloudesley Shovell when he perished with four of his ships off the Scilly Isles in 1707 – the event that precipitated the race to find a better way of establishing longitude. As a young captain, it was Cloudesley Shovell who had captured the Dutch fluyt *Schiedam* from Barbary pirates in 1693, and who then escorted her to Tangier, where she was used in the evacuation of the city by the English the following year. In another connection, the coin is very likely to have passed through Port Royal in Jamaica, the conduit for most of the Spanish coins to reach England at this period, and could even have been taken by an English privateer from a ship of the Spanish Main. I could not have wished for an artefact more closely linked to so many threads in this story, some of which only became apparent to me as I handled the coin and pondered the history that led to it being lost on that fateful day in 1707.

Even more so than with my previous novels, the ongoing investigation of an actual shipwreck has provided the basis for scenes of diving and discovery in this story. The opening through the cliff where Jack finds the coin really exists, above a cannon site that I discovered off the Lizard peninsula in Cornwall in 2013. The artefacts found there included a worn Spanish silver coin, one of many to have been discovered along that coast. Not far away in the cove of Jangye-ryn is the 1684 wreck of the *Schiedam*, the ship that had been captured by Cloudesley Shovell, lying on the seabed just as described in the novel. It had been buried under sand for years, but in a real-life Jack Howard moment my fellow diver Mark Milburn and I rediscovered it while snorkelling over the bay in the summer of 2016. Since then we have recorded many fascinating artefacts, including cannon and cannonballs, mortars, lead shot for muskets and pistols, concretions containing muskets and tools, and hand grenades with their wooden fuses still intact. Other artefacts found in earlier excavations include small columns and pieces of architectural marble that may have been taken from a house at Tangier, just as Pepys sees in Chapter 8 being taken down to the harbour during the evacuation of the city a few weeks before the shipwreck.

In December 2016, our press release on the site was taken up widely by the media, and articles with photos of me underwater appeared on the BBC and ITN sites, as well as in *Diver* and *Scuba* magazines. The process of discovery is continuous; while I was finishing this novel, we found further artefacts, washed ashore during a storm in February 2017, and we are certain that much of the wreck remains to be uncovered.

The remarkable historical backdrop to the wreck of the *Schiedam* includes the involvement of none other than Samuel Pepys, the famous diarist of 1660s London, who in his 'day job' was Secretary to the Admiralty and a passionate promoter of the Royal Navy, without in any way being a nautical man himself. Having been appointed under Lord Dartmouth to help oversee the evacuation of Tangier – the port inherited by Charles II as a dowry with his Portuguese wife Catherine of Braganza, but which had proved disastrously expensive to maintain – he decided to write a diary again for the first time in almost fifteen years. The most recent edition, *The Tangier Papers of Samuel Pepys* (edited by Edwin Chappell for the Navy Records Society, 1935), contains other primary documents, as does the other main source, Enid Routh's *Tangier, England's Lost Atlantic Outpost, 1661–1684* (London, 1912), including the account of the loss of hand grenades to the Moors in 1680 at Charles Fort outside the city walls that Jack remembers during his dive in Chapter 3 and Pepys in Chapter 9 (Routh, op. cit., p. 179).

The Tangier diary is far more prosaic than Pepys's earlier diary, and is important not so much as a literary achievement as a unique day-to-day account of the final dramatic months at Tangier, including Pepys's excursions to negotiate with the besieging Moors; but there are occasional flashes of the old Pepys in his acerbic comments about some of the officials at Tangier, and about his own health and private affairs. He reserves his most damning judgements for the governor, Colonel Kirke, who on 7 October took Pepys to see some 'old Roman little aqueducts', and whose wife we glimpse in Chapter 8. Pepys's mention of the Knights of Malta – 'Got a copy of the letter of thanks from the Knights of Malta to our King on the redemption of some of them with the rest of the Christian slaves' (24 July 1683, in Chappell, op. cit., p. 319) – was my inspiration for the inclusion of the Knights in the storyline of this novel.

One of Pepys's responsibilities was to assist in negotiations with Ali Ben Abdala, the chieftain of the nearby town of Alkazar, the man chosen by the Moroccan sultan to besiege Tangier. The Alcaïd's fictional son in Chapter 9 and his shooting skill is inspired by Pepys's account of one occasion when they were joined by Ali Ben Abdala's son, 'a pretty youth', who 'exercised very neatly' when there was 'great shooting with the small shot' (28 September 1683).

Pepys mentions the *Schiedam* and other fluyts or 'flyboats' several times in his diary, but his most extensive reference to the ship is among his correspondence in the Admiralty Papers, held in the National Archives, where he concerns himself with the salvage and financial affairs after the wrecking – including, for reasons that are not easy to explain, considerable efforts to exonerate and reinstate the pay of the lamentable Captain Fish, who 'lies abed and cries instead of having saved any of the wreck'.

Among the nefarious activities known to have taken place in Tangier was coin-clipping, in which Spanish gold and silver hammered coins, already irregularly shaped and often clipped at the mint to achieve the desired weight, were clipped further to remove bullion; the alteration of coins in this way was the basis for my idea that some merchants might have over-stamped their coins with marks such as the Star of David, something that was further inspired by the Jewish merchant tokens used in the Caribbean from at least the eighteenth century onwards, including those of the Brandão family of Jamaica (R. D. Leonard, 'Tokens of Jewish merchants of the Caribbean before 1920', in R. J. Doty and J. M. Kleeberg, *Money of the Caribbean*, The American Numismatic Society, 2006, pp. 219–48).

In the historical backdrop to this story, the Inquisition is not the only agency to have had anti-Semitic policies; at Tangier, the 'Barbary Jews' were banished in 1677 by the then governor, Sir Palmes Fairborne, though in 1680 a few were allowed back in, and in 1683, shortly before Pepys arrived, Governor Kirke decreed 'that the trading Jews of Barbary must lodge in tents outside the walls and only come in by day; only those of proved fidelity might sleep in the town' (Routh, op. cit., p. 276). Whether or not Portuguese Jewish merchants were present in Tangier at the time of the evacuation is unknown, but given the previous Portuguese ownership of the town and the extent of the Sephardic Jewish diaspora, it seems likely.

João Rodrigues Brandão – owner of the fictional Star of David stamp – actually existed; he was my ancestor, through

346

my four-times-great-grandmother Rebecca Brandon, part of
the Sephardic community in London. The Brandão family
were *conversos* or 'New Christians' in Viseu and Porto in
northern Portugal, where they prospered as merchants but
lived under the constant threat of persecution by the
Inquisition for their concealed faith. Because the men of the
Inquisition were fastidious record-keepers and much of
their documentation survives in the Portuguese National
Archives, it has been possible to build up a detailed picture of
the Brandão family in the seventeenth century – including
João's considerable wealth and his interests in the tobacco
trade with Brazil, and the long periods that he and his wife
and children spent imprisoned at Coimbra. João's grandson
Daniel, Rebecca's father, fled to London in the mid eighteenth
century, and others of the family escaped to France, Holland
and Jamaica, where the Brandons of Port Royal and Kingston
were part of the community of Jewish merchants who
provided brokerage for the pirates, and where many of their
descendants continue to live today.

The buildings of the Inquisition still exist at Coimbra,
including the tribunal chamber, the cells where João and his
family were imprisoned and the square where the condemned
endured their auto-da-fé, either an act of public penance or
burning at the stake, the latter being the fate suffered by at
least one of my Brandão ancestors in the sixteenth century. In
common with most Portuguese Jews, they would probably
originally have been expelled from Spain in 1492, and would
have traced themselves back to the Jews who had fled the
Holy Land during the Roman period; it is conceivable that
they might have included 'Christian Jews', sympathetic to

Christianity, as suggested in this novel, and that they might have lived in the north-eastern region of Spain.

One of the Portuguese Christians sympathetic to the Jews in the late seventeenth century was Father António Vieira, a Jesuit whose report to the Pope on the conditions that he had experienced when he himself had been imprisoned resulted in the Inquisition in Portugal being suspended from 1674 to 1681. The words quoted by João Brandão to the tribunal in Chapter 10 are authentically those of Vieira. Whether or not Vieira went to Potosi, in present-day Bolivia, to the Cerro Rico, the Mountain of Riches, is unknown, but in Brazil he devoted himself indefatigably to the improvement of conditions for the indigenous people and the downtrodden, earning the name the Apostle of Brazil. According to most accounts, he died in Salvador, Brazil, persecuted in his last years by those who wished to undermine him, having left Portugal for the last time in 1681 when the Inquisition was reinstated.

For Vieira, as for the Pilgrim Fathers, the New World would have offered the possibility of a 'Celestial City', as Pepys's contemporary John Bunyan termed it in *The Pilgrim's Progress*; the attraction would have been heightened as religious persecution in Europe plumbed new depths of barbarity. At the same time, the behaviour of Europeans unleashed in the New World, some previously morally constrained, others drawn to it precisely because they were not, would have shown the temptations and dangers of such places – with Port Royal, like Tangier, being the antithesis of the Celestial City – and led to the redoubling of efforts, religiously motivated or otherwise, to ensure that the dark side of human nature did not win the day.

★ ★ ★

The circumstances of present-day mining at Cerro Rico in Bolivia, including the employment of boys, the health problems that they suffer and the veneration of El Tío, the devil-like spirit of the underworld, are much as described in this novel. Few examples of the equipment of the seventeenth-century mint survive, having become redundant with the adoption of milling in the eighteenth century, but those that do exist can be seen in the collections of the Casa de la Moneda at Potosi. During the Spanish colonial era, as now, most of the mine workers were descendants of the Inca peoples of the Andes, but a proportion of them – as well as those used to man the mills in the mint, referred to by their masters as 'human donkeys' – were African slaves. The mass grave in Chapter 19 is based on an actual mass grave discovered in 2014 in Potosi, containing some four hundred skeletons of the colonial era that may have included both slaves and free labourers who worked in the mines. In 2011, a large sink-hole appeared at the top of the mountain, a result of collapse within the huge complex of tunnels below, so a scenario on the scale of the collapse in Chapter 22 of this novel is a very real possibility.

Laurentius was a deacon of Rome who was murdered during the persecution of Christians by the Emperor Valerian in AD 258. The circumstances of his death as presented in the Prologue are drawn from Church tradition, including the edicts of the emperor ordering the confiscation of Church treasures, the attempt by Laurentius to distribute them among the people, and his famous defiance of the city prefect, when he proclaimed that the true treasures of the Church were the poor and the suffering, and that 'the Church is truly rich, far richer than your emperor'. His execution by roasting on a gridiron was one of the more horrific martyrdoms of the Roman period. He is said to have given the Holy Chalice – the cup used by Jesus at the Last Supper, also known in medieval tradition as the Holy Grail – to a Roman soldier named Proselius, with instructions for him to take it for safe keeping to Laurentius's home town in Spain. The same tradition states that the cup had been brought to Rome in the first century AD by St Peter, and that it had been passed to Laurentius by Pope Sixtus II before his own martyrdom earlier in the same persecution.

Nothing else is known about Proselius except that he too was said to have been Spanish. My account of his rescue of the Chalice from the catacombs is fictional, but the description of the underground passages and tombs is closely based on my own exploration of the Catacomb of Callixtus while researching this novel. Proselius's destination in Spain may have been Osca, modern Huesca in the north-east near the Pyrenees, the town thought to have been the home of Laurentius. As for the Chalice itself, assuming it existed, its most likely appearance is much as Jack surmises in the final chapter, a simple pottery vessel rather than one of glass or metal, and certainly not the bejewelled Grail of Arthurian legend. Intact examples of goblets and bowls of the type that may have been used at an event such as the Last Supper were found in the caves at Qumran, site of the Dead Sea Scrolls, and can be seen on display in the Israel Museum in Jerusalem.

★ ★ ★

The *Black Swan* and the slave-market discovery at Port Royal in Jamaica in this novel are fictional, as is the island Santo Cristo del Tesoro. However, the wreck is based on an actual discovery made by a team from the Institute of Nautical Archaeology at Port Royal in the 1990s. During the excavation of a group of buildings some sixty metres from the 1692 shoreline, divers found the lower timbers of a ship that had clearly been driven over the wharf and up the street during the earthquake, ramming into the wall of a building before coming to rest. It is most likely to have been HMS *Swan*, a vessel known to have been careened at the time and therefore out of ballast, and more easily lifted above the wharf by the wave. Like my fictional *Black Swan*, HMS *Swan* was originally a Dutch vessel, captured by the English in 1672 when the two countries were still at war, but rather than being a pirate ship she had been used against the pirates, carrying out numerous patrols during her years of service in the Caribbean.

Stories of lost treasure abound in Cornwall, many of them based on ships carrying bullion known to have been wrecked off this coast. One of the more persistent concerns Henry Avery, 'King of the Pirates', notorious for ransacking the Grand Mughal's fleet in the Arabian Sea in 1695, for further filling his coffers in the Caribbean and then retiring with his treasure allegedly intact. Avery was a Cornishman, born probably near Plymouth in 1659, and began his career in the Royal Navy, perhaps serving as a junior officer by the time of the evacuation of Tangier. Whether or not he was present at the evacuation is unknown, but the suggestion in the novel that he may have been given temporary command of a transport vessel is consistent with other junior officers being given commands at the time. After leaving the navy, he became an illicit slave trader – the basis for my fictional arrangement with the Howard family, in which he absconded with money meant to underwrite legitimate trade – and then embarked in earnest on his career as a pirate, supposedly amassing more treasure in the few years he was active in the mid 1690s than any other pirate before or since.

The involvement of the fictional Howard family in Atlantic trade at this period is based on the real-life activities of the Gale family of Whitehaven, who are ancestors of mine. Four brothers who were all sea captains, including my ancestor Matthias Gale (1677–1751), began as officers in the Royal Navy but then became merchant captains and prospered in the tobacco trade with the American colonies, where they owned land. Matthias's brother Lowther, the basis for the fictional Lowther Howard in the novel, is the only one of the brothers known to have ventured into the slave trade, though unsuccessfully – his ship the *Nancy Galley* was taken by an enemy privateer on his one and only voyage to the Guinea coast, in 1711. However, another of the brothers, George Gale (1671–1712) – whose wife was the grandmother of George Washington – had slaves on his plantation in Maryland, and the fact that anyone prospering from the tobacco trade at this period was ultimately profiting from slave labour is the basis for Jack's disquiet about his own family's wealth in the late seventeenth and eighteenth centuries. Both Matthias and George were present at the first trial of pirates by the Virginia Admiralty Court, and witnessed the hanging of pirates in cages at Cape Henry in Virginia; the fourth of the brothers, John Gale, was captured in 1726 with his ship the *John and Betty* by the pirate Willam Fly, whose execution in chains that year is often seen to mark the end of the 'golden age' of piracy.

Henry Avery disappeared mysteriously in the Caribbean, never to be heard of again, but one tradition is that he returned to Cornwall with his treasure, buried it and died in obscurity without ever having recovered his loot. The parish record that provides the key to Jack's discovery in Kynance Cove is fictional, but is based on an actual Victorian account of wrecks off the adjoining parish to the north. The idea that Avery's treasure might have been lost in a shipwreck, and not buried, was inspired by my own explorations at the cove, and by actual wrecks known to have taken place there. In 2014, I took my gear down the cliff path and dived through the Devil's Bellows, just as Jack does. I was chasing rumours of a seventeenth-century Dutch wreck in the gully at the seaward end of the tunnel, and among the rocky ledges I did indeed find fragments of blue-and-white Delftware consistent with that date. There was too much sand in the gully to determine whether other artefacts might survive, but the idea of treasure off Kynance is not just speculation – a few hundred metres away, at Rill Cove, is a wreck of the early seventeenth century where divers have found thousands of Spanish colonial pieces of eight, many of them of silver from the Cerro Rico in Bolivia, where the action in the later part of this novel takes place. The Rill Cove wreck is a protected archaeological site under UK law, but Mark Milburn and I are licensed to dive there and are planning renewed investigations as soon as the sand levels drop enough to reveal artefacts and allow excavation.

For me, linking these real-life discoveries of my own with Jack's adventures represents a natural confluence, to the point where the two have become almost seamlessly intertwined. From the outset, a guiding tenet of these novels has been that the diving and the archaeology should be based as closely as possible on my own experiences, and it is exciting for me now to draw this inspiration from ongoing projects and not just from past expeditions. Much of the investigation of the *Schiedam* took place in real time as I was researching and writing this novel, with days being divided between writing and diving, and calls coming in about new discoveries just as Jack experiences them in the novel. This relationship gives my own life and my fictional imagination a dynamic that might never have happened had I not embarked on these novels almost fifteen years ago. In the final chapter of this novel, Father Pereira talks of Jack being a dreamer by day, and of being able to act on those dreams to bring the adventures of his imagination to life; after ten novels in this series and numerous adventures of my own along the way, living Jack's life for me has become far more than just an act of the imagination.

The edict that coins of Charles II should be buried in Tangier, remembered by Pepys in Chapter 8, is from Josiah Burchett's *A Complete History of the Most Remarkable Transactions at Sea* (London, 1720, p. 405), and is quoted by Chappell in the frontispiece of *The Tangier Papers of Samuel Pepys* (op. cit.).

The entries from Pepys's diary in Chapter 5 about feeling abominable and in Chapter 7 about artefacts are both fictional, though inspired by his actual writings in the surviving Tangier diary; that is also the source of the order of Lord Dartmouth quoted in Chapter 7. The fictional entries for 1684 are possible because Pepys's actual diary for that final period at Tangier, if it ever existed, is lost.

The proclamation for Avery's arrest that Jack reads in Chapter 4 is an actual document, issued by the Privy Council of Scotland on 18 August 1696, as is the late-seventeenth-century chart of west Cornwall by van Keulen that Jack has on his wall; both can be seen on my website. You can also see images of the coin, videos of me diving through the Devil's Bellows and on the wreck of the *Schiedam*, extensive accounts of the Brandão family and the Inquisition in Portugal, and much else related to the novel, as well as updates on the exciting discoveries that my team and I are continuing to make on shipwrecks and other underwater sites around the world.

www.davidgibbins.com
www.facebook.com/DavidGibbinsAuthor

THE JACK HOWARD SERIES

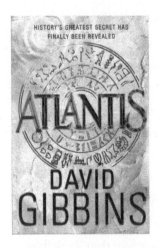

ATLANTIS

On a dive in the Mediterranean, marine archaeologist Jack Howard gets very lucky. He and his team uncover what could be the key to the location of Atlantis. But while Jack's discovery is beyond his wildest dreams – it comes at a terrifying price. Suddenly he is locked in a game of life or death with consequences that could destroy thousands of lives . . .

CRUSADER GOLD

Diving for lost Crusade treasure, Jack Howard discovers something wholly unexpected. In an English cathedral library, a long-forgotten medieval map is unearthed. What unfolds is a thrilling but lethal quest, stretching from the fall of the Roman Empire to the last days of Nazi power and the darkest secrets of the modern Vatican. The clock is ticking for Jack – and the stakes are already too high . . .

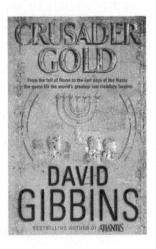

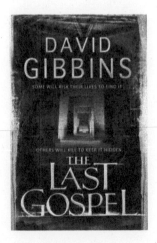

THE LAST GOSPEL

What if one of the Ancient World's greatest libraries was buried in volcanic ash and then rediscovered two thousand years later? What if what was found there was a document that could shatter the very foundations of the Western World? When Jack Howard uncovers the greatest secret ever kept, he must confront deadly enemies determined to ensure it goes no further.

THE TIGER WARRIOR

1879: Lieutenant John Howard witnesses something so unspeakable it changes him for ever. His subsequent disappearance is never solved. Present day: Marine archaeologist Jack Howard makes an astonishing discovery on a deep-sea dive. What's the connection? Jack doesn't know yet, but he's about to find out . . .

THE MASK OF TROY

Greece, 1876: Henrich Schliemann, raises the Mask of Agamemnon and finds something extraordinary. The secret will follow him to his grave. Present day: Jack Howard uncovers a shipwrecked galley, and a link to Schliemann and a Nazi operation of unimaginable horror. Soon he becomes embroiled in a desperate chase across Europe, but this time Jack risks losing something of even greater value . . . his own daughter.

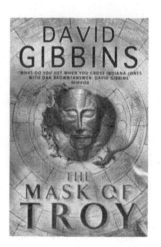

THE GODS OF ATLANTIS

A lost Nazi bunker in a forest in Germany contains a dreadful secret. In the submerged Neolithic citadel of Atlantis, Jack Howard discovers an ancient fragment of writing in the ruins. Could there be a horrifying new version of Atlantis, a priesthood of darkness? Have the Reich concealed traces of evil and will a wrong move trigger unimaginable destruction? Jack must uncover the truth before it is too late.

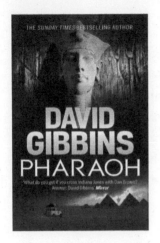

PHARAOH

1352 BC: Akhenaten the Sun-Pharaoh rules supreme in Egypt . . . until the day he disappears into the desert. 1884: A British soldier stumbles upon a submerged temple containing evidence of a terrifying religion. Present day: Jack Howard and his team are excavating an incredible underwater site. Diving into the Nile, they enter a world inhabited by a people who have sworn to guard the greatest secret of all time . . .

PYRAMID

1892: A British soldier emerges from the depths of a Cairo sewer, trapped for years in an ancient underground complex. He is dismissed as a madman and his story is lost to the world. Present day: When Jack Howard learns of the soldier's story, he risks everything in a dangerous expedition to find the truth. Jack and his team are taken back through Egyptian history to the spectacular reign of Akhenaten, the Sun-Pharaoh – and keeper of an incredible secret . . .

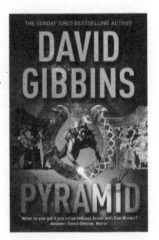

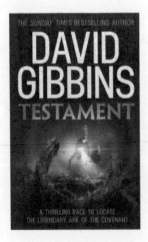

TESTAMENT

586 BC: Jerusalem has fallen. In desperation, the temple priests look to the greatest navigators ever known to save their holiest of treasures. 1943: A group of Allied codebreakers know nothing of the ancient artefact hidden on board a ship whose fate they have just sealed. Present day: Exploring a wreck on the continental shelf, Jack Howard makes a startling discovery. Now he must fuse past and present as never before in a desperate mission for humanity.